THIS CRUEL BLOOD

SOUL BITTEN SHIFTER 4

EVERLY FROST

DISCOVER THE EVER REALMS

Seven series. One world.

Suggested Reading Order:

Bright Wicked
Storm Princess
Assassin's Magic
Soul Bitten Shifter
Supernatural Legacy
Dark Magic Shifters
Kingdom of Betrayal

Break rules. Bite back.

CHAPTER ONE

$\mathscr{T}$he flames remind me of a man I once loved.

Firelight turns the night sky above me golden, the funeral pyres burning so hot that the heat is icy across my skin.

Smoke rises like finely crafted ropes from each pyre, up and overhead, before dispersing far above me.

On the other side of the pyres, packs of supernaturals are huddled in blankets, recovering from the battle we fought today.

Beating back the past is too hard tonight.

I nearly lost my alpha today, fought beside women whose strength is forged out of pain and heartache, and now all of the unresolved memories from my past are crashing back to me in a wave I've been keeping at bay for far too long.

I fought another battle like this once, except that I attempted it on my own—and I lost. Badly. Catastrophically. I owe my life to people who were strangers to me at the time; people who took me in despite not knowing me at all, and have become pivotal in my life now.

Tessa Dean approaches me at a cautious prowl. The concern in her eyes nearly kills me. She's fierce, the blood of old gods running through her veins. She's capable of killing every supernatural here on a whim, but her biggest concern is keeping us all safe.

I catch the way she assesses me as she approaches. Nothing seems to escape her. Certainly not the fact that, unlike everyone else, I'm not snuggled up in a blanket, chatting quietly, devouring soup, and recovering.

Instead, I'm standing apart. I'm dressed for a fight in my knee-high black leather boots over black leggings. My top is also black, and my long ebony hair is pulled up into a topknot to keep the strands out of my face. My guns and daggers rest at my waist, and I can't stop staring into flames that make my heart hurt.

Tessa bumps my arm with the lightest touch. "You okay, Iyana?"

There's no lying to her, not least because she has the power to see my deepest impulses—read my sadness—if she chooses to. Although I doubt she would. She respects my privacy as much as I respect hers.

I take a deep breath and focus on the bright flames, the way they quicken and slow as they burn. "Memories are hard."

Her cautious expression softens. She understands what it means to fight the past, the way it shapes our minds and hearts.

"The fire reminds me of someone..." I try to say more, but speech sticks in my throat, a painful constriction around my vocal chords.

Aiden Brand wasn't right for me. He may have made my heart race and my body heat with a single touch, but he was closed off to love long before he met me.

Tessa doesn't push me, but she leans a little closer, a gesture of comfort that makes me want to reassure her and take away her worry.

"I'll be fine," I say, nodding—convincing myself that I don't need to relive these memories tonight. I'm safe. The people I love are safe. I'm determined to keep it that way.

I square my shoulders. Tessa was on her way to the forest surrounding the clearing when she veered in my direction. She stopped when she saw me, and I know she'll stay with me as long as I need her...

But she deserves this night, everything she's fought so hard for. She and Tristan Masters can finally be together without any barriers between them.

"I'll keep an eye on things here," I say to her.

She wraps her arms around me, supportive, firm. Gentle. I allow the tension in my body to seep away, relaxing in the warmth of her gesture.

"Love you, Iyana," she says, pressing her cheek to mine. It's a wolf's gesture—an affirmation of the bond between us. I might be a vampire, but I'm part of her pack.

"Love you, too, Tessa," I whisper as she stalks away into the dark, every step she takes revealing her strength and grace as an alpha, her long ruby-red hair as brilliant as the flames burning nearby.

As soon as she disappears into the distant trees, I prowl around the pyres to find a quiet place—unobtrusive—and stand guard near the pack members huddled in blankets.

We are three packs united in a common purpose and a new future. Old hatreds are gone.

I scan the group for Danika, the hawk shifter, and Cody, Tessa's beta. Cody was once a wolf shifter and is now completely human. I'm not worried when I can't see either of them. They, too, disappeared into the forest a little while ago, and may not return for the rest of the night. They both deserve this happiness.

I remain guarding everyone from a distance until the moon is high and their conversations die down. Many of them find a place to sleep where they are, nestled in blankets under the stars and warmed by the pyres. Others take themselves off to the tower nearby.

Maeve, the witch, rests with Reya, the lion shifter. Luna and Lydia, the card mage twins, are already asleep close by, as is the rest of Tessa's pack, and the fae warriors gathered around them.

Hours pass, midnight comes and goes, and the night enters its darkest point, dawn still at least two hours away.

I'm exhausted, but I need to stay awake until the sun rises—to feel the darkness around me and resume my natural rhythm.

I normally sleep during the day, and I've forced my body to operate during sunlight hours for too long now.

Needing to move, I circle the pyres to the far side again. I'm not surprised that the flames continue to burn brightly. The fae lit the pyres using their power over sunlight while the sun was still shining, and the flames have burned high since.

I'm about to pass around the fires, yet again—a constant restless prowl—when a loud crackle within the pyre to my left makes me spin.

I scan the flames, but nothing appears out of place.

There's another *pop* and then—

Sparks burst outward, a chunk of wood hurtles past my shoulder, and flames rear up within the fire, rising as high as my head.

A figure appears within the blaze, a man's silhouette crouched, head down, the fire licking around his form and turning his skin the color of amber.

Dear fuck. Only one person I've ever met has the power to stand within a raging fire, let alone translocate themselves *into* it.

Did I conjure him with my thoughts?

I force myself to breathe.

"Aiden?"

He rises up, his muscular physique backlit in amber. He's naked from the waist up, wearing only a pair of dark suit pants as if he came from a cocktail party—except that he's missing the collared shirt and jacket that should go with the pants.

His shoulders are slumped and the flames flash across his chest in a pattern that disturbs me, as if the fire is drawn to spots on his chest for a reason I can't identify.

Even so, the heat curls around his body without burning him or his clothing.

He's a pyromancer. Fire is his to control in any way he chooses. He can attack with it, defend with it, or... *warm* with it.

He lifts his head.

His eyes are the deepest blue, like navy, shadowed beneath his furrowed brow. His hair is a dark brown, swept back on top, while the tilt of his head reveals the tattoo inked above his left ear, an intricate design of flames that sweeps around the side of his head where his hair is shaved.

When he speaks, his voice is the deepest baritone, reaching me over the popping of the fire.

"Ana." He pronounces my name, not as Iyana, but as Ah-na, the way he used to address me in rare, unguarded moments—the moments when there weren't walls between us.

I'm too shocked to move as he steps down from the pyre and takes a knee on the grass in front of me, his head bowed, but I recognize immediately that it's an involuntary pose.

His knee buckles, his right arm hangs at an awkward angle, and his chest...

Oh, fuck...

Bullets nestle across the front of his chest—so many bullets—their flat bases visible in the surface of his skin. They must be the cause of the flashes across his chest that I saw before—the fire was reflecting off the metal.

Three bullets rest in his left shoulder, three more across his left ribcage, and four across the location of his heart... But none of them appear to penetrate beneath the surface.

My jaw tightens and my reflexes kick in.

"Aiden!" I throw myself forward, catching his shoulders, attempting to support his heavy torso as his other knee buckles and he loses his balance.

His skin is warm to the touch, but he didn't bring the flames with him when he stepped from the pyre, so I'm not in any danger from them.

Aiden's head drops to my shoulder, his uninjured shoulder curving against my chest. Other than speaking my name, he's intensely quiet and I don't dare to breathe.

"Aiden?" I whisper, my cheek pressed to the top of his head. "Talk to me."

My heart hammers in my chest when he doesn't respond.

I need to help him, but he is a threat to everyone here.

No matter what he wants for himself, his actions are dictated by the demon I tried to kill—Banta Sol—a weapons dealer who has no care for anyone but himself, and who kills without a second thought.

Shouts rise from the other side of the pyre.

My friends may have been settling down to sleep, but they are all warriors, many with heightened hearing.

There's no way they missed my shout or the unusual popping of the fire.

Reya hurtles around the pyre first, her lioness side visible in the animal shape of her amber eyes and the flow of her tousled, flaxen hair. "Iyana!"

She races toward me with Maeve close on her heels.

A violet glow grows around Maeve's hands. The witch's ash-colored hair is streaked with violet, the same color as her magic, and her eyes are cedar brown.

Her wand was molded to her palms, so she is never without her magic. The molding of her wand was once used to cage her, but she overcame it. At seventeen years of age, she's the youngest member of Tessa's pack.

"Stay back!" I cry, unable to hold out my hand to stop my friends from coming closer since I'm using all of my strength to keep Aiden upright. Panic rises inside me. "He controls the fire. He could burn you!"

Reya and Maeve skid to a stop a few paces away. Maeve crouches, arcs her hands through the air, and immediately, a protective violet shield forms between them and me.

Aiden groans against my chest. "I'm not here to hurt you." He tips his head back so I can see his face and bloodshot eyes. "I'm here to warn you."

He grips my forearm, his palm hot and tight around my limb.

A hard, sharp object scrapes down my arm as he shakily attempts to shift his grip to my hand, pressing the object into my fist.

I stare at what he's given me. A fang, its tip still sharp, but broken at the top.

It's one of my fangs.

Banta Sol ripped them both out before he left me for dead.

Aiden may as well be holding my heart in his hands.

"If I can find you," Aiden says, the flames glinting in his dark blue eyes, "so can Banta."

CHAPTER TWO

I'm frozen as I stare at my broken fang.

Seven months ago, I went after Banta Sol without backup, trying to bring down his crime ring by killing the demon, himself.

I spent nearly a year planning my mission, successfully infiltrating his organization, and gaining Banta's trust—or so I thought.

I planned my attack on a night when Aiden was away. I chose that night, not only because I thought Aiden's absence would give me a better chance at taking Banta down, but because I didn't want Aiden to be forced to hurt me.

Nothing prepared me for the united power of Banta's other four lieutenants.

When I tried to escape, they chased me, beat me, and tore out my fangs. I incurred so many injuries on the night of my near-death that my memories of the event are scattered and incoherent.

Now, I resist the urge to press my fingers to my gums—to the new teeth and fangs that Helen gave me when she repaired all of the injuries Banta's men inflicted on me. Although it was Tristan who rescued me, it was Helen—a powerful witch—who healed me and kept me safe at Hidden House, a shelter for those in need.

I take a sharp breath, inhale the smoky scent of the pyres and Aiden's skin, deeply aware that he needs medical help, but also that I can't trust his word that he's here to warn—and not hurt—me.

Banta controls him. Could be controlling him right now.

Demons manipulate their victims through the power of suggestion. They have the uncanny gift of being able to figure out what a person wants and convincing that person they can help them achieve their goals. It's how they suck their victims in. For that reason, demons make excellent businessmen and live easily among humans.

But Banta's power of suggestion is stronger than most. He can make a person do things they don't want to do—and they have no choice but to comply.

His power of compulsion doesn't fade until his victim completes whatever task he sets for them.

It means I have to question every move that Aiden makes.

Every. Damn. Move.

"Banta knows you're alive," Aiden says quietly, his body becoming heavier as he leans against me. He takes a deep breath, but he can't hide the tremble in his arms or the tension around his mouth that betrays his pain. "You were seen about a week ago in the eastern lowland. He's been tracking you ever since."

Damn. It's my own fault I was seen.

When Tessa went missing, Danika and I headed into Baxter Griffin's territory and roughed up a few shifters while trying to find out what had happened to her.

We weren't exactly quiet about it. News would have traveled fast to Banta's compound, which sits on the outskirts of the eastern lowland.

"He's paranoid that you're going to come after him," Aiden continues. "If you want to live, you need to come with me."

"Go with *you?*" I finally close my fist around my broken fang, accepting the emotional pain that comes with it. "You're in no shape to go anywhere."

I saw enough before Aiden collapsed against me to know that the bullets embedded in his chest have to be removed very carefully.

Right now, they're acting like plugs, stopping the worst of his bleeding. Depending on how big the bullets are—how deep they go—he could bleed out if he tries to remove them. Each one will need to be handled carefully, removed one at a time, and each wound stitched.

Unfortunately, Maeve can't heal him. When Tristan was hurt, she told us that her knowledge of healing spells is very limited and because of that, she can do more harm than good if she tries to help.

I'll need to ask the fae to help, since they have at least one healer—a woman with coral pink hair whom I saw from a distance yesterday.

But I circle back to the agonizing reality: I can't trust Aiden right now.

His presence could be a ploy of Banta's making.

"Aiden," I murmur, an ache growing within my chest. "I can't go anywhere with you."

As if he chooses to believe I won't go with him because he's too wounded, he pushes off me, wobbly and trembling, making it as far up as to sit back on his heels.

His hand shakes as he waves at the bullets. "These are fucking nothing. I just need some help to get them out. I'll be fine."

I lurch forward, my hands closing around his face. "But what about your mind?"

I want more than anything to believe that Banta isn't dictating Aiden's actions right now—that his sudden appearance isn't part of a game to get to me, or worse, to hurt my friends.

Aiden grips my hand with his. "My mind is my own, Ana. You have to believe me." He searches my eyes as deeply as I'm searching his. "I saw you through the flames. I didn't tell Banta that I'd seen you, but I made the mistake of telling someone—" He coughs and a droplet of blood rests on his lip before he swipes it away. "I told someone I thought I could trust, but Banta forced them to betray me."

He gestures to his chest with the same hand on which his blood is smeared. "This was Banta's way of trying to make me tell him where you are—"

"Then how can you claim he's not compelling your actions now?" I ask. "If he interrogated you, he would have used his power—"

"No," Aiden says. "The pain was too much. It kept my head clear." He gives a bitter laugh. "If I'd known I could escape his control by inflicting pain on myself, I would have done it every fucking time he gave me an order."

His hold on my hand hasn't wavered and I don't fight the contact. The press of my palm against his cheek. His hand over mine.

"I jumped through five fires all over Oregon before I landed here so he wouldn't be able to follow my trail," Aiden says.

I want to believe him. *So badly.*

If I could believe him, then I could call for help—call for the fae healers, take him inside, hear his story, and connect for the first time without lies between us.

I infiltrated Banta's operations by getting close to Aiden. To do that, I spun countless untruths to gain Aiden's trust.

I was so determined to take Banta down that I didn't think about what I was doing to my own heart. Or to Aiden's.

"How can I believe you?" I whisper, shaking my head, a deep pain cutting across my chest.

It's not the first time I've wished that my heart didn't beat. There are some vampires whose hearts beat so slowly that other supernaturals believe they don't have a pulse.

My own heart hammers and thuds and can break just as completely as anyone else's.

Aiden's response is quiet, but the tension in his body—the firmness of his grip—increases with every passing second. "I want to prove it to you," he says. "But I don't know how."

What really worries me is that Aiden got inside the Spire in the first place.

He can use a flame in one place to translocate himself to a flame in another place, and, ordinarily, fires as huge as the funeral pyres would be like a beacon to him.

But the Spire and its surroundings are protected by the strongest of old magic. Even Helen couldn't locate this place when we were searching for Tessa, and she might be the most powerful witch alive.

Aiden claims he saw me in the flames, but he shouldn't have been able to detect the fires within the Spire's grounds.

Unless Banta somehow already knows how to find the Spire.

I draw the only conclusions that I can, the tension within my body heightening to unbearable levels as I shake my head. "Banta sent you to get me. He worked with Ford Vanguard, so he must know about the Spire and how to find it."

I wave my hand at the bullets. "He fucked you up badly enough to convince me that he hurt you, and then he sent you to bring me back. This is all an elaborate ploy—"

Aiden's response is instant. "I don't even know where I am right now, Ana. Banta's deals always went down in the city—"

I'm already pulling away. "Stop talking." I wrench my hand free and lurch to my feet.

It's taking every shred of anger inside me to shout down the voice of empathy that tells me he's hurt and in horrible pain. "Get the hell out of here, Aiden. Go back to Banta and get help before you pass out from blood loss."

I have no good options available to me. Nothing that can keep my friends safe that also won't hurt Aiden.

I need to warn Tessa. Warn my friends. We have to be ready for whatever the demon has planned.

"That's not happening," Aiden says. "I'm not leaving until you believe me."

He groans as he attempts to rise back to his feet, his muscles bunching, a sheen of sweat building across his chest and shoulders.

His legs wobble, and he nearly doesn't make it up—but he persists, eventually making it far enough, even though his left arm hangs more loosely at his side and he leans in that direction.

"What are you? A damn child?" I snap. "You're going to pass out any second now. Get the fuck out of here before you do."

"Nope," he says, popping his 'p' like I sometimes do and tilting his head to the side. "I'm not leaving unless you come with me."

For a precarious moment, he sways as if he's going to fall on his face, but then he remains standing. Just to fucking annoy me.

I grit my teeth. "And when you pass out, I'm going to pitch you into those flames," I say, pointing to the pyre on my right. "Your power will trigger, and you'll be whisked back to the fire you first came from—right back to Banta."

Aiden twitches—the barest indication of fear—a rare sight that surprises me.

He holds his hand out to me. "Come with me, Ana. There are things you don't know. You have to run with me. Right fucking now."

"*Run?*" I whisper.

My heart pounds harder inside my chest as I fight the scattered memories of when I ran from Banta the first time: a cold breeze against my cheeks; my motorcycle sliding out from under me because I couldn't control it; the echo of my uneven footfalls slapping the pavement as I escaped across one of the bridges between the eastern and western lowlands; the heavy footfalls of the men pursuing me.

None of it is clear now. All I know is that I somehow made it into Tristan's territory. After that… it's a blur.

I failed in my mission to take down Banta Sol because I was alone, but I'm not alone anymore. I'm part of a pack with alliances that make us unstoppable.

I'm aware of Maeve and Reya standing at my back, and all of the women with them, ready to fight beside me: Luna and Lydia, flicking their cards into the air, prepared to use the cards as weapons, if needed. Neve, the snow leopard with silver hair and pale blue eyes, and Nalani, the panther shifter with olive skin and the darkest eyes, both standing with claws extended, their cats ready to be called.

A quick glance tells me that the fae queen, Calanthe, has joined them. She stands with her daughter and a group of fae, forming a semi-circle behind my pack.

They're all armor-clad, holding diamond-tipped spears, many pointed at Aiden. Their power is strongest during the day, so they wouldn't be able to put out any fires that Aiden creates, but even so, they are a force to be reckoned with.

An army of friends watches my back, and all of my fear falls away, the memories receding under the sheer fucking force of my friends' strength.

"Iyana?" Maeve calls from where she remains on a knee, maintaining a shield of magic between us and the other women. The shield curves around at the sides and I hope Maeve has the power to extend it around all of the women if she needs to. "What do you want us to do?"

"Stay back, but stay ready!" I return my attention to Aiden as I harden my heart. "I'm sending him on his way. And then I'll figure out how to deal with Banta."

Aiden squares his shoulders and rises to his full height. Only moments ago, he was stooped, visibly in pain. But now...

Watching the cold come over him is like watching the sun go down. All of his soft edges disappear. The fire reflecting in his eyes is like a cold burn. Whatever pain he's feeling from his injuries, he's hiding it now.

My worry that he's here to trap me increases.

The man I'm looking at now is the pyromancer whom Banta chose to stand at his right hand, the cold-hearted criminal the demon sent to take care of anybody who got in his way.

"You give me no choice, Ana," Aiden says.

He rolls his shoulders and curls his fingers into fists, a deliberately controlled movement.

I take a sharp breath as flames from the nearest pyre leap toward his hands, arcing across the air so fast that I can hardly follow their path before they curl around each of his fingers and light up his palms.

I circle around him, my fangs descending halfway, their silver tips peeking between my lips. "I don't like to drink blood, Aiden," I say. "But that doesn't mean I won't drink yours."

He pauses, suddenly still. Suddenly wary. "You have new fangs."

My lips twist. "You thought I was fangless after what Banta's men did to me?"

His response is flat. "Vampires don't regrow their fangs."

I snarl. "I guess I'm not as helpless as you anticipated."

I don't wait for him to make the first move. My goal now is to get him the hell out of here before he hurts anyone. The only way to do that is to knock him out.

To do that… I need to bite him.

Just one bite.

I'm not an ordinary vampire and he fucking knows it.

CHAPTER THREE

A cold smile grows on my face—cold enough to match his.
I'm a rarity among vampires.

The venom of other vampires fills their victims with euphoria while the vampire drains them of their blood, killing their victims through blood loss.

My venom knocks my target out by slowing their heartrate. If I inject enough of it at once, I can stop their heart nearly instantly.

Biting one of Aiden's enemies was how I finally gained his trust.

Before I can step toward him, fire leaps from his palm, hitting the ground at my feet and flaring upward—a warning shot.

I cast a scathing glance at the burned grass. My knee-high leather boots protect me from the heat, and the fact that he used a cautionary shot indicates he'll only hurt me as a last resort.

Advancing on him as he flings another fireball at my feet, I step right through the flames and aim a punch at the bullets in his shoulder.

I'm prepared to break my knuckles on the metal ends, but it will be worth the pain I'll cause him—pain I intend to use to drive him to his knees so I can sink my fangs into his shoulder.

He extinguishes the fire around his fist and catches my hand before I can land the blow, twisting and attempting to force me to the ground.

I react just as swiftly, using my left knee to aim a hit right across his groin. He releases my hand to block my leg, so I draw back my fist for another punch—which he also blocks.

Harnessing my natural speed, I attempt to rain blows on him with my fists, feet, knees, elbows—but he moves as fast as I do, blocking every single knock.

Crimson lightning suddenly crackles in the distance, casting electricity across the sky, and I'm distracted by the two thunderbirds in the distance where they perch on the rocky platforms jutting from each side of the Spire.

Their hearts send lightning thumping through their bodies, but the sudden crackles indicate they aren't happy. The ruby bird spreads her wings, and even from a distance, her suddenly sharp eyes gleam like fiery suns in the thick darkness around the tower.

I flinch when she rises from her perch and beats her wings with a thunderous *boom* that sends lightning crackling through the air around her.

Aiden also jolts at the thunder reverberating around the clearing, releasing me and twisting toward the birds with a shout. "What the fuck is that?"

The thunderbirds are the last of their kind and he won't have seen one before. I hadn't, either, before yesterday.

Leaving the platform, the ruby bird soars down toward us, flying frighteningly low across the space above our heads.

Aiden drops to the ground, but I remain where I am, standing tall as my hair billows in the wind her wing beats creates.

The ruby bird is bonded with Tessa. I'm certain she won't hurt me.

With another booming beat of her wings, the thunderbird banks and soars away toward the forest on my right. Despite all of the darkness within my memories, my heart lifts to see her fly.

I spin back to Aiden, preparing to take advantage of his shock to grab him—except that he's already moving, throwing himself forward.

I scream as his arms close around my hips and he lifts me off my feet, flinging me across his uninjured shoulder so fast that the air whooshes out of my chest.

He runs with me toward the pyre, and I have two choices.

I can drive my knee into the bullets around his heart and—potentially—kill him.

Or I can attempt to bite him—maybe the back of his neck if I can reach it. My venom will knock him out and I can get away from the flames he's running toward before his power stops protecting me from their heat.

Attempting to use my stomach muscles, I try to twist and sink my teeth into his shoulder, but his arms are clamped so tightly that I can't twist close enough.

In another three steps, we'll reach the pyre.

Damn him for forcing me to risk his life.

With a scream of effort, I drive my knee into his chest, trying to avoid the location of the bullets.

The impact causes him to veer off course, and I sense the way his breathing changes, rasping out of his mouth. I can't believe that he remains on his feet with all the pain he must be feeling, but he corrects his path right away.

I scream, "I can't go with you!"

His response is a roar. "I won't let you die again. Not when I can do something about it."

His declaration hurts my heart.

He thought I'd died. He would have found out that I was alive at the same time Banta did. I never attempted to contact him to let him know I was okay.

I let him believe I was gone.

I squeeze my eyes closed as Aiden hurtles into the flames. He leaps right into the center of them and then stops as the heat envelops us on every side.

A scream of terror rises to my throat as the flames jump higher, curving inward.

I brace for the burn, but Aiden wrenches me off his shoulder, pulls me close, and wraps his hand around the back of my head, his other arm around my backside, gathering me as close as he can.

The fire rises up around us, beating at my back, and for a horrible second, I wonder if this is the end that Banta has designed for me—to burn in this fire.

My survival instincts kick in, and I fight with everything I have to escape Aiden's hold, kicking and pushing against him. But his power over the flames is a force I can't defeat, pressing in on me with all of its heat like a physical weight.

I'm forced to become still, my heart pounding in my chest.

A cocoon forms around us, a buffer of power—not quite like air because it's hazy and hot—becoming heavier and thicker. It has to be some sort of protective layer, keeping us from burning, and now I'm trapped because fighting my way out of it means stepping into the flames.

Aiden draws back far enough for me to see his face as the cocoon thickens. "Please trust me," he says.

My lips part. Tears stream down my cheeks, evaporating in the heat.

I whisper, "I can't. We can't ever trust each other."

His jaw hardens, his expression becoming cold again. "I will do everything in my power to make sure you trust me. Even if it kills me."

His gaze becomes distant, and I can only guess that he's searching for another fire somewhere—a flame powerful enough to jump both of us into.

For a moment, I second-guess my decision not to believe him. If he planned to take me to Banta, he would surely already know which fire he wanted to jump into…?

His expression brightens and he refocuses on me. "I have it. A safe flame for us."

The pulse of his power ripples through me, but, just as I sense myself lift, becoming weightless in his arms, shapes move beyond the fire above me.

A giant shadow covers us and crimson lightning ripples through the air, striking right into the pyre and washing across my back.

My head snaps back to witness the power descending on us from above.

CHAPTER FOUR

*T*he crimson thunderbird's talons rake through the flames, ripping through the cocoon of power around me, tearing a gash through it.

In the same instant, an angry scream splits my hearing and Tessa throws herself off the thunderbird's back, right into the fire.

The strength of her entrance parts the flames and forces the cocoon Aiden was building around us to split completely, driving a wedge between the flames and creating a tunnel through them.

She crashes into me, ripping me out of Aiden's arms, her scream echoing around us like a physical force that makes me want to slap my hands over my ears.

At the same time, I groan with relief because she's here and she can cut through any lie to see the truth.

She'll know if Aiden is lying.

"Iyana!" she cries, her blue eyes blazing. "I've got you!"

Her strength and speed take my breath away as she scoops me up and leaps from the fire with me in her arms.

In the same instant, Tristan hurtles through the flames behind her.

His wild, raven black hair whips across his face, his crisp, green eyes piercing, and his muscles bunching as he leaps from the ground on the other side of the fire.

He barrels into Aiden, his broad shoulders colliding with Aiden's chest as he lifts Aiden off his feet.

Tristan moves so fast that, within the space of a blink, he and Aiden exit the flames and roll across the grass.

Smoke rises from Aiden's back as he attempts to jump to his feet in time to face Tristan, who leaps back into the fight, steam lifting from his shoulders and one hem of his jeans ablaze.

Aiden's hand darts out, calling the fire to himself. It blazes around his hands and chest, lighting up his entire torso in deadly swirls.

He braces and gives a roar that would stop any other supernatural in their tracks—but Tristan doesn't even flinch. He shifts into his wolf form, shedding his burning jeans at the same time and leaving them to smolder on the grass.

His wolf is massive—a sleek, black-furred beast that reaches Aiden's waist.

Tristan is unstoppable. He's a descendant of Cerberus, the guardian of the gates of Hell.

A little bit of fire isn't going to slow him down.

Even if Aiden is now encased in more than a *little* fire.

Aiden's entire body blazes and his eyes glow amber, the same color as the flame he throws directly at Tristan's wolf.

Tristan's wolf avoids the blow, adjusts his course, and leaps at Aiden's chest, ignoring the blaze as he attempts to snag Aiden's shoulder and pull him down.

Aiden reacts swiftly, his fist smacking into Tristan's wolf's neck, splashing fire around them both. The punch barely slows Tristan down. His claws scrape down Aiden's side. Aiden roars with pain but jolts to the side to avoid the worst of the cut.

The fight between Tristan and Aiden happens so quickly that Tessa has barely slowed down with me while it continues. She drops low to the ground, gathering me up in her arms before she reaches for my face and shoulders and rapidly checks me over. "Iyana! Are you okay? Are you hurt?"

"I'm okay." I gasp. Exhale. "I'm okay."

My eyes are wide as the fight between Aiden and Tristan becomes even more ferocious.

My heart lurches because as much as Aiden poses a threat to everyone here, I don't want him to die because of me. I want the threat of Banta Sol to be over. I want the pain of the past to be healed.

I don't want Aiden killed.

But to get between Tristan and his target is to take my own life into my hands.

"Please, Tessa!" I cry. "I don't want Aiden to die."

She stares at me, a hint of crimson flashing across her irises, but it disappears and doesn't flood her eyes. "Who is this man to you?" she asks me urgently.

I'm already tugging out of her arms, needing to launch myself between the two men before they tear each other apart. I'm in disbelief that Aiden has lasted this long. I need to stop them—

"No. Wait," Tessa orders me, grabbing me and pinning me with all of her strength. "Stepping in front of Tristan right now is suicide." She gives me a commanding stare. "Explain to me why this man is important to you."

I'm grateful that Tessa didn't use her power to invade my deepest emotions, but I need her to know that, despite my complicated history with Aiden, he's meaningful to me.

"Aiden is Banta Sol's first lieutenant—"

Tessa's snarl is instant, her teeth sharpening and her claws snapping out. "He obeys the demon who hurt you?"

Her gaze passes swiftly across my face. I guess she's flashing back to the day we met when I told her it took Helen six months to reconstruct my face and body after the damage Banta did to me.

"Aiden had no part in that," I say in a rush. "He wasn't there that night. He would have tried to help me." *Maybe. Unless Banta forced him not to.* "He came here to warn me."

Tessa's eyes are luminescent but growing wider by the second as she flashes a glance at the fire blazing around Aiden's body. "Wait..." she whispers. "The flames remind you of him."

I guess she remembers what I said to her earlier in the night. But it feels as if she sees so much more than I want her to.

I give her a quick nod. "I can't let him die."

"Quickly. Tell me about his power. What is he? A fire mage? A warlock?"

I'm already at my screaming point. Every second counts right now, but Tessa's order is undeniable. She needs to know what she's up against before she takes him on.

"He's a pyromancer," I say, speaking so quickly that it comes out in a garbled rush. "He can't create fire from nothing. But once he has access to even the smallest spark, he can make a firestorm. He can do anything with it. See with it. Kill with it. Even use it to move from place to place."

My summary of Aiden's skills makes Tessa stiffen. Her bright eyes meet mine, and her soft 'hmm' tells me she realizes Aiden's power poses a greater risk to her and Tristan than if he were a magician.

Tessa and Tristan are resistant to all magic except old magic, but the flames Aiden controls aren't magical. He doesn't create fire like a mage or a warlock might. The natural world can still hurt my alpha and her true mate.

Tessa presses her lips together when her gaze falls on Tristan, as if she's acutely aware that he won't stop. Not when he perceives a new threat to the people he loves after everything he already fought against.

Fuck knows, he's justified to want to end Aiden.

All Tessa says is, "Okay."

Her hair flies around her face as she tips her head back and cries, "Danika! I need you!"

I search the night sky where Tessa is looking, trying to see past the golden haze of the pyres. Above us, the ruby thunderbird has been coasting in the air, hovering close to Tessa, but now she lifts upward, circling higher and higher.

That's when a smaller form appears beneath the thunderbird's position and circles lower, descending in a rapid swoop.

Danika's hawk soars down from above, her gorgeous honey-colored feathers glistening in the dark. She dives toward Aiden and Tristan, her hawk shrieking so shrilly that she knocks both of them apart.

Tristan's wolf leaps backward, out of Danika's path, but Aiden ends up plastered to the ground, lying on his side. His biceps strain as he tries to push himself back up and his roar becomes desperate, the sound drowned out by Danika's scream.

Off to the side, Tristan's wolf snarls, his teeth bared as he paces, unable to enter the space that Danika targets as she swoops over and over at Aiden until the pyromancer throws his hands over his ears. He's completely pinned to the ground.

"Cody!" Tessa cries, another call for help.

From the other side of the clearing, Cody appears out of the darkness and runs toward us, his legs pumping. He's wearing low-slung jeans and nothing more. Not even shoes, his bare feet flying. He's broad-shouldered, his biceps as large as Tristan's, his waist lean. His hair is sandy blond, and his brown eyes are the color of hickory. Despite his lack of other attire, he's carrying two guns.

His gaze is raised to the sky above us, his focus solely on Danika, who drops through the air toward him.

He skids to a stop and pitches one of the guns up to her. "Danika!"

Her wings sweep close to her sides as she plummets to the ground, following the arc of the weapon. In one breathtaking move, she shifts back into her human form, deftly snatches the gun out of the air, and lands next to Aiden.

Her scream fades, even though she has the strength to maintain it in her human form.

Standing over Aiden, ignoring the flames still licking across his skin, she arms the weapon—a deadly *click-clack* in the suddenly deafening silence—and takes aim at his head. "Don't fucking move unless you want to die."

Danika is shorter than I am, her light brown hair tousled and falling past her shoulders, the golden highlights softly illuminated by the firelight. In contrast, her gold-flecked hazel eyes are hard and angry.

She's butt-naked and furious.

Tristan's wolf takes one look at her and halts where he is, growling softly before he resumes his human form. He shifts so quickly that he's a mountain of human muscle again before I even blink. Retrieving his jeans, he swiftly pulls them on, apparently unconcerned that one leg of the pants has burned off to the mid-calf.

In the meantime, Cody takes a knee and now aims the other gun he's holding at Aiden.

The pyromancer freezes as he lies half on his side, his fists punched into the ground where he was trying to push himself up.

One of the bullets in his shoulder, and another across his heart, must have been dislodged during his fight with Tristan because blood leaks down his chest and drips to the ground.

My heart remains in my throat when Tessa releases me so I can take a step toward him. My movement seems to be enough to draw his gaze to me. Without looking away from me, he very slowly inches upward onto his knees, not making any sudden moves while he carefully splays his arms.

The firelight he was controlling dies, the flames glinting across his muscles and fading, leaving him bent partially over his knees.

I'm more worried about the fact that Aiden has *stopped* fighting now. The seven pyres burning nearby give him access to unlimited fire. I once watched him raze an entire compound to the ground within minutes because Banta had ordered him to take out a rival's stronghold. He did it with the smallest flame—a lighter that he always kept in his pocket.

Aiden could fill this whole clearing with wildfire within seconds and burn everyone to death.

Instead, he kills the remaining light around his fists and raises his head to look directly at me. "I will do anything to protect you, Iyana. Even if it gets me killed."

CHAPTER FIVE

*M*y heart remains in my throat, but Tessa is quiet beside me.

She's relentless when someone she loves is in danger, but she isn't rash or prone to violence when it's not necessary. In fact, she hates violence. More than anyone I've ever met.

"Let's figure this out. Together," she says to me. "Stay close to me."

She also gestures to her pack—my friends—behind me.

The violet glow of Maeve's shield of magic fades as the ashen-haired witch lowers her arms, allowing Tessa's pack to follow us. At the same time, Queen Calanthe mobilizes the fae, who spread out to form a protective circle around our position together with the other packs.

Everyone is quiet, and I'm grateful that the packs and the fae seem to be waiting for instructions from their leaders instead of acting out of fear or anger toward Aiden. Even Bridget, Tristan's delta, who is usually hot-headed, remains calm as she waits for her alpha's commands.

Tessa crosses the final steps to Aiden's position and I remain close on her heels, even though everything inside me wants to surge ahead and deal with this situation myself.

Tessa is my alpha. I trust her with my whole heart. I have to keep trusting her now.

As she walks, she seeks Tristan across the clearing and the

connection between them nearly knocks me off my feet. They adjust their positions together—not like a mirror of each other—but in a way that complements the other. Even their breathing is visibly synced.

Tristan takes up position directly behind Aiden while Tessa prowls toward him.

It leaves Aiden with Danika pointing a gun at him on his left, Cody aiming at him on his right, Tristan behind him, and Tessa stopping in front of him.

Aiden stares up at her before his focus returns to me. His expression is blank now, his cheeks pale, while the blood continues to drip down his chest.

"Aiden," Tessa says. "You're clearly hurt and in need of medical attention, but unfortunately, we can't trust you. So we're going to talk for a few minutes. Your responses will determine whether or not we help you. Do you understand?"

A muscle in Aiden's jaw tightens, but it's the only betrayal of his emotions before he nods.

Tessa surprises me when she murmurs to me, "Sit with me, Iyana."

She lowers herself to the ground, folding her legs under herself. I notice that she chooses a spot just outside of Aiden's reach. Her flannel shirt is long enough that it skims the grass when she sits and folds her hands in her lap, a demure pose that conceals all of her ferocity.

I feel the tug of the bond between her and me drawing me closer to her. Following her lead, I kneel beside her, but I can't seem to alleviate the anxiety I feel.

Tessa's voice is soft, but I sense her speech carrying to her pack and the other supernaturals. "My home is protected by old magic," she says to Aiden. "But somehow, your power allowed you to puncture the shield around us to see within these grounds."

Aiden's brow furrows. "Old magic is a myth. It doesn't exist."

Tessa doesn't contradict him. "Nevertheless, this is my home, Aiden, and you've invaded it. You need to state your intentions here, but I warn you, I will know if you lie." She spares a glance at Tristan before she turns back to Aiden. "You should know that we hate liars."

It was one of the first things I discovered about Tristan after he helped me—he won't tolerate lies. It wasn't until I found out about the minds of Cerberus—one of which was the Deceiver—that the source of his hatred was revealed.

"I'm here for Iyana," Aiden says. "Banta Sol is hunting her, and it won't be long before he traces me to this place. I have to get her out of here before his men arrive."

Tessa shakes her head. "But that's the problem. You're Banta's first lieutenant—"

"*Was*," Aiden snarls. His fierce gaze rakes over me. "I *was* Banta Sol's first lieutenant."

I draw a quick breath. Aiden joined Banta's organization when he was a teenager. He has stood at the demon's right hand for the past decade. It would have taken something catastrophic for Banta to demote him.

"What happened?" I whisper.

His jaw tenses. "*You* happened." His gaze pierces mine. "I wasn't there when he killed you that night. When I found out about it—when I thought you died—I wanted to end him, but I couldn't."

"Because of your brother," I murmur. Family was the reason Aiden got embroiled with Banta in the first place. A reason I could understand.

He gives a terse nod.

Tessa's expression is closed off beside me, but she says, "Explain your situation to me, Aiden. And remember, I hate lies."

Aiden exhales slowly. "I joined Banta's operations when I was fifteen. My brother, Lucas, was ten years old. Our parents had abandoned us because Lucas is an Unknown."

"An Unknown?" Tessa asks. "What is that?"

"Magically repressed," Aiden says. "His powers didn't manifest when we were kids. For all intents and purposes, he may as well be human. Except that Unknowns are dangerous. When their powers are finally revealed, they can't control them.

"At first, they have what are called flicker fits—smaller blasts of power. But when their repressed power finally bursts through, they can't control it. They kill everyone around them. Lucas had his first flicker fit when he was ten. That's when our parents left. I guess I was grateful they didn't kill him like some parents do."

Tessa is tense beside me, her claws suddenly digging into her jeans across her knees. I don't know the full extent of the violence she faced as a child, but I know how deep her feelings run about being rejected by family.

"How did Banta Sol come into all of this?" Tessa asks.

"He caught me raiding a dumpster behind a night club he owns," Aiden says. "He said he could protect my brother—stop the fits, help Lucas control his power when it finally fully manifested. He promised to protect us. In return, all he wanted was my loyalty."

Tessa sighs. "Loyalty sounds simple," she says. "But I'm guessing it cost much more."

"At first, I followed Banta by choice. He treated us like his sons. Gave us everything we needed," Aiden says. "Eventually, I came to realize that my mind was no longer my own."

A crease forms in Tessa's forehead. Because she grew up secluded from other supernaturals, there are many species she hasn't been exposed to. "What is this demon's power?"

Aiden's jaw tenses so suddenly that his teeth crack. "He tells you to do something and you don't even fucking question it. You just do it. It's only afterward, when you find yourself standing over a body with blood on your hands, that you start to think for yourself again. But by then, it's too late." Aiden's eyes blaze. "Because that person you killed—they've got family. Friends. Now Banta's your only ally."

Tessa is intensely still, although her focus has shifted to Tristan. His black hair falls across his face, but his green eyes are alert between the strands. The silent communication between him and Tessa is so powerful, it makes me shiver again.

Tessa's lips soften. Tristan gives her the barest nod.

I can't be sure what they're saying to each other, but Tristan knows better than anyone what it's like to lose himself to the control of another being. The minds of Cerberus destroyed his family for generations before he and Tessa overcame them.

"You must have many enemies now," Tessa says to Aiden.

Aiden grinds his teeth. "Too many. It doesn't matter that my targets all deserved it. You see, that's what makes Banta so clever. He reads you. He gets to know you—understands your nature better than you know it yourself. He never tells you to do anything that is so contrary to your beliefs that you'd rebel against it."

Tessa purses her lips. "Then what is this?" she asks, gesturing to his chest. "Clearly, this didn't happen because you obeyed him."

I lean forward, wishing I understood the injuries he has sustained

—the pattern of bullets seems far too deliberate, but the way they're stopped in his chest is confusing.

Aiden's cold smile grows colder. It never fails to surprise me how a man with the power to control a warming fire can carry a heart of ice in his chest. "This time, he pushed me too fucking far."

"How?"

Aiden's eyes narrow. "I've answered enough of your questions."

Tessa stiffens as she stares at Aiden. When she glances my way, I catch the fading crimson in her eyes, the telltale sign that, while I was focused on Aiden, she finally used her power to discern his impulses.

Fuck, I would give anything to know what she knows right now—to be certain if I can trust him.

Her lips are parted slightly as if she's taking a quick breath, and when she speaks, her voice is harsh. "Iyana, I want you to move away from Aiden."

I freeze where I'm poised, leaning forward, nearly breaching the gap between me and Aiden. I'm so close to him that I inhale the fiery scent of his skin. I'm suddenly aware that Tristan has also tensed, his muscles bunching, his focus on Tessa as if they're once again communicating with each other.

"Iyana," Tessa says. "Move away from him. *Now.*"

A shiver passes through me at what she might have seen in him that has suddenly made her so worried. The bond between her and me plucks at my heart, urgently pulling me toward her—and away from Aiden.

Just as I move, Aiden's hand snaps out and wraps around my wrist, a firm hold.

The sudden blaze in his eyes is my only warning of his intentions.

He sweeps his free hand toward Tessa. In the same instant, firelight arcs from the nearest pyre, lights up his hand, and blasts through the air at her.

Tessa's reflexes are second to none.

She leaps backward so fast that her whole body is a blur as she flies out of reach of the firebomb. But she has her own dangerously hidden gift.

As she soars backward, her wolf's energy launches from her body, its form a blaze of emerald light as it takes shape, its eyes as crimson as hers right now. It's an insubstantial creature that may as well be a dagger, the pain I've seen it inflict taking down the strongest creatures.

It all happens so fast that I'm still trying to pull out of Aiden's hold when Tessa's wolf appears. If the wolf weren't jumping toward us, I would clobber Aiden myself, but as it is, I have to spin to the side to avoid its fury, yanking Aiden with me.

Aiden's shout of surprise at the wolf's appearance breaks across the clearing, but his apparent determination to keep hold of me is his undoing.

Tessa's wolf passes through his upper chest and bullet-riddled shoulder and lands on the other side of him.

Aiden's hand opens and I slip easily from his hold as he slumps over his knees, his face ashen, his lips colorless.

He grips his chest, over his heart.

He must be in horrible pain, but the fucking stubborn man will never admit it.

With a roar of anger, he lurches upright.

Flames from the pyre leap across the distance, flooding his entire torso again. He lurches toward Tessa, taking a menacing step. "Just fucking end me already! It's the only way you'll stop me."

Behind him, Tristan is preparing to shift.

At his side, Danika and Cody have adjusted their aim.

Aiden is surrounded by deadly power. If he wants to die, he's going about it the right way.

"Aiden!" I shout. "Enough!"

Racing forward, I snatch Aiden's blazing hand into mine and draw his wrist to my lips, fire and all.

Flames leap around my face, the heat scorching.

His focus snaps to me.

I was hoping for a chance to bite him when he wasn't using his power, but he's given me no choice. If he really doesn't want to hurt me, he'll extinguish the flames he's controlling before they burn me.

The fire around his wrist dies the scantest second before my hair would catch alight and my skin would burn.

"Do it!" he snarls at me. "Bite me. But make sure you use enough venom to kill me, Ana. Otherwise, I won't stop until I take you away with me."

Closing my mouth around his wrist, I taste ash and the heat of the extinguished flame. My lips draw back, and my fangs descend, breaking the surface of his skin.

At the moment that his blood touches my tongue, the rush takes over. The venom within my gums releases and I shake with the awful euphoria that fills my mind and body.

My fingernails dig into his arm as I fight the desire to keep injecting him.

If I do, I'll kill him.

The smallest amount of my venom will knock him out; too much is lethal.

I grip his arm hard, my fingernails breaking his skin, as I mentally scream at myself to stop.

I'm aware of Tristan, his hand raised to Tessa, as if he's telling her to wait. He knows about the lethality of my bite, although I've never revealed this side of myself to Tessa. I'm also aware of Danika and Cody and the beads of sweat on their foreheads, the way their muscles tense as they prepare to use their guns if they have to.

"Ana," Aiden murmurs, his lips softening, a slight crease forming in his forehead. "Do it already."

I'm stunned. *He really wants me to end him?*

The problem is… I've already injected enough venom into him to knock out two men Aiden's size.

By now, his pupils should have dilated. He should be losing mobility. His legs should be wobbling, his head lolling.

I injected enough venom that he should have hit the fucking grass already.

Instead, he's wide awake. In fact, the brightness of his eyes increases, the distant firelight seeming to dance across his skin even though he extinguished it.

The tension around his mouth increases as he searches my eyes. "Why won't you kill me? You know I'm a threat to you and everyone you love."

I slowly withdraw my fangs, trembling as I stare at the puncture wound in his wrist. My venom spills from the bite; two silver streams mixing with his blood, evidence of the amount of poison I injected. A whole fucking lot of it.

My eyes are wide with shock. "I already did."

Aiden's lips part. His eyebrows rise. It's a moment of surprise that ends too quickly when darkness spreads across his face.

He will have felt my bite—even with the slight numbing agent in my saliva—but his speech tells me he doesn't believe I injected any venom into him.

"I thought you were done lying to me," he says.

I want to shout at him to look at his wrist—to see the venom seeping from the wound—but all I feel right now is panic.

Unless I subdue him, my friends will have no choice but to end him.

I slip to the right, wrap my arms around his chest, risking that he'll whisk me away into the flames with him again. I sense his muscles bunch, see the flame rise in his eyes, feel the heat only moments away...

"Aiden Brand," I say, arresting his attention for the second that I need. "I will never lie to you again."

My declaration has the intended effect. Surprise. Disbelief. Anger. Hope. The light in his eyes changes as each emotion rages across his face, but I don't stop any longer to see the impact of my promise.

Darting forward, I sink my fangs into his neck, losing myself to the rush as my venom pours into him—so much venom that I risk his life. And risk my heart because I don't want to lose him.

Just when I think I've failed—when the heat of flames gathering around his body grows to levels that scorch my skin—his legs bend, his head tips forward, and his weight suddenly bears down on me.

I buckle under his bulk, dropping to the ground so that we don't fall, making sure his head doesn't hit the grass.

We land with him sprawled over me, my arm hooked around his shoulders, my legs pinned, but it's a discomfort I welcome, because he has finally passed out.

Frantically, I press my free hand against his chest, panic billowing through me as I pray I haven't killed him.

CHAPTER SIX

*R*elief fills me as Aiden's heart resumes beating, a regular *thud-thud.*

He's alive.

I knocked him out and saved his life and now…

He's our captive.

The clearing has fallen quiet. Warm arms wrap around me, helping me to support Aiden.

Tessa rubs my back while Tristan and Cody bend to take Aiden's weight from me, working together to lay him on the grassy ground in front of me.

They don't take him away, leaving him close, and I recognize the wolfish gesture. They're treating Aiden as if he's mine—treating him like they would treat a wolf's mate—making sure they don't separate him from me.

It's only when the pressure of his body against my chest lifts that I'm aware of his blood dampening my black T-shirt. Even though his chest rises and falls, it's a slow, shallow movement since my venom has slowed his heart.

My own heart feels raw—raked through.

Once Cody finishes helping Tristan, he steps back and hurries to Danika, reaching for her where she stands with her gun lowered. She catches my eye before he wraps her in his arms.

She and I were at Hidden House together. We never delved too much into each other's pasts, but she knows what Aiden means to me. She'd be able to surmise all of the turmoil his appearance has created within me now.

I don't catch what Cody says to her, but she leans into him, and I'm reminded of the way they worked in unison to guard Aiden just now. One of the fae women hurries forward and passes Danika a pair of jeans and a T-shirt, which she quickly pulls on.

Ella and Jace emerge from the shadows behind Cody and Danika. Ella's long hair is such a pale shade of blonde that it resembles daisy petals, while her eyes are the color of brown treacle. She was already at Hidden House when I arrived there and the trauma of her past had left her fragile, but with Tessa's help she fought through it.

Ella is now the alpha of the eastern lowland pack. She and Jace went through hell to be together. Jace is as tall as Tristan, but his hair is honey blond, and his eyes are a deep green.

They're both quiet, and I suspect they were waiting in the background for a lot longer than I was aware.

Ella makes her way toward us, exchanging a quiet nod with Tessa before she kneels beside Tristan, opposite me. Jace remains standing at her back.

Queen Calanthe also makes her way gracefully toward us, the last of the leaders to join us. Her dark brown hair is streaked with forest green. She is a springtime fae and has the power to control water and the growth of plants.

She kneels at Aiden's feet.

Aiden and I are now surrounded by the three alphas and the Fae Queen—Tessa on my right, Calanthe on my left, and Tristan and Ella opposite me. Cody and Danika remain close on Tessa's right, while her pack remains at our backs.

Tessa has already indicated that she's reserving judgement about Aiden's fate, but now the other leaders will have their say.

Ella's voice is low, a soft growl. "It's hard to tell how much blood he's lost or the damage that has been caused by these bullets in his chest, but he clearly needs a healer or he won't make it."

Tristan's focus shifts to me. "How long will your bite keep him under, Iyana? Will it be long enough to heal him without him becoming agitated and fighting back—given that it's clear he won't trust us?"

I chomp down on my lip as I look between them. "You don't want to kill him?"

Ella's eyebrows shoot up. "Of course not. We trust Tessa's judgement. Whatever's going on with this man, we need more information before we pass judgment on him."

I take a deep, shuddering breath, shaken by the relief that courses through me. My feelings for Aiden are jumbled up in a storm of hate and love that I didn't think it was possible to feel.

Tristan's crisp, green eyes remain levelled with mine, but his expression is softer than before. "How long before he wakes up?"

I'm suddenly aware of the tilt of Tessa's head, the way her warm hand has paused on my back, and the curiosity in her gaze. I haven't previously revealed this aspect of my power to her before, although Tristan is aware of what my bite can do.

My voice scratches in my throat. "I used enough venom to keep him unconscious for a few hours. Any more would risk killing him, and I don't want that."

"A few hours should be more than enough to heal him," Calanthe says.

She's dressed in her indigo armor, even though she was resting only moments ago. All of the fae seem incredibly comfortable in their armor—even sleeping in it—as if it's a second skin to them.

"Since Helen is no longer here with us, I will ask one of my healers to help him," Calanthe continues. "Unfortunately, my own power over water wanes at night—as does the fae power over ice—so we will be little help when it comes to counteracting his pyromancy if he wakes up sooner than anticipated. However, if you wish, I can send Essandra to help guard him when the sun comes up. Her power over ice should extinguish any fire he might try to make."

"Thank you," Tessa says. "In the meantime, my pack will take care of guarding Aiden. I don't want to treat him like an enemy, but we can't take any chances, given the damage he could do with his power." She turns back to the queen. "We should also be ready in case this demon, Banta, attempts to attack the Spire."

Calanthe responds without hesitation. "We will protect the Spire's perimeter. It's our honor to have the chance to guard this place of magic again. Now that we know we have a new enemy in this demon, we won't take any chances."

My breath catches at the way these two powerful women are talking. The reality is that Banta Sol is my problem. I'm the reason Aiden is here.

Banta is after me.

I'm the one who has brought about the threat to the safety that Tessa fought so hard to give all of us.

My heart suddenly pounds inside my chest as I wonder if… maybe… I should have allowed Aiden to take me away. By leaving, I could have taken the threat with me.

As if she hears my thoughts and anticipates what I'm about to say, Tessa's hand suddenly slips from my back and lands on my arm, a firmer hold than before.

"No," she says. "I've been down that road, Iyana. I'm not letting you walk that path alone." Her deep, blue eyes compel me to listen and believe her. "You and Danika pulled me back from the darkness. Now, I will be here for you."

Tessa presses her lips together as she contemplates Aiden. "As for this man, we'll be there for him, too, if he chooses to let us help him."

Speech sticks in my throat. "Thank you," I whisper.

"Okay, then. Let's get him away from these fires and inside the Spire as quickly as we can," Tessa says.

Opposite us, Ella rises to her feet. "I'll check in on you soon. In the meantime, I'll make sure my pack remains calm. With your permission, Tristan, I'll ask Carly to look after your pack."

Tristan gives her a nod. "I'd appreciate that. I'll stay with Tessa for now."

"Ella?" Tessa reaches for the blonde-haired alpha before she can leave. "Your pack needs to heal. If you need to leave in the morning, I'll understand. We've got this covered."

Ella reaches across to Tessa. "Thank you, Tessa. I trust you to handle this."

Tessa gives Ella a firm nod, after which Ella and Jace quickly navigate toward the shifter packs, while Calanthe rises and begins calling instructions to the fae. Within moments, the fae army has mobilized around us, heading toward the outskirts of the Spire in all directions, while Ella's and Tristan's packs gather in the background.

Soon, only Tessa's pack remains with us—along with Tristan.

"Your pack needs to heal, too," Tessa says to him.

His jaw tightens, since her unspoken message is that he might need to leave her to take care of his pack. He shakes his head with a low, soft growl. "Carly can care for my pack for another day."

Tessa doesn't give up. "We're safe here," she says, firmly. "I've got this. Your pack needs their alpha."

"We'll talk about it," Tristan replies, apparently the only concession he's prepared to give right now.

He and Cody bend to lift Aiden—Cody at his feet and Tristan at his head—but Maeve steps forward, small flares of violet light playing across her palms. "I can lift and carry him into the Spire with my power, assuming he isn't immune to my magic?"

Her question is directed to me, and I shake my head. "Not to my knowledge." Unlike Tristan, whom we had to physically carry down a flight of stairs because he's immune to all magic except old magic.

I'm suddenly aware of Tessa's intense scrutiny on Aiden as Maeve's power flares, a sharp burst of violet light that spreads along the grass around Aiden's body and then rises up around him.

Tessa visibly relaxes when Maeve's magic curls around Aiden and lifts him off the ground, the violet haze spreading beneath him like a physical force.

"Okay," Tessa says, so calmly that I'm sure I imagined her tension. "Let's get him inside and heal him as fast as we can."

Tristan walks beside Tessa, while I stay close to Aiden's side, trying not to step within the sphere of Maeve's magic in case it lifts me off my feet.

I'm comforted when the other women of Tessa's pack, along with Cody, fall in behind us.

Maeve speaks quietly to me as we walk, her cedar-brown eyes darkening when we leave the burning pyres behind. "I don't have Tessa's ability to clearly see a person's impulses, but I sense deep conflict within this man's mind," she says. "Do you believe his word that he came here to warn you and not to harm you?"

My fingers hover over the bullets embedded in Aiden's chest.

"He and I have a complicated history," I say. "But he never hurt me." My response diminishes to a murmur. "I believe his intentions are honest."

"Then we need to make sure he doesn't die," Maeve says. "In the meantime, I have to warn you that if he makes any move that threatens you, or any person here, I won't hesitate to wrap him up in so much pain that he'll wish he didn't exist."

It's not an idle warning. Maeve was forced to obey Mother Zala, a witch who taught Maeve how to use her magic to inflict pain and suffering.

"I understand," I say. "I wouldn't expect anything less."

Some of the tension leaves Maeve's shoulders.

Soft footfalls sound, and Luna appears on my left. She's petite, wearing a flowing skirt and loose sweater, a sharp contrast to the armor-clad fae. When she reaches me, she flicks a bright square of paper into the air, where it turns softly, the card keeping pace with me with every step I take.

The card depicts a human heart speared with a dagger. It was one of the first cards Luna showed Tessa, and I know too well what it means: a heart turned upon itself, in pain, unable to heal.

Luna's sage-green eyes are wide, her cheeks flushed peach, the color so marked that it's discernable in the dark. She doesn't speak. Has never spoken. Her sister, Lydia, usually voices Luna's thoughts for her, but in this instance, Lydia is resolutely quiet where she walks a step behind her sister.

With a quiet exhalation, I accept the card, plucking it gently from the air.

It's time to take ownership of the dagger I drove through my own heart seven months ago.

CHAPTER SEVEN

*T*ogether, we move at a rapid pace, approaching the Spire within minutes.

The tall, black tower sits at the edge of the cliffs where the ocean waves crash—a sound that I've quickly become accustomed to. The Spire has fifteen levels and a platform jutting from each side near the top.

The two thunderbirds have resumed their perch above us, one on each platform, their wings folded to their sides. It fascinates me that their hearts beat lightning around their bodies, the pulses curling across the night sky.

The sapphire bird is bonded to Calanthe's daughter, while the wilder ruby bird is loyal to Tessa in a way that seems to have surprised the fae.

The ruby bird's talons curl around the edge of the platform as she leans over it, following our path as we approach the low dais at the foot of the tower, her sharp focus never leaving Aiden.

I'm grateful that Aiden is unconscious. If he were awake, he would be a greater threat, but the pallor of his skin concerns me.

"Where should we take him?" Tristan asks Tessa, but my alpha defers to me.

"Iyana?" Tessa says. "You know his power best."

"Any room without a fireplace in it," I say. "Not that that leaves us with many options."

I didn't spend much time exploring the Spire after the battle yesterday, but my quick tour confirmed several crucial details. For starters, every room is lit with lamps filled with magical flames and I have no way of knowing whether or not Aiden can control the fire within them.

Also, the majority of the rooms don't have doors, only arched and open doorways, so there's no way to constrain him without taking him to one of the cells on the lower floors—rooms that Fenrir apparently used to cage supernaturals over the years.

Neve speaks up from the other side of Aiden. "There's a room adjacent to the kitchen on the first floor," she says. She's partially shifted, her snow leopard evident in the shape of her pale-blue eyes. "It has a table we could put him on and no fireplace. I saw it earlier when we were preparing food."

I give a quick nod. "That will do."

"This way." Neve hurries ahead of us as we navigate through the entry room, which is shaped like a semi-circle and contains five sets of stairs on the circular side. Etched into the top of the arches above each are numbers listed in groups of three, from one to fifteen.

She leads us up the first staircase—the sapphire light glowing across her alabaster skin—and along the first hallway we reach, past the enormous kitchens, and to a smaller room next to it on the far side of the tower.

"Here," she says.

The room contains a wooden table, its surface and legs chunky, appearing roughly hewn together with several wooden chairs. The far wall is lined with hooks, from which aprons hang.

Yesterday, Tessa told me that some of the old magic in this tower is still functioning, like the weather shields around the windows, which don't contain any glass. The first floor is so close to the cliff's edge that I can see the water spray rise outside the window where the ocean waves must be hitting the rocks.

Each of the room's corners contains a lamp that rests above eye-level and is lit with dreaded flames.

"What about the lamps?" I ask Tessa. "Are they natural fire?"

"Those flames are old magic, built into the fabric of the Spire itself," she replies, confidently. "They aren't ordinary flames. He won't be able to control them."

I exhale a breath of relief at this news.

Tessa directs Maeve to place Aiden on the table, after which she's quick to organize the rest of the pack, asking everyone except me and Tristan to remain outside on guard. Her pack fans out along the hallway outside the room, but before Maeve leaves, she catches my arm. "I'm sorry I can't help with his healing."

"It's okay," I say.

A moment later, before Maeve can leave, a petite woman hurries into the room. "I'm Elen," she announces. "Queen Calanthe sent me."

Her eyes are ash-gray, her hair a soft coral pink. Unlike most of the other fae, she's wearing a blouse and a skirt, which makes me think she's not a warrior like the others. Her high-cut top is a pale blue while her skirt is deep amethyst, and her skin is the palest gold.

She heads straight for Aiden, speaking quickly. "You left the bullets in. Good. They must each be taken out and the wound beneath treated before the next bullet is removed, or he could lose too much blood. I need hot water, towels, and pliers—or some other instrument I can use to remove the bullets."

Maeve immediately jumps into action. "I'm on it."

Tessa and Tristan pull up chairs on the far side of the room, watching closely while the fae woman continues to lean over Aiden, examining each of his wounds.

Her lips press harder together, her expression growing grim. She gives a low 'hmm' before she says, "These bullets reek of a magic I've never come across before."

"Is it dark magic? Like a warlock's?" I ask.

"It feels different." Elen pulls back sharply. "Many of the bullets are aimed at his vital organs—perfectly positioned to cause death if they continued on their path. My guess is that whoever did this was using the threat of the bullets as a form of coercion. Trying to make this man do something he didn't want to do. Or to reveal something he didn't want to reveal."

My throat constricts as my anger rises. I can't stop my fangs from descending. "You're saying he was… tortured?"

She looks me in the eyes. "I'm sorry. It's the most likely explanation." Returning her attention to Aiden's wounds, she continues, "Until I remove the poison of this magic, he won't heal."

My breathing quickens and my grip on Aiden's arm tightens. "Banta Sol's power is the manipulation of minds," I say. "He never exhibited any control of magic like this. Someone new must be working for him."

The last dark magician we encountered was the warlock, Silas, but Tessa killed him days ago, so this magic can't be his.

Off to the side of the room, Tessa and Tristan are alert, both of them leaning forward slightly. Their chairs are positioned close enough together that their shoulders are touching and their bodies never lose contact.

Tristan's growl breaks the tense silence. "My conflict with the eastern lowland pack allowed Banta Sol's operations to flourish," he says, his sharp eyes promising violent justice. "Now that our packs are at peace, it's time to end him."

Tessa's hand lowers to Tristan's knee, as if she's urging him to remain calm. The visible change in their breathing from slow to rapid tells me that neither of them likes the idea of sitting this fight out.

"We need more information about this new supernatural," Tessa says. "Elen, can you tell us anything about the identity of the person who did this? Are there any magical indicators?"

Elen considers the bullets carefully before she exhales slowly. "The grooves on the edges of each of these bullets indicate they were fired from a gun *before* they hit him. The supernatural who controlled them is powerful enough to not only stop the bullets' trajectory despite the speed they would have been traveling, but to also guide their path to ensure they hit where they did."

"How would that be possible?" Tessa asks, casting me a worried glance.

"Perhaps the bullets were already spelled so that the supernatural could latch on to the spell midair and control them that way?" I suggest.

Elen shakes her head. "I can't tell you how it was done, only that the person who did this is extremely powerful."

I worry at my bottom lip. "Tessa, you can pluck bullets from the air. Could you control them, too?"

She shakes her head. "I don't think so."

Before I can say more, Maeve hurries back into the room holding an array of metal instruments. Danika follows her, walking more slowly with a bowl of steaming water. They place all of the objects on the table before they back out of the room again.

"We'll stay on guard," Maeve says.

Elen hands me the pliers. "You will help me remove the bullets," she says. "This bullet above his heart first. But you must wait until I tell you."

After latching on to the bullet she points at, I wait as a dark glow grows around Elen's hands, centering on the bullet I'm holding. The dark light is deathly cold. A shiver spears down my spine, and my instincts scream at me to get away from it as fast as I can.

"What is that magic?" I demand to know.

Elen barely glances at me, but her ash-gray eyes suddenly flood with darkness, such pure black that I jolt. It's the same ebony that floods Banta's eyes. Pure evil.

"The poisonous magic must be removed from his body before I can heal him," Elen says, her voice harsh and tense. "Don't interrupt me again."

My instincts fire. I grab her nearest wrist with my free hand. "You may be a fucking pretty rainbow of pastels, but I don't know you. You *will* answer my questions when I ask them."

Her black eyes flash across me. "Darkness attracts darkness," she says. "All fae healers learn this fact early in our training. The only way to draw out malicious magic like this is by using darkness as a poultice. Unfortunately, it is my burden as a healer to walk the fine line between the light and the dark that removing this magic requires. Believe me, it isn't a task I enjoy."

I'm aware of her arm shaking beneath my grasp, but I don't think it's because she's afraid of me. The look in her eyes is one that I've seen many times on Tessa's face. The inner war between light and dark.

Slowly—carefully—I remove my hand.

Elen refocuses on Aiden, and I close my eyes against the dark light she's creating, hating the cloying cold it produces, until she finally says, "Pull the bullet out, please."

The bullet slips free, Aiden's blood beginning to flow, but the light beneath Elen's palms quickly becomes golden and warm, chasing away the dark like a rising sun. Within seconds, Aiden's broken flesh knits together, new skin forms, and the bullet wound seals.

One bullet removed. Seven to go.

CHAPTER EIGHT

*A*s Elen directs me to clamp the pliers around the second bullet, she says, "You're right to distrust the dark light, Iyana. Each time I deal with it, I become a little less sensitive to its nature, a little more accepting of it. It's difficult to fight a power when it would be so much easier to give in to it."

I swallow hard. She's talking about dark powers, but I've learned that lies are much the same. One lie leads to another. Once one is told, it's easier to lie again. And again.

My response is small this time. "Thank you for healing him."

She pats my arm before she concentrates on the next wound. "Now that I know I can successfully heal one wound, I'll try to take the malice from the rest of his wounds. Prepare yourself, please. This won't be pleasant."

I brace as she concentrates her power across Aiden's entire torso. The dark light beneath her palms spreads from his shoulder, across his heart, and down to his ribs, radiating around each of the wounds. The cloying cold is nearly unbearable and my eyes water with discomfort.

I force myself to remain where I am, my head bent, water trickling down my cheeks, but I'm ready to help as soon as Elen asks me to. While the chill in the air increases to such sharp levels that goose-bumps rise all over my skin and I start trembling with the cold, the tears streaming down my cheeks are hot.

I suddenly have to face the fact that I'm not solely crying because of Elen's magic.

There were moments—significant moments—when I was with Aiden that I forgot my mission. There were even times—reckless times—when I considered abandoning it.

"Iyana?" Tessa's gentle voice breaks through my thoughts.

The act of opening my eyes releases a wash of tears down my cheeks.

My throat is scratchy as I try to find my voice. "Yeah?"

Tessa glances at Tristan before she speaks again, and the strength of the connection between them hits me like a hammer. The connection between Aiden and me had felt unbreakable, too.

Then I chose to break it.

"You don't have to tell us anything about Aiden that you don't want to," Tessa says. "But we're here for you if you need us."

I bite my lip as the temperature around me plummets even further, but Elen's focus is complete, and I finally sense the darkness lifting. Within myself, a deep darkness also needs to lift. I've kept so much to myself that talking about what happened feels like a release.

"I wish I could remember the details of that night," I say, quietly. "When I went after Banta, I was so certain I could take him unawares. My plan was to put a bullet in his head before he could make a move to control my actions, but somehow... He must have got inside my mind. I couldn't kill him. His men showed up, and all I could do was try to escape."

"And Aiden?" Tessa asks, gently.

"I made sure he wasn't there that night. Or he would have stopped me. Helped me. Taken the beating for me." I shrug as if it means nothing, except that it means... everything. "I never told Aiden who I was or why I was there." I swallow. "I could have trusted him and told him what I planned to do, but I didn't. I betrayed Aiden's trust when I lied to him."

Tessa presses closer to Tristan as I speak. Maybe she's remembering the pain she felt when Ford Vanguard ripped her away from him. She asks the question I've been dreading—the one I know I don't have to answer, but I want to. "Did you love him?"

I square my shoulders and face her. "I *used* him," I say. "To get close to Banta." I suddenly realize that I'm gripping Aiden's hand and, reluctantly, I let it go. "I didn't realize what it would cost me." I take a deep, shuddering breath. "What it would cost him and me."

She rises from her seat, breaking her contact with Tristan, to reach for me, her sapphire eyes glistening. "But did you love him?"

"I did."

The moment I speak, I exhale what feels like a ton of fear and doubt.

"Then you have to fight for him," she says. "No matter what it takes."

My lips part, my breath short. "What are you saying?"

"I'm saying that you have a battle ahead of you, but I'll be right there with you."

My heart suddenly hammers. "You want to go after Banta. But, Tessa, you've only just found peace."

"He's the final part of Ford Vanguard's empire," she says. "We have to take him down."

I want to believe that we can, but the doubt I thought I'd conquered comes crashing back to me. I shake my head emphatically. "Banta Sol's ability to control minds is beyond anything I've ever experienced. Are you certain that you would be immune to his power?"

Tessa falters a little. She's never rash, always thinks through her actions, which is what I love about her—and why I trust her with my life.

"Demons use dark magic, yes?" she asks. "If that's the case, then Tristan and I are both immune. We can take him out."

Behind her, Tristan rises from his seat and begins a slow prowl in front of the wide window.

Outside, the first hint of dawn spreads across the sky, a lightness to the color of the air despite the heaviness in the room around me. Across the view, the ocean spray begins to sparkle where it mists the air.

My fingers twitch against the cloak at my waist, prepared for when I need to activate the protective suit that Helen designed for me so I can walk in the sunlight.

"Demons have been around since the dawn of time—like angels," Tristan says. "Angels are pure light magic, but their weapons can be infused with old magic."

A new tension grows around Tessa's eyes. Tristan was struck with an angel's spear that was infused with old magic and it nearly killed him.

"We can't be sure what magic or weapons Banta controls," Tristan says.

Tessa presses her lips together into an unhappy line, her brow furrowing. "I'm not sitting this out."

Tristan stops prowling and considers her through the black strands of his hair, the curve of his lips softening. "You might need to," he says, with a growing smile. "And not only for your own sake."

She stares at him before her expression clears and her hands shoot to her stomach. "You can't know that already," she says. But she doesn't sound so certain as she continues. "Can you?"

He breaks into a grin as he strides toward her, sweeping her up into his arms. His lips crash against hers, but it's a brief touch before he nudges her cheek with his. "I will fight beside you in any wars you need to fight, Tessa Dean," he says. "But from now on, I'll be fighting for both of you."

Tears sparkle in her eyes and she smiles as she kisses him.

My heart leaps to watch them and, for a blessed moment, I forget my troubles.

They're going to be parents.

It's unclear to me how Tristan knows that already, but he seems completely certain.

My happiness for them is tinged with a sudden pang of sadness that I quickly push away. I can't have children. Can't become pregnant and give birth.

And given the way my venom works, I highly doubt I could create another vampire—not that I have ever considered doing so, given the threat that vampires pose to humans.

My inability to have a child is a fact that I reconciled with during my time with Aiden when I started to ask myself: *What if?*

What if I could have children, and what if our lives weren't filled with danger... Would I choose to have children with him? The answer was *yes*, but it was all a hypothetical that I put carefully away.

"Congratulations, sweetie," I whisper to Tessa, but as I speak, a new sense of dread overcomes me.

Again, I wonder if I should have allowed Aiden to take me away. Tristan and Tessa have so much more to lose now, and Tristan's warning still rings true: We don't know for certain that either of them will be completely immune to Banta or any weapon he controls —or supernatural, for that matter—since he seems to have a new powerful ally standing beside him. An ally who tried to hurt Aiden tonight.

I nearly leave Aiden's side, ready to tell Tessa that it's too dangerous, that I have to fight this battle alone, when the dark light fades from beneath Elen's palms. The chill around me disappears and the fae woman gives a long exhalation of relief.

"It's done," she says. "We can focus on removing the remainder of the bullets now."

I put aside my intentions to speak with Tessa and Tristan for now and reach for the pliers again. Just as I close the instrument around the bullet resting against Aiden's ribs that Elen points to, my instincts fire.

My focus flashes to Aiden's face, my gaze landing on his navy-blue eyes as they blaze at me.

Fuck!

He's awake already!

CHAPTER NINE

*A*iden lurches upright in a rush, rising with a fierce roar that sends a shiver down my spine.

Elen's healing power dies around her hands and she immediately leaps away from him, running toward Tessa and Tristan, who have immediately braced at the side of the room.

I remain where I am as Aiden launches himself off the table away from me, ramming into the wall so hard that the *thud* vibrates in my hearing. The pliers clatter to the ground—a jarring sound—since his movement wrenched them out of my hands.

Aiden's focus flies to the lamps on the walls as his fingers twitch, but he doesn't appear to make a grab for the flames yet.

It's only going to take him a minute to switch from defensive to offensive, and I don't want him to escalate—especially when he discovers he can't control the flames here. He already declared that old magic is a myth. He won't easily believe that the magic in the Spire exists.

I flash an appeal at Tessa that I hope she'll read correctly: *Please let me handle this.* I catch her responding nod and the way her fingers wrap around Tristan's arm, urging him to stay with her, before I spin toward Aiden.

"Easy, Aiden," I say, lifting my hands and stepping between him and Tessa and Tristan. "You're among friends now."

"Where the fuck am I?" Aiden shouts, his dark blue eyes flashing around the room from the open window, to Tessa and Tristan—and Elen hovering behind them—then back to me.

"You're safe," I say, keeping my hands lifted away from the guns and daggers resting at my waist.

"Safe," he snarls, edging around the table toward me. "Fuck *safe*. What about *free*, Ana?"

My heart plummets. "You're not a prisoner here."

"I'll always be a prisoner," he says, his voice low and harsh. "Here or with Banta."

My focus darts to the bullets still in his chest. We didn't finish healing him. He's still hurting, and the pain must be messing with his ability to rationalize his situation.

I force my legs to move, backing carefully away. I'm conscious of Tessa and Tristan, their increasingly angry growls. They will understand Aiden's fears—the fear of being restrained and imprisoned—but they will protect me and their packs above all else.

He may have revealed his inner turmoil to me about working for Banta, but Banta chose Aiden as his first lieutenant because the pyromancer is fucking dangerous, even without flames at his disposal.

"You're not a prisoner," I say, maintaining the distance between us while he edges around the table toward me. "It doesn't have to be that way."

"More fucking lies!" he shouts, his fiery eyes flashing.

His muscles bunch before he launches himself forward and barrels into me, lifting me off my feet with another roar that chills me.

I drop my weight, making it harder for him to hold on to me, but before I can actively fight back, there's a flash of violet light from the doorway.

Maeve crouches there, both arms extended.

She promised me that if Aiden threatened me, she would wrap him up in pain. She shrieks a spell as the violet light hits him in the side of his exposed torso, and he collapses to his knees, dropping me at the same time.

I land lightly, crouched in front of him.

His shoulders hunch, but his focus is suddenly on Maeve. "I know you," he says, a low, threatening rumble. "You're one of Mother Zala's witches."

Maeve jolts and her eyes fly wide. She remains with her arms extended, but whatever second spell she was about to utter seems to die on her lips. She collects herself, her head lowering with determination. "Not anymore," she says. "I have a new life now."

Aiden's eyes are hard and cold, his lips pressed together. It's the hard look I learned to identify before he lashes out and kills someone.

"Aiden," I say, my voice carrying a stern warning as I reach for him. "Calm the fuck down."

"Or what?" he asks, swinging back to me. "You'll kill me? You've already proven you won't."

With a roar that chills me, he launches himself to the side, running at Maeve.

She shrieks a spell just as Aiden reaches the opening.

Violet light fills the space within the doorway, blocking his path.

Aiden doesn't stop running. He bashes into the magical barrier. Violet light splashes around him, rippling across the opening at every contact point between it and his body, but the barrier holds. He's trapped inside this room—a captive. Which I promised he wouldn't be.

With another roar, he punches his fist into the barrier. And again and again. Each hit splashes more magic around him and Maeve screams on the other side of the light, her arms shaking.

The corridor behind her isn't the largest, but Luna and Lydia stand ready with their cards, the shifters are all partially shifted— lion, snow leopard, and panther—and Danika and Cody flank Maeve, ready to defend her.

At the side of the room, I'm aware of Tessa and Tristan, both partially shifted now. Tessa's warning growl tells me I have one more chance to get Aiden under control before she acts to subdue him with the full force of her power.

"Aiden!" I shout. "*Calm the fuck down!*"

I grab the nearest chair and launch myself at him, leaping forward for momentum, breaking the chair across his back.

The pieces of wood clatter and roll across the floor.

Aiden stills before he whirls to me, his eyes blazing.

Okay, so I poked the bear.

His focus shifts dangerously to the guns and daggers at my waist and I suddenly regret not removing them before I entered this room. Too late now—unless I pitch them through the window. But then he'll see that the window doesn't have glass in it. He'll realize it's an avenue of escape, and I don't want that, either.

I back away from him, reluctant to engage in another fight with him because that will escalate the situation. "Let us help you," I say. "You can trust—"

He doesn't let me finish. "Why would I believe anything you say to me?" His voice is sharp, but his footfalls are careful, calculated, as he propels me toward the wall.

His back is now to Tessa and Tristan, the most vulnerable position he could be in, and I suddenly second-guess his intentions. He didn't survive years at Banta's side by trusting anyone. Until maybe... *me.* And then I proved to him just how dangerous trust can be.

"You're a practiced liar." He snarls. "Without any care for collateral damage."

I stiffen. "And you're a fucking criminal without any care for anyone."

As soon as I speak, I regret it, because I know it's not true. He loves his brother. Protecting Lucas has always been Aiden's first priority. He also risked his life to come here and warn me about Banta.

Aiden shrugs his shoulders, but it's a kind of feigned nonchalance. "I don't care about anyone, huh?" His smile makes me shiver. "Let me prove you wrong."

He extends his arm, his palm out, stretching toward the nearest lamp.

He's attempting to call the fire to his fist.

I wait a beat for him to discover that he can't control this fire and I brace for his response when the realization hits him. Shock pins me to the spot when a blaze of light rushes from the lamp into his hand. The golden flames wash across his body, lighting up his eyes.

He shouldn't be able to control this fire!

His muscles bunch as he snatches me from my feet, his arms wrap tightly around me, and he pulls me up against his chest. The cold bullets still embedded above his heart dig into me when he pulls me close.

His power strikes, and an inferno erupts around us, a wall of flames leaping skyward between me and my friends.

Tessa screams my name, her cry breaking through the sound of the roaring blaze. The fire is too thick to see past it, but my bond with her tells me she's approaching fast, the outline of her figure leaping toward me.

My cry dies in my throat as Aiden's power grips me, my body becomes weightless, and he takes me with him into the fire.

CHAPTER TEN

$\mathcal{W}$ e crash through the flames.

The firelight around us changes and my body feels as light as air, as if I could float away if it weren't for Aiden's power keeping me in one place. Sooner than I expect, my sense of weightlessness ends and my body plummets back into place.

We're surrounded by fire. Every way I look, the firelight is a haze that stops me seeing where we've landed. All I sense right now is the closeness of Aiden's body, the way his chest rises and falls, his rapid breathing, and the press of his hands against my back and my head.

A cocoon of power has formed between us and the flames, its edges hot and hazy, but the fire we landed in must be extreme, because as soon as I take a breath, the heat rages into my chest.

"What did you do?" I gasp. The fact that he took hold of flames made from old magic shakes me. "If you hurt my family, I swear I'll fucking kill you!"

"I didn't hurt them." His arms are like steel around me, the expression in his eyes becoming wild as I continue to struggle against him.

"Stop moving!" he orders me.

"Take me back." I glare up at him, forced to acknowledge the danger of fighting him while we're standing in a new inferno. "Right now."

"No." His expression hardens and his arms clamp tighter. "If you care about your friends, you'll lead the danger away from them. Banta's after you and me—not them."

My eyes widen as I stare up at him. He sounds so much like Tessa. She believed she had to fight her battles alone—that it was her responsibility to keep us away from danger. She was so determined to make sure we were safe that she pushed us away.

"He can't beat my friends," I say, gritting my teeth with determination. "You saw how strong Tessa and Tristan are."

"Exactly!" Aiden says. "Imagine what Banta will do if he controls them? He's only as strong as the people he commands. With your friends at his disposal, he'll be unstoppable."

A shudder passes through me, violent enough that he clamps his arms around me again. Tristan and Tessa weren't sure that Banta couldn't hurt them. They considered the possibility that he has a weapon that could be used against them—and they didn't discount the chance that his power of suggestion could manipulate their minds. Everything Tessa did to end Ford Vanguard was so that her strength couldn't be used against her will.

I can't bring this danger into her life.

Especially not when she's pregnant.

"You're right," I whisper. "I have to lead Banta away from the people I love." My grip on Aiden tightens—as tight as he's holding me. The threat to my family isn't only from Banta, but also the supernatural who controlled the bullets that still decorate Aiden's chest. "But Banta didn't shoot these bullets into you," I say. "What happened, Aiden? Who did this?"

"There's no time to explain right now," he says, his expression so coldly blank that I struggle to breathe. "We need to get out of these flames."

"Like fuck we do," I snap, reacting with anger to the wall he just put up between us. "You put us here. You chose these flames." I release him to point at the furnace around us, a reckless move. "Tell me what I need to know."

Aiden snatches my hand to stop me from breaching the hazy cocoon of his power. "This fire is different. It's spelled to incinerate anyone who steps into it. It wants to hurt you."

I consider the sweat dripping from his forehead and the urgency in his voice.

Perhaps he's not as in control of this fire as he wants to be.

Silently, I make a vow to get answers, but only after we make it out of these flames. That's *if* we can...

I try to see through them, but the flames blaze in every direction —above and around us. They're so high that we're standing up in them, and still surrounded by their heat. This is definitely not a fireplace. Not a bonfire, either, because it extends too far in either direction.

"Where the hell are we?" I demand to know.

"We're standing within the bed of flames beneath the room where Mother Lavinia kept her prisoners."

My eyebrows rise. "*Beneath* the room?"

He gestures upward with minimal movement, not disrupting the protective cocoon around us.

Squinting to see through the flames, I convince myself that I can make out long, wooden panels, each nearly a foot wide, and situated maybe two feet above our heads. It looks like there are narrow gaps between each of them.

"Those are the floorboards," Aiden says. "The room above us is surrounded by these flames—even up each side. Mother Lavinia designed it this way to keep her prisoners in line."

Mother Lavinia was the mother witch of the coven where we found Tessa after Ford Vanguard captured her. She told me about what happened to her inside this place, but it was what occurred afterward that really affected her. It was here that Cody died and Tessa's humanity broke.

This is where she pushed me away.

I try to shake off the memories, reminding myself that if Aiden wanted to kill me, he would have done it already. I squeeze my eyes closed, wishing I could trust him as fully as I trust Tessa, Tristan, Danika, Cody, and all of the women from Hidden House.

Right now, I have no choice.

"Stay close while I find a place to make an opening in the floor above us," Aiden says, drawing me against his side while the flames crackle and pop around us.

The cocoon of his power moves with us while we step along what feels like uneven, rocky ground, some sort of cavern cut from rock and soil beneath us. We pass beneath what could be metal supports under the floorboards and, through the flames, I make out the shape of the beams above us.

Aiden stops us after several paces and then tips his head back. "There are gaps in the floorboards above us. I can push them up here," he says. "Keep close. I don't want the fire to reach you while I'm distracted."

Until I met Tessa and found a leader I'm willing to follow, I was used to calling the shots—being the one to take the step forward. My natural inclination is to reach up and help Aiden, but I recognize how dangerous that would be.

I lean closer to him, wrapping my arms around his chest. His muscles bunch as he reaches upward.

At the same time, I sense the firelight around us change slightly, shifting and becoming darker around his fist; as if the cocoon of his power is thinner there and the fire is trying to get inside.

He taps his fist against the floorboards above us, his muscles straining, his torso stretching. "My goal is to push the panel up so we can replace it once we've gone through," he says. "Punching a fist-sized hole in it won't do us any good. I also need to maintain the barrier of my power so we don't damage the spells that are keeping the flames under control. Hold on."

He braces, then he drives his fist upward. The wooden panel creaks and lifts, the nails going with it, revealing a glimpse of another ceiling far above us.

Aiden repeats the process twice more, pushing up two more panels. Wood groans and the nails wrench from their positions.

Finally, Aiden slides all three panels out of the way.

The cocoon we're in prevents the air above from rushing in, but even if it didn't, I have a sense that the room we're about to ascend into doesn't exactly contain fresh air.

Aiden lowers his fist and wraps one arm around my waist. "I'm going to lift us out now, but it's going to take some effort because the fire doesn't want to let us go."

I smirk at him. As if he's strong enough to jump up through the hole while holding me. But I'm willing to watch him try. And a little afraid of what might happen if he doesn't succeed.

I'm completely at his mercy right now.

He grips the edge of the opening above us with his left hand—his bicep flexing and his stomach muscles tightening where I'm pressed against him—gripping me tightly with his right arm, as if he's going to perform a chin-up with me in his arms.

With a heave, he wrenches us upward.

Just as my feet leave the rocky ground, his left fist releases the ledge, punches upward, and a blast of flame shoots from his hand into the air above us.

Sudden weightlessness fills me and my vision blurs as I'm jolted up toward the blast of fire and out of the pit. The new flame engulfs us, heat licking around my torso, but Aiden's power protects me from injury as we drop to the floor beside the opening he made.

My head spins with what just happened.

He must have translocated us the short distance between the pit into the plume he shot into the air, jumping from the flames below into the one he created above us.

I find my feet while Aiden bends to the panels he pushed aside, fitting them back into position and thumping them into place with his fist.

While he's busy, I take a quick look at the room around us.

For a cage, it's deceptively homely.

The corner to my far right is filled with piled-up rugs and pillows. A small bathroom sits to my left. The wall I'm facing contains a floor-to-ceiling mirror, in front of which are two clothes racks with both men's and women's clothing.

My jaw tightens with anger to see them. When we came to rescue Tessa from this place, she was wearing a cobalt blue dress with a plunging neckline and a tight, short skirt. Similar evening dresses hang on the rack. My alpha prefers flannel shirts and jeans, but no doubt she was required to wear what the mother witch demanded.

Glancing down, I make out the glow of the flames through the cracks in the floorboards, the threat of fire close by and visually present. Lastly, I eye the staircase at the side of the room, which leads upward—the only escape.

Aiden finishes pushing the panels back into place and then, to my surprise, he stays right where he is, hunched over with his back to me.

He's quiet for so long that I tiptoe around him, but I keep my distance and remain standing. "Aiden?"

"Why haven't you left yet?" he asks.

I'm asking myself the same thing. The only answer I have is: "Because I need to know what I'm up against."

I remind myself that Luna and Lydia can track me here. It was only when Tessa was within the Spire's grounds that we couldn't find her.

She'll come for me, and in the meantime, I need answers. About Banta. About Aiden. Even about myself, since my venom didn't have the intended effect on him.

I add, "My friends will find me soon enough."

"They won't," Aiden says, startling me. "The fire surrounding this room is one of a kind. It won't stop burning and it will prevent anyone from sensing our presence. That's why we're safe in this room." He looks up at me. "But not once we ascend those stairs."

I narrow my eyes at him, considering whether he's lying to keep me here. Then I remember Helen saying that Tessa's presence was coming in and out as we tracked her. Luna and Lydia detected her presence when Tessa was on her way here, but when Helen used her magic to follow Tessa's movements, there was a patch when Tessa disappeared off the radar again. It could have been while she was in this room, so it's possible Aiden's telling the truth.

If so, I'm not sure if I should be happy about it.

"We can hide here from Banta until I figure out a safer place to take you," Aiden says.

"Stop doing that," I snap. "Stop trying to protect me."

His grin is raw and violent. "Never."

But he groans as he lies down on the floor, rolling onto his back and closing his eyes. "I'll tell you everything you want to know." He takes a ragged breath. "But first, I need your help with these bullets."

It's about fucking time he stopped being such an asshole and asked for help.

I've already had plenty of time to study his wounds. We only succeeded in removing two of the bullets, but at least Elen removed the poisonous magic that was keeping him from healing.

Since I don't have pliers anymore, what I need now is some sort of implement with which to pull out the bullets and then... I'll need to figure out how to seal up the wounds since Elen isn't here to use her healing power on him.

One problem at a time.

I hurry to the racks of clothing, where I choose a thin metal clothes hanger and unwind it so that I'm left with a pliable piece of wire. I can wrap it around the bullets to pull them out, but stitching him up is going to be more difficult. The little bathroom is no help—

all it contains is a toilet and a sink. No cupboards that might contain something useful.

Returning to the racks of clothing, I grab the softest dress I can find, along with several shirts with sleeves that might—in a pinch—be long enough to wrap around Aiden's chest to keep pressure on the wounds.

"No need to stitch," he mumbles, lying still with his eyes closed. "I'll heal fast enough."

"Hmm." I'm hoping that's true now that Elen drew away the darkness of the magic that was used to hurt him. "I hope you're right."

He's very still when I lean over him. "Aiden?"

He doesn't answer me.

I listen for his heartbeat, finding it steady, but he doesn't react when I wind the coat hanger around the nearest bullet.

He's unconscious and I suddenly find the silence oppressive. Only moments ago, I was surrounded by a hundred warriors—three packs and all of my friends—and now...

I push away all of the conflicted feelings I have about Aiden and focus on my task. I choose to start with the bullets that appear to be embedded less deeply since the bleeding won't be as bad.

After that, I work fast. Some of the bullets are so close together that I don't have much choice but to remove them all before I can press wadding to them and tie it tightly.

By the time I'm done, I'm sweating, and my hands are shaking.

It's a good thing I'm not attracted to the scent of blood because it's everywhere. On the floor. On my clothes. On my hands.

I double check that the makeshift bandaging is secure around Aiden's chest and shoulders, and then I sit back on my heels.

He looks so peaceful right now. Not like a ruthless killer.

With Aiden beside him, Banta was able to take down all of his rivals and become the sole source of black-market weapons in Oregon and beyond. Ford Vanguard was just one of Banta's customers. Humans and supernaturals alike come to him when they want untraceable weapons.

Now, Aiden seems to be finally breaking away from that life. And he seems determined to take me with him.

After I clean up the space around us as best as I can, using another evening dress as a mop, I sigh into the silence.

Even though I know I won't get an answer, I whisper, "How did you survive these bullets?"

Let alone remain standing at the Spire. Especially after I bit him the first time.

And how the hell did he take control of the old magic fire?

I rub my face, knowing I won't get answers anytime soon, and now I have a choice to make.

The battle yesterday drained all of my strength. My body cries for sleep now that the first rays of dawn must be threatening to break the sky outside.

I consider carefully whether or not to leave this room and allow my friends to find me, even if I don't abandon Aiden here.

But if he isn't lying to me, then Banta will find me here, too, if I climb those stairs. I can't take the chance that Banta will find me first —not when Aiden is still recovering.

Tessa and her pack will be going crazy with worry, but it's the lesser of two evils. I can't risk putting Aiden, or myself, in danger— not until he's healed.

Having rationalized my decision, I grab several cushions and rugs from the corner of the room.

I carefully lift Aiden's head and slide one of the pillows under him, then pull a blanket to his chin. He doesn't stir when I touch him, but when I check his pulse, I find it steady.

After withdrawing my guns and daggers from my belt, I pull off my boots and shimmy out of my leggings, releasing my tucked-in shirt. It will have to make do as a nightshirt.

After positioning pillows next to Aiden, I lie down on them beside him and turn inward, my head fitting neatly into the crook of his neck.

It's an all-too-familiar position, but my instincts tell me this is where I should be.

I pull the blanket over both of us and try to sleep.

CHAPTER ELEVEN

I wake to find Aiden's arm curled around my shoulders and my head pressed to his chest.

I'm immediately aware of the strength of his breathing, his steady heartbeat. Even though blood is not in my diet, if there's anything a vampire can hear, it's a heart beating. Especially this close to my ear.

The healthy *thud-thud* lifts any remaining worry I had about his wounds.

He must notice the change in my breathing because he turns a little, the blanket bunching between us.

I tip my head back to catch his half-smile. His eyes are bright and clear, his lips curved and relaxed, the tension gone from around his mouth. It's a sharp change from the anger and desperation of last night.

"Do you remember that time you patched me up after the knife fight with that young bear shifter?" he asks, his voice quiet.

"Uh-huh," I murmur. "You could have used your power to kill him, but you didn't."

He gives a slight shrug. "That kid was scared. I had no reason to hurt him."

Lying in his arms like this suddenly feels too close. Too vulnerable. It's so much easier to keep my feelings for him at bay when I'm angry at him. These quiet moments feel dangerous.

I disentangle myself from his arms, drawing myself up onto my knees. My hair has come loose, the long, black strands falling across my shoulders and down the top of my shirt, where the upper buttons have come undone.

"I need to check your wounds," I say.

He lies silently while I grapple with the knots I tied in the makeshift bandages. I wasn't taking any chances when it came to putting pressure on the wounds last night.

Finally succeeding in removing the bandage from his shoulder, I'm happy to find his skin smooth and healed beneath.

"This looks good," I say, moving onto the bandage around his ribs next. As I gently peel up the wadding, relieved to find these wounds also healed, I keep my tone light. "You promised me answers. Will you tell me what happened?"

For a second, I think he isn't going to reply, but he says, "Banta was throwing a party for his latest business partner. It was one of those exclusive events at Banta's compound. You remember them?"

Parties with drugs and women. Banta's lieutenants never took part in the festivities. They were the muscle to make sure nothing got out of hand. It would explain why Aiden's wearing suit pants.

"I was watching over the crowd when I suddenly saw the flames at that place—what did you call it? The Spire?" Aiden asks.

I give a quick nod.

"The power of those fires hit me so suddenly that my own power nearly triggered. I had to leave the room before I burned a hole in the wall. Lucas came after me to check that I was okay—"

"Lucas was there?" When I was with Aiden, Lucas was never part of Banta's activities. He was kept in seclusion, which is why I only met him a few times. I remember him as a quiet twenty-year-old, with hair as dark-brown as Aiden's but eyes that are a pale green, his face slightly more rounded, his jaw less chiseled.

A muscle in Aiden's jaw flexes as he grits his teeth. "After you 'died,' Banta started bringing Lucas along with him to parties."

I sigh as I recognize the tactic Banta was employing. "Banta was reminding you of what you have to lose if you betray him."

Aiden's eyes brighten, but in a dangerous way—a haze of heat growing across his shoulders. "You were my woman," he says. "When you tried to kill Banta, he questioned my loyalty."

Aiden's gaze is unrelenting, and I suddenly read much more into his statement. I grip the bandage in my hand. "What did he do to you?"

Aiden doesn't flinch. "He interrogated my mind."

I stiffen. Banta attempted to break into my mind when I attacked him. It felt like daggers jabbing at my head. I didn't anticipate how relentless Banta would be, and the battle to keep him out of my mind incapacitated me for long enough that his lieutenants arrived.

Aiden continues. "Allowing him to interrogate my mind hurt like hell, but, of course, I gave him permission do it. I had nothing to hide. You were very careful not to reveal anything to me while we were together."

I squish the bandage in my hands. "I wanted to be sure you wouldn't get caught up in my betrayal if I didn't succeed."

Aiden sits up beside me, closing the gap between our bodies, but he doesn't reach for me. The final dressing remains around his heart and I need to check that wound, but the fact that Aiden is sitting up is a good sign, and right now, there are truths I need to face.

I exhale carefully, trying to calm my rising heartrate. "I lied to you so many times about who I am."

"Convincingly," he says, giving me a slow nod, but the tension in his jaw fades. "You played the part well."

I have no comeback because, while I lied to him, he was always honest with me. He never hid who he was, whom he worked for, or what he was thinking. In fact, he actively pushed me away in the beginning.

He pauses, a careful silence before he speaks again. "I have to ask you... That first night I saw you. Those guys in the bar who were hassling you—did you pay them to do it?"

Sound sticks in my throat. I'd done my research on Aiden—observed him for long before that first night. He never mistreated a woman. A couple of times, I even saw him quietly escort a woman away from a potentially dangerous situation before she could get hurt.

So I'd put on a dress for the first time in years—a flimsy summer frock that buttoned down the front. I'd already ascertained that Aiden would be in the bar that night, taking a payment from the owner. I also knew that a few of the regular wolf shifters would be there—members of Baxter Griffin's guard who had hair-trigger tempers.

It took very little to make them mad.

They grabbed me, and Aiden stepped in.

I give a quick shake of my head. "I got in their way. They overreacted." I wasn't worried about what would happen if Aiden didn't intervene. I could handle them, although it would have blown my cover.

"Huh." His gaze becomes distant before a fleeting smile dances across his face. "I don't remember much about them. All I remember now is you."

His fingertips trace the contours of my face, feather-light against my temple, my cheekbone, and my jaw, coming to rest beneath my chin.

He speaks as his fingers send the most tantalizing shivers through me. "These blue eyes. These lips... The teardrops on your eyelashes... Everything about you was vulnerable. Open. Like you had nothing to hide."

He withdraws his hand.

"It was far from the truth, wasn't it?" he asks.

I bite my lip. I never revealed to Aiden that I was a trained fighter, or that I knew my way around firearms.

I *did* reveal the power of my bite, though. We'd dated for two months, but he was keeping me at arm's length until I 'panicked' during an altercation and bit his assailant—the young bear shifter with the knife.

I patched Aiden up afterward and—*finally*—he invited me into the compound and let me into his life.

Now, he sits back a little, as if he's returning to the present. "Even though Banta was satisfied that I had nothing to do with your attack on him, he saw what you meant to me. He kept Lucas close after that. A reminder of what else I had to lose. Which is why Lucas was at the party last night."

"What happened?" I ask, quietly.

"Lucas followed me out of the room. He wanted to make sure I was okay." Aiden exhales a deep breath. "I told him that I saw you through the flames." Aiden's eyes blaze again. "I should have kept it to myself."

"You told your brother? But *he* wouldn't tell Banta."

"I underestimated the hold that Banta has been developing over him," Aiden says. "Lucas left the room and within minutes, there was a bag over my head, and I was dragged to the wet room."

I shudder. *Wet work*, they call it when they interrogate someone. I never saw it happen. While I played my part as Aiden's devoted girlfriend, I was invited to parties and glimpsed the inner workings of Banta's operations, but I was never part of them.

Aiden's lips twist. "I could hear Lucas shouting in the background as they dragged me away. He was saying that Banta promised not to hurt me. Then I heard a *thump* and he stopped shouting." Aiden's jaw tightens. "I don't know what happened to him after that."

I reach for Aiden. "Banta won't hurt Lucas. Your brother is his leverage over you."

Aiden's shoulders hunch, his muscles flexing. "All this time, I thought I was protecting Lucas by accepting Banta's help. Instead, I condemned him to a powerless life of being controlled by a demon." Aiden meets my eyes. "I fucked up, Ana."

I lean forward, wishing things were different between us. Wishing I hadn't lied as many times as I had. That he didn't believe he was alone.

"You were a teenager when you joined him," I say. "You did the best you could at the time."

"I'll never know if that's true," he says. "I'll never know if things could have been different for my brother and me if I'd made different choices."

I give Aiden a soft smile. "In another life, maybe."

Holding my breath, I finally reach for the wrapping around his chest, exhaling my relief to find the skin over his heart perfectly healed beneath the dried blood.

Carefully, I remove all of the now-ruined clothing I used to bandage him. My hands are light across his chest and back. I force myself to remain business-like as I remove the last of the wadding.

It's difficult to push away the memories of exploring his muscles and planting kisses across the hard planes of his chest, of the way he'd wrap me up in his arms as if I were his reason for breathing.

As I wad up the material and pile the pieces beside me, Aiden leans forward, making me pause as he closes the gap.

"Thank you," he says.

Determined to keep my distance as much as I can, I clear my throat and focus on what else I need to know.

"Banta Sol controls minds, not bullets," I say, remembering the grooves in the edges of the bullets I pulled out of Aiden last night. "The bullets you were shot with should have passed right through you. How did they stop mid-flight?"

Aiden's head is tilted to mine, his breathing quiet and in control. "It was Banta's new first lieutenant. A guy I've never seen before. He has skin like he's made out of bronze and he controlled the path of the bullets. Banta called him 'the Metalworker.'"

I search my memory for any mention of a supernatural by that name, but I come up empty. The fae healer, Elen, said that the bullets were being used as a coercive technique.

"It was a sick game," I whisper. "To force you to give up my location."

Aiden gives a terse nod before he exhales slowly. "The first thing Banta did was make sure I didn't have access to fire and then he attempted to interrogate my mind, but this time, I didn't let him."

My eyes widen. "You resisted? Successfully?"

Aiden shrugs, but the tension in his shoulders is visible, his muscles clenched. "I don't know how I did it, but he was fucking angry about it. That was when he brought in the Metalworker, who shot a bullet into me every time I refused to tell them what I saw in the flames." He points to his shoulder and his left rib. "The first bullets were painful, but the Metalworker got frustrated when I still wouldn't talk."

Aiden's fingertips rise to rest across the patch of skin where the bullets were once embedded in the flesh over his heart. "These ones were a death threat. The longer I refused to answer, the deeper he drove them into my chest."

"Fuck," I whisper. My heart clenches and I wish that the myths about vampires not having beating hearts were true. Right now, I would give anything for my heart to be dead and cold. Unfeeling. "What else can this Metalworker do?"

"Given that he controlled the gun without touching it, my guess is that he can use anything metallic at will," Aiden says. "You'll need to leave your guns and daggers behind before we leave this room."

I stiffen. "I'm not abandoning my weapons."

"Anything metallic can be used against us," he says, leaning forward so suddenly that I gasp when he runs his hands up my sides, stopping his upward stroke beneath my breasts. "Even the underwire in your bra." His expression hardens. "You're wearing an instant dagger right now, Ana. Positioned directly beneath your heart."

My shirt is caught under his hands, the movement lifting the material to expose my hips. My left thigh presses against his leg and the warmth of his skin seeps through.

I fight my body's response to how close he is to me—the way he could light a fire within me with not much more than the brush of his hand against my arm, the lightest kiss...

I shake myself. "It won't matter what weapons we carry," I say. "If this Metalworker knows what he's doing, he'll make sure he carries any metallic objects he needs to do his work. Just like you carry a lighter."

"*Carried*," Aiden corrects me. "It was the first thing they took when they jumped me."

I assumed as much, but I narrow my eyes at him. "How did you make the jump to the Spire if you didn't have access to fire at your end?"

"I used the spark from the final bullet," he says. "I didn't think I could do it with a flash that small, but I caught it."

"Then I'm bringing my guns with me," I say. "If I have to fire a bullet to create a spark to get us out of a tight spot, then I will."

"I'd rather you didn't," he says, drawing back a little, the tension increasing in his shoulders again. "The Metalworker could turn that bullet on you faster than I can create a blaze big enough to jump through. I'm used to working with an open flame, Ana. Using a spark felt lucky the first time. I can't guarantee I'll be able to do it again."

His old name for me keeps rolling off his tongue, but the more often he says it, the more I want to hear it. I can't let that continue. "You need to stop calling me that," I say.

"You mean 'Ana'?" he asks, a crease forming in his forehead.

"Ana never really existed," I say. "She was a construct. Nothing more."

He's quiet for a moment before he reaches for my hand. His voice whispers across my lips as he leans in closer. "Then I look forward to getting to know the real you."

He pauses. "Iyana."

CHAPTER TWELVE

*a*iden continues speaking on the next breath as he encircles my hand with his big one. "We're still better off not carrying anything metallic on us."

I consider the daggers and guns I took off last night, all placed neatly on the floor.

My protective cloak sits next to them. It has the appearance of a folded-up umbrella, but it's made from a magical substance and I'm suddenly extremely grateful that there's no metal in it. The magic gives it form and allows it to morph into a transparent layer over my clothing, or into a larger tent if I need cover to sleep during the day.

Still, I'm going to feel naked without my weapons.

I scowl at Aiden. "Okay, but I'm not happy about it."

His smile grows, and it's anything but cold. "I understand if you're angry with me. I'm just happy that you're alive." His jaw tightens. "I plan on keeping you that way."

As he moves away from me, beginning to rise, the inside of his arm catches my attention. I snatch hold of it, stopping him halfway to his feet.

Like me, he doesn't seem to like being grabbed, but I ignore the way he jolts as if he has to stop himself from retaliating.

I turn his wrist so he has to look at it.

Two puncture marks scar his skin where I bit him. He may have healed from the bullet wounds, but not from my bite.

His jaw tightens. "It doesn't mean you tried to take me down."

"You really think I lied about trying to knock you out?"

"Maybe."

I purse my lips. "You don't trust me because I didn't tell you the truth about who I am. And I don't trust you because Banta controls—*controlled*—you. I think that puts us at an impossible impasse."

He sinks back to a kneeling position. "Then we need to draw a line in the sand right now. We put the past in the past and let our future actions speak for us."

"You're asking me to have faith in you."

"I am." He pauses. "But I also need to have faith in you. We both have a lot to lose."

He's asking for the chance to start over. To be able to leave the lies of the past behind. The way that lifts a weight off my shoulders takes my breath away.

I force myself to resume breathing. "At this point, I'd prefer to call the shots, so… as an act of faith… what's your plan?"

He doesn't close in, keeping his distance. "Your point about the Metalworker carrying what he needs is a good one. We should anticipate that he'll arm himself with the weapons of his choosing, but being surprised by a nail wrenched out of wood or knives flying out of a cutlery drawer isn't my idea of fun."

He pauses. And, as an act of faith, I wait.

"There's a place we can go," he says. "It's secluded—and heavily guarded. The supernaturals who live there lead very simple lives. They don't like anything metallic, so it's the perfect place for us to stay while we figure out what to do." He rubs the back of his head, squinting at me. "The only problem is that I won't be welcome there."

I narrow my eyes at him. "Why not?"

"It's a community of dryads."

"Tree folk?" My eyes widen. "I thought dryads were extinct."

He shakes his head. "They want us all to think that. They're very protective of their community. Axes and blades are forbidden." He grimaces. "So is fire."

"Ah." I rise to my feet, my shirt finally falling past my backside. "Then we'll have to convince them they have nothing to fear from you."

I pause. My accusation that he doesn't care about anyone repeats back at me. My voice is quiet and small this time, mostly because the weight of responsibility has settled back onto my shoulders. "We *will* get your brother away from Banta, Aiden."

He rises to his full height, towering over me, a haze of heat around his chiseled chest. He slips his hands around my waist and draws me toward him.

Since we arrived at this place, I've settled far too quickly back into our old ways. The ease with which I used to let him touch me, how natural it felt for his hands to be on my body...

My instincts don't tell me to pull away. They never did.

He draws me close, stroking the hair off my shoulder and following its fall down my back, his palms warm through my shirt. "Banta will keep Lucas safe for as long as he wants to control me and can use my brother's safety as a threat." His hand rises to the underside of my jaw, his fingertips tangling in my hair. "My first priority is getting you to safety."

I attempt to clear my throat of the lump that's forming in it. "If Banta's tracking us already, then we'll need to move fast once we ascend the stairs out of here."

He nods. "I need a box of matches or some other fire source that I can use to jump through."

"What about the fire beneath us?" I ask. "Can't we jump back through it?"

He tenses suddenly, a rare shudder passing through him as though he's immediately repelled. "I'm not traveling through that fire again," he says, a bite in his voice.

I tip my head to the side, considering the sharpness of his response. "Aiden? What is it?"

He exhales slowly. "Fire speaks to me, Iyana. I hear its voices. The places it's been. The lives it's taken."

I'm surprised. "You never told me that before."

He shifts a little. "I guess I hid some things from you, too." He clears his throat as he takes a step back. "The fire beneath our feet has consumed too many souls. If I could find a way to extinguish it, I would. But for now, I don't want to jump through it again unless we've exhausted all of the alternatives."

No wonder he was so jumpy while we were standing in the middle of the flames.

He turns toward the bathroom. "Let's get cleaned up."

While Aiden heads to the sink and turns on the water, I reach for my leggings and boots.

I'd give anything for a shower and a change of clothing right now. My shirt is bloodied, and my clothes smell like smoke from the pyres. The fae did their best to syphon the smoke upward, but I stood by the fires for hours.

The blood and smoke won't encourage the dryads to trust me. Of course, even if I could wash both scents off, we're about to jump through another fire, so I resign myself to my current state of dishevelment.

Leaving my leggings and boots at the side of the room, I scour the racks of clothing for alternative attire. I'm disappointed to discover that the only women's clothing is dresses, while the men's shirts and pants are too big for me.

After a little thought, I grab one of the dresses with a black, corset-style bodice. After checking the bodice for wire supports, I take my dagger to the base of it and carefully cut off the attached skirt.

I'm left with a supportive bodice to wear, which will also do away with my need for my current bra. I'm grateful that I'm wearing stretchy leggings that don't have any sort of zipper or metal buttons, although I wish there were clean pants here that didn't have blood on them.

My knee-high boots are a problem. I could cut out the metal zippers with my dagger, maybe puncture holes up the sides of the boots and lace them with ribbons, but it would take a long time. Or I could go barefoot...

I'm considering my options—none good—when the sound of violently splashing water in the bathroom draws my attention.

Turning, I nearly let out a laugh. Aiden is trying to wash the blood off his chest—not a laughing matter—except that he's trying to angle his torso under the little faucet and the water's spraying right up into his scrunched-up face.

"Fuck!" he exclaims, darting backward and swiping the water from his eyes.

As a pyromancer, he has a natural dislike of water, although he suffered through a shower each day—at least, when we were together.

Glaring at the sink, he reaches out to cup his hands beneath the flow of water instead, splashing it over himself and attempting to scrub at his chest with his hands.

He's making an almighty mess.

I clear my expression and don't let out a sound.

Quickly scanning the men's clothing, I select a new shirt and a pair of suit pants that I judge to be about Aiden's size—but only after checking that the zipper and buttons on the pants are plastic.

I also grab a definitely-too-small shirt that looks softer than the rest before I make my way to the bathroom.

Dropping the clean clothes outside the door where they won't get wet, I bundle up the smaller shirt.

"Here," I say, interrupting Aiden. "Let me help."

Angling toward the sink as he steps aside, I wet the shirt like a sponge and turn back to him.

He glowers at me as I wipe his shoulder first, carefully cleaning up his neck and along his hairline, before working around his big shoulder muscles and down his biceps. Rinsing out the cloth, I start in on his chest while his glare remains.

I'm matter-of-fact, scrubbing without mercy at the blood that sticks, and he doesn't complain, becoming still the longer I work.

When I glance up at him before I move to the skin across his heart, I find his eyes are closed, his breathing deeper and more relaxed than before.

I falter a little, since it's rare to see him look so peaceful.

His eyes open—but slowly—a piercing light in them. He insists that he needs an external flame to use his power, but sometimes... in these moments... I glimpse an internal fire, as if he carries a spark within him. My only explanation is that it's a remnant flame from the fire he controlled before, the smallest flare that he holds on to.

I quickly focus back on what I'm doing, wiping clean the final spots of blood before I place the cloth into the sink.

"Let me check to make sure I got it all," I murmur, my voice catching in my throat as I turn back to him. His muscled chest glistens with water, his biceps flexing slightly as he lifts his arms as if he's going to reach for me, but he lets them fall again.

He remains quiet as he allows me to check across his chest and stomach, up and behind his shoulders and his neck, but just as my fingertips slip away from his jaw, he catches my hand, entwining his fingers with mine.

His other arm encircles my waist as he pulls me close to him, the dampness from his chest soaking into my shirt. His pants are saturated, too—both from his own attempts to get clean and my ministrations.

He gives a visible shiver, and I'm not sure why until heat blossoms between us—a sudden hotness across every inch of his skin that touches mine.

Steam rises from his shoulders and between us, the droplets of water evaporating before my eyes. The dampness disappears from my shirt and from the material of his pants pressed against my thighs.

I gasp as the warmth spreads right through me, across my stomach and down to my toes—and up through my heart, around my chest, and across my back, where his arm rises.

He might need an open flame to use fire, but his internal heat has dried him off within seconds.

He gives me a lazy smile as his lips continue to hover above mine. His chest is dry now, the material of our clothing between us crisp again.

"That's better," he rumbles.

My head tells me to keep my distance, but my heart is a freaking mess right now.

When I planned to kill Banta, I was prepared to face Aiden afterward, to explain my betrayal, but I believed that he would understand why I concealed my intentions from him.

Then, when I failed... well, all I had was my determination to heal and recover. To become myself again.

Now, there's a question in his eyes as his fingers unfurl from around mine and glide across to my hip, slipping beneath the hem of my shirt to press against my lower back.

The heat from his fingertips is startling against my cool skin, leaving a tingling trail from my hip to my back.

My quick inhale draws me closer to him, my mouth brushing against his bottom lip. In that brief contact, I taste the ash of warm coals, along with the last hint of steam that rose from his body.

Despite my move toward him, he holds back in a way he never did when we were together.

Our relationship is much more precarious now.

Before, I was the woman he loved.

Now, I'm the woman who could get him killed.

CHAPTER THIRTEEN

$\mathcal{E}$ ver so slowly, Aiden's other hand slips into my hair at the nape of my neck, the edge of his big palm resting against my jawline and his thumb brushing my cheek.

His gaze is steady, the question in his eyes remaining painfully clear.

"I don't want to complicate things more than they already are," he says. "You need to tell me what you want."

I press my lips together, the scent and taste of his lips lingering within my senses.

I *missed* him.

I want more of him.

And just for a few moments, I want the past to be healed.

Arching upward, I slip my hands across his back, my fingers flexing against his defined muscles.

Nudging my lips against his, I inhale the ash that makes my head spin and my body ache for his touch. The memories of nights spent by a fireplace return to me, the recollections too acute to push away.

I moan against his lips when he finally responds, his lips fitting to mine, claiming every part of my mouth as he eases me back against the wall.

His hard chest presses to mine before he breaks the contact to graze my neck with his kisses—scorching touches down to my neckline.

Returning to my mouth, he reaches for the buttons at the front of my shirt, taking his time releasing the top one, as he continues to kiss me, his tongue tasting mine, before he breaks the contact again.

I sigh as he trails kisses down my chest, between my breasts, proceeding lower with every button he releases until he reaches my lower stomach.

Easing my now-open shirt aside, he curls his fingers around the top of my underpants, tugging them downward—but only an inch—his tongue swirling against the skin he exposed.

I rock a little within his hands, already wanting much more, but he kisses his way back up to my mouth, pulling me close as he guides my right leg up beside his thigh.

He may not want to access the fire beneath our feet, but flames are never far from the surface of his skin. My naturally cool body temperature is like an icy lake dragging his warmth into my body as he presses close, and his fingertips trace my cheeks and lips.

His dark blue eyes blaze at me, becoming like an amber flame against a deep night sky. "I never forgot how fucking beautiful you are."

I stiffen. My heart falls and a cold chill comes over me.

The face he sees now isn't the one I used to have.

I suddenly feel like stone beneath his hands, and no amount of heat can warm me.

He notices the shift in my posture immediately, responding by drawing back a little, a wary light entering his eyes. "Iyana? What is it?"

Speaking slowly, I'm careful only to reveal what I can about Hidden House, but I need to share the truth. "This face took six months to reconstruct, along with other parts of my body that were injured."

I squeeze my eyes closed. It's the moments of silence during the fight for my life that repeat on me.

The quiet inhales between kicks to my head and stomach.

The sharp pebbles beneath my hands as I tried to crawl toward the darkness beneath the bridge on Tristan's side of the river.

The final silence when I couldn't breathe anymore. The dark haze that descended, until only one sound registered: a spine-chilling growl.

I didn't know who—or what—made the sound until I woke up in Hidden House: Tristan's wolf.

I press back against the wall, my arms dropping to my sides. "This is not the same face and body you used to know. Please don't tell me it's beautiful."

Aiden steps back fully, allowing me to find my feet.

My shirt floats down around my thighs and I quickly button it up at the top, needing to reassert the physical barrier between us.

His expression is closed off as he scoops up the fresh clothing that I brought for him to wear before he slowly turns back to me. "I wasn't there for you that night," he says. "But I'll sure as fuck be there for you now."

My eyes widen because beneath his hard exterior, I catch a glimpse of something more painful.

Remorse?

I want to tell him that he has nothing to regret. He wasn't responsible for any part of what happened.

His emotion is fleeting and then concealed, and, before I can speak, he turns his back to me and strips off his old pants, keeping his underwear on before he pulls on the fresh clothing.

I study the tense lines of his body, the determined set of his lips. Whatever he was feeling when he kissed me, his more vulnerable feelings seem buried now beneath a quiet rage.

It doesn't scare me. Instead, my heart warms a little. I told him to stop trying to protect me, but I'm remembering my own words to Tessa when she tried to push Danika and me away for the second time, and then I remember her words to me at the Spire.

I don't have to walk this path alone.

Respecting Aiden's silence, I focus on what I need to do. I grab the bodice, my leggings, and my boots—conceding that I'll just have to wear the boots as they are for now. After waiting a moment for Aiden to finish in the bathroom, I hurry back to it and close the door.

Splashing water on my face, I check myself in the mirror; the flush in my cheeks, the darkness in my blue-gray eyes. My lips are pink, but drier than I was hoping they'd be—a sign I need to feed.

Aiden hasn't eaten for a while now, either, but from past experience, I know that he can go up to an entire day without hunger as long as he has access to the energy he needs from fire—and he's had plenty of that.

After pulling my black hair up into a topknot, I slip into the bodice and secure it at the front. It's a little too small across my breasts, but supportive enough, and I can move well in it, which is what matters.

Within minutes, I'm dressed and ready to exit the bathroom.

I catch the flare of heat in Aiden's eyes as he watches me walk past him, his gaze following the lines of my face to my exposed neck and shoulders, to my cinched-in waist, my hips, and all the way to my booted toes.

Despite his appreciative scrutiny, he keeps his comments focused. "It's impossible to tell the time in this room, but I would guess we slept most of the day," he says. "Still, the sun may not have set yet, and I don't want to take any chances with your safety, so we may need to wait longer to be sure."

I give him a small smile as I retrieve my umbrella from the floor. "I don't have to worry about sunlight anymore," I say, patting the contraption.

"Because you have an umbrella?" he asks.

I respect his skepticism. The cloak is cleverly disguised, and given that it rains so regularly in Portland, an umbrella isn't out of place.

When I press the base of the handle to trigger its magic and touch the side of the umbrella to my stomach, the suit deploys with an efficiency that takes Aiden by surprise.

The material is designed to remember my body—uniquely synced to me—but it will also mimic whatever I'm wearing while forming a transparent layer around my exposed skin. Helen really outdid herself with it and I'm eternally grateful for how skilled she is. Because of her, I don't have to hide during the day anymore.

Aiden crosses the gap between us, running his hand across my shoulder, then up across my face. His touch is muted through the protective layer, but the warmth from his fingertips seeps through, a reminder of his kiss only moments ago.

"Good." He steps back, remaining all business. "We will jump through multiple fires across the city to make it harder for anyone to follow our trail. The dryads' home is located in the forests of the North Cascades National Park, and the closest fires are miles away within the tourist areas. We'll have to jump as close as we can and then hike the rest of the way."

I itch to reach for my weapons, but I make myself leave them in a neat pile before I stalk toward the staircase. The way out is a single flight of stairs leading up to a wooden door at the top. Presumably, it isn't still locked, but I guess we'll find out soon.

"Stay close," Aiden says as he joins me at the base of the stairs. "I'll need your help looking for a way to light a fire as soon as we open the door at the top."

As I ascend the staircase behind him, I attempt to wet to my lips, finding them painfully dry—and it isn't just because of the persistent tension between Aiden and me.

"Aiden," I say, snagging his arm and halting him. "We have another problem."

He tilts his head. "What is it?"

I can't stop my fangs from descending a little, the tips of them making speech difficult. "I'm thirsty."

CHAPTER FOURTEEN

*A*iden pauses on the step. "If I thought it would make a difference, I'd offer you my blood."

"Nourishment is going to be an ongoing issue for me," I say, rapidly thinking through my options.

It was certainly one of the few truths I told Aiden when we were together: I don't drink blood.

Instead, I crave mercury.

The toxic silver liquid is my source of hydration and energy, and it isn't easy to come by. It would be extremely unlikely that the dryads would have a supply of it.

If I have to, I can make do with zinc or cadmium. Zinc is found in some human multi-vitamins, which the dryads are unlikely to have, and also in some vegetables, which they might have, but I'd have to consume a lot of them to make a difference.

Ugh. I'm more likely to bring vegetables right back up than to digest them.

There's a case of thirty vials of mercury back at the Spire, but I can't go back there because of the possibility that Banta and the Metalworker will follow us.

I shudder at the realization that the fae wear armor that appears metallic. I can't imagine what the Metalworker would do to them if he can manipulate their armor around their bodies.

There's plenty of mercury at Hidden House. In fact, it's the ideal hiding place for me—I successfully hid from Banta for seven months there.

But I can't take Aiden with me, because its location and purpose must be kept secret. The lives of the women who shelter there depend on it.

Tessa faced the same problem when Tristan was mortally injured. Although he already knew about Hidden House, the minds of Cerberus were in control of him at that time, and I watched her grapple with her decision, weighing up the risks. She would never have endangered the women at Hidden House if there had been another option.

For a moment, I wonder if Aiden would believe that I have a place to disappear into, and whether he'd let me go on my own. Maybe he would. In fact, if the flash of guilt I saw in his eyes is any indication, he might insist on it.

Except that it would mean leaving him to his own fate.

I chose that path once.

I can't do it again.

Not when I have another option—even if it's a dangerous one.

I manage to retract my fangs before I speak. "I have a stash of mercury hidden in a storage unit on the eastern outskirts of the city," I say. "It's near Oregon Park. We could jump there on our way to the dryads."

Aiden shakes his head when I give him the address. "That's within walking distance of Banta's compound. It's too dangerous."

I glare back at him. "It's the only workable option unless you're willing to take me back to my friends."

His jaw clenches. I knew he'd hate that option more, since there's no way Tessa will let him leave twice.

"I don't like it," he says.

My smile is humorless. I imagine he's having the same gut reaction that I had to leaving my guns and daggers behind.

I bare my fangs again. "You won't like what happens if I don't get food."

He gives me a wary glance, his eyes narrowing slightly as he contemplates me.

I was always careful to be well-nourished when we were together —hence the stash near Banta's compound—so he never saw me hungry.

"What happens if you don't get your mercury?" he asks.

"I get hangry," I say. "And I mean *very*."

He can't hide his smile fast enough.

I arch my eyebrows at him. "You laugh now. You won't if it happens. I may not drink blood, but I can sure as fuck spill it."

He swallows his grin. "What about long term?"

I shrug, as if it's nothing. "Oh, you know. Coma. Death. I've never tested it to find out."

He's suddenly very serious. "How long could you go without mercury before that happens?"

I give it some thought. "A week, at a guess. Maybe less because it's my only source of hydration." If I try to drink water, I just hurl it up again. Many other liquids have the same effect. Sharing a hot chocolate or a glass of wine with friends means nursing the cup in my hands and not drinking from it.

"That's fast enough to be a problem if we have to hide out for a while." Aiden presses his lips together. "Are you sure Banta didn't know about your stash at this storage unit?"

It's a valid question, but I shake my head. "The storage units are contained within a warehouse owned by a paranoid mage. The entire place is spelled so you can't step foot within it unless you've been vetted and given access. I was very careful because mercury isn't all I have stored there."

"All right. Let me see if there's a flame we can jump into." His gaze becomes distant, and I assume he's searching for a path across the city.

Within seconds, he refocuses on me. "There's very little fire around there. Our choices are a smoldering cigarette on the pavement within the warehouse grounds—but I can't guarantee I can jump using a flame that small, not with two of us. Or there's a dumpster fire, but it's a few blocks over, so we'll be exposed while we walk the distance to the warehouse."

I resume my ascent toward the door at the top of the stairs. "Try the cigarette," I say. "I trust you to make the jump."

I sense him pause and I turn to ask him what's wrong when I realize I told him that I trust him.

I guess I do in this instance.

He's paused on the step down, but he's tall enough that now we're eye height. The way he tips his head exposes the tattooed flames that sweep across the skin above his ear. Banta requires all of his lieu-tenants to shave a part of their skull and ink it with their power.

"You trust me, huh?"

I give him a quiet smile before I turn and reach for the door. I'm not terribly surprised to find that it opens right away. Tessa and Cody were the last prisoners here and they were outside when we arrived, so it stood to reason the door was left unlocked.

I'm prepared to move fast now, but I halt abruptly when I exit into the homely-looking lounge room beyond. "I know this room."

We didn't exactly go through the buildings here after Tessa left, but she pointed us to this place, telling us where to find Ella's bracelet... On the mantelpiece above the fireplace.

"You've been here before?" Aiden scans the room for a second, as if he thinks that the Metalworker could be waiting for us already.

I give a terse nod. "On the day that Tessa Dean annihilated Mother Lavinia's coven."

"Tessa Dean did that?" Aiden looks impressed. "Banta had an alliance with Mother Lavinia. She supplied all of his spells. He asked me to find out who killed her. He thought maybe Ford had done it."

I pin him with a piercing gaze. "Tessa killed every last witch in this place as retribution for hurting her beta. That's how far she'll go to protect the members of her pack."

"Including you," he says, a glimmer of respect in his eyes. "Then she's a powerful ally to have."

"And a dangerous enemy."

It feels like I lived years in the last week, but no doubt word is still spreading about what Tessa did—defeating the witches and then Ford Vanguard.

Striding to the mantelpiece, my hand closes around the box of matches sitting on it before I hand them quickly to Aiden.

He doesn't waste time striking the first match.

An edge of tension disappears from his shoulders when the open flame appears. He always seems calm when he's contemplating fire, but I know his relaxed posture won't last long.

He pockets the matches while holding the burning match between us. His arm circles my waist, drawing me closer. The nearness of his body sends pleasant sensations whirling through me; the strange combination of feeling at home—but also invigorated—and at the edge, there's a need for more that I push away as hard as I can. Thank fuck for my protective suit muting his touch.

"Close your eyes," he whispers, his lips hovering at my temple.

"Why?"

"Because this might be a bit alarming."

I arch an eyebrow at him. "More alarming than being rushed into a burning pyre?"

He winces. "Yes."

Worse than that?

I immediately shut my eyes, allowing him to gather me tightly against him as I brace for his next move.

CHAPTER FIFTEEN

*T*here's a puff of air on my cheek as if he blew gently on it, and then—

Whoomph!

Heat rushes around me and my eyes fly open, despite my resolve to keep them closed. Fire billows from the match held in his fingertips, accelerating as if it's streaking from his hand—an amber firestorm that forms wide rings encircling us from our ankles to the tops of our heads.

His lips are still pursed lightly, the gleam in his eyes beyond bright as the firelight builds within them.

Dear fuck, he just fanned that little flame into a wildfire.

I don't have time to rationalize his power any further because my body becomes weightless, the amber light streaks past me in a blur, and the cocoon of Aiden's power solidifies around us, keeping us together as we jump.

We come to a jarring halt, wrenched apart.

There are no flames to cushion us this time.

My knees hit the pavement and my surroundings come into sharp focus. I recognize the inside of the warehouse, the overhead ceiling soaring far above us. We've landed in the middle of one of the walkways between storage units inside the warehouse.

Aiden rolls to a stop nearby, leaping back to his feet, his focus on me. A faintly smoldering cigarette butt lies on the pavement between us, hardly glowing anymore, and I'm impressed that he pulled off the jump.

"We need to move," he says. "Assuming Toad is at Banta's compound right now, he'll be able to sense us and get here in twenty minutes, tops."

Toad is the unlikely name of Banta's tracker, a snake shifter who can use his senses to detect and distinguish our scents—merely by tasting the air. He's an expert at singling out a scent on the breeze, even with all of the city smells around him, although the closed-in warehouse walls should help us for now.

"Which way do we need to go?" Aiden asks.

Rubbing my knees, I hurry back to my feet, pointing to the right. "The next walkway over," I say. "It's the seventh unit from the end of the row."

The warehouse is lit with dim fluorescent lights and the only windows are high up around the top. The glow of streetlights beyond the windows tells me that it's later than we thought.

Now that the sun has well and truly gone down, I have no concerns about retracting my protective cloak. I pluck at the front of it, pinching the magical substance between my thumb and forefinger and pulling it outward.

The suit responds quickly, sliding off my body like a sheet of material before it folds in on itself, back into the shape of an umbrella —which I quickly clip onto my waistband.

The walkway we jumped into is deserted, but when we turn the corner, I spy another person at the far end of the row, and a second person halfway along on our left.

The closer of the two is exiting their storage unit, the one at the end of the row is entering theirs. Both are wearing sweaters with hoods, making them impossible to identify, and they disappear from sight quickly.

A number of bounty hunters use this warehouse, and they won't want to stay here for long, let alone be recognized. When I became a bounty hunter, I thought I might be entering some sort of fraternity —a family of sorts—but I quickly discovered that it was each hunter for themselves.

I stop outside unit number seven and place my hand on the scanner at the side of the wide door. My palm pricks in multiple places as the system takes my blood.

When the door clicks open, I wipe my bloodied palm across my pants leg, leaving silver smears, before I pull Aiden inside.

The door automatically seals again.

The anteroom is rectangular—only as wide as the door we passed through—and very dimly lit. It looks like a dead end, but a second level of security flashes, taking my body print, before the second door slides open.

The internal lights flicker on as soon as we enter, revealing the sizeable interior.

The upper portion of the right-hand wall is lined with weapons, while ammunition and other supplies are stored in a row of waist-high cupboards beneath them.

The back wall contains a clothes rack with an assortment of clothing, both combat and casual, along with several boots.

There's a small bathroom tucked into the corner to the left behind us, and the left-hand side of the wall is plastered with notes and maps: all of my research into Banta. Every piece of intel I gathered.

What really seems to have caught Aiden's eye is the gleaming motorcycle propped up on a stand in the middle of the room.

"Do you think you could take the bike with us when we jump next?" I ask. It's a throwaway question, since I don't really think it will be possible, but he seems to be seriously considering it.

He circles the bike a few times, deep in thought, while I head toward the clothes rack at the back of the room.

Checking each of the three jackets hanging there, I choose the only one that has a plastic zipper—I don't relish the idea of the Metalworker ripping a zipper off my jacket and strangling me with it. The one I choose is not my favorite, but it's better than nothing.

I also ditch my knee-high boots in favor of ankle-high ones with an elastic side panel instead of a zipper.

Then I grab a material bag and shove some underwear, T-shirts, and another pair of leggings into it before I join Aiden at the bike.

"It would be useful to have a means of transportation through the forest, but the Metalworker could dismantle it and kill us with the parts," he says, following with a shrug of his broad shoulders. "I don't think I could jump with it, anyway. Small objects are okay, but objects as large as this will rip out of my hands. It's much easier to jump with a person than an object."

I run my hand across the bike's sleek paneling. This motorcycle saved my life multiple times. If I'd had it with me when I was trying to escape from Banta, I'm sure I would have gotten away.

Taking Aiden's warning about carrying objects seriously, I return to the cupboard beneath the weapons and pull out my case of mercury. The case itself is compact, but with thirty vials inside it, it's also damn heavy.

"What about this?" I ask.

Aiden nods. "That should be fine, but tuck it into the front of your jacket just in case."

"Right after I drink some." I snap the case open and retrieve one of the vials, anticipating the way the silver liquid will cool my insides and ease the dryness in my lips. I never quite realize how parched I am until I hold mercury in my hands. I guess I'm glad, because otherwise I might panic.

Dehydration is torture to vampires.

The funny thing is that I don't remember anyone telling me that I would need to drink mercury on a daily basis.

Vampires are made, not born. We don't remember anything about our human lives before our creation, which is just as well, because there's nothing human about us after we've been changed.

As for needing mercury instead of blood, I woke with the knowledge that the silver liquid was my food source. If I hadn't known what to ask for, I would have starved.

To say that my sire was angry when I refused to drink blood is an understatement. Apparently, he had high hopes for his new 'daughter.'

He managed to supply me with mercury for the first two months of my vampire life before he banished me from the hive and washed his hands of me.

After that, I had to learn to survive quickly.

Uncapping the vial, I lift it to my lips, the silver liquid washing down my throat, cooling my body.

"Stop! Don't drink that yet!" Aiden's shout makes me jolt, but I've already swallowed half of the vial.

A droplet spills across my hand as I swing back to him. "What's wrong?"

He prowls toward me, his focus blazing on the vial. His lips are pressed together so hard that they're white, his jaw is clenched, and his chest rises and falls rapidly.

His heartbeat punches in my hearing.

"I've been fucking stupid," he says.

He's suddenly so agitated that a heat wave rises across his shoulders, and I take a step back from him. I'm a little concerned he might combust on the spot. The box of matches in his pocket would certainly facilitate it.

"The Metalworker told me he'd tear you apart," Aiden says. "But I didn't think he could mean it literally."

The heat wave grows around his chest, his palm scorching as it closes around mine before he extricates the vial from my frozen grip.

"Aiden," I whisper. "What are you talking about?"

"You just drank heavy metal, Iyana. It's spreading through your bloodstream right now. If he can control metal in its liquid form, then he could rip you apart from the inside."

"But..." I stare from the vial Aiden's holding to the open case. "I don't have a choice—"

I flinch as the door behind me creaks. I could convince myself that it was a result of the natural shifting of the walls, except for the imminent threat the Metalworker poses to us.

Aiden spins toward the sound, at the same time reaching for the box of matches in his pocket. "Grab the case! We're leaving!"

The soft scratch of the matchhead against the box breaks the tension as he lights the flame.

Just as his free arm closes around my waist, the inner door explodes outward, the metal surface buckling and folding in on itself as the side of the unit rips outward, leaving a gaping hole behind.

At the same time, a force wraps around my chest, squeezing so tightly, I don't have breath to scream before I'm wrenched out of Aiden's arms.

CHAPTER SIXTEEN

*a*ir rushes around me. The case of mercury flies from my hands and the vials shatter against the walls and floor.

I'm yanked to a stop, my arms and legs jolting before I float above the paved walkway outside the unit where the lights have all gone out.

My entire body is out of my control, from my head to my toes.

I fight to control my movements, but I can't do a thing. My arms are pulled out at my sides and my legs bend against my will so that I end up kneeling in space.

A hooded figure stands in the shadows no more than four paces away from me.

He raises one hand toward me, far enough away that I couldn't kick him even if I could control my legs.

A glowing cigarette butt rests loosely between the fingers of his other hand. Other than his outstretched arm, his posture appears relaxed, as if holding me in the air requires no effort at all.

The two metal doors, both folded in on themselves so that they're a quarter of their original size, now float on his other side, and it suddenly feels as if they're trophies. An exhibition of his strength.

There's no doubt in my mind that this man is the Metalworker.

He begins pushing back his hood, but I only catch a glimpse of a bronze jawline before Aiden's shout breaks across us.

The pyromancer's footfalls are drowned out by the sharp crackle of exploding fire as he rages through the storage unit's now jagged entrance.

"Let her go!" Aiden roars. Flames burst around his body, lighting up his skin so that his silhouette glows beneath his clothing and waves of heat billow across the air, buffeting me where I float.

Aiden draws his arm back as he runs, punching his hand forward to release a fireball that hurtles toward the Metalworker.

The Metalworker's posture remains impossibly relaxed as the folded doors zip into the space between himself and the fireball, their surfaces overlapping and acting as a single shield to protect him from the attack.

The flames explode against the metal surface, fire splashing like liquid around its edges.

I'm close enough to the explosion that the heat scorches my torso, but the flames don't reach me.

Skidding to a stop ten paces away from the Metalworker, Aiden releases two more orbs in quick succession, lobbing the first high and shooting the second low.

The Metalworker anticipates both of them. The two doors separate—one up, the other down—to deflect the fire, while the flames splash like molten lava toward the unprotected space between the shields.

But Aiden wasn't done. While the two shields moved into separate positions, he took another shot square at the Metalworker's chest—a third, slightly delayed fireball.

All three were fired in such quick succession that the doors are still deflecting the first two blows, and the Metalworker has nothing to protect him from the third fireball.

Or... I guess that was Aiden's intention.

He's running toward me, his arms outstretched. He only needs to touch me, and he can jump us both out of here.

The Metalworker's extended arm moves at the last moment, his fist clenching and jolting toward his chest as if he's grabbing and pulling something.

Immediately, my body obeys him.

I fly so fast into position in front of him that my back arches and a scream tears out of me.

"No!" Aiden's eyes widen with horror as I become the Metalworker's shield for the third fireball.

The blaze fills my view, its heat like a hungry animal—a living beast that wants to destroy whatever organic material it touches.

Aiden's roar of effort reaches me before the fire halts, hitting an invisible wall between it and me with only an inch to spare.

I can't see Aiden beyond it, and I can only imagine the strength it took to stop the fire in its tracks. It swirls and spreads, an angry wall of amber extending across the air in front of me while I try to breathe.

The Metalworker laughs softly into my ear, uncomfortably close as he draws me up against him so that my back is plastered against his chest.

He's holding me so close to him that his heartbeat is a slow, steady thump in my hearing. My feet remain off the ground and, from the corner of my vision, his bronze skin gleams across his jawline, neck, and high cheekbones.

He's slightly taller than me, so, with my feet off the ground, my head is level with his.

For a second, his cheek presses to mine. His metallic skin is cold—dead—sending a chill through me.

When his arms close around me, they're hard, his contoured muscles pressing into my ribs and across my shoulders. It's his grip across my upper back that alarms me the most. All he has to do is slip his hold higher and he'd have me in a chokehold.

There isn't a fucking thing I can do about it.

"Let go of me, asshole," I snarl, as I struggle against his power.

He grunts when I attempt to drive my elbow into his stomach, but the sound he makes can't be because I hit him.

Every move I make is met with resistance. Every signal I send to my limbs is hopeless. It's like trying to push against an invisible barrier.

He counters every attempt I make to free myself by pushing me in the opposite direction, jolting me around like a puppet.

My eyes water with frustration and anger as the flames in front of us finally disperse, revealing Aiden standing, fists clenched, three paces away. His hands blaze and the fire remains around his entire body, but he's standing incredibly still, as if he's holding his breath.

He resumes breathing as soon as he sees me.

His eyebrows draw down and his shoulders hunch when the Metalworker jerks me hard against his chest again.

I whimper when the Metalworker molds my back against his front so painfully that my head tips back and my legs are forced to either side of his thighs.

The Metalworker clicks his tongue, shaking his head at Aiden. "Aiden, Aiden," he says. "That was a little too close, don't you think? You could have killed her."

Aiden's eyes blaze in the darkness. "I won't let you hurt her."

The Metalworker shrugs. "Can you stop me?" His hold suddenly loosens around me, and I try again to struggle against his power, but instead, I find myself jolted back against him. The movement is smoother this time, as if he's getting better at controlling me—as if the first few times he pushed me around were practice.

"She's so full of metal right now, I can make her body do *whatever* I want," he says.

I gasp as I jolt forward, bent at the waist, the back of my thighs pressed to the front of his.

Against my will, my hands rise, reaching for the top clasp of my bodice and slipping it open to reveal the tops of my breasts.

Dear fuck. I have no control.

Aiden's voice is guttural, an animalistic fury in his eyes. "I will kill you, you fucking—"

The Metalworker holds up his hand—the one he was controlling me with before. "I have no problem turning her into my shield again, Aiden."

At the edge of my view, the Metalworker is still loosely gripping the cigarette butt and when he speaks, he waves it around, the expressive movement of his hand trailing the little light through the air.

Aiden follows its arc and I guess it's like an open taunt to him. The Metalworker can offer Aiden all of the flames he wants, but Aiden can't use them against him while the Metalworker controls me.

Damn my thirst! Damn my blood!

The Metalworker wrenches me upright again, forcing my back to arch as he presses his cheek to mine. The side of his hoodie rests between us, and I still can't see his face fully, his skin a gleaming surface that reflects the increasing firelight Aiden is creating.

I can't control my body, but I decide to try my voice again.

If I can get the Metalworker talking, distract him—even make him angry—he might make a mistake, because right now, he's too fucking cool and in command.

Opposite me, Aiden is a mountain of fury with no outlet, little sparks bursting across the backs of his hands.

We need a way out. *Somehow.*

"How did you know we'd come here?" I ask, waiting a beat to see if the Metalworker forces me to close my mouth. "And how the hell did you get inside?"

His bronze lips curl into a smile as he finally pushes back his hood. Without being able to turn my head properly, I can only just make out his features.

His eyes are a darker shade of bronze, his eyelashes finer than I was expecting, every detail of his face following natural contours, but made out of metal. His hair falls to his shoulders, glistening bronze strands like fine wire.

"As for getting inside this warehouse, I have my ways. But knowing you'd be here was simple: Your food stash is here, Iyana," he says with a smile. "I figured you'd run out of mercury, eventually. I thought it might take weeks, and I've learned to be patient. I didn't think I'd be rewarded so quickly."

He makes another soft sound of satisfaction as he waves the cigarette in front of me in what feels like a more deliberate move this time. "I guess Aiden wasn't able to resist this tiny light."

I'm incredulous. "You planted that?"

Across from us, Aiden tenses, his shoulders squared. Then he starts a slow prowl back and forth, never taking his eyes off me as he moves. His pacing forces the Metalworker to shift me ever so slightly to the side so he can keep Aiden within his sights.

The Metalworker raises his voice as he throws the cigarette butt onto the ground near Aiden's feet. "I'm impressed, Aiden. You jumped through a bullet's spark last night, and tonight you transported Iyana through the smallest glow. You're becoming stronger—but you're growing more desperate."

Aiden snarls and flames jump around his shoulders. It's astonishing to see them light up his body while his clothing remains unburned.

I force the Metalworker's taunts to roll off me. "How did you know my stash was here?"

I was so careful. I always covered my tracks. I know when I've picked up a tail, and I'm practiced at shaking them. I was sure nobody ever followed me here.

"It's easy to gather information when people don't realize they should fear you," the Metalworker says. "I used to think that my ability to blend into the background was a bad thing—until I learned I could use it to my advantage. Tailing you was easy."

My brow furrows. It sounds like he was following me for a while. It had to be back before Banta hurt me, since I haven't come to this storage unit since then.

"I know you, don't I?" I ask, hoping to coax the answer out of him.

"Of course you do," he snaps. He sounds almost disgruntled. "But you thought I was nobody. You dismissed me like all of the others."

Who is he?

Someone I wronged in my past? Someone I knew as a human? Or someone I overlooked more recently?

Whoever he is, the only way we're going to escape him is if he lets go of me for long enough that Aiden can grab me.

"Well, you're obviously somebody," I say, softly. "But if you're here doing Banta's bidding, then it means he controls you just like he controlled Aiden, so you can't be *that* powerful."

I was hoping to goad him into reacting, but I succeed a little too well. He wrenches me around so that I'm facing him.

He shucks off his cloak fully and for the first time, I can see all of his features.

I was correct that he's a little taller than me—Aiden's height, and just as broad in the shoulders. He's wearing an ivory collared shirt rolled up at the sleeves, which reveals the contours of his biceps, and navy-blue pants with a bronze belt.

It's hard to tell from his metallic features, but he looks a bit younger than Aiden and I.

For the second that I'm floating in front of him, I sense Aiden brace, as if he's going to leap for me, but the metal man's hands snap around my wrists in a crushing grip that makes me wince.

"I choose to follow Banta," he snarls. "He lets me do whatever the fuck I like."

Damn, he *sounds* young. Which could mean he's more likely to be provoked into an angry outburst that I could work to my advantage.

"Really?" I ask. "Then what's stopping you?"

His lips twist and a cruel light glints across his bronze eyes. "I could crush your bones right now and Banta wouldn't care," he says. "As long as he gets your blood, he'll be happy."

My blood? I stare at him. "What has my blood got to do with anything?"

A slow smirk grows across the Metalworker's face, his bronze eyes sparkling now. "You aren't the only one capable of playing a game, Iyana."

"What the fuck are you talking about?" I demand to know, struggling once more against the metal man's hold.

To the side, Aiden has also frozen, his quick glances from the Metalworker to me indicating that he doesn't know what the metal man is talking about, either.

The Metalworker leans toward me. "Banta's going to bleed you dry."

CHAPTER SEVENTEEN

*P*anic builds inside me, and I hate the feeling of not being in control.

Of not knowing what's going on.

Until the night I fought Banta, I was confident and always knew my next move; nothing could shake me.

But now there are cracks. Vulnerabilities that I didn't have before.

All I know right now is that I need to get away from this guy.

Concentrating on my hands where he grips my wrists, I force my fingers to obey me.

Make a fist! I shout at myself. *Make a fucking fist!*

The Metalworker's grip trembles, the first sign of alarm in his widening eyes as my fingers slowly furl inward.

It takes every shred of my concentration to keep them there. The muscles in my right arm shake as I fight to pull against his hold, gritting my teeth, shuddering with effort.

His lips press together, his eyebrows drawing down, and a glimmer passes across his face—from one side to the other—as if his bronze exterior faltered for a second.

I didn't see who he was underneath it. Don't care right now.

I just want him the fuck away from me.

With a violent scream, I pull my fist back with all of my might and slam it forward against his forehead. The impact of my knuckles against his metal face is hard enough to shift my bones—possibly crack them—but I don't stop.

The moment I strike him, his power falters even further.

My legs are free.

Arching backward midair, I use all of my strength to smack my boot into his neck and push off him. He still has enough control of me that I don't hit the ground, but I make it halfway across the walkway.

I scream. "Aiden!"

Aiden doesn't waste a second. Now that the metal man isn't controlling me, Aiden's already running toward me, his feet splashing fire across the pavement, his hands reaching for me.

Just before he reaches me, a new voice sounds—a voice that is so calm, it soothes my frayed nerves, but so sharp that it somehow cracks across the walkway. "Freeze, Aiden."

It's a voice I know too well.

Not Banta. Not now.

Aiden hits an invisible wall, collapsing to the ground as every limb in his body suddenly seems to lose strength. His lips part with a visibly harsh breath and his shoulders wrench backward, his torso straight, held as tightly as I was being held by the Metalworker.

Aiden might be frozen, but I'm still free. I throw myself forward, wrapping my arms around Aiden's torso, ignoring the heat of the flames still licking around his body. "Aiden," I whisper. "Jump! Please!"

Aiden's chest rises and falls rapidly, his eyes blazing, sweat beading on his forehead, revealing the effort he's making trying to fight his way free of the compulsion to obey Banta's command.

Banta Sol strides toward us along the walkway, his shoes striking the hard pavement, his whispering voice continuing to act like a soothing balm on all of my fears. His presence explains how the Metalworker got into the warehouse in the first place—Banta would have simply told the proprietor to let him inside.

Banta isn't as tall as me, but he doesn't need to be. Physical strength and force have never been his go-to. Silver-gray hair sweeps back from his head, his eyes are a pale shade of brown, and he wears a thick, silver-white beard cut neatly around his jawline.

I've never been able to ascertain his real age, but he appears to be in his late fifties—his skin slightly weathered but in a way that makes him look wise, not old. He's impeccably dressed in a dark gray suit, his shoes polished and shiny.

"You don't need to fight me anymore, Iyana," he says, reaching my side, his hand closing around my shoulder and tugging me away from Aiden. "You're at peace. You're right where you should be."

I fight the lethargy seeping through my body, the sagging sensation within my limbs right before I'm wrenched away from Aiden, the Metalworker taking control of my body again. He drops me to the ground a few paces from Aiden, forcing me into another kneeling position—not that I'm really fighting it now.

Banta's speech echoes around my head and I tell myself: *It's okay. I'm at peace.*

Banta turns from me and bends to Aiden—to where the pyromancer is now slumped over his knees. Banta pats his shoulder. "Stay there, Aiden."

Despite the order, Aiden struggles, his shoulders bunching, his jaw clenching. He told Tessa that Banta didn't give him orders that went against his inner nature, but now... Banta clearly has.

Banta ignores Aiden's efforts as he reaches me again, dividing his attention between Aiden and me while the Metalworker watches on. Banta leans down to brush his fingertips across each of my cheeks, one after the other.

"*Breathe*, Iyana," he says, as if he's trying to help me. "Everything will be as it should be."

His eyes are deceptively gentle. Somehow, he manages to exhibit empathy—a chilling kindness—despite being the one inflicting the pain.

My thoughts are rapidly becoming cloudy, and I find myself focusing on what he told me to do: *Breathe and trust that everything will be as intended.*

As I relax, I sense the Metalworker release his hold on me. I guess it takes a lot of energy to keep me under control—and he knows Banta has me now. My shoulders slump, but I breathe normally and calmly.

Just as I'm about to surrender completely to the compulsion in Banta's speech, a moment of clarity returns to me: When Aiden tried to convince me that his mind was his own, he told me that the pain the Metalworker inflicted on him was too much. It had kept his head clear.

He said he wished he'd inflicted pain on himself every time Banta gave him an order.

Now, pain is my only hope.

When Banta leaves my side—apparently satisfied that I'm under his control—I force myself to find enough clarity to pull my lower lip into my mouth, as if I'm trying to moisten it.

Instead, I bite hard, allowing my fang to descend far enough to pierce my skin.

The pain clears my head instantly.

Surfacing from the pull of Banta's commands, I'm afraid that I'll only have moments before he gives me another order and, if I slip under again, I don't know if I'll have the strength to pull myself out.

My heart hammers inside my chest as I stare at Aiden, where he also kneels only a few paces away from me.

He's so close.

He's shaking. Maybe with rage. Maybe with desperation.

The worst part is that his fire is gone now. Without the heat, the air is chilling around me.

My focus flicks to the abandoned cigarette butt, which lies on the concrete floor only a few paces to my right. Then to the box of matches tucked into Aiden's pocket.

The cigarette butt is so cold now that it's a long shot, but the matches will need to be withdrawn and struck—seconds we won't have.

I'll only get one shot at this. I can't make the wrong choice.

I wait another beat for Banta to give the Metalworker his full attention.

"Well done," Banta says to the metal man, his voice oozing with pride. "The van's waiting outside the warehouse. I'm relying on you to keep Iyana in line. I'll take care of Aiden."

I launch myself to the right, snatching up the cold cigarette butt, raising it to my lips and dragging on it.

Oxygen and a spark make fire. All I need is a spark.

Please burn.

My hand closes around Aiden's wrist a split second before the Metalworker catches sight of me and shouts from the side. "Iyana! Stop!"

His power wraps around me, a sharp tug, ripping me away from Aiden—but Aiden's hand is already in my mouth.

My fangs tear through his palm so savagely that I taste blood and flesh between my teeth.

I don't inject any venom. This time, I'm aiming purely for physical pain.

Aiden's eyes shoot wide as I'm torn away from him. I try, but don't quite succeed, in retracting my fangs fully before my rapid movement causes more damage.

I fly backward, lifted off my feet, thumping into the Metalworker's hard chest before his arms close around me.

"That was a fucking stupid move, Iyana," the metal man says, his grip painfully tight around my ribs and my limbs frozen again under his power.

Opposite me, Aiden looks down at what I left in his hand.

The glowing cigarette burns in his bloodied palm.

Pain and fire blossom in his eyes.

He launches himself to his feet and runs toward me, every muscle in his body straining.

Despite not wanting to see him hurt, I pray he remains in pain because, if the agony subsides, Banta will be able to control him again.

Fire bursts within Aiden's palm, the tiny flame I gave him growing and wrapping around his arm, spreading up to his shoulder before it explodes across his chest.

I don't know how he's going to get me away from the Metalworker so that we can jump. It feels impossible, but Aiden's speed indicates he intends to use sheer brute strength alone.

Banta's pale brown eyes shoot wide, a cruel twist forming on his lips as he starts to shout, "Aiden! You will obey—"

Aiden doesn't seem to hear him.

I guess I really tore into his hand.

The Metalworker's shout of alarm is harsh in my ear as Aiden reaches us without slowing down.

Aiden barrels into us, fire blazing around his entire body as he tackles us. Tackles *me*.

His arm scoops around my stomach, but I recognize the split-second moment—the burst of tension in his muscles—when he must realize he can't wrench me from the Metalworker's control.

He has no choice but to close his other arm around the Metal-worker, too.

Heat and flame billow around us—so hot that it snatches the breath from my chest.

My body becomes weightless, telling me that we're about to jump.

All three of us. Together.

CHAPTER EIGHTEEN

*T*he world—the flames—everything rushes past me so fast.

Aiden's arm is locked around my waist, his bleeding hand splayed at my side.

The cocoon of his power forms around me—but only partially around him, as if he's concentrating it across my body alone.

Despite the sense of weightlessness, I feel more whole than I did moments ago—more myself—and I suddenly realize that I'm free from the metal man's control.

My body is my own again. My bite gave Aiden freedom, and his power has given me the same.

My liberty is a relief that burns hot within me.

At the same time, I'm frighteningly aware of the fight between the two men, which is difficult to see through the flames that surround them.

My only sense is of the tension in Aiden's arm around my waist, the flex of his bicep.

We have moments until we crash into whatever flame Aiden is taking us to, but if he lets go of me during the jump... I don't know what will happen.

I press closer to him, trying to see through the immense wash of amber around us. He told me that jumping with people was easier than with objects, but the metal man is anything but flesh and bone right now.

The cocoon of Aiden's power around me pushes back the fire so I can finally see the two men, who are in startling proximity to me.

The Metalworker's bronze fist is wrapped around Aiden's neck.

Aiden slams his free fist down on the Metalworker's arm, thumping him again and again, trying to make him let go.

My sense of weightlessness shifts.

We're about to land and maybe that will help us, but I can't take the chance that the Metalworker will crush Aiden's neck before we reach our destination.

Without thinking about it, I lurch forward and sink my fangs into the Metalworker's shoulder.

Heat billows around me as Aiden's power stretches thin, the protective cocoon receding dangerously. Now that Aiden has proven himself invulnerable to my venom, I have no confidence that I can kill the metal man, but at the minimum, I'm determined to distract him for long enough for Aiden to free himself.

As soon as my fangs sink through his shirt and pierce his skin, the Metalworker's glistening eyes snap to me, shooting wide.

The metallic sheen across his body ripples away from the bite mark, withdrawing across his shoulder and neck and revealing flesh —and now blood soaking through his shirt.

With a snarl, he shouts at Aiden. "Your brother is a fighter, too, Aiden. If you don't give yourselves up, he'll pay the price."

With a roar, Aiden rams his fist down once more and the Metalworker's flesh-and-blood arm drops away from Aiden's neck.

It was his only anchor to us. He flies backward through the flames, ripped away from us, disappearing instantly.

It all happens so fast that a second later, we crash into the ground.

My leg hits something hot and metallic and for a horrible moment, I'm worried that the metal man has landed with us...

But the next thing I know, I'm falling forward onto my hands and knees beside Aiden.

There's a loud *clang*, and an overturned trashcan wobbles behind us, its fiery contents spilling across the pavement.

I'm suddenly aware of thumping music and multi-colored lights.

I look up into the startled faces of a group of teenagers who are holding beer cans. Many of the teens are still in the act of jumping out of the way, while others are shouting.

Aiden grabs my arm, scooping me back to my feet. "Run!"

As he moves, the fire spilling from the trashcan rushes from the ground up to his bloodied hand. We run together across a paved backyard in what appears to be suburbia.

Aiden punches his fist forward, shooting the flame ahead of us, where it stops midair.

He tugs on my arm, and I don't hesitate, racing with him, and leaping upward.

The fire takes hold and then I'm weightless again, intensely aware that the fire Aiden shot into the air came with us when we jumped, and I can only assume he drew it with us so we didn't leave a fire behind.

I wrap my arms around Aiden's waist, determined not to let go of him.

His body is tense for the few seconds it takes to jump.

There's no time to talk about the threat the Metalworker made against Aiden's brother.

I tip my head back to see his face, since his heart is beating far too fast right now, but the only emotion I get from him during my brief glimpse of his features through the fire is a deep focus. Deep determination.

He told me once that he learned to put away his emotions—contain them, box them up—because they could impair his judgement when he needs his entire focus to survive.

I'm not sure if we'll jump right to the forest where the dryads live, but I suspect he will want to jump through at least one more fire first to obscure our trail.

I recognize the sensation of landing before it happens—a tug and a sense of heaviness within my limbs. I roll through logs and out of an open fireplace into what looks like a well-lived-in lounge room.

Judging by the wooden paneling and the hewn furniture, it's some sort of a cabin.

Aiden is close behind me, both of us shooting to our feet to face the woman who has swung around in the lounge chair at the side of the room.

Her teeth sharpen and her claws extend. "Who are you? How did you get in here?"

Her features partially shift, her eyes taking on the shape of a wolf's, when her gaze rakes over me.

"Vampire!" she snarls, her sudden fear evident in the way her pupils dilate.

I'm painfully aware of the crib beside her chair and the peacefully-sleeping child wrapped up in blankets inside it.

She won't know I don't drink blood.

Our hands shoot up, fingers splayed. Aiden's injured hand is so bloody that it drips across the stone hearth as he inches toward the front door.

"We're not here to hurt you," I say. "We just want to leave."

"Then fucking leave," she snarls, moving to stand between us and her baby.

Aiden hurriedly bumps against the door—his back to it—but I reach for the handle first. There's no way I'm letting him leave a bloody handprint on this door as a reminder of our unwelcome visit.

"I'm sorry," I whisper as we slip out.

We're lucky she lets us go. I have no doubt that if she wasn't determined to stay beside her child, she would have attacked us.

As she should have.

Aiden tugs me into a run again, aiming for the wheelbarrow next to the wood chopping block positioned off to the side of the front porch.

Above us, the stars sparkle, and I'm aware of the depth of a forest that spreads beyond us.

"Where are we?" I gasp.

"Upper Highlands wolf shifter territory," he says, his voice strained. "Banta won't expect me to jump here, given how territorial the wolves are."

I spin back to the lone cabin, remembering what Tessa told me about her upbringing. She grew up in a cabin on a mountain, where she was banished from the rest of her pack. It wasn't this one—her old pack is the Middle Highlands pack—but the cabin we left has the quiet seclusion that I suspect she grew up in.

I don't have another moment to think about it.

Aiden shoots fire into the air ahead of us, which spreads across the space once more until we jump into it.

Again, I sense it come with us—and I'm glad, because leaving fire behind in the forest could start a devastating blaze.

I'm breathless as we land again, this time crashing out of another log fire—which turns out to be an open campfire. Tents surround it, but I don't see any people—not yet, anyway.

We pick ourselves up and Aiden tugs me into the trees before the campers come out of their tents to see what all the commotion is about.

I fully expect to jump again, but Aiden guides me farther along into the woods without creating any more fire, keeping up a quick pace until the campsite is well behind us.

"Where are we now?" I ask, finally comfortable that we're out of earshot.

"The North Cascades National Park. That was our last jump," he says. "Banta will have trouble following our trail. We've got at least a week's head start now." He waves his uninjured hand around. "Thanks to your friend, Tessa Dean, there are no more witches to help transport him instantly from place to place. He'll have to follow us by road and then on foot."

I'm relieved that we don't need to jump again, but I'm also conscious of Aiden's wound now that we're safe.

I hurt him badly. Regret is a nasty feeling inside me. I can't let it fester.

I reach for him. "Aiden? Let me check your hand."

He backs away from me, bumping into the nearest tree before turning away from me. "I need a minute alone. Wait here, please."

I guess the box in which he's keeping his fears for his brother isn't so tightly closed, after all.

He stumbles into the dark trees, his silhouette blending into the forest now that the fire has faded from his body.

I stare after him before I make a decision. I know only too well what it looks like when someone pushes me away—Tessa did it with as much desperate aggression as she could. I'm not letting it happen again. Not even if Aiden said, 'please.'

"No," I whisper, even though I'm sure he's out of earshot by now—and he doesn't have a wolf shifter's or a vampire's hearing. "I'm not waiting here."

I hurry after him, treading carefully, but trying not to be too quiet so I don't startle him.

Following the faint sound of his heartbeat, I step between the trees while the undergrowth becomes denser and also more damp.

Up ahead, I make out the soft bubbling of a creek—a shallow sound that makes it a little harder to follow Aiden's steps.

When I finally step onto the creek's bank, I find myself standing at the edge of a moonlit stream, the shallow wash of water streaming across glistening rocks at a gentle downward angle.

The height of the moon tells me it's nearly midnight, approaching the deep dark of night—the time when I feel most comfortable in my skin.

Aiden sits beside the tree on my right-hand side, nursing his wounded hand.

He's quiet.

He can't have missed my arrival, but he doesn't ask me to leave.

I lower myself to the mossy ground beside the nearest tree, giving him space. I'm certain that I'll end up with a damp backside, but it's the least of my concerns right now.

Determined to let him speak first, I watch the water flow as it carries random leaves and twigs away with it.

As a bounty hunter, I learned to deal in secrets, but it wasn't until I lived at Hidden House that I realized how important it is to respect a person's silence.

Even if I'm increasingly desperate to check his wound.

Finally, he says, "It's my own fucking fault. I left my brother there. I should have tried harder to get to him."

My heart squeezes as I hear what he's *not* saying: He chose my safety over his brother's.

Rising to my feet, I relocate myself beside him, making no comment about his family or his choices as I reach for his hand. "Show me your wound."

He allows me to take his hand and turn his palm up, but he makes a growling sound in his throat when I make a move to touch the wound. I'm tempted to ask him if he has any wolf shifter heritage because it's exactly the defensive *back-off* sound Tristan would have made.

I ignore Aiden's narrowed eyes as I peer at the injured flesh.

There's too much blood to see the damage properly, and only one easy way to clean it that doesn't involve dipping his hand into the creek water, which looks all sparkly but could just as easily carry parasites and all sorts of animal droppings.

Lowering my mouth to his palm, I allow my fangs to descend just the slightest before I gently swirl my tongue against his skin, careful not to scrape him with the tips of my teeth.

I may not crave blood like other vampires, but I produce the same numbing agent in my saliva when I allow my fangs to descend. It allows other vampires to drain an initial amount of blood under the guise of a passionate kiss. The victim doesn't feel pain until it's too late.

The numbing agent I produce is not quite so effective as it is for other vampires—a trade-off, it seems, for the different effect of my venom. Aiden would have felt my bite yesterday, just as he'll continue to feel the pain of this wound, but it should take the edge off his discomfort.

Gently running my tongue across the wound, I pause at the fleshy part of his palm, relieved to discover that I didn't do any structural damage to his thumb or forefinger. I'm grateful that I must have retracted my fangs just in time.

I continue to clean the wound by gently pressing my tongue against it, but I'm at a loss about how to help him after this.

I have nothing to wrap around the wound this time. No bandages. No spare clothing. I'll need to ask him for a strip off the hem of his shirt, since the material in my structured bodice isn't an option.

When I look up, prepared to ask him for his shirt, I find him reaching for me.

Gasping, I release his hand as his other arm swiftly circles around my back.

"Come here," he orders me, before he deftly pulls me toward him as if I weigh nothing.

My legs slip to either side of his hips so that I'm straddling him in a kneeling position while he pulls me as close as possible to his chest.

Lowering his injured hand to my thigh, he tips his head, his lips nudging mine.

A fine sheen of rain begins to fall around us, but nothing has ever felt more natural than being pressed against him like this. There isn't any question in his eyes when he kisses me again, only a certainty that seems to burn deep.

"Fuck, I missed you," he murmurs, stroking the back of my neck, brushing the little wisps of hair, before easing back the collar of my jacket to access the top of my shoulder.

His touch trails down my side before he presses his lips to mine again, slow and gentle, taking his time exploring the curves of my mouth with his lips and tongue.

The taste of lingering fire on his skin is intoxicating.

I anchor myself by gripping his shoulders, leaning into his kiss. Even though he isn't controlling an active flame right now, he may as well have lit my body like a match.

The flare of need grows inside me, heightened by the hard press of his body between my legs.

There's a part of me that doesn't want to break this moment by asking for more. He's dealing with a lot right now. I don't want to be nothing more than a distraction from the worry he feels about his brother.

His kiss deepens, but his touch against my side remains light and I find myself breathing evenly with every stroke of his tongue against mine, relaxing into the pleasure, until he slowly breaks the contact.

He remains quiet, but he keeps me close.

I look up to find his eyelids half lowered, his breathing deep, his jaw relaxed, and his forehead clear of all its tense lines as he leans back against the tree trunk, pulling me with him.

He rests his injured hand over mine where I'm touching his chest.

Exhaling slowly, centering myself again, I say, "I'm sorry about your hand. It was the only way I could think to wake you up."

"Banta did this. Not you," he says, unbelievably calm.

I tip my head back to check his expression and gauge his state of mind. "We will rescue your brother," I say.

He takes a deep breath and meets my determined gaze. "There are only two people in this world I care about," he says. "Once you're safe, I will make sure nobody hurts my brother."

I consider Aiden carefully—listen to the increasingly harsh edge of his voice—realizing I was totally wrong about him being calm.

He's angrier than I could have imagined.

The kind of quiet anger that scares me more than if he shouted and burned everything around him.

It's the kind of anger that will explode when he chooses.

His hand closes around mine, a strong grip despite his wound.

I shiver when he says, "I'm going to burn Banta's empire to the ground."

CHAPTER NINETEEN

*R*ising to his feet, Aiden pulls me with him before he glances up at the round moon, visible between the trees on either side of the waterway.

"We need to follow the creek north," he says, pointing upstream. "The dryads' home is likely to be near the water source that this stream comes from."

"How do you know that?" I ask, stepping to the left and following the trail of moss along the stream's banks. "I'm assuming you haven't been here before."

He shrugs as he walks beside me. "It's a calculated guess. Dryads need water to grow their environments. So it would make sense that they should be located near the largest water source."

I squint at him. "What you're really saying is that you don't know where they are. We could walk around in this forest for weeks and not find them. Am I right?"

He tips his head with a sudden grin that seems to banish all of his anger. "More or less. But Banta won't find us, either."

I blow out an exhale. "Do you know anything else about the dryads that could help us find them?"

"I know a few things," he says, his answer a little cagey for my liking. He gives me a smirk. "They're creative. If you see an unusual plant, chances are they made it."

"I'll keep an eye out," I say, unconvinced about how helpful that will be since much of the foliage around us is unfamiliar to me.

In all of my remembered life, I've lived in cities. Venturing into the forest in the western lowland controlled by Tristan was one of the first times I'd immersed myself in nature.

Aiden returns to his previous serious tone as he steps lightly along the creek's bank. "I'm concerned about your food supply."

I sigh. "The Metalworker demonstrated very effectively that mercury is going to get me killed. I have to find an alternative."

Somehow.

"You haven't exactly eaten for a while now, either," I say.

Aiden shrugs. "Fire is my food. I'll be fine for another day."

I navigate around the protruding roots of a tree. "I guess we can be hangry together, then."

Aiden's focus suddenly shifts farther along the creek's bank where the moonlight sparkles. The light brightens there, and at first, I think it's the moonlight glinting on the moving water, but then Aiden snags my arm and draws me down to the ground, pointing.

"Do you see that?"

The glow across the water's surface increases until I make out what looks like a small blue ball of light, dancing along the surface.

I saw a light like that at Hidden House. It was the night that we took Tristan there after he was injured in the fight with the angels. We were all gathered in Tessa's room after we bonded as a pack.

The brilliant dancing light had glided toward Tessa. She didn't know I was awake and I didn't follow her when she left the room.

The light bouncing along the stream ahead of us now is similar, but, as it draws closer, I realize it isn't the same. Its edges are uneven, as if it were made of blue flames that are all crammed into a small space.

"What is it?" I whisper.

"It's a will-o'-the-wisp," he says.

I blink at him. What little I know of will-o'-the-wisps, they're either innately good or extremely evil.

They will either light the way for someone who is lost and lead them to safety—or lead them to their death.

I sigh. "We need to follow it, don't we?"

"We don't have much choice," he replies, rising to his feet. "Where there's a dryad, there's usually a will-o'-the-wisp. They often live symbiotically. If we follow it, we'll find them."

"Sure, we might find the dryads. Or we might step off a cliff," I say, following him quietly. "Or into a pit. Or get stabbed in the eyes. Or get stung by poisonous wasps..." I continue listing off all the horrible ways the will-o'-the-wisp could lead us to our deaths. "But as long as it's going the same direction we were headed, anyway, I'm willing to follow it for now."

He gives me a lopsided grin. "I'd be sad to lose my eyes," he says.

My brow furrows at the fact that he picked that calamity specifically. "Sadder than if you walked off a cliff?"

"Yeah." He grins. "At least I'd see you on the way down."

I roll my eyes at him. Somehow, despite all that's going wrong around us, he can draw a smile out of me.

I fall silent after that, and we follow the meandering stream and the will-o'-the-wisp north for the next three hours.

It never strays from the water—and nobody is in close pursuit of us—so I slowly find myself relaxing more and more.

We keep a quick pace, but it feels as if, no matter how far we go, the scenery doesn't really change. Other than a thickening of the trees on either side of us, and a deepening of the stream, which retains the same sparkling, calm flow across pebbles.

Finally, the air brightens a little and I cast a glance at the emerging sunlight that filters through the canopy of branches overhead.

Dawn is less than an hour away. I'm still carrying my protective suit, so I'm not worried about my skin being burned, but my energy levels are low and, without a supply of food, I'll need to sleep soon.

I'm also conscious that, despite his assertion that the fire was sufficient sustenance, Aiden's energy levels will be dropping, too.

"We should stop to rest," I say, stepping away from the stream's edge to check out a small clearing immediately to our left.

"I don't want to lose the will-o'-the-wisp with the rising sun," Aiden says, rubbing his forehead.

As he speaks, the ball of light stops moving, rising slowly upward to the nearest tree, and settles into a fork between its branches, as if it, too, needs to rest.

Aiden takes another glance at it before he gives me a quick nod of agreement. He runs his hand across the fronds of a fern growing around the nearest tree before he follows me into the clearing. Water droplets fall from his fingertips, trickling off the fern and puddling on the ground beneath it.

He gives a shiver, reminding me of a cat that accidentally stepped into a pool of water and is trying to shake its paws off. "There's water everywhere."

I hide my smile when he flicks his hand to get rid of the liquid before he wipes his palm across his thigh to dry it. The fact that his discomfort around water has increased in the last hour probably means we're on the right track.

Taking care to stand in the shadows well out of any hint of sunlight, I unclip my umbrella, turn the handle, and press its base.

It springs outward, deploying into a tent that extends across the space above us while the magic in its edges seeks the width of the clearing, slowly curving down toward the ground and shutting us in.

Aiden watches me carefully as the canopy plunges us into darkness moments before a starry night sky appears across the magical canvas above us.

The false view gives a sense of depth that easily tricks my mind into believing we're standing beneath a vast night sky that stretches as far as the eye can see.

It's high enough inside for both of us to stand up, and wide enough that we'll be able to lie down to sleep inside it. Not that Aiden is going to relish sleeping on the damp ground.

He remains standing, quietly focused on me. "How did you come by this kind of magical object?"

He was confronted by Tessa, Tristan, Tessa's pack, and even the fae army back at the Spire, but he hasn't met Helen.

I decide to keep her existence to myself for now. After all, she has chosen to conceal her whereabouts from the world for... well... I'm not really sure how long. Centuries, possibly. Nobody stays at Hidden House unless they need a safe and private place to heal. Even Helen, its creator.

Even though I won't reveal the umbrella's origins, I want to be as truthful as possible. "It was a gift from someone who cares about me."

His surprise is brief—his eyebrows raising, a slight tilt to his head —before he hides it.

"Yeah," I say, my voice soft. "There's a person out there who cares about a defective vampire."

"That's not what I was thinking," he says, his expression suddenly shuttered. "The determination of the wolf shifters to protect you back at the Spire is evidence that you have powerful friends who love you. I'm surprised by the power that would be needed to create this object."

I avoid answering the lingering question in his eyes about how I came by the umbrella, focusing on my friends, instead. "I belong in Tessa's pack now," I say, unable to conceal the peace that truth brings me.

Now his forehead creases. "I believe you, but how does a vampire fit in a wolf shifter's pack?"

I smile. "Tessa isn't like any other alpha you've ever met. Neither is Tristan."

"So I saw," he says, his gaze becoming slightly distant. I imagine he's remembering the way Tessa's wolf leaped from her body, as insubstantial as a ghost, and yet as powerful as a thousand daggers as it soared through his body. "Can you explain her power to me?" he asks.

"She's Ford Vanguard's daughter," I say, wondering if he knows Ford's true identity.

His brow furrows. "How is that possible? Ford Vanguard was human, not supernatural. Banta told me so."

I shake my head. "Ford Vanguard was Fenrir."

Aiden stares at me, his eyes narrowed. "You're talking about the old god. The War Wolf, himself."

I nod. "A creature of old magic. So is Tessa. She's one of the last."

Aiden folds his arms across his chest as he restates the belief he expressed at the Spire. "Old magic is a myth. The old gods died out at the beginning of time."

"Not all of them," I reply. "And not their descendants."

Aiden rubs his forehead, and I sense he's having trouble believing me as he steps around the now-covered clearing. "If what you're saying is true, that would make Tessa Dean one of the most powerful—"

"She is."

"Then you can't take the chance Banta will control her," he says.

"I'm not sure he could," I say. "A demon's power is dark magic. Tessa is immune to all magic except old magic, and there are no other old magic creatures alive to harm her."

Except Tristan. But he and Tessa fought hard to be together, and he would never hurt her.

"What about the rest of her pack?" he asks. "Are they immune or could they be used against her—like Banta could use *you* against her?"

I shudder. It was the threat of leverage that caused Tessa to push us away, but this new threat is worse because, if Banta were to control me and Tessa didn't know, she'd trust me. Banta could send me back to her with a purpose of his own making and she wouldn't question me.

"Well, I'm not going to jeopardize her safety," I say. "Or the safety of anyone else I love."

Aiden's expression softens before he starts pacing around the tent. It takes me a moment to realize that he's testing the ground, pressing his foot down in places. Every step he takes squelches a little. "This canopy can't cover the ground, can it?" he asks.

"You could use your power to dry it out," I suggest.

He gives it thought but presses his lips together. "Any spark of fire could get the dryads' attention in a bad way."

"That might not be a terrible thing," I say. "They might come to us."

"We should only take that path as a last resort because they'll interpret it as an act of aggression," he says. He considers the damp earth for another moment. "Maybe a small amount of heat will do."

Drawing the box of matches from his pocket, he counts the remaining sticks, since each one is potentially a lifeline for us. Cupping his hand over the side of the box, he flicks a match only the barest amount before I hear it flare.

Immediately, he closes his hand across the flame—so fast that I don't even see the fire. A haze grows around his fist as he continues to hold his fist closed. The heat grows rapidly, radiating from his body and filling the space around me with warmth.

The look of concentration on his face is intense as he pockets the box and bends to the ground beneath us, carefully opening his hand and hovering his palm above the wet earth.

Not a single flare of fire licks across his skin. Instead, warmth diffuses outward. He closes his eyes briefly, rolling his shoulders. I sense the heat spreading across his body as he lowers his other hand, palm flat, above the ground.

Steam rises gently from the earth as the dampness beneath our feet begins to evaporate, forming a gentle mist, not quite visible, but I feel it when I glide my hand through the air.

Aiden continues his task carefully until the leafy ground beneath us is mostly dry, but I'm not sure that he could be happy with the level of humidity in the air now. He's traded one problem for another, it would seem.

"Here, let me help with the steam," I say, taking care as I step to the glowing slit in the side of the tent, where it's designed to open.

Sticking the toe of my boot through it—since I don't want to take the chance that I'll push my unprotected hand into sunlight—I prop it open for long enough that some of the steam slips out. Not much, since it would be better if it could be held open at the top. "Maybe you could...?"

"Maybe this is okay," he says, surprising me when his arm slips around me from behind, tugging me back inside the tent. "I have to desensitize myself to the water around me sooner rather than later. Or I'll never make it through the rest of my time in this forest."

It feels so natural to stand within the circle of his arms that I nearly forget to reassert the physical distance between us.

Being with Aiden was never something I had to second-guess. At first, building the relationship was calculated on my part, but I very quickly slipped into his life like I belonged there.

It was never hard to be with him, never a challenge, and—*damn*—the nights were good. There were moments—many of them—when I forgot why I was with him, and that our relationship was going to come to an end, eventually.

Needing an excuse to pull away from him, I reach for his injured hand. "Let me see how this is healing."

He holds back, scrunching his fist. "Only if you promise to clean it again."

I meet his lazy smile—the hint of a challenge—the sudden heat in his gaze. He was always so relaxed about sex, would wait for me to come to him—until we got started, and then the bedroom belonged to him.

"I don't think that's a good idea," I whisper.

He leans forward, slowly and carefully, until his lips hover over mine, his arms relaxed around me, his breathing calmer than mine suddenly is. "The flame between us is as strong as it used to be. Sooner or later, we're going to have to stop fighting it."

It's something I don't want to fight at all right now, but I already learned that when it comes to Aiden, I can't separate the physical from the emotional.

I loved him and there's too much that needs to heal between us. Still... the humidity has gathered on his lips and cheeks, moisture resting across the patch of chest that's visible beneath the collar of his shirt, and I'm aware of the mist I'm inhaling and exhaling—a little too rapidly—as he lowers his hands and curves them around my hips.

"Say the word, Ana, and we can pretend there's nothing else outside this tent. Nothing but us, here and now," he says. "No demons —real or in our past together."

His thumbs brush each of my hips, firm and tantalizing as he tugs me closer to him until the front of my thighs press to his.

The heat he's controlling fills the air around me, an intoxicating mix of steam and warmth. My lips part as I drag air into my chest and wrap my hands around his biceps, stroking his skin through the material.

"You said we shouldn't complicate this," I whisper.

His eyes blaze and, for a moment, I'm afraid he'll light up in amber, but he appears to control it. "Last night was the first night I went to sleep knowing I wasn't under Banta's control. Today is the first day that I walked my own path. Tomorrow?" He shakes his head. "I'll probably be the dryads' prisoner. I don't want to lose this chance to be with you when there aren't any chains around us."

What he's proposing is far too alluring.

My heart tells me to be careful—that I could hurt him as much as he could hurt me.

But my body tells me that all I need to do... is say *yes*.

CHAPTER TWENTY

I lean into Aiden, aware of the tension in his muscles as he waits for my answer.

I don't hesitate any longer, pressing my lips to his.

It's a light kiss, testing his response.

He relaxes, the tension easing from around his mouth, allowing me to follow the shape of his skin, the curve of his upper and lower lips.

Gentle touches at first, before I nudge his lips apart and taste the heady heat of burning coals—the fire that promises every pleasure.

I'm surprised when he allows me to take the lead, lets me slip the top few buttons of his shirt undone, but within moments, he breaks our kiss and captures my hands.

Lifting my arms above my head, he runs his hands all of the way down the insides of my arms to my chest, making me shiver.

Gripping my waist, he dips his head and claims my mouth, his lips demanding that I open and let him explore my tongue, every stroke making my breathing erratic.

"Fuck, Iyana," he says against my mouth, his voice husky, his lips barely parted from mine. "Don't expect this to be quick. I meant it when I said I want to get to know you all over again."

I shiver within his arms, my head tipping back a little, my toes curling within my boots. My topknot is loose and I slowly reach up to pull out my hair tie and allow my hair to fall to my waist.

I tell myself that even if I couldn't separate the physical from the emotional before, I can do it now. I'm ready for everything he's promising me.

"Show me," I whisper.

His eyes blaze. With a groan, he lifts me off my feet, elevating me for the few steps it takes to carry me to the side of the canopy.

He must have memorized where the trees were located because there's a hard surface at my back when he returns me to my feet, while the cloak around us mimics the night sky, making it feel as if we're standing in a wash of stars.

His lips crush mine again, his tongue tasting my mouth while his hands press around my waist for a long moment before he pulls back a little.

Dropping kisses at both corners of my mouth before ascending to my temple, his touch becomes light again, the contrast between the heavy presses and light touches making my skin tingle.

His fingertips trail across my collarbone to rest at the top of my bodice, sliding through the moisture gathered on my skin, his thumbs moving in swirls, dipping just beneath the top of my bodice before retreating.

I reach for the top clasp of my shirt, wanting the barrier between us to be gone, but he entwines his hands with mine, stopping me. Giving me another lazy smile. His thumbs brush the inside of my palms, then my wrists, tracing the sensitive skin up to my elbows before he draws my right wrist up to his mouth and runs the tip of his tongue across it.

He groans against my skin, the vibration of his mouth making me jolt as if he'd closed his mouth over my center.

I struggle to control the growing ache between my legs—my lips parted, and my breathing coming fast.

Still holding my wrist with one hand, he deftly reaches out and unfastens the top two clasps of my bodice, revealing the upper curve of my breasts. But he doesn't make any move to touch me there.

His gaze meets mine as he draws his tongue from my elbow back to my wrist, swirling all the way to the base of my thumb, the fire in his eyes a force that heats my body, making me jolt again.

Fuck-damn. All he's done is kiss my arm and unfasten two buttons and my body has responded with complete and utter need, the heat between my legs undeniable.

Still, he takes it slow, fully in control as he slowly reaches out and draws his fingertips through the dew gathered across the top of my breasts, slipping down the inner curve to unfasten another two clasps.

The air is light on my increasingly exposed skin. His touch is so gentle, he could be whispering across my skin, his fingertips slowly gliding to the base of my breasts in a way that heats me to my core.

When he rests his hand against my sternum, making no move to undo any more clasps, I lean forward, attempting to take back a little control.

He reacts swiftly, pulling me toward him. His leg was resting between mine, and the movement draws me up against his chest so that I'm straddling his strong thigh muscle.

I gasp as the pressure of his muscle between my legs rubs against my center and a burst of pleasure strikes through me.

Tipping my head back, I meet his smile as he allows me to grip his shoulders, but when I rock against him, his hands clamp around my hips, halting me.

"Not yet," he murmurs.

Oh, give me patience. My body wants everything.

He drops a kiss to my lips, a light nudge before he presses lingering kisses down my neck to my collarbone, making me sway against him. Peeling aside the top of the bodice on each side, he lowers his head to the side of one breast, his fingers lightly teasing the skin of the other.

With a moan, I lean back into the surface of the tree behind me, Aiden's strong thigh still between my legs, his knee also propped against the tree.

I'm on tiptoes to stay balanced and I arch back to plant my palms against the surface behind me, bracing as his tongue presses against the side of my nipple, curving around it while his other hand cups my other breast lightly. The distinction between the touches—one firm, the other light—makes my head spin.

"Aiden?"

"Hmm?" His voice vibrates against my breast as he painstakingly explores every inch of it.

My eyes close. "I want more."

He isn't swayed—doesn't speed up—continues stroking my skin until I think I'm going to lose every sane thought in my head.

"See the thing is," he murmurs, as he slips another two clasps of my bodice free. "I knew what Ana liked." His lips curve into a smile as he raises his eyes to mine, his speech challenging me to maintain that Ana was a construct and not the real me. "But you're new to me."

His thumb swirls across my nipple, making me gasp.

"I need time to figure out what you like," he says.

I exhale a heavy breath, unable to stop the curve of my own lips as I accept his challenge, and all of the pleasure he's determined to give me. "Let me help you with that."

I dart forward, seeking his lips. "I like your lips."

He responds by claiming my lips, his tongue stroking mine, exploring my mouth as thoroughly as I'm now exploring his.

With a moan, I reach for his shirt buttons, slipping the top ones free and running my hands across his exposed muscles, all the hard lines, soaking up the sense of fire and freedom beneath my palms.

"I like your skin," I whisper.

He hooks his arm around my backside, drawing me high up on his thigh so that my pointed toes barely touch the ground. The pressure on my center only increases the ache within me.

"And I like when you undress me," I say, a demand in my voice and my eyes.

He gives me a slow smile, finally reaching for the bottom clasps with his free hand and pushing aside my bodice, his fingertips grazing my stomach all the way to the top of my leggings.

I shrug the bodice off my shoulders, allowing it to drop to the ground. The humidity in the air increases with every breath I take and my pulse pounds when he tips me back over his arms, supporting my head with one big hand as he tastes every inch of my breasts and stomach, lifting me higher for better access.

He holds me there until I'm moaning with need. Then his lips clash against mine, he clasps my back, and he hooks my legs around his hips to draw me away from the side of the canopy and lower me onto the ground.

I catch the intense fire in his eyes as he reaches for my leggings, his actions demanding now, and a thrill of anticipation shoots through me.

After deftly pulling my leggings down across my hips, he lowers his mouth to my pelvis, running his tongue across the front of my underpants, his hands hooked into the top of them, tugging them lower—but not as far as to expose my most sensitive center.

Dragging at my leggings, he follows the descent of my long pants down my legs with his lips, nudging my inner thighs, then my calves as he pulls off one boot, then the other, then removes my leggings entirely.

My breathing is beyond ragged as he draws his palms up between my legs, tugging aside my underpants to stroke his fingertips across my mound, working toward my center.

When he stops before he reaches it, I nearly scream.

"Tell me," he says, a firm command as he rears up over me.

I force myself to focus. "I like you when you're naked," I say, tipping my chin, daring him not to comply.

The heat in his eyes grows as he breaks the contact between us, rising back to his feet and swiftly removing all of his clothing.

Suddenly, I'm the one who is still dressed.

He lowers himself over me, pressing my knees to either side as he glides up to kiss me. The memory of fire seems to linger within his chest. I trace the faint amber swirls across his shoulders, down his pecs, to his lower stomach.

He rears back before I can touch the hardest part of his body.

His voice is barely controlled when he says, "If I didn't think you needed your underwear, I'd rip it off you."

I let out a groan, the knot of need deep in my stomach growing tighter as he pushes my legs together and lifts my hips off the ground to slip off my underpants. The minute my pelvis is exposed, his hand cups me, his thumb finally stroking against my sensitive nub.

The heat in his finger is sharp, striking through me, making me gasp.

With a lazy smile, he draws the first two fingers of his other hand into his mouth before rearing up over me and sliding them inside me.

His fingers are as warm as his thumb, the sudden heat bursting within me, driving the ache deeper.

"Fuck, Aiden." I groan as his hand moves and I rock against him, finding only more need, as if the heat of his hand can only build my pleasure and not release it.

"Tell me again what you love," he says, a demand for an answer as he hovers between my legs, his hand pausing.

He asked me to tell him *what* I love, not whom, but all I want to say is: *You.*

I can't because I have no right to make that claim.

I clamp down on my emotions, allowing the physical to take dominance. Slipping my legs around his hips, I draw him toward me, my body more than ready for his.

"I love fucking you," I say.

He makes a satisfied growl in the back of his throat, and I glimpse again the intense fire in his eyes—the need he's controlling. He withdraws his fingers and positions himself over me before he grips my hips, bracing me.

He pauses again, a moment where I take a breath, my body ready, but my heart trying to hold itself together.

Drawing my hips toward him, slowly at first and then hard, he fills my body with his.

I meet the thrust, wanting it—*needing* it—moaning as the deepest ache builds. Gripping the ground as best I can, I brace as he withdraws and thrusts again, this time faster.

Every inch of my body explodes with an agonizing pleasure... every nerve suddenly triggering.

I'm tingling all over, crying out as he continues to control my hips. Every thrust is like a flare of fire until I'm burning with need. Moaning. Needing.

More.

As his movements grow wilder, he shifts from between my legs, repositioning himself over me without withdrawing, gathering my legs around his hips before he plants his hands on either side of my head, his eyes blazing into mine.

But instead of speeding up, now he slows down, each unhurried move grinding against me, teasing out every possible moment of ecstasy.

I release my hold on the ground to flex my palms against his chest. Steam rises around us, the remaining moisture on the ground evaporating and forming droplets in the air, making our skin glisten and the air sparkle.

When his lips crash against mine, I taste the dew on his mouth and I fall into the fire in his eyes.

My body feels like molten metal beneath his touch, and I lose all sense of my edges, aware only of his touch, his body, and the building wildfire between us until there's nothing but the crash.

I tip my head back, crying out as wave after wave of an orgasm rips through me, and I let go of every thought—every regret—allowing the final crash between us to wipe away the past.

Aiden crashes with me, his breathing erratic as he gathers me up into a sitting position, our bodies still joined. We're slick with dew, but he doesn't try to shake it off or dry our skin, his chest heaving against mine.

"Fuck," he whispers, tangling his hands in my hair, trailing kisses down my neck and up to my lips. He pauses, his eyes blazing at me. "Iyana."

He seems to enjoy saying my name, and it's almost as if he's challenging me to change my mind about what I want him to call me.

When he slowly lowers us back to the ground, I slip to the side, my upper leg hooked across his hips, my body nestled beside him. The forest floor is prickly beneath me, but I find it hard to care as I settle into a long moment of waiting for my breathing to return to normal.

I sigh when he pulls me back on top of him, and his hands move with heated sweeps across my back, soothing all of my sore muscles, relaxing me more than I've felt in weeks. I close my eyes, allowing myself to let go of any remaining tension as he kneads the aching muscles in my shoulders.

He remains quiet, holding me close, making no move to separate from me—which is unusual for him. When we were together before, he was the first to leave the bed.

I trace the familiar lines of his chest, the muscles that are even more honed than they were a year ago, and I consider the faraway look in his eyes.

"Aiden?" I murmur. "Where are you?"

He doesn't answer me right away, continuing to stroke my back. "When we were together, I took it for granted," he says. "I didn't think there would ever be a time when you wouldn't be in my bed and in my life."

My breath catches. "And now?"

"Now I know that nothing is certain." He buries his hands in my hair again, cupping the back of my head. "Everything can change in the blink of an eye, and you don't have a fucking chance of stopping it."

I lift myself up higher, studying his eyes, the curve of his lips, the faint tension in his expression. "Aiden... what is it?"

With a firm shake of his head, he rears up beneath me, claiming my mouth again, the heat in his touch snatching all of my questions from my lips.

CHAPTER TWENTY-ONE

J wake to a heavy silence.

It feels like we could be the only living beings in the whole world right now.

Aiden is like a hot water bottle next to me, keeping me dry and warm from the dampness and the cold—but not everything is comfortable right now.

Stretching against his chest, I check my lips.

Dry.

Damn. The half a vial of mercury I drank last night isn't going to last as long as I wanted to believe it would.

"Thirsty?" Aiden asks, his voice a low rumble against my ear. I guess the quick press of my fingers to my lips didn't escape him.

"Are you sure my blood won't make a difference?" he asks.

"I'm certain," I say, reaching for my discarded bodice. Unlike when ingesting water, I don't hurl up blood, but it won't sustain me for long. "Although it could be a last resort if I'm truly desperate."

Like setting off a fire to attract the dryads' attention.

It seems we might face multiple last resorts tonight.

Despite being in a completely unusual situation, we settle into our old routine of helping each other dress.

He does up the clasps at the front of my bodice. I do up the buttons on his shirt, then I check his wounded hand.

I'm pleased to find that the bite I gave him is healed, but the puncture marks on his wrist where I injected him with venom back at the Spire have remained. It's been a while since I bit someone, but the pierce points seem to be taking a long time to fade. Still, I'm relieved that he no longer has any open wounds.

"It's a fucking shame," he says, staring ruefully at his hand.

It takes me a second to realize why he's disappointed to be healed.

With a heated smile, I bare the peaks of my fangs and run the tip of my tongue across his palm.

He immediately pulls me up against him, the heat in his eyes undeniable. He gave me two more orgasms last night before we finally fell asleep, but my body still wants more. It's like I'm trying to make up for lost time.

"We should conserve our energy now," I say, my voice husky, betraying my need despite my attempt to be practical.

"I'm hungry, too," he says, drawing me close and demanding access to my mouth.

A fiery heat trickles through my body from my lips where he kisses me, right down my chest into my heart.

It's so sudden and sharp that I feel like my heartbeat stops for a moment before it resumes beating, a growing warmth making me feel more alive than before.

I drag in the heat from his mouth like it's mercury, soaking in the energy that tingles across my skin, surprised by how much more awake I feel now that he's kissing me.

What's more surprising is that he's still able to create heat since it's been hours since he lit the match that he used to dry the ground.

"Aiden?" I murmur against his mouth when he eases back. "Where is your fire coming from right now?"

He nudges my lips again, his tongue slipping across the sensitive curve in the center of my upper lip, making me sigh. His focus seems completely consumed by his exploration of my mouth and I'm not sure if he's going to answer me.

Finally, he draws back far enough to give me the briefest smile. "From you."

I laugh a little, my breathing rapid as he drops his lips back to mine, light touches like delicate promises. "I don't have any fire to give you," I say.

He stops kissing me so suddenly that I blink at him.

His forehead is fiercely creased, a muscle tensing in his jaw. "You have no fucking idea what it feels like to be around you, do you?" He takes my hand and places it over his heart. "The moment I first saw you, I knew I needed you in my life."

My lips part as pain strikes through my heart. Despite the ache, I try to keep my tone light. "Oh? What was your first thought?" It's a playful question and I'm not sure I expect him to answer it.

"You mean when those guys were hassling you?"

"Yeah," I whisper.

His response is a deep rumble. "You won't like it."

I arch my eyebrows at him. "Well, now I *really* want to know. Why wouldn't I like it?"

The heat in his eyes grows—a glow that reminds me of the deepest flame—while his arms tighten around me. "Because it wasn't very polite."

I let out a laugh. "Tell me. I can handle it."

He pulls me closer. Hard up against him. His eyes glitter at me. "I thought: I need to fuck that woman."

My breath catches. "You're right, that's not very polite."

He tips his chin, his lips pressed together, as if to say *I warned you.*

I slip my hands up his chest and lightly against his neck before I curl my fingers into his hair, nudging his lips with mine. "Then why did you wait two months to get what you wanted?"

He took his time with me, taking me out, drawing me into his world before he finally invited me into his bed.

"Because I knew a good thing when I saw it. I needed to be sure that my occupation didn't alarm you."

"Were you surprised when it didn't?"

He traces the contours of my cheeks and chin. "I should have been smart enough to realize that you accepted my lifestyle too easily." His finger rests lightly across my jaw as his expression becomes deadly serious. "I never lied to you, Iyana. Not once."

"I wish I could say the same," I whisper. "I wish I could have told you who I really was."

His arms slide down my back, a gentle pressure. "Hey, we drew a line in the sand, remember?" he says.

I give a quick nod, although I'm not certain we can bury the past so easily.

"We should get moving," I say. "We need to find that will-o'-the-wisp. Assuming it's still out there…"

Aiden exits the tent before me to check that the sunlight is gone. Once he gives me the all-clear, I pinch the side of the tent like I did to remove my suit and tug it inward. Instantly, the cloak folds in on itself, resuming its umbrella shape.

The humidity outside the tent washes in on me and I'm aware of the droplets of water already resting on Aiden's face. He must be acclimating to the dampness because he doesn't shake it off. At least, not right away.

"Let's head back to the creek," he says, brushing his forehead and flicking his fingers like an unhappy cat before he sets off toward the bank of the stream again.

I'm surprised to find the will-o'-the-wisp waiting right where we left it, illuminating the fork in the branches of the tree it ascended into. As we approach, it floats toward the ground, its luminescent blue flames flickering before it sets off along the creek's bank again.

I pick up my pace as I follow it. The reality is that I can probably only make it through another two days, at most, without some sort of sustenance. If the dryads don't have something I can eat, then staying with them will no longer be an option.

Aside from the increasingly dire food situation, I'm also ignoring the fact that we don't have a plan beyond hiding from Banta in the short term.

Finding a safe place to figure out what to do next seemed like the right call yesterday. Today, I need more certainty.

The problem is that I tried to defeat Banta once and failed. His power over my mind was too great—over Aiden's mind, too. Using pain as a shield will only protect us from Banta for so long, especially with the Metalworker on his side.

Lightly brushing Aiden's arm as we walk, I say, "We need a plan beyond hiding with the dryads. I won't last long without a supply of mercury. Hiding out indefinitely is not an option for me."

His expression is shuttered as he turns to me, the moonlight only partially brightening his face. "Staying with the dryads will be temporary, but I'm hoping they might be able to help us beyond sheltering us."

My forehead creases. "How?"

He blows out a quiet exhale. "By helping us beat Banta at his own game."

I consider Aiden carefully before I focus back on the path ahead, trying not to get my feet caught in the vines that trail across the ground. "What game, Aiden?"

Aiden seems more guarded than he was before, and it surprises me because he never told me a lie, but maybe... he kept things from me and I'm about to find out what they are.

"There's another reason why I want to find the dryads," he says. "One I didn't tell you because it involves cutting through that line in the sand that we've drawn."

I take a deep breath, mentally preparing myself. If there's anything I don't want between us now, it's more secrets. "Whatever it is, you can tell me."

He pushes aside the vines hanging from a branch in our path. "It's about the night you went after Banta. He sent me on a mission, but I didn't tell you what it was."

"Yeah," I whisper. "It was why I chose that night. You wouldn't tell me where you were going, or why. At the time, it didn't matter. I was just glad you wouldn't be there. I didn't want you caught up in the fight."

Aiden gestures to our surroundings. "I was here," he says. "Walking along this creek like we are right now—except that I didn't have a will-o'-the-wisp to guide me then."

My eyes widen. "Why would Banta send you here? Does he know about the dryads?" *And what could Banta possibly want from them?*

"You already know that Banta's primary dealings are in weapons, and he mostly deals in mass weaponry like human firearms," Aiden says. "But he's always on the lookout for a new weapon. Something he can sell for a higher price: wands, magical weaponry, armor. You name it. Sometimes he sells to private individuals, other times to corporations. He even sells to humans. The problem is that he can't completely corner the market."

I nod. "He couldn't branch into the eastern states because another demon ran the black-market weapons trade there."

"The demon, Oliver Draven, who ran Draven Industries, had an unbreakable hold on the market, and powerful allies to protect him," Aiden says. "But when it comes to rare weapons, Banta has a knack for finding them. It's the reason he was so useful to Ford Vanguard, who was always looking for rare items. Banta sent me here that night to find the rarest of weapons."

My forehead creases. "What kind of weapon would be hidden in this forest?"

"The mythical kind." Aiden tips his head at me. "The kind that can kill any supernatural, no matter how strong they are."

I jolt. "*Any* supernatural?" I'm suddenly thinking about Tessa. I'm not completely sure about Tristan, but Tessa can survive even an otherwise fatal bullet wound as long as her wolf's energy survives. It's why her biological father, Ford Vanguard, survived through the centuries. "How can you be sure this weapon even exists?"

"I can't," Aiden says. "But ever since I met him, Banta has been trying to find the dryads' home. At first, he didn't explain why. Finally, he told me that the dryads have guarded a deadly weapon since the time of the old gods. Two days before you attacked him, he told me he had new information. Apparently, Ford Vanguard had let something slip about dryads in this National Park, but it's still a hell of a lot of ground to cover looking for them."

Aiden pulls up short, staring at the trees around him. "This is about as far as I got before I turned back that night." His eyes blaze at me. "There's no phone reception out here, no way for Banta to let me know what was happening—but I felt it, Iyana. Somehow. I knew you were in trouble. I had to go back. When I got there, I was told you were dead."

My voice sticks in my throat. "I nearly was," I whisper. "It's only because of the help I received from strangers that I'm alive."

As we've been walking, the vines dripping from the trees around us have become much thicker, some patches of them forming thick curtains through which I can't see.

I suddenly look around. "Where did the will-o'-the-wisp go?"

Aiden follows my gaze from the vines hanging off the trees so far that they trail into the stream—all the way to the other side.

The bouncing blue light is nowhere to be seen.

"We need to proceed carefully," Aiden says. "I don't know why the will-o'-the-wisp would have disappeared here."

I cautiously push aside the wash of vines in front of us, peering around them before I hold them to the side to step through.

Aiden follows me and the vines swish closed behind us when I drop them. My hand is as damp after touching them as if I'd dipped it into water.

While I flick the droplets from my fingertips, Aiden scans our surroundings. The trees are much closer together and our path is becoming narrower. Beneath our feet, the ground slopes slightly upward, but it shouldn't be steep enough to drain our energy too much.

He pushes on ahead of me, picking his way through the blanket of vines covering the ground.

"When you went after Banta that night," he says, "Banta's first theory was that Ford Vanguard had sent you. He thought that Ford had deliberately given him false information about the dryads' location, knowing that Banta would send me out to this forest. It pissed Banta off that Ford perceived him to be weaker without me to guard him."

I rub my arms. "I didn't want you to be there." I hurry to continue. "Not because of how much you could hurt me, but because I didn't want to face your reaction when I took my shot at killing Banta."

Aiden gives me an unexpectedly confident smile, lightening the mood. "But it was mostly because you knew I could beat you," he says.

I snort. "Keep believing that, fire man."

My brow furrows again. I wonder if Banta knew that Ford Vanguard was Fenrir, a creature of old magic. It seemed to be a secret that Ford guarded at all costs. But if Banta knew, then maybe Banta's need to find this mythical weapon was more about ending Ford than Aiden was aware.

Carefully, I ask, "Who did Banta want to kill with the weapon?"

Aiden gives me a harsh smile. "Nobody. Or so he told me. He said he wanted to sell it to the highest bidder. But not before he figured out how to replicate it."

My eyebrows rise at the sheer audacity of it. "He wanted to make more of these weapons?" I can't stop a shiver running down my spine. "The damage that a weapon like that could do in the wrong hands... Do you know what it is?"

Aiden shakes his head. "I don't. And I didn't get any closer to the dryads to find out. Although I sense we're getting close now."

I pause and crouch to examine the thick vines sliding along the ground. They're a rich, green color, like emeralds, and they glisten with water droplets. "You said we should look out for unusual plants," I say.

Up close, these vines carry delicate amber flowers with tall, wavy petals that—oddly enough—look a lot like rising flames. There are so many of the flowers along some of the vines that they resemble delicate rivers of fire.

I gasp when the nearest vine shrinks away from my touch.

Making sure I didn't imagine the movement, I reach out again.

This time, the vine slithers away like a snake, disappearing among the vast wash of greenery covering the forest floor.

"Iyana." The warning tone in Aiden's voice grabs my attention.

His arms are held out at his sides, his gaze darting around the small clearing.

The space around us is rapidly becoming smaller as a circular wall of vines rises up from the ground, closing in around us.

The thick, ropey plants are tangled and entwined in such a way that they look like closely-knit lattice, and they rise higher than our heads, curving in around the top of us.

"Well," I whisper, as the closing vines block out the dappled moonlight, "I think we found the dryads."

CHAPTER TWENTY-TWO

*T*he vines with the fiery fronds continue closing in around us, their bodies rustling like whispers.

Aiden and I quickly reposition ourselves so that we're standing back to back, our hands raised while the vines continue to rise up off the ground, mimicking a drawstring bag that's slowly pulling closed at the top.

"Stay close," Aiden says.

For a moment, I consider if the vines are actually the dryads themselves, but I don't think so. This has to be some kind of defense mechanism. I imagine the ground for miles around their stronghold is covered in vines like these, waiting to trap trespassers.

The only question is whether or not we'll be crushed to death. I don't have my daggers—or claws like a wolf shifter—to try to cut through the thick vines, and I'm sure I'd only be met with more vines if I tried.

Aiden still has his box of matches, but the greenery will be too damp to burn easily—and lighting a fire might be the most antagonistic move we could make.

"Your box of matches!" I gasp, as the wall of vines closes in so tightly that it presses against my upraised hands. "You need to give it to them."

Aiden's back is stiff against mine. The quickening tension in his muscles is a signal he disagrees. "They're all I've got."

I reach for his hand, entwining my fingers with his. "You've got me."

He turns his head—the closest either of us can get to facing each other with our backs pressed so firmly together.

I lean into him so I can nudge my cheek to his. It's a wolf shifter's gesture of love and protection—not a gesture a vampire would normally make—but Tessa's traits have rubbed off on me, and the move feels completely natural.

Aiden relaxes, exhaling quietly before his arms shift. A moment later, he holds the box of matches up. There's no space around us to place it on the ground, so he carefully pushes it against the wall of vines in front of him.

From my position, I can barely see what's happening, but the amber fronds on the vines all around him suddenly swirl, folding around the box and taking hold of it.

With a smooth ripple, the vines carry the little box to our left, where a gap opens up, revealing a swiftly forming tunnel of vines barely wide enough or high enough for us to walk through in single file, stooped over.

The box quickly disappears along it.

The amber fronds all around us flatten in the direction of the tunnel, a ripple that reveals their white undersides so that the space around us suddenly gleams with ivory and emerald.

I eye the vines warily. "Are we supposed to follow the tunnel?"

"No fucking idea," Aiden says. "But it's the only way out."

The fronds unflatten, revealing their amber side again, before they flatten once more, pointing to the tunnel. This time, the gesture feels impatient.

"I'll take that as a *yes*," I say, carefully pressing against Aiden so I don't touch any of the greenery as I bend to make it through the small space. I tug him with me, keeping hold of his hand for as long as I can before the size of the tunnel makes it impossible to hold on.

His footfalls are quiet behind me, and I find myself checking constantly that he hasn't been separated from me, but every time I glance back, I find his eyes brighter in the dark—the fiery light in them never seeming to fade.

The tunnel goes on and on and my back begins to ache, my thigh muscles burning from walking at a crouch for so long. I finally have to pause, at which point Aiden closes his arms around me from behind and pulls me down into his lap.

We sit without speaking—his body curved around mine, the back of my head against his shoulder—while we catch our breath.

The box of matches is long gone and the tunnel stretches ahead of us with no end in sight. Despite the closed-in space, the air is fresh, the slim gaps between the vines somehow allowing a slight breeze to pass through.

It's also quiet. So quiet.

I don't want to break the silence, but there are things I need to say, and a fair chance I'm walking to my death—whether to be killed by the dryads or to die of starvation.

Tipping my head back, I say, "I never told you that I loved you."

I expect him to stiffen, maybe feel confronted—or even angry—that I'm telling him this now, after all the deception of the past, and all of the opportunities to tell him in the last day, but instead, he presses his lips to my temple. "I didn't tell you, either."

The tension leaves my body on my next exhale. "Then... I guess we need to survive this so we can tell each other how we feel one day."

I sense him grin, the change in the shape of his cheek where it presses against my forehead. The brightness in his eyes suddenly lights up the space around us. I want to ask him again how he's accessing his power right now when he doesn't control an open flame, but he already insisted it was because of me, and I'm sure it isn't. How could it be?

Taking a determined breath, I glide upward—as far upward as I can rise—and tug him with me. His hand trails across my back before he lets me go and we continue onward.

Twenty minutes later, my muscles are screaming again.

Sweat drips down my face, chest, and legs, and I'm ready to drop when the vines suddenly shift around us, spanning outward and opening up to form a clearing about five paces wide in every direction. The moonlight is dappled, a broad canopy of branches intermingling across the space above our heads.

The change in our surroundings is so sudden that I pull up sharply, but my back is too stiff to allow me to move much. I have to go slowly, stretching out my spine. Behind me, Aiden groans as he drops to his knees, wincing and straightening his upper body.

Ahead of us, the vines rustle, parting to allow multiple figures to pass through before closing behind them.

There are ten newcomers: five men and five women. They're wearing emerald-colored tops and pants that are cut in simple designs: tank tops with a V neck and long, fitted pants. Their feet are bare and their hair is long—the men wearing their hair braided back, while some of the women wear their braids piled up on their heads. Their skin ranges from the palest white to the darkest brown, and their complexions are all flawless.

The women each have high cheekbones and rose-bud lips, and the men have strong jaws and muscles that flex as they fold their arms in unison.

They don't appear armed, although their weapons are certainly all around us in the shape of the vines, trees, and even the blossoms gleaming within the leafy canopy above.

Aiden and I draw closer to each other. I'm still trying to ease the cramp in my lower back, pressing my palm to it. Aiden takes over, kneading my lower back as he steps up beside me.

Before he can say anything, four of the men speak in turns.

"Why—"

"Are—"

"You—"

"Here?"

I blink at them, my gaze darting from one to the other. The speakers are all standing on different sides of the clearing and yet their voices blend as smoothly as if they're one person.

Three of the women swiftly follow, their speech also blending in a way that makes them sound like a single entity despite their different tones.

"State—"

"Your—"

"Purpose."

I close my eyes, since trying to follow them from one to the other as they speak around the circular clearing is making me dizzy.

"We need shelter," I say, focusing on the man standing directly ahead of me.

He has long, light-brown hair braided back from his face, his skin is light brown, and his eyes are a sharp green that picks up the emerald in his clothing. He is not a small man, his enormous biceps flexing as he folds his arms across his chest.

"We need your help," I say.

Six of them, both male and female, speak a word in turn, their voices varying from melodic to deep. "We do not shelter his kind. He is too dangerous."

Their eyes all turn to Aiden, and I force myself to breathe slowly, silencing the angry retort that rises to my tongue. "Aiden has given up his matches. He has no access to fire now. He isn't a threat to you."

They all shake their heads in unison—a slow, firm movement. "*You* are his fire."

My eyebrows draw down, a glare forming, but I'm more confused than anything else. I'm a fucking vampire. If I were a fire mage, or a Solstice fae, I'd understand how my power could combine with his. But I'm nothing more than a woman with sharp fangs, venom that only sometimes works, and who has taught herself a few combat skills for the purpose of survival. Not to mention, I'm completely reliant on a rare, heavy metal as my only food source.

Before I can snarl a response, Aiden catches my arm. "They have a hive mind," he murmurs to me. "You won't change their mind unless their queen changes it for them."

"Then what do we do?" I cast a desperate glance at the wall of vines around us. Even the tunnel we came through has closed up now. "There's no way out or back."

He takes my shoulders and stares deep into my eyes—so deeply, it scares me. "Promise me, you'll stay alive."

I grip his hand, dread rising within me, but I respond to fear with anger, snapping back, "I don't plan on dying anytime soon, Aiden—do you?"

He grips me harder, the amber flare in his eyes an unwanted confirmation that—somehow—there is a flame within him that is separate to the external fire he can control.

"Aiden?"

He scares me when he runs his hand through my hair, his expression softening. "Remember when I said I wouldn't let you die again?"

My breathing becomes more rapid as my anger dissolves and the dread rises again. "You said you'd never stop protecting me."

"Yeah," he says, his gaze following the lines of my face. "Never."

He steps back from me, taking a knee before he bows his head and extends his arms at his sides. "If you won't shelter me, then I ask that you shelter this vampire. She doesn't drink blood and isn't a threat to you."

There's a pause.

Then, they say, "We will shelter her. But only her. As for you, you know the location of our home. We can't let you leave alive."

"I understand," Aiden says, without flinching. "All I ask is that you end me quickly."

Wait... what?

It happens so fast that I'm still lurching forward when one of the vines darts toward Aiden, whips around his neck, and squeezes tightly.

"No!" My fingers close around the emerald rope, pulling with all my strength. It releases him as quickly as it wrapped around him. The force of my pull causes me to fall backward, where I scramble to right myself.

"Aiden!"

He tips toward me, and I catch him, trying to wrap my arms around his broad shoulders and support his weight.

"Aiden!"

Red welts blossom across his neck—five puncture points with scratches around them. My knees are curled beneath him, partially supporting his torso as he slumps within my arms.

"What did you do?" I scream at the dryads, who remain silently watching us. "What the fuck did you do?"

Five dryads answer me. "He will not wake up." They step toward me. "You will come with us."

"Like fuck I will." I shove at their reaching hands, punching one-handed as hard as I can.

They pause in their efforts to grab me, standing far enough away that I can't hit them, but close enough that they're crowding me.

"We will not hurt you," they say.

"Like I care about myself right now," I scream at them. "Back off!"

They don't. Instead, the vines slither inward, the circular wall around me tightening so fast that I feel like I can't breathe.

I try to grip Aiden's face, his shoulders—try to make him look at me. His eyes are half-closed, his lips turning blue, and his breathing is shallow. His palm brushes my cheek, and despite the increasingly far-away expression in his eyes, he doesn't look away.

"Don't blame them," he murmurs. "They're protecting themselves. As they should."

Anger rises inside me, so much anger that I'm raging at him. "You knew they were going to hurt you, didn't you?"

It's a wild accusation, but he doesn't deny it, and it suddenly feels so true. He told me that he could lose everything in the blink of an eye and there wouldn't be a chance to stop it from happening.

My voice lowers. "Why, Aiden?"

"I knew it was possible," he rasps. "But I decided last night that I wouldn't fight it." Aiden's voice becomes softer. "I can't keep Banta out of my head. You nearly ripped my hand apart freeing me from him. There's no way out. He'll fucking take over again when he finds me. You're safe now. He can't force me to betray you, hurt you... or leave you."

I jolt. Shiver. My heart squeezes inside my chest. "So you're *choosing* to leave me."

"I would never choose to leave you," he says.

Even though I chose to leave him.

Tears are hot behind my eyes. I fight them—don't want to shed them—but it's impossible. "Aiden, don't go."

"Stay where you're safe," he whispers. "Hate the dryads if you have to, but stay with them."

His head is heavier, his body weight so immense that I'm losing hold of him. I wrap my upper leg around him, trying to keep him upright. My arm trembles across his back from the strain of holding his shoulders. Even so, I press my other fist above his heart. "There has to be another way. I won't accept this—"

"Ana," he says, his hand slipping away from my cheek. "You can't save me. You were never going to free me."

His voice trails off, his head drops to the side, and his eyes close.

His heartbeat stops.

CHAPTER TWENTY-THREE

*M*y arms are shaking, and my brain won't work. I can't think. Can't seem to function.

It all happened too fast.

It's not happening.

I should be raging at the dryads. I should fight them, tear them apart, take my revenge, but all I can do is hold Aiden close, my palm still pressed to his silent chest.

I want to believe that I'm strong, that nothing can affect me, that I'm as hard as steel... but I'm not. I'm a mess of vulnerabilities, of pieces I'm constantly trying to pull together.

I'm scared and full of regrets.

I rock slowly on the spot, my leg still hooked around him, my heart in denial. Complete denial. If I accept that he's gone, then I won't make it. I won't be able to hold it together because I refuse to believe that Aiden and I won't have another chance.

I'm vaguely aware of shifting vines to my left, a new figure running through them and bending down to me.

She's a child. Maybe only eleven years old. She's wearing the same style of emerald-green clothing as the others, but her body is decorated with vines that are so fine, they appear as threads twining around her arms, up her neck, and across her rosy cheeks. Her skin is like porcelain and luminescent in the moonlight. Her glistening, black hair falls freely down her back, and her large, gray eyes peer up at me as she crouches beside me.

"I will take him now," she says, and it's a moment before I realize that she spoke completely for herself without any of the other dryads chiming in or finishing her statement for her. "The earth will give him the care he needs."

I shrink away from her when she touches me, tightening my arms around Aiden, trying to protect him from her.

"You must trust me," she says, her gray eyes becoming wider. "This man can't live until he has died. But we must act quickly now."

She isn't making any sense. I open my mouth to tell her so, but I can't speak.

Suddenly, all I can do is cry. Ugly tears, pouring out of me as I bend my head to Aiden's chest.

The girl glances at the dryads. "She's in shock. Help me carry her."

The dryads move in unison, crowding in on me again, but I turn on them with a snarl, my fangs descending so suddenly that they cut my lower lip. "Touch him and I'll bite you."

The girl doesn't seem perturbed. Her hand darts out, the lightest brush, but it scratches my skin, leaving three distinct pinpricks of blood across the back of my hand.

I stare at her, aghast. "What did you... do...?"

My vision blurs. The moving figures of the dryads shift in and out of focus as my legs and arms go numb. I fall back against a soft surface that rises slowly beneath me, lifting me up. The vines that cover the ground and had formed the tunnel around us curl around my arms and legs, a moving bed on which I lie.

Desperately, I try to hold on to Aiden's torso, then his arm, then his hand as my fingers lose feeling and drop away from him.

No.

Please.

The last thing I see is the girl's face, her luminescent eyes large in my vision as she leans over me.

"Rest now, young one," she says.

~

I wake up with a gasp.

I'm lying on a soft surface in a small room.

The wall on the right-hand side contains the enormously wide trunk of a tree that looks as if it grew up in the side of the building—or the building was constructed around it. Two of its branches spread across the ceiling above me.

The wall on the left is made of a paper screen with simple wooden squares to give it structure.

A small, decorative alcove sits opposite me with a scroll hanging at the back, and a single blossom growing right up through the floor. The flower isn't like anything I've seen before—the petals of a large, golden sunflower sit at the base, while a budding peach-colored rose grows in its center, a combination of two blossoms.

The soft surface I'm lying on is as smooth as silk and a pure ivory color, although it's not much more than a mattress on the floor.

A figure stirs at my head, and I spin, crouching on the mattress, my hands out, prepared to defend myself.

The girl from the clearing kneels at the top of the bed as if she's praying, her head down and her eyes closed, her posture making me pause.

My sense of relief that I'm not being attacked is short-lived.

Aiden.

Pain shoots through my chest and I grab at my heart, unable to do anything about how much it hurts.

"Easy, Ana," the girl says, opening her eyes and twisting toward me.

I snarl back at her. "That's not my name."

Her eyebrows rise. "It's what Aiden called you."

"Where is he?" My fangs descend a little, my protective instincts in full swing. "What the hell have you done with him?"

"There is no hell here, Ana," she replies. "Only regrowth and new beginnings."

I don't know what the fuck she's talking about. I repeat, "Where is Aiden?"

The girl tips her head slightly to the side, her black hair falling across her shoulders while her forehead creases. She purses her lips. "Aiden is not with us anymore."

I close my eyes, groaning as I rock forward. "I know he's dead. Where did you take him? I need to see him—"

"No," she says, her fingertips brushing my arm.

I jolt away from her, remembering the way she knocked me out the last time she touched me.

She quickly removes her hand but raises it, palm up, in a calming gesture. "You don't understand," she says. "Aiden is gone, but your friend is alive."

I rub at my eyes, stopping when they sting. My skin is so puffy, my eyes so sore, my lips so fucking dry.

"You were crying in your sleep," she says. "You're dehydrated. I can help you with the pain."

"I don't need your help," I say. "You've *helped* enough."

Ignoring my declaration, she says, "I've brought you some new clothes. You might be more comfortable in them." She pats a neat pile of emerald-green material folded at her side.

I'm aware that my jacket lies folded beside the bed alongside my boots, although I'm still wearing the uncomfortable bodice and my leggings. My clothing is sweaty, dirty, and bloodied. My hair will be a mess and my cheeks—when I press my fingers to them—are swollen from crying.

"I don't want new clothes," I snap, but my voice breaks as I continue. "I need to see Aiden."

Despite my anger, she remains calm, and I'm not sure what it would take to unsettle her. "Then you should come with me." She glides to her feet and waits for me to follow her. "My name is Clara," she says. "If your name is not Ana, what is it?"

"Iyana," I say.

My footsteps are stiff, and my arms and legs ache, when I force myself to stand. Aiden wanted me to stay here, where he thought I'd be safe, but he didn't know I have other places that are far safer than here. I chose not to tell him about Hidden House and now...

Fuck. The regrets keep piling up on me, a weight that's going to crack open my heart.

I tell myself I need to see Aiden, say goodbye, and then I'll leave. There's safety and mercury at Hidden House. I can ask Helen for help. She can get word to Tessa and her pack, I can explain the whole situation to them, and all of those strong women will stand by my side. They'll help me figure out a way to beat Banta Sol.

Somehow, I will find a way to rip that demon's heart out.

By doing so, I can free Aiden's brother, too. Aiden didn't make me promise to help Lucas, but killing Banta and freeing Lucas go hand in hand.

As for the dryads, my feelings are a storm of anger and resolve. I understand their need to protect their community from a pyromancer. It was because of my fear that Aiden could set the entire Spire alight that I tried to drive him away when he first appeared to me.

But I didn't try to kill him. I don't know how I can trust a community that will judge a person so completely that they take their life because of *what* they are, not *who* they are.

Clara slides open the paper door, but I pull up sharply when bright morning sunlight floods the space outside the door. I vaguely make out the shape of a porch before I'm forced to step back.

My hand flies to my waist—reaching for my protective suit—only to find it gone. It's not sitting with my jacket and boots, either.

I glare at Clara where she pauses a pace inside the door. "What have you done with my cloak?"

She tips her head to the side, as if my missing umbrella shouldn't matter to me. "You don't need that here."

"I can't walk in sunlight," I snap, squinting to try to see through the glare to what lies beyond it.

Clara appears unperturbed. "Then you'll need to walk in faith." She steps into the light, her voice calling back to me. "Either you want to see your friend or you don't."

"Wait!" I call out, but she doesn't reappear, leaving me inside the room on my own.

Anyone else might be able to see past the brightness of the porch, but my eyes don't do well in sunlight. Cupping my hand over my face and separating my fingers slightly, I hope to be able to make out my surroundings.

It's no use.

I prowl back and forth in the middle of the room before my gaze lands on the mattress on the floor behind me.

It will have to fucking do.

Stripping the sheets off the mattress and pulling it up off the floor, I heave it over my head. It's thin enough that each side drops down beside me, but thick enough to form a barrier that will protect my head and sides—even if my front and back will be in danger of exposure, depending on the angle of the sun.

I'll have to walk carefully, but I can always drop to the ground and crawl beneath the mattress if I have to.

I don't care if I look ridiculous.

Fuck my pride.

Checking that my grip on the underside of the mattress is secure, I take a deep breath and step into the light.

CHAPTER TWENTY-FOUR

*I*mmediately, the sunlight fades and I find myself immersed in shadows.

I stop right where I am, hesitant to peek around the edges of the mattress to find out why the light changed so suddenly.

At least I can now finally see beyond the porch to the area beyond.

The dryads' home is breathtakingly beautiful. Wooden homes sit among enormous trees, which grow at regular intervals around the area.

The branches of each tree spread across the sky, reaching out and intertwining with the next tree's branches to form a thick shield above us. Gardens filled with exotic plants surround the homes and trees, and dryad children play among the plants.

A nearby group of children chases each other around the clearing, but when they run across the lush grass, the shadowed branches above follow their movements, stopping the sunlight from reaching them.

A furtive, upward glance tells me that the tree branches have formed a thick canopy over my head, too, casting me into such complete shadow that I don't feel the heat of the sun.

I sense a presence nearby and I swing to find Clara standing so close to me that I nearly hit her with the side of the mattress. Unlike the children, she stands in full sunlight.

"When humans learned how to fly in metal contraptions, the

dryads had to protect themselves from being spotted from the sky," Clara says with a heavy sigh. "They're connected with the trees, and the trees now form a moving canopy that protects everyone from being seen from above."

"But not you," I point out.

A fleeting smile plays on her lips. "The sunlight hides me," she says. "I'm more visible in the dark."

I'm not sure what to make of that, but I turn my attention back to the children and the strange phenomenon of the trees. I don't know much about plant growth, but I do know that most plants need sunlight. "How do the dryads thrive?" I ask.

"It's difficult for their children to grow up in the shadows," she concedes. "But they found a way. See?" Clara gestures to three patches of sunlight that stream onto wide stones in the clearing ahead. "Those stones are the only places where the sunlight consistently hits the ground. The children can take turns standing in the light for a few minutes each day, but only if they know it's safe. It took many years for the dryads to reach the right balance between protecting themselves and allowing the light through. Every risk must be balanced."

I narrow my eyes at her in thought. "You keep saying 'they' as if you're not one of them. But you must be their queen if they listen to you."

Her lips part and her eyes shoot wide before she relaxes and lets out a soft laugh. "They don't have a queen. They make decisions collectively. Every dryad has a voice, no matter their age. And they all listen to each other."

My brow furrows. "If you're not their queen, who are you?"

She exhales a quiet sigh. "I'm here to light their way when they need me. And in return, they gift me with armor of their making." She lifts her hand to show me the thread-like vines decorating her skin. The way she turns her arm in the sunlight that streams through the parted branches above makes the threads gleam. "We look after each other," she says. "The dryads and I."

Slowly, I slip the mattress off my head, taking wary glances at the canopy overhead. It feels like a huge risk to expose myself like this, especially around dryads who didn't hesitate to protect themselves from strangers, but I take a step forward, testing the magic of the branches. I'm grateful when they follow me with each step I take.

Clara told me to walk in faith, but I didn't imagine she meant it quite like this.

She seems pleased when I take another step forward.

As I pause at the edge of the short staircase to the ground, she says, "Your friend is this way."

Clara glides ahead of me, navigating her way through the beautiful space around me. I soon come to recognize that the grass is different where she walks—a path of deeper green. Although the trees shade me, their branches part to allow the sunlight to follow Clara, and I try not to step too closely to her in case I enter the sun's rays.

She stops every now and then to speak with a dryad, but her speech is hushed. Much farther along the path, she bends to a girl sitting on her own at the base of a tree. The girl is focused on a tiny blossom shooting from the earth, each of its petals a different color, as if she's experimenting with her power.

"I like this one," Clara says, brushing her fingertip across a gleaming petal the color of gingerbread. The girl smiles as we walk away, but the slight press of her lips when she looks at me confirms she's wary of me.

She should be. I'm thirsty, hungry, and a mess of grief and anger.

The path grows darker the farther we walk until the canopy above us is nearly completely knitted together. It casts deep shadows around us, and I find myself breathing more easily now that I don't have to trust the trees to shadow me.

I'm surprised to discover that the darker our surroundings grow, the brighter Clara becomes. Her skin glistens, her black hair gleams, and her silhouette begins to sparkle.

Seeing her light up the darkness, I now understand why she walks in sunlight. From above, she must glimmer like a reflection on water, but in shadow, she would be a beacon betraying the dryads' location.

"What are you?" I ask, since she revealed she's not a dryad, but I'm sure I've never encountered a creature like her before.

"I'm a will-o'-the-wisp," she says, making me pull up short.

"Was it you?" I ask. "The light guiding us here?"

She gives me a small smile. Then, with a graceful gesture, she forms a fist and uncurls it.

A glowing orb of light forms above her palm and floats away from her, dancing gently around the edges of the clearing we've now entered.

The ground here is covered in moss, while white toadstools grow at intervals along the path, their surfaces bright in the darkness.

"How old are you?" I ask, suddenly wondering if Clara's child-like appearance is a deception. After all, she called me 'young one.'

"I've lived with the dryads for hundreds of years," she says.

At my raised eyebrows, she explains. "Will-o'-the-wisps age backward. We begin as light, but once we find places we wish to call our homes, we form corporeal bodies that are 'old' by most standards. The longer we live, the younger we appear. One day, I will return to my light form again."

She takes a deep breath and gestures at a wall of vines ahead of us.

"When that day comes, this is where I will come to rest."

The wash of vines is decorated with tiny flowers that form a rainbow of colors. Each one shimmers in the light radiating from Clara's body, making it appear as if sparkles are falling down the vines.

She pulls aside the plants and I step into another circular clearing, this one larger than the area we left behind.

An enormous tree rests on the other side of this new space, its branches spreading above us and its leaves lush and thick. Vines fall from the outer branches to form thick, unbroken walls around the edges of the entire area so that the tree is forming the cave we now stand in.

It's so closed in that it would be completely dark except for the pool of water in its center, which glows as if it's filled with luminescent silver.

I gasp to see that Aiden lies within the pool, floating on his back. Unlike the rest of the pool, his body is like a dark chasm—his silhouette barely recognizable—as if the light reaches everywhere but him.

I hurry to the edge of the water, but Clara grabs my arm before I can step into the pool.

"No," she says. "You must not touch these waters."

I recoil from her touch, but I don't try to go any farther. "Why not?"

"These are the life waters," she says. "They will kill the living."

"*Life* waters? If they kill people, they should be renamed."

She shrugs before she gestures to the pool, but she does it slowly, releasing another orb of light from her palm. It floats across the pond and hovers over Aiden's face, revealing his closed eyes and peaceful expression.

Too peaceful.

He looks… blank. Empty. Like a shell.

"Aiden hates water," I whisper, before I drop my head into my hands. "You need to get him out of there."

"He's right where he should be," Clara replies.

I spin to her. "What are you talking about?"

She purses her lips, the light radiating from her skin making her appear ethereal in the darkness. "What do you know of supernaturals who are magically repressed?"

My brow furrows deeply because I'm not sure how this answers my question. "Not much," I admit. "Their power is unknown because it hasn't manifested, and until they control their power, they're dangerous."

The corner of Clara's mouth rises into a smile that makes me shiver. "No, Iyana. In fact, a once-repressed supernatural is *more* dangerous once they're in control of their power. Then, they are creatures to be feared."

A shiver rages down my spine so suddenly that I wobble. Aiden's brother is magically repressed, but if he will be more dangerous once he can control his power, then he could be a powerful ally in my fight against Banta—or a dangerous foe if Banta controls him.

Clara waves her hand, creating another globe of light that dances across the air. It's so bright that it leaves streaks in my vision before it hovers above Aiden's chest.

"Magical repression is a sign that ordinary genetics have been displaced," Clara says. "An unexpected power is going to manifest that has nothing to do with the person's parentage or heritage. They may even be a supernatural that the world hasn't seen since the time of the old gods."

The furrow in my brow deepens as my confusion increases. "That's all nice to know, but I'm not sure what it has to do with Aiden lying in a pool of water."

Clara remains unruffled. She exhales heavily as she stares at the tree opposite the pool.

"Did you know that Aiden is magically repressed?" she asks.

I'm startled. "That's not possible. He's a pyromancer. He controls

fire. Very effectively, actually. He knows what he is. *I* know what he...
was." My voice chokes because speaking about Aiden in the past tense
is too hard.

Standing in this place watching him float in water is too hard.

And it's sure as fuck too hard not to wade in and pull him out.

I shake my head because I've had enough. "I don't care if you think
he was magically repressed—"

"Not *was*," she says. "He *is* magically repressed."

I stare at her, my breathing suddenly erratic. "What are you
saying?"

"I'm saying that Aiden's death is not what you think." She peers
back at me. "It's my nature to shine light into dark places. I sensed a
cage around Aiden's power as soon as you began following my light
alongside the stream. The fact that he can lie peacefully in the waters
of life proves that his power has not fully emerged."

I struggle to accept that what she's saying is true. "Then what
about the fire he was controlling?"

"Somehow, he must have found a way to tap into a surface aspect
of his power, but he hasn't fully manifested it yet."

My hands are trembling despite my efforts to calm myself. All of
this time, I thought I knew who Aiden is.

I was the one who lied about my life, not him.

"Would he have known?" I ask, not sure if she will be able to
tell me.

Clara gives a quick shake of her head. "It's unlikely."

My throat is so dry now—not helped by my rapid breathing—but
I'm suppressing my need to drink, although these surprise revelations
aren't helping my nerves. "How does this water help him?"

The corners of Clara's mouth turn down as tension fills her face.
"Some supernaturals believe that putting a magically repressed
person through trauma will reveal their power. It's a barbaric practice
that breaks the supernatural and deconstructs their sense of self."

Her tension eases as she gestures to the pool again. Little orbs of
light dance away from her palm, lighting up the air around us. "But
these waters... the life waters... will gently draw out his true nature.
They will show us who Aiden really is."

Clara turns back to me with a confident smile on her face. "The
Aiden you knew has died," she says. "Now we will wait and see who—
or *what*—rises in his place."

CHAPTER TWENTY-FIVE

$\mathcal{M}$y heart is in my throat.

Clara's telling me that Aiden is alive, despite his silent heart, but she's also telling me that he is something else. *Someone* else.

That is, assuming I can take her word at face value.

"How long will we have to wait?" I ask.

"It's a lengthy process," she says. "To open the shell that houses a seed can take years. But without breaking the protective outer layer, the seed inside can never grow."

"*Years?*" I clasp my trembling hands in front of myself. "I don't have that long. I'm being tracked by a demon who wants me dead. If he finds me here..."

"The dryads will take care of him," Clara says. "Demons control others through persuasion, yes? The hive mind of the dryads is impossible to control."

I swing to her. "Are you sure about that?" It's my turn to peer at her, my eyes narrowing. "Or are you confident about your safety here because you're harboring a weapon you know can kill any supernatural?"

Aiden told me it was Banta's goal to find this weapon and use it to his benefit. Aiden, himself, was hoping to use it against Banta.

Clara's response is a gentle 'hmm.' She stoops to pick a flower from a stem growing at her feet.

"It's true that the dryads are guarding a weapon," she says. "But it's impossible to retrieve."

"Why?" I ask. "Where is it?"

"It's here," Clara says. "See?"

An orb of light floats from her outstretched palm, bobbing through the air as it ascends to the tallest branch above us. A vine twines around the branch that the orb lights up. The orb follows the vine's path to another branch from which the vine finally descends.

Hanging at the end of the vine is a dagger, the greenery securely wrapped around its handle, holding it, dangling, at the highest point of the cavern.

The dagger's tip points directly downward at the spot where Aiden lies in the pool. It looks as if the dagger would pierce his heart if it fell.

High above us, Clara's orb of light slowly rotates around the weapon, revealing that it's a simple design. Its handle appears metallic, as is its blade, and it looks like any dagger I might carry. It's nothing out of the ordinary.

"That's the weapon?" I'm slightly disappointed. "It's just a simple dagger."

Clara is quiet beside me. "Sometimes the simplest weapon is the most effective."

She gently blows on the flower she's holding between her fingertips and lets go of it at the same time.

The flower floats through the air before it drops to the surface of the glistening pool.

I gasp when the flower disintegrates, curling up and blackening, as if the pool were acid.

"What looks like water isn't simply water," Clara says.

I take a hasty step away from the edge of the pool, suddenly taking note of what Clara said before: The fact that Aiden can lie peacefully in these waters proves that his power has not fully emerged. I'm suddenly worried about what will happen when he does wake up.

"If that dagger isn't a simple dagger, then what is it?" I ask.

She tips her head to the side and answers my question with one of her own. "What do you know of the old gods?"

"Again, not much," I say. "I know of the time of the titans, the jotunn, and the emergence of the new gods, but I don't know anything in detail."

Clara nods, as if this doesn't surprise her. "As you would expect, many of the gods—old and new—played games to gain power. Over time, their alliances shifted back and forth, but there was one old god who was genuinely impartial. He cared only about his craft."

She points at the dagger. "He was Vulcan. God of the Forge. It was said that a weapon crafted by him would win any war. Destroy any supernatural. But getting him to make a weapon for you? Now *that* was the challenge. He made weapons like creating art. They were not to be bloodied with war. Then, he was betrayed."

"What happened?"

"His eldest son stole the weapons Vulcan had made and sold each of them for the highest price. Vulcan was angry at his son's betrayal, but the real tragedy happened when one of the stolen weapons was used to kill the titaness, Theia. She was the Goddess of Silver and Gold. It's rumored that Vulcan was secretly in love with her, and her death destroyed him. He was so overtaken by grief and rage that he ripped out his traitorous son's heart and fashioned that dagger from it."

I stare at her. "I'm sorry… He did *what?*"

She shrugs. "It's unclear whether the story is literal or metaphorical. Either way, the dagger is said to be made from the heart of Vulcan's son."

I shudder. "What happened to all of the other weapons?"

"Vulcan spent the rest of his days finding them and melting them down. But he couldn't bring himself to destroy the dagger, which he gave to the dryads to keep hidden from those who would abuse it."

I stare up at the branches overhead, following them back to the tree's trunk and down to the ground, noting the way that the water sits only inches away from the base of the tree.

If what Clara says is true, then what looks like a dagger might not be a dagger. She said it is impossible to retrieve. For all I know, it could kill me to touch it.

"You have choices now, Iyana," Clara says. "You can try to take the weapon and use it to kill your enemies. Or you can stay here, be patient, and wait for Aiden to wake up."

And then take the dagger.

"I'll starve if I stay," I say. "You don't want me here if I'm hungry."

"I may have a solution for that," she says.

I can only imagine what she's going to say. "I don't drink blood," I respond quickly, screwing up my face. "If you're thinking of giving me animal's blood—don't."

"I wasn't." She gives me a patient look. "I know you don't sustain yourself on the blood of others. Come with me, please."

I pause before I follow her. *How did she know I don't drink blood?*

Snagging her arm, I ask, "How do you know so much about Aiden and me?"

She pauses. "As I said, I shine a light into dark places."

I narrow my eyes at her. "You're implying that my body is a dark place."

"It is," she says, returning my sharp gaze without flinching. "But your mind is darker. Too dark for me to see inside."

My grip on her arm tightens. The memory of Banta trying to control my mind comes back to me. "Stay away from my mind."

Her lips part slightly and her voice lowers to a whisper. "It's in my nature to be drawn to dark places, Iyana. Just as it's in *your* nature to crave the hottest flame. We both fight our obsessions."

She draws back sharply enough to dislodge my hold, but she composes herself, her features peaceful again. "You need to drink. Come with me now."

Clara leads me from the cavern, but instead of heading back to the main stronghold, she turns left and takes me around the outside of the wall of vines.

It's brighter out here than it was inside the cavern, although the branches overhead are so thick that they continue to shelter me from the sun.

We stop at what I'm sure is the other side of the tree that sits inside the cavern. While we were inside, the enormous tree looked like a glistening giant.

On this side, it appears bent over and twisted. Squinting upward, I try to make out the way its branches spread to one side, forming the protective canopy over the cavern, but it's difficult to see because of the ever-shifting leaf-cover above me.

Clara runs her hand along the tree's rough bark until she stops and twists her fingers around one of the vines twining down the tree's trunk. She gestures for me to approach. "You may drink from these vines," she says.

"I'm sorry?"

"All of these vines absorb the elements from the earth, including the heavy metals you crave," she says.

I find it difficult to believe her, given that she just got finished telling me that things aren't what they appear—water isn't water, and all that.

At my hesitation, Clara says, "Walk in faith, Iyana. Drink in faith. Or not. It's your choice."

I consider what I have to lose. Worst case—my life, if whatever sap the vines contain is poisonous to me. Best case—I won't starve. It's a big risk, but slow starvation will lead to death, too. And it means I can stay here. There's no way I'm leaving Aiden here now that I know he's alive.

Whatever time I have to spend waiting for him to wake up, I won't waste it. I'll figure out my next move, figure out how to retrieve Vulcan's final weapon from its place above the acidic water, and how to beat Banta without endangering Tessa or her pack.

Closing my eyes, I sink my teeth into the soft vine, piercing its surface.

Lukewarm liquid fills my mouth, a lot more fluid-like than I was expecting. It tastes like a combination of candy and apples, but beneath the sweetness is a metallic flavor like copper. I swallow before I think about it, and the sap slips down my throat, warming me as it goes.

It's like swallowing an ember. Heat spikes across my chest, dominating my senses as it spreads through my arms all the way to my fingertips, then down my legs to my toes. I may as well have slipped into a warm bath, and I sigh against the vine as the dryness in my lips eases.

After drinking until I've had enough, I finally pull away to see that the liquid seeping from the broken vine is a silver color like the mercury I usually drink.

"How is this possible?" I ask.

Clara gives me a smile. "The forest provides," she says. "Now, will you come with me, and we can get you properly cleaned up?"

I nod, feeling much stronger now that I've eaten, but I pause before I leave the tree. "I'll need to drink from this every day. Is that okay?"

"That's fine," she says. "You can check on Aiden at the same time. I'm sure you'll want to see him each day."

As we return to the main stronghold, I take note of the winding path and the landmarks along the way: the changing plants, the trees whose trunks are different colors. Now that I'm not so stressed, I notice the subtle differences between the plants and the trees, some with unusually shaped or colored leaves.

One of the trees has a trunk that is the same bronze as the tips of Danika's feathers. Another has violet leaves that remind me of Maeve's power.

I'm sure that my mind is making connections because I need to stay linked to my pack. The bond between Tessa and me is rising to the front of my mind. It's new, but it's strong, and it tugs at me so suddenly that I stumble.

Ahead of me on the path, Clara turns back. "Are you okay, Iyana?"

I right myself quickly. "I'm fine."

At my reassurance, she continues onward, leading me back past the playing dryad children toward the cabin where I woke up.

"I will leave you here for now," Clara says, squeezing my arm briefly. "Get yourself cleaned up and when you're ready, come out and explore your new home. I'm sure the dryads would like to meet you properly."

The tug within my heart remains as I step inside the simple hut and pull the paper door closed.

I don't try to shake off the connection with my pack, needing the reminder of the people who care about me—people I consider my family—and the knowledge that they must be trying to locate me.

Luna and Lydia will be using their cards to try to pinpoint my location. Tessa is likely to have sought Helen's help, too. Aiden said that the dryads' home is heavily guarded, and I saw the proof of that when we arrived here—but he never encountered the strength of Luna, Lydia, or Helen, who are all skilled at locating someone.

Once again, I'm in turmoil about whether or not my friends will be in more danger if they come looking for me, but I push my uncertainty aside. I won't choose to take the danger to them, but if they find me, we'll forge a way through it.

Scooping up the emerald-green clothing, I discover that my suspicions were correct—the top and pants are exactly the same style as the clothes the dryads wear.

I'm a little confused about where I'm supposed to wash up until I study the walls around me more closely and discover that the panels in the wall opposite the tree form an opening into a small bathing room.

It contains a sink, a wooden seat-like contraption that reveals itself to be a toilet, and a shelf piled high with towels. A cup rests on the counter beside the sink and I'm fascinated by the toothbrush fashioned from wood and soft bristles that must be from the fine stems of some sort of plant. Other basic grooming equipment sits beside the cup—a wooden comb for my hair and a cake of soap that's a pale lime color.

I discover that there isn't a heating system when the water at the sink comes out cold, and I sorely miss Aiden's warmth. But I make use of the towels to minimize the freezing impact of the water by dampening a smaller towel and wiping it over my body to get clean.

Once washed, I dress and find that the underwear and clothing Clara gave me is surprisingly soft and comfortable to wear, made out of a fabric that is as smooth as silk, but as breathable as cotton. Even the bra is structured in a way that supports me without making me feel like I'm being clamped into a vise.

Damn, I could get used to this underwear.

What I don't have is a mirror, but I do my best to make myself presentable by feel alone. While I'm brushing my hair, trying to get the knots out of the long, black strands, I suddenly remember the card Luna gave me. I had tucked it into my leggings pocket back at the Spire.

Quickly retrieving it, I consider the image on it, which depicts a heart speared with a dagger. Back at the Spire, I interpreted the card as the heart that is unable to heal, a representation of my regret about my past, but now...

It's unsettlingly symbolic of the story Clara told me about the dagger that Vulcan crafted out of his son's heart.

Luna and Lydia struggle with time. They don't see the present, past, and future the same way I do. For all I know, when Luna gave me this card, she might have been looking ahead to the moment when I stood beside the life waters today, gazing up at the elusive dagger hanging high above me.

I try to remember the way Luna looked at me when she gave me the card. Her sage-green eyes were wide, her cheeks flushed so brightly peach that she'd practically glowed in the darkness around us at the time.

The memory of the anxiety in her expression suddenly hits me.

A shiver runs through me at the possibility that Luna was trying, not to comfort me, but to warn me about what I'm going to face.

CHAPTER TWENTY-SIX

I tuck the card into the pocket of my new pants before heading outside again, resolving to always keep the card with me.

As soon as I push aside the paper door at the side of the room, I'm greeted by two dryad women. One of them holds a pile of towels while the other carries a platter of multi-colored soaps.

The woman with the towels has flawless brown skin and long, mahogany-brown hair braided and piled on top of her head. I recognize her from the group that surrounded Aiden and me.

The other woman is new to me. She has white skin and shorter hair the color of sunflowers, the strands escaping from the short braids sitting across her shoulders.

They speak back and forth, each uttering a single word in turn. "We've come to help you bathe."

I blink at them, hoping they don't mean that they're here to *personally* bathe me. Now *that*, I don't need. I wave my hand awkwardly in the direction of the little bathroom. "Oh, I've already washed up."

They stare at me for a long moment before they speak in turns. "But that water is freezing."

I shift my weight from one foot to the other. "Yeah, well, I've had worse."

Both women cover their mouths with their free hands, hiding smiles. "Oh, dear," they say. "You really are as tough as you look."

The one with the golden hair deftly juggles her plate of soaps while she reaches out to tug on my arm. "There's a better place to bathe," she says, still speaking in turns with the other woman. "Come with us. We will show you."

"Oh-kay." I hold my breath as I step out onto the porch. The women were already standing in shadow, so it's not so daunting as stepping into full sunlight like before, but I have to remind myself to trust the overhead canopy to protect me from the sun.

A deeper shadow immediately falls around us and I let out my breath.

The women lead me down the steps, but we turn to the left this time, heading along a narrow path that skirts around the gardens where the children are still playing.

Within moments, the women draw me past the main compound and into a quieter part of the forest. It's hard to keep my bearings, but if the cavern where Aiden lies is north, then we're now walking west.

My feet are bare—I didn't think to grab my boots—but the forest floor is soft and welcoming against my skin. Similar to the path to the cavern, the light overhead fades and the canopy becomes denser the farther we walk until, once again, I'm traveling in near-darkness.

Finally, the women draw me toward a section where there are distinctly separate portions of vines hanging from multiple trees. It's difficult to see beyond or above them, but I make out strangely cup-shaped leaves along the branches above us.

Pulling aside the greenery in one section, the women say, "Come inside."

This cavern is much smaller than the one in which Aiden lies. With three of us standing inside, we take up half the space. The ground is covered in luminescent toadstools while, once again, a tree stands on the opposite side, providing the ceiling and the infrastructure from which the vines fall to enclose the space.

As soon as we step inside, the vines light up, glowing softly fluorescent along their lengths. Because the women are still holding the vines apart for me to proceed, I can see that the vines have lit up outside the cavern, too.

"You will know when someone is already in one of the shower cubicles because of the vines," the women say.

They place the towels and soaps on top of a patch of bigger toadstools on the far right that provide a quaint sort of table. Then they gesture to a circular row of blue toadstools on the ground.

"Once you step past that line, the water will flow. But be sure to undress first." They smile again as they back out of the space. "Otherwise, your clothing will be soaked."

"Wait," I say before they can leave. "What are your names?"

Their foreheads crease. "We are dryads. We don't need names."

"Right. Okay." I guess that means I'll have to call them *golden-hair* and *mahogany-hair* from now on. It feels like labeling them somehow, but until a better option presents itself, it's the best I've got.

After letting them go, I take their warning about undressing seriously and make sure to remove all of my clothing before stepping beyond the blue toadstools.

A rain shower falls around me, the droplets warm on my skin, gentle enough to feel calming, while firm enough to allow me to clean myself—properly, this time, since I'm not relying solely on a cloth.

I'm not sure exactly how the water system works, but I imagine it has something to do with the cup-shaped leaves I saw from outside the cubicle. Perhaps the leaves gather rain water, warm it, and then tip and allow it to fall down. I make a mental note to ask the dryad women when I finish showering.

I allow myself to enjoy the calming sensation of the water for a few moments before I tell myself I don't know how long the shower will last, and I quickly scoop up a cake of soap and lather and scrub myself until I'm clean.

The wet strands of my hair fall around my shoulders as I step out of the shower area and dry myself thoroughly, taking deep breaths, grateful to finally feel as if I'm starting fresh.

A lot has happened today, and I'm still processing what it all means. We found the dryads, which means I'm safe from Banta for now, but I don't have the weapon yet, and Aiden…

Aiden's future is more uncertain than it ever was.

I don't know what will happen when he wakes up. I don't know who he'll be, or whether or not he'll remember me.

I scrunch the towel in my hands, needing to close my fists and feel like I can control this small part of my world—even if it's only the act of crumpling a piece of material.

Even when Tessa pushed me away, I had a plan. A simple one—

find her, convince her that she wasn't alone, then fight any battle she needed to fight. Beside her.

Too much is out of my control right now. I can't control Aiden's transformation. I can't control Banta's plans for me—whatever they are. I can't predict what moves Tessa might make to find me.

But I remind myself that I *can* control the small things. I can control each breath I take. I can control how I respond to this new environment and to the dryads. And… even though I feel like my feelings are in turmoil… I can recognize what Aiden means to me.

Everything.

He means more to me than I thought I'd ever be lucky enough to find.

He told me that he would never stop protecting me, but now it's my turn to protect him.

CHAPTER TWENTY-SEVEN

On my way out of the shower area, I pick up the towels and the tray of soaps, piling them in my arms.

The women are gone, but I'm okay with that.

The vines at the sides of the clearing outside the shower cavern ripple in a way that points me in the right direction. Even without them, I've memorized the path and I follow it confidently now, taking note of other paths diverging left and right.

Halfway back to the center of the territory, I'm surprised to come across a dryad girl, sitting on her own at the base of one of the trees.

I stop when I realize that it's the same girl Clara and I passed earlier on our way to the life waters. Clara had stopped and complimented her on the multi-colored blossom she was creating.

I take a closer look at the girl this time, noting her dark, straight hair that gleams with ruby red highlights in the muted light. It reminds me of Tessa's hair and once again, I find myself drawing similarities with my life outside the dryads' home.

This girl's skin is light brown, and her eyes are deep gray—a similar shade to Clara's, but darker—and I judge her to be a little younger than Clara in appearance, maybe only ten years old.

The girl's expression now is anything but tranquil. She stares fiercely at a flower sprouting from the ground in front of her. Its petals are different shades of purple, which again, reminds me of Maeve's power.

The vehement unhappiness on the girl's face is a surprise, given that the dryads I've met so far don't seem to betray anything other than serenity. Even when they were threatening Aiden, they appeared to have complete control of their emotions.

I crouch beside the girl, placing the towels and soaps on the ground, not sure why she's unhappy with her creation since it looks perfect to me.

"It's beautiful," I say.

Her focus intensifies, the light playing in her gray eyes. "It's only beautiful on the surface."

As with the first time Clara spoke with me, it takes me a moment to realize that the girl spoke solely for herself.

Casting a glance around to verify that she's alone, I catch glimpses of the other children playing between the trees much farther along the path.

Carefully, I sink all of the way to the ground.

"What makes you think its beauty is only surface deep?" I ask.

"Because I don't control its heart," she says, looking up at me.

Her eyelashes are incredibly long; her big, gray eyes somehow dominating my entire field of view while she sits very still.

"Control isn't beauty," I say, quietly. "Being wild is beautiful, too."

"That would be true if this flower were wild," she says. "But it isn't. Its heart is in a cage."

A shiver runs through me. The girl's speech reminds me so much of Tessa, who fought tooth and claw to free herself from the cages that others tried to place around her.

I tip my head, trying to guess what the girl is trying to tell me about cages, hearts, and how they relate to flowers, of all things. "What do you mean by—?"

Quick footsteps interrupt me. Clara hurries along the path toward us. "Iyana! There you are." Her smile is bright as she reaches us. "You found the shower?"

I rise to my feet. "Yes, thank you. It was very pleasant."

"I'm glad to hear it." Clara beams at me before she leans down to the girl. "Drina, darling, you've worked hard today. It's time to rest."

Drina? Not only does the girl speak for herself, but she has a name.

When I look down at her, I find Drina's scowl has been wiped away, her expression as tranquil as it was earlier today.

She smiles up at Clara before rising to her feet, wiping her palms down her emerald-green pants, and heading in the direction of the main compound. She veers off the path a few steps along, and I don't see where she goes next.

I watch her disappear with a puzzled smile. "Her name is Drina? The other dryads told me they don't need names."

Clara turns away to lead me along the path. She gives a breezy wave. "I had to give them names or I'd be saying, 'Hey, you,' all of the time."

"That makes sense." I decide to ask her about the two women who showed me where the showers are. "There were two women earlier— one with golden hair, the other with reddish-brown hair. Do you have names for them?"

"Assuming I'm thinking of the same women, I call them 'Sunflower' and 'Mahogany,'" she replies.

My eyebrows rise. "Plant names that match their hair?"

She shrugs. "It fits."

I guess it does. I dismiss my remaining questions and take in the quiet hum of the dryads' back-and-forth voices and the sounds of the children playing as I make my way back to my cabin.

It's so incredibly peaceful here. If I had a home like this, I would kill to protect it, too.

"Rest assured that you're safe now," Clara says, pausing on the porch. "You're free to explore as much as you like, but I would urge you to find a routine. Otherwise, the days can become a blur in a quiet place like this."

I give her a nod. "Thank you, again."

She leaves me and I consider how erratic my routine has been lately. Still, if I'm going to be here for an indefinite period of time, I want to assimilate as best I can into the dryads' way of life.

After checking on Aiden again, I spend the rest of the afternoon observing the dryads, making mental notes about what appear to be customs—most of which revolve around the children.

The young ones play for an hour, then rest, then take turns standing on the Sunlight Stones with an adult, then they play again.

A group of nearby adults tends to the gardens around the cabins while watching over the children from the sidelines—only intervening when it looks like one of the younger ones might stray onto the Sunlight Stones when they shouldn't.

When I explore the eastern side of the dryads' territory, I find sections that are dedicated to different crafts. In one section, some of the adults are busy fashioning wooden items—from small things like bowls, to larger planks of wood for a new home that's being constructed nearby—while another section is dedicated to dryads who are spinning and weaving plants into clothing.

Yet another section of the compound is set aside for the cultivation of medicinal plants. I only know this for sure because I find Sunflower there and she welcomes me to sit with her while the dryads explain that the plants they nurture can treat all sorts of ailments, from muscle aches to sleeplessness.

After that, I find the path that leads to the outer perimeter of the compound, wanting to check out their defenses.

I discover that the density of the vines eventually becomes impenetrable until it forms a wall around the dryads' territory. The boundary is made from the same emerald-green vines with fiery fronds that Aiden and I encountered. On our way here, it was frustrating not being able to pass through them, but now I find the thick barrier comforting. Banta will have a lot of trouble getting through it.

But… so will Tessa.

Turning away from the boundary wall, I'm startled to find a male dryad standing farther along the path, watching me closely.

CHAPTER TWENTY-EIGHT

$\mathcal{I}$ recognize the scrutinizing dryad from the group who surrounded Aiden and me when we arrived.

His light-brown hair is braided back from his face, his skin is pale brown, and his eyes are a sharp green. Once more, his biceps flex as he folds his arms across his chest.

I pause where I stand.

"Hello," I say, when he remains quiet.

He inclines his head but doesn't say anything, and I wonder if it's difficult for him to express himself without his brethren around.

Despite his intimidating height and muscular physique, I don't get a dangerous vibe from him—not that I can really tell, since all of the dryads wear the same peaceful expression.

"Are you following me?" I ask.

Again, he inclines his head.

"Why?"

His forehead creases, in a moment of thought. "Protect," he says, looking a little pleased with himself when he speaks.

"You're here to look out for me?" I ask.

He inclines his head.

I dismiss any misgivings I have about his intentions and step closer. I don't really have any choice but to approach him since he's standing at the side of the only path back to the center of the territory.

"I understand you don't have names," I say when I draw closer. "But it's important for me to understand who you are."

"Dryad," he says, and I hear the words he would say if there were more dryads present: *I am dryad.*

I try again. "Do you have a name that I can call you?"

A smile plays around his mouth, as if he's amused by my need to give him a label. Without a word, he bends to the ground, running his hand across the mossy substance covering the path.

Immediately, a patch of bright green grass springs up, each blade slender.

"Ryegrass," the man says, pointing to the plant he created before turning his thick finger toward himself. "Rye."

I take a guess at his meaning. "You want me to call you... 'Rye'?"

He nods.

I allow myself to smile. "Nice to meet you, Rye."

He points at me. "Iyana." Then he spins on his heel, much more agile than I was expecting for such a big guy, and inclines his head down the path. "Come."

He doesn't wait for me to respond, striding along the path ahead of me. Two steps along, he abruptly stops, turns, and appears surprised that I haven't immediately followed him.

I guess he's used to moving in unison—with one mind—with the other dryads, and doesn't realize I won't be as in sync with him as they are.

"Come," he says again, his forehead creasing as he visibly struggles with speech. "Important."

"Okay." I hurry to catch up to him, walking where he can see me so he's aware of where I am as I try to fall into stride with him.

He leads me through the central compound, where he diverges off the path to smoothly scoop one of the children away from a Sunlight Stone, depositing the little boy into the arms of a woman also reaching for the child.

Rye returns to the path without missing a beat and continues on as if we never stopped. It's definitely taking me a minute to get used to the way the dryads move so much in tune with each other. The path Rye leads me along weaves to the south and is paved with stones —which is different to the other paths—and the shadowed clearing we converge on is bigger than any other.

He strides right into it, but I stop and catch my breath.

A central tree sits in the middle of the clearing, its enormous branches thick and entwined with those of the trees around the clearing, keeping us in darkness.

Unlike in the other clearing, the ground here is free from toadstools. Instead, it's covered in a smooth sort of moss that glows, casting light upward. Patches of the trees also glow, along with the vines that form the walls around the clearing.

Mahogany—the woman with the reddish-brown hair—is here, along with the other men and women who surrounded Aiden and me earlier. They're running through a series of combat moves, their movements so fluid that they seem to flow through the space, each one of them moving in time with the others, but not in unison.

They move as if they are all opponents.

It's like watching a highly experienced tai chi class moving through an elaborate sequence, but if the moves were sped up, they would be performing combat moves like elite warriors.

"Here," Rye says, pausing ahead of me, another smile playing around his lips. "Join."

Damn, I want to.

But how the hell am I going to move in sync with them when I don't have their hive mind? I can see myself bumping into one of them and upsetting their rhythm. Worse, I might topple someone and cause an accident.

"I don't think I can," I say, mentally plotting my path out of here, even though I'd love to at least stay and watch their moves.

When I take a step back, Mahogany breaks off from the group, slipping neatly between two dryads as they spin away from each other.

She joins Rye, slips her hand into his, and glances up at him.

He returns her gaze and it's as if a silent communication passes between them. It's so much like Tessa and Tristan that a pang of envy flashes through me.

I'm not sure if Rye and Mahogany are a couple—or if the dryads even form couples—but the way Rye's expression softens when he looks at Mahogany indicates he feels more for her than he does for the other dryads.

He immediately relaxes into his speech again. "Don't be worried," he says, speaking in turns with Mahogany. "We can teach you."

Mahogany gives me a smile before they continue. "We're as

patient as the trees," she says, speaking in turn with Rye. "You don't need to feel pressured to excel on your first day."

As they speak, the others stop working through their drills and form a quiet row in the background, soft smiles on their lips as they wait for me to respond.

"Okay," I say. "But I'll need your help."

Mahogany takes my hand and draws me to the center of the group, where the others form a circle around me. "We're willing to give help, if you're willing to receive it," she says, speaking in turn with four of the others while Rye remains quiet this time.

"First you need to breathe," she says, standing behind me and reaching forward to place her palms flat on either side of my ribcage, so that she's practically hugging me from behind. "Once you're relaxed, you'll start to hear the forest like we do."

I'm definitely not relaxed, stiffening as soon as she touches me. I don't feel like I know her well enough—or have built up anywhere near enough trust—for her to be standing so close to me right now.

"Relax," she says, her voice combining with that of two other women, who all speak at the same time. It has the effect of echoing the word *relax* around me.

The other two women stand on either side of me, running their palms down my biceps to my wrists as they wrap their hands around my arms. Their hair and skin glisten in the light of the moss glittering at our feet.

"Let go of your fear," they say.

I fight every instinct in my body to throw them off, but then Rye steps up in front of me. "Close your eyes," he says, speaking with two of the other men, both of whom have dark skin and black hair braided back, their bodies not quite as large as Rye's, but bigger than the average male supernatural.

"And breathe," Mahogany and one of the other women say in turns.

I do as they say—not because I'm letting down my guard, but because I need to center myself or I'll never figure out what my instincts are telling me right now.

Fight. Relax. Let go...

The moment my eyelids close, silence descends around me.

I'm acutely aware of Mahogany's palms against my ribcage as I breathe in and out, and the other women's hands around my arms, lifting my limbs slightly away from my torso—but I'm also aware of the quiet breeze brushing across my cheeks and the smooth moss beneath my feet.

And then... when I listen beyond the sound of my own breathing... I'm suddenly aware of a deep heartbeat. It thrums through my feet and thuds up through my heart—

My eyes fly open.

Rye smiles at me, tipping his strong chin. "You heard it," he says, speaking in turn with the two dark-skinned men.

"What *was* that?"

"It is our heartbeat," he says, speaking in turns with Mahogany and the others. "We created this clearing with acoustic moss so that we can focus and really connect with each other. When our children are old enough, we bring them here to learn how to listen to each other."

I eye the trees and vines around me, suddenly aware that the moss beneath our feet also covers the trees in patches, which must be why the clearing glows so much despite the dark. It's a good thing that the canopy above us is so thick, or the light might be visible from above.

"Close your eyes and listen," Mahogany and Rye say.

Exhaling, I shut my eyes and open my senses, allowing the steady thudding beat to drum through me, calming me.

The woman to my right runs her hand along my arm so softly that at first, I barely notice it, until she gently tugs my arm in that direction.

At the same time, Mahogany eases her grip on me, supporting my torso while allowing me to sway toward the woman. Then the other woman gently tugs me the other way so that I sway back that way.

"Let go," Mahogany whispers, an echo of my own thoughts.

Within seconds, I sense more hands guiding my legs, my back, my torso, and my arms, moving me in a sequence that I recognize as a punch-kick combination, but so slowly that it's like a dance.

I can't stop my smile and have to suppress my desire to open my eyes and take over the movement, allowing the dryads to move me to the beat of their hearts.

They speed up a little and I can't really tell whose hands are whose anymore as I lose myself to the rhythm.

My senses expand even further, and suddenly, the beat echoes distinctly through each of them so that I'm aware of where they stand and how they're moving, even though my eyes are closed.

Until, finally, I realize that only Mahogany is still holding on to me.

I keep my eyes closed, moving through the routine, hyperaware of where the dryads are and what they're doing—every smooth glide, every fluid kick and turn—until they slow down and stop.

I open my eyes. Exhale.

I find myself standing in the middle of three rows of dryads, as if I belong there. I certainly didn't topple any of them.

I feel more alive than I've felt in years.

Tessa talked about being in sync with Tristan, and I saw with my own eyes the way they were melded—breathing together, anticipating each other's responses. I don't think that what I experienced just now with the dryads comes close to the connection that Tessa and Tristan have, but I got a glimpse of it.

Rye turns to grin at me, and Mahogany smiles when I glance at her.

"A vampire will always hear a heartbeat," they say, sounding pleased with their conclusion. "You may train with us every afternoon, if you wish."

"I'd like that," I say.

I tell myself that I might be waiting for Aiden to wake up, but I plan to make the most of every minute of it.

CHAPTER TWENTY-NINE

*A*fter spending the remainder of the afternoon with Rye, Mahogany, and the rest of the dryad group that I'm quickly coming to call "the warriors," I return to my cabin as the sun begins to set.

When the moon rises, the biggest change happens within the central compound. While my body responds to the moonlight by becoming more alert, the dryads slow down, their movements becoming more lethargic. Rye and Mahogany take themselves off to a cabin a few rows away from mine, and the other warriors also disperse.

At the exact moment that the first full rays of moonlight filter through the overhead canopy, all of the adults who were watching over the children open the paper screens at the sides of their cabins in unison.

Like my cabin, each has a giant tree in the side of it and a decorative alcove at the back with a different plant on display. The children immediately head back to their parents and then the families curl up in full view of each other to sleep.

It surprises me when nobody shuts their doors.

I pause on the porch of my new home, watching curiously as the greenery around the houses grows up and across each porch and covers the sleeping dryads like blankets.

Visually following the path of the vines from one home to

another, it looks like all of the families are now connected as they sleep. Not just them, but also the homes in the distance, too.

I'm even more surprised when the vines creep toward my own cabin, but they stop at the bottom of the steps, hovering there before settling back to the ground.

I guess I'm not really one of them yet.

Since all of the children seem to have gathered in the central cabins, I scan the sleeping dryads for Drina, the girl who said her flower's heart was in a cage.

I don't see her among the families, although I'm sure she must be there somewhere.

I'm on the verge of stepping down to look for her—casually, of course, since I don't want to go around peering into people's homes—when Clara's soft voice sounds from the side of the porch, making me jump.

"The dryads are at their most vulnerable at night," she whispers.

I consider her carefully, since I'm not sure why she's pointing out how vulnerable they are right now.

Her silhouette glows softly, making her look a little taller than her apparent eleven-year-old stature. Her skin glows and her black hair glistens in the stream of moonlight that shines freely on her. In contrast, the branches above me continue to cast me into shadows.

She continues. "Given your vampiric nature, this makes you ideally placed to watch over them." She pauses. "If you choose to take on that role."

"The role of a guardian?" I ask, surprised by her suggestion.

"If you choose."

I give it some thought. When I believed that the dryads had killed Aiden, I never would have considered becoming their protector. But in the space of a day, a lot has changed. I know that Aiden is safe and alive. I've been welcomed into the dryads' home. And I believe that— one day, hopefully soon—Aiden and I will walk out of here. Together.

Clara turns away, but not before she says, "It's in my nature to stay awake all night, but if I did that every night, I'd rarely be awake at the same time as the dryads. So I try to change my routine every now and then. I often sleep after midnight and through the morning. If you need me tonight, I'll be patrolling the perimeter."

Remaining on the porch, I consider my choices.

When I was at Hidden House, I started up a routine in which I slept from lunchtime to midnight so I could be awake in the morning when Tessa needed to train.

Here, I want to be able to train with the dryads in the afternoons, but I also want to resume my nighttime rhythm as much as I can. I decide to aim for a routine where I sleep as soon as dawn breaks and then wake at midday.

Exhaling a deep breath, I head down into the gardens, glancing at the homes as I pass by. It's too difficult to tell if Drina is asleep in one of them, so I stop looking and enjoy the silence and the time to myself.

The air is incredibly fresh. The silence is equally refreshing. It reminds me a little of the garden at Hidden House where the silver flowers grow. There's a similar glow to the air here.

My heart tugs again at the thought of Tessa. Being part of a pack wasn't something I ever expected to happen to me as a vampire, but I committed to it with my whole heart. Or maybe *part* of my heart, since another part of it belongs to Aiden.

Now that I'm alone, I find myself heading north to him again.

The path grows darker the farther I travel away from the central compound until I'm walking in darkness, but my eyes adjust quickly. I can never see so well as I can at night.

I pull aside the vines and step into the cavern where Aiden lies, finding the water even brighter now that night has fallen. Aiden's silhouette is dark in comparison. If Clara hadn't illuminated his face earlier, I wouldn't be able to tell that it's him.

Somehow, not being able to see his face makes his current situation more painful.

I drop to the soft, mossy ground as close to the water's edge as I dare and rest my chin in my hands.

"Wake up soon, Aiden," I whisper.

For the next two weeks, I slip into a new routine, and the days pass a lot faster than I thought they would.

I wake in the middle of the day to the sounds of the children playing and, after attempting to make myself presentable without the benefit of a mirror, I snatch up some towels to take with me and head straight for the northern cavern to check on Aiden.

While my thirst is the greatest when I first wake, and I need to feed on the vines at the back of the cavern as soon as I can, I always go to Aiden first.

Each day, I have to steel my heart to see him lying in the life waters, where he floats quietly, unmoving.

Not being able to be near him becomes more unbearable. With the passing days, I step closer to the water's edge. Dangerously close.

Craning forward to make out Aiden's features, I tell myself I can see the shape of his lips or his eyes, even though I can't.

There's a part of me that's afraid I'll come back one day and discover him gone. That whatever power he's destined to discover within himself will obliterate his memories of me and he'll simply... get up and walk away.

It feels like an irrational fear, but I can't seem to shake it.

Some days, I plot a visual path up the tree and along its branches to the knife dangling from the center of the ceiling, but the water laps too close to the base of the tree for me to try climbing to it. Yet.

Its position right above Aiden also gives me pause.

I tell myself that as soon as Aiden wakes up and no longer lies beneath the dagger's blade, I'll take my chances retrieving it.

After feeding on the vines and staying with Aiden for a while each day, I take my towels to the showers to freshen up before I spend the afternoon training with the warriors.

I don't have names for all of them, but I've come to know their differing personalities—the ones with a sense of humor and the ones who are always serious.

Each day, I become more skilled at training with them, letting go of my reliance on what I can see and learning to listen to their synchronized heartbeats within the training cavern.

Even so, there's an ache in my own heart that gets bigger and bigger. I miss my pack—Danika, Tessa, Ella—and their friendship. I miss Helen and her wisdom. And Luna and Lydia with their quiet power and their way of getting in my space when I need them.

While I'm forming friendships with the dryads, and especially with the warriors, Clara is the one who seeks me out the most. Every evening when the moon rises, she meets me on my porch to ask me how Aiden is doing. Each day I tell her the same thing: He's still sleeping.

Every now and then, I encounter Drina, the young dryad girl, on one of the paths back to the central compound. Sometimes, it's when I'm returning from seeing Aiden. Other times, it's on my way to the training cavern.

After some observation, I've ascertained that she doesn't sleep in a home with the other dryads or play with the other dryad children, which I find strange.

When I carefully ask the others about her, they give me blank looks and remind me they don't have names; they are all dryads. Even Rye doesn't seem to know whom I'm talking about.

After a while, I give up asking questions and simply keep a lookout for her.

Each time, I find her kneeling on her own at the base of a tree, her dark, crimson-highlighted hair falling around her shoulders as she leans forward, her small hands hovering over a new creation. Mostly, it's flowers. Some days, it's plants that remind me of objects—a golden bracelet, an ivory wand.

Then, at the end of my first two weeks with the dryads, she creates what looks like a book.

Usually, the look of concentration on her face is so deep that I don't want to interrupt her, but on the day of the book, I can't help myself.

Crouching quietly, I keep my voice low so I don't startle her. "That's incredible, sweetheart."

Even without touching it, I can see that the book's spine is made of wood, and its pages are splashed with color that doesn't quite form images.

"It's forbidden," Drina says, so bluntly that I'm surprised.

"Books are forbidden?" It's not as if I've ever seen a dryad reading a book, so it's possible they don't even have books.

"No," she whispers, looking up at me with her big, gray eyes while the colors on the pages in front of her continue to swirl across the fine paper she created. "This knowledge is forbidden."

CHAPTER THIRTY

My brow furrows as I focus on the image that pulls together on the page Drina created. It nearly takes shape, but it quickly disintegrates again.

"This knowledge... Who made it forbidden?" I ask, since the dryads don't have a leader who could make rules like that.

Drina doesn't answer me. The colors wash toward the center of the page and I catch sight of what could be—*possibly, if I use my imagination*—two figures standing in an amber clearing. Then the image fragments once more.

"What story is this?" I ask, trying again for answers.

A deep crease forms in Drina's forehead. "I don't... remember..."

Her shoulders slump, but when I reach out to comfort her, she says, "It's okay. It is as it should be."

I feel as if a cold breeze blew across my skin, and I'm not sure why.

I've become so used to walking in the shadows of the trees now that I don't think about the danger of the sun anymore. Even when Clara comes near to me, with all the sunlight shining down on her, I've discovered that the canopy prioritizes the shadows over me, casting darkness over whichever part of her body is near to mine.

Normally, I revel in darkness, but right now, crouching beside Drina, the shadows feel too deep. The quiet laughter of the children along the path as they play feels somehow too punctuated.

Before I can speak again, Drina shuts the book and puts it on the ground, where vines begin to slither across it.

She rises to her feet, standing no higher than my shoulders.

Her gray eyes flash at me, a compelling glance. "You should take the book before I'm compelled to bury it in vines."

She slips away, her bare feet silent as she turns off the path and disappears into the trees.

I purse my lips in thought. She has never left one of her creations behind like this before, and curiosity burns brightly within me.

I drop to the ground and reach for the book, fighting the growing vines to grab hold of the book's spine.

I nearly lose my grip when a vine scratches the back of my hand and my survival instincts tell me to let go before the vines bite me. I ignore them, grabbing hold of the other side of the book and pulling two-handed with all of my might.

The book slips free, but not before another vine snakes upward, whipping out at me as if to strike my face.

I dart out of its path, the book in hand, kicking back with my foot and knocking the vine to the side before I spin and glare at the growing pile of plants slithering across the path like hissing snakes.

"Behave!" I snap at them. As if they can understand me.

At my command, their movement slows, but I have no illusions I had anything to do with it.

My sharp movement caused the canopy above me to also shift quickly, the shadows coming with me while the sunlight suddenly shone down on them. The bright light seems to take the sting out of them and within moments, they lie still again.

Holding the book close to my chest, I stride away down the path toward my cabin. It's nearly time to train, and I'll be late if I delay, but I close my paper door and sit on my bed to open the book and study its pages.

I don't expect to see much. It's Drina's creation and she said she couldn't remember the story that was forbidden, so it will only show the extent of what she knows.

A wash of amber flows across the first page, starting at the spine and spreading toward the page's edge before vanishing. It's as if a watercolor painter is creating and then erasing their work in the next second.

On the second page, a similar wash of color appears and disappears like a wave from the spine to the edge, except that it's alternating strokes of silver and gold this time.

When I turn the page, the silver bleeds through from the previous page, blossoming across the image I first saw—two figures turning toward each other, but they're barely more than silhouettes, their features obscured.

The next page is blank.

So is the one after that.

I turn another, just in case I discover something new, finding it also blank.

I prepare to close the book when crimson color suddenly spills across the page, so dark and thick that it's like blood gushing across the paper.

I jolt, nearly drop the book, and shudder as the blood continues to spill and fade, spill and fade...

A droplet of silver appears in the middle of it, running in the opposite direction of every other image—toward the spine. Then another drop, and this time, I'm aware of the damp on my upper lip.

Oh, fuck.

Brushing the back of my hand beneath my nose, I discover that my nose is bleeding.

Another drop of my silver blood falls to the page before I snap the book shut and hurry to the bathroom.

Grabbing a towel with which to catch the blood, I sink onto the closed toilet seat to wait for the bleeding to stop.

It's been years since my last nosebleed. It happened in the first few months of my vampire life before I was able to source regular doses of mercury. At the time, I put it down to settling into my power. I don't understand why it would happen now when I have a plentiful supply of food—and what feels like a supercharged source of food, at that.

Drinking from the vines is like swallowing energy. It eases my thirst within moments and makes me feel completely hydrated, fully energized, and warm from my head to my toes. It can't be bad for me, or I would surely have noticed adverse effects before now.

A different thought occurs to me that makes me wonder...

Maybe I'm getting *too* much of it?

I certainly haven't been measuring the amount I'm drinking. With mercury, I only need as much as would fill a shot glass each day. I could be overdosing on *too much* goodness here.

Pushing aside my unease, I resolve to simply reduce my intake tomorrow.

When my nosebleed finally stops, I rinse out the towel as best I can and then I push the book beneath the towels on the shelf.

I feel a little guilty about hiding it. And also, a little silly. After all, any number of dryads saw me carrying it into my room, but I tell myself I don't really have anywhere else to put it, anyway.

Leaving the book behind, I spend the rest of the afternoon training with Rye and Mahogany before I return to my cabin, where I find Clara waiting.

As usual, she asks me how Aiden is doing.

"Still sleeping," I say, standing beside her in the shadows while she glows in the moonlight.

For once, I'm a little envious of Clara's freedom to stand in the light. It feels like forever since I was able to feel the moon's rays on my skin.

Even when she moves close to me—or reaches out to squeeze my hand—the branches move to shadow whatever part of her body is touching mine, prioritizing my protection. It's lifesaving during the day, but not so welcome at night.

"Okay, then," she says, gliding toward the porch steps, but she suddenly stops and peers at my face. "Iyana?"

I don't know what she's asking until my nose tingles and cold liquid slips down my upper lip.

Not again!

"Fuck," I whisper, leaning forward and cupping my hand to catch my silver blood. "Excuse me."

Hurrying inside to grab a towel, I hold it beneath my nose, emerging from the little bathroom to find Clara standing in the middle of my room, her silhouette backlit by the moonlight outside.

"Are you okay?" she asks, folding her hands in front of her, her suddenly intense focus on me a little unnerving.

"It's nothing to worry about," I say, my voice a husky nasal sound now that my nose is full of liquid. "It'll stop soon."

She tilts her head and, with the light behind her, I can't really see her expression. "Has this happened before?"

"Earlier today," I say. "But before that, not for many years."

"I wonder why it's happening now, then?" she asks—her tone unusually light and breezy—and she doesn't give me time to answer before she takes a step back. "Well, if you're sure you're okay?"

"Yes, please don't worry about me."

I sink to my bed when she leaves, curling my legs beneath me to wait it out. I'm relieved that she shut the door behind her. Even though the dryads are sleeping now, I don't want one of them to wake up unexpectedly and see me like this.

This time, it takes so long for the bleeding to stop that I work my way through multiple towels and end up staying in my cabin until midnight, not daring to go out. The blood flow isn't fast, but it's constant, and *so* cold.

My blood has never been warm, but the liquid trickling from my nose makes me shiver to the point where I'm pulling my only blanket around myself, trying to get warm. My breathing is erratic, my entire body shakes, and I curl over, trying to hold myself together.

I've never had a fever—not in my remembered vampiric life, anyway—but I imagine this is what a fever feels like.

Fuck, I miss Aiden.

I haven't cried since I thought he was killed, but big, ugly tears roll down my cheeks as I huddle, shivering, trying to catch the blood and not make a mess of this beautiful, earthy room. Trying to breathe, too, since crying is *not* fucking helping.

By the time the night reaches its darkest point and the nosebleed finally stops, I'm too tired to stir myself—too exhausted from crying.

I slip under the blanket and fall asleep despite the call of the moonlight.

CHAPTER THIRTY-ONE

*W*hen I wake at midday the next day, I'm wrecked. My body aches, my face hurts, and my head feels like it's full of dust.

Despite sleeping what I estimate was nearly twelve hours, it feels like I fought a battle all night, and the sleep I *did* get hasn't refreshed me. Not at all.

Dragging myself out of bed, I stumble to the bathroom and wash my face in the freezing water. I don't want to go outside until I'm sure I don't have any silver blood left on my chin, neck, or shoulders that might alarm the dryads. Or at least, make them curious. My silver blood isn't exactly normal. Of course, they might have green blood for all I know, so it might not bother them at all...

Not having a mirror leaves me paranoid that I missed a spot, but once I'm satisfied that I've done the best I can, I grip the sink and try to focus myself.

I'm so thirsty.

After all the blood I lost, I should be craving mercury—desperate to get back to the vines near the life waters—but I find myself cupping my hands beneath the running waterspout, gathering water in them, and raising it to my mouth.

My tongue darts out to taste the liquid, finding it cool and sweet. When I swallow a little, I fully expect to bring it back up and I brace for the awfulness, but...

My stomach doesn't revolt. The water stays down.

Even more surprising, I want more of it.

This can't be...

My brow furrows as I stare at the water still pooling in my hands. Releasing it with a splash, I grab the cup by the sink, fill it, and gulp the water down, gripping the edge of the sink with my other hand.

The freezing water cools my tongue and clears my head. I wait a full five minutes, but still, I don't bring it up.

I turn off the tap and back away from the sink, bumping into the opposite wall as I stare at the cup I left precariously perched at the side of the sink.

I don't drink water.

Last night must have muddled my senses somehow. I tell myself that I need to feed. I'll get myself to the vines and then everything will be back to normal.

Reaching for the last towel on the shelf, intending to dry off the final water droplets from my chin, my hand lands on the book Drina gave me.

I'm wary of looking at it again since the nosebleeds started when I opened it yesterday. It's not as if merely opening a book should cause a nosebleed, but the association is too strong for me.

I don't want to trigger another episode because of anxiety. Not least, because I'm all out of towels.

Taking deep breaths, I change into fresh clothes—pulling on a pair of pants and a shirt—grateful for the dryads who launder clothing for me each day. Realizing that they'll bring fresh towels too, I relocate Drina's book to beneath my mattress.

I feel more like myself by the time I slide open my door and head out into the central territory toward the life waters. I pause along the way to greet Sunflower and say *good morning* to the children.

As always, they think it's hilarious that I'm greeting them this way when it's clearly the afternoon already. Their smiling faces and laughter lift my mood and, by the time I reach Aiden, my heart feels lighter. I can nearly forget about last night.

Until I step into the cavern and the darkness weighs in on me.

The life waters don't seem to glow as brightly today and it only serves to make Aiden's form more indistinct.

In contrast, when I raise my focus to the dagger hanging over him, it seems brighter, its blade glistening.

Quietly, I pace around the water's edge to the base of the tree, mentally plotting each move it would take to reach the weapon—leap up to the lowest branch, then swing myself up to the next branch. Up again and to the right.

The safest course—without pushing up through the canopy into what could be sunlight above—is to balance my way along a branch that extends below, but parallel to, the branch from which the dagger hangs. Then it will take a final leap up to snatch the dagger—and fall into the life waters, unless I can manage to leap far enough that I make it to the next branch in the same jump.

I exhale a sigh and exit the cavern, intending to head around to the vines to feed, when I find Drina sitting directly outside in the middle of the walkway.

Her shoulders are hunched while her hands hover over a new creation that sprouts directly up on the mossy path.

This flower is simpler than any of the others I've seen her create.

A pure white daisy.

The color of its petals reminds me of Ella Griffin's ivory hair, and a sharp pang shoots through my heart at the memory of the wolf shifter who fought to recover her pack from her father.

"I'm not strong enough," Drina whispers, so quietly that I nearly don't catch her speech before I kneel in front of her.

"Drina?" I lean forward, almost touching her but thinking better of it. "Are you okay, sweetheart?"

Her eyes glisten as she looks up at me. "I can't control it."

My heart squeezes again. Today, more than any other day, she reminds me so much of the family I've left behind. She has hair like Tessa. Eyes like Helen—far too wise. And she creates flowers that remind me of Maeve one day, and Ella the next.

Thinking of what the warriors told me, I say, "Then maybe let go."

"No!" Her response is far more vehement than I was expecting; a sharp rebuke that vibrates through me like an echo. "To let go is to surrender."

"I don't mean to surrender," I say, taking a deep breath to calm my suddenly racing heart. "I mean to let go of whatever's holding you back, whatever's caging you. Be *wild*."

Her expression brightens. "Maybe I can—"

Whatever she was about to say, her voice is drowned in a rush of wind through the treetops.

My focus shoots up to the canopy above us as it shakes and shivers so loudly that it sounds like a jet engine taking off.

I poise on the verge of jumping to my feet. "What the—?"

Drina is pale as she rises to her feet, suddenly towering over me, her crimson-highlighted hair falling down her back, her focus on me and not on the violently shivering branches.

"I can't stop it now," she says, her eyes glistening. "He's here."

CHAPTER THIRTY-TWO

I jump to my feet. "Drina?"

Without another word, she spins on her heels, disappearing into the forest, her dark hair flying behind her as she races away into the shadows.

"Drina!"

Above me, the branches continue shaking, the vibrations running through the ground at my feet and up into my body, making my head spin.

What the fuck is going on?

I'm torn between running after Drina and returning to the center of the compound, but I choose the central area, launching into a sprint along the path.

Up ahead, I'm finally close enough to catch glimpses of the main gardens through the trees where the dryad parents and children are scattering.

I can't hear them beneath the sound of the crashing wind, but it looks like they're shouting as they scoop up the youngest ones and disappear into their homes.

The warriors are gathered in the center of the clearing ahead, while the vines that often slither across the paths are rising up around them.

Each of them faces the southeast side of the compound—the direction between the training cavern and the other work areas.

Before I can reach them, they break into a run, quickly disappearing along the southeastern path.

Every home I pass as I race through the central area has its doors closed now, and the children are nowhere to be seen—neither is any other dryad. I don't see Clara anywhere, either.

Speeding up, I sprint along the path the warriors took, my heart in my throat as my imagination goes wild.

Drina's cryptic comment that "he's here" could mean anything. It could be another dryad—or worse, it could be Banta, since I warned the dryads about him.

I push myself to run as fast as I can. I'm quicker than the dryads, who have strong cores, but they have the benefit of being able to use their power to remove any obstacles in their way.

Chasing after them along the southeastern path, I reach the wall of vines at the perimeter. The dryads ahead of me are running through a sudden opening in the boundary and it's quickly closing.

I manage to reach it just in time to slip through behind Rye, who immediately spins and catches hold of me.

"No," he says, holding me tightly and physically blocking me from going farther.

I crane around him, trying to see the other dryads, who are ahead of us now. "What's happening?"

Rye's speech is a little stuck now that he's alone with me, but his single-word command tells me everything.

"Danger," he says.

He's trying to protect me, but I glare up at him before I attempt to peer around him again.

A little farther ahead, the other dryads have stopped in the same sort of clearing that Aiden and I were herded into. Vines rise up all around it—their fiery fronds rippling like an angry wildfire, ready to strike as they close in.

A single figure kneels within the rapidly closing circle of vines—a man with dark brown hair the same shade as Aiden's, the strands falling across his face as he holds his hands up, his shoulders hunched. The dryads close in on him.

My eyes widen with surprise.

"Lucas!" I cry, trying to wrench myself free from Rye's hold, desperate to get to Aiden's brother before the dryads decide to kill him.

"He's my friend!" I shout, leaning around Rye to be heard by the others. "Please! He won't hurt you!"

They've completely closed in around him, and now I can't make out what's happening.

My fear level rises. I wasn't able to go looking for Lucas—and Aiden made it clear that he wanted me to stay here—but now that Lucas is here, I'll do whatever it takes to keep him safe.

I look up into Rye's eyes, taking a deep breath and trying to calm myself, since I know that the dryads respond much better to reason than anxiety.

"Please, Rye," I say. "He's Aiden's brother. He won't hurt you."

Rye's arms clamp around me as he lifts me off my feet, turns, and puts me back on the ground so that we're both facing the group. At the same time, the other dryads separate, revealing Lucas, still alive.

Relief courses through me, but it doesn't last long.

Lucas raises his head and now I can see dried blood across the side of his head all the way to his jaw.

The dryads can't have done it because it isn't fresh. The front of his T-shirt is a mess, the material torn and splattered with blood that also stains his jeans. There are cuts all up the inside of his arms, which I can see as he continues to keep them raised. They look a hell of a lot like defensive wounds.

"Iyana?" he asks, his voice scratchy and rough as he peers at me across the distance, a deep crease forming in his forehead.

Rye makes a sound in the back of his throat, and I sense he's trying to speak but can't without the other dryads. He quickly gives a resigned sigh and, to my relief, releases me.

I race toward Lucas, but I haven't taken more than a few steps when one of the vines behind him darts between the watching dryads, encircles his left wrist, and pulls tight.

His focus snaps to it, a fierce glare as his muscles visibly flex and he wrenches his arm to the side, pulling the vine so hard that, to my shock, it snaps.

I'm so surprised that I nearly stop running.

Lucas's angry voice slurs. "What the fuck was… that…?"

The stem of the vine slithers away while its broken head drops to the ground, leaving large pinpricks of blood on his wrist.

He sways, his eyes glaze over, and he falls forward, about to land on his face.

"No!" I throw myself across the remaining distance, sliding through the greenery to catch him. I expect the vines on the ground to impede my momentum, but they form a smooth surface beneath me—similar to the training cavern—and I reach Lucas in time for his head to land on my thigh. I catch his shoulders at the same time.

To my enormous relief, his heartbeat sounds loud and clear within my hearing.

"Don't worry, Iyana," Mahogany says, speaking in turns with another two dryads as they bend over me and Lucas. "The vine didn't hurt him. He will wake up."

I squeeze my eyes closed, trying to calm my own racing heartbeat, relieved that Lucas is okay and that they don't intend to harm him.

My next worry is that the dryads will keep Lucas sedated once they realize he's magically repressed like Aiden. That they'll put Lucas in the life waters, too.

I accepted that fate for Aiden because I was too late to prevent it—his heart had already stopped—but he should have been given the choice.

I won't let it happen that way for his brother.

"Can you please bring him to my cabin?" I ask the dryads, knowing it's only a matter of time before Clara reaches us. Her power will allow her to see that Lucas is magically repressed, and I want to be on my own turf when she does in case I have a battle ahead of me to decide his fate.

I've barely finished speaking when Clara appears at the edge of the clearing.

"Iyana!" She hurries toward me where I'm still kneeling, holding Lucas. Her voice is breathless, and I note the rapid rise and fall of her chest. She must have run as fast as she could to reach us.

She stands next to me, somehow looming over us despite her shorter height, as her gaze darts from Lucas to me.

"Who is he?" she asks.

"He's Aiden's brother." Steeling myself for Clara's response to Lucas's presence, I tip my head back to scrutinize her. "I assume you can see what he is."

She peers down at him before she gives a short nod, her expression closed off. "I can."

"He deserves to make the choice for himself—"

She shakes her head, quickly cutting me off. "Only one person can occupy the life waters at a time. We can't do anything to help this man discover his power until Aiden wakes up."

I let out my breath, hugely relieved, but I prepare for another fight. "Can he stay with me?"

Clara's lips press together before she says, "How well do you know him?"

"Well enough to trust that he won't hurt me," I say with as much certainty as I can, even though fear grows at the back of my mind—the same fear I had about Aiden when he appeared at the Spire. *How can I be certain that Banta doesn't control Lucas's mind right now?*

The only evidence that his mind is his own is the wounds on his body. That much pain would *have* to free him from Banta's control.

Clara is quiet for a moment and I'm aware of the stillness of the dryads as they wait for her to make a decision. She might not be their queen or their leader, but they seem to look to her for guidance.

"Very well," she says. "But you need to be careful."

The vines that stand around us curl inward, wrapping around Lucas's shoulders and torso, and I slip out from beneath him as they lift him into the air.

Supported by a platform of greenery that ripples across the ground, his unconscious form moves ahead of me along the path back to the central territory.

"Thank you," I say to Clara.

She catches my arm, a warning tone entering her voice. "You should be aware that this man's mind is a dark place, Iyana."

When I first met Clara, she told me that it's in her nature to shine a light into dark places, and that's how she knew that Aiden is an Unknown.

I take a deep breath and challenge her for information. "Then you should be able to see into it. Tell me what you see?"

"I can't," she says with a rueful smile. "His mind is as dark as yours."

Too dark to see.

"I'll be careful," I promise Clara, before I hurry after the group of dryads escorting Lucas into the main compound.

CHAPTER THIRTY-THREE

The vines carry Lucas as far as my porch before the dryads take hold of him and convey him inside for me, carefully placing him on the mattress.

I'm surprised when his big body takes up most of the bed.

His dark brown hair is a sharp contrast against the ivory material, his features more chiseled and less rounded than I remember. Even his shoulders seem broader, his chest larger, his muscles more pronounced.

He's changed a lot in the seven months since I last saw him.

"How long will he sleep?" I ask Rye.

"Another hour, at least," he says, speaking in turn with Mahogany.

"We will bring medicine for his wounds," three of the women say, their back-and-forth voices sounding completely normal to me now.

Clara hovers in the background and when the dryads move to close the door as they leave, she stops them. "Bring the medicine, but leave this door open at all times."

When I open my mouth to argue, she gives me a firm look, and I quickly press my lips together.

I'm sure she's trying to keep me safe by ensuring that everything that happens inside this room is visible from the garden, but there are things I need to ask Lucas when he wakes up, and I don't want our conversation to be observed.

I focus on my most important job first: tending to his wounds.

Hurrying to the bathroom, I'm grateful to find the supply of clean towels replenished, although it makes me remember the book I slipped under the mattress. Lucas is currently lying on it and I'm sure he'll notice it when he wakes up. But I'll deal with that when it happens.

I dampen one of the towels before I return to Lucas and set about cleaning his head wound first.

The wound itself baffles me. It isn't a cut like a dagger or a claw would make. It looks more like a sort of burn mark, where the impact busted open his skin, making him bleed, while the blast cauterized the surrounding skin.

It's the sort of wound I would associate with Aiden's fiery fist. Maybe. Even that doesn't quite fit.

My concern about brain damage is somewhat relieved by the fact that the dried blood indicates the wound happened some time ago and Lucas was conscious, functioning, and talking before the dryads knocked him out.

When I push aside his hair to check the rest of his scalp, I pause to see the shaved area at the side of his head above his left ear. It's the same location where Banta requires all of his lieutenants to tattoo their scalps, but so far, Lucas's has only been shaved.

My heart sinks a little to see what appears to be razor cuts across the area indicating that the shaving was recent.

Despite Lucas's inability to use his power, Banta must be preparing him for a place in Banta's empire.

It's the last thing Aiden would want.

I hold on to my anger, conserving it. It won't do me any good right now.

When the female dryad returns with a pot of ointment, I give her a grateful "Thank you" before she leaves me again.

After slathering the ointment over Lucas's head wound, I turn my attention to his chest and arms, carefully removing his torn shirt by ripping the seams before methodically cleaning and treating the cuts and bruises one by one.

I'm confronted by the number of bruises across his chest—some older than others—and I proceed carefully, keeping my touch light.

I'm turning away to scoop the final bit of ointment from the pot when he jolts.

His hand wraps around my wrist so suddenly and tightly that I gasp, spinning back to him.

He's half-up, his stomach muscles clenched, his grip on my arm painful. "What the fuck is this?" he snarls. His voice trails off as he stares at me, his brow furrowing, then clearing. "Iyana?"

"Lucas," I say, my eyes wide. I'm frozen beside him, pain shooting through my wrist. "It's me."

"It's you." He seems to recognize me, but he remains half-raised off the mattress, scanning the room from the tree to the paper screen and across the bright porch. He doesn't seem to realize that he's still crushing my arm. "Where am I?"

"You're with the dryads," I say, my voice strained.

Dear fuck, I wasn't wrong about his muscles. When I first met him, he was young, quiet, and polite. Now, there's an edge in his speech that wasn't there before, and his grip is far stronger than I imagined it would be.

I force myself to breathe around the pain, lowering my voice as I try to catch his attention. "Lucas... You're hurting me..."

His focus flies from our surroundings to his fist before he rapidly unfurls his fingers from around my wrist, leaving bright red marks where he gripped me. "Fuck."

I slowly rub my wrist, easing the blood flow back to my hand as he carefully maneuvers himself into a sitting position.

"It's okay," I say, gently turning my wrist to make sure he didn't break my bones.

"It's really not," he murmurs. "This isn't how I wanted to see you again."

Without taking his eyes off me, he reaches for the pot of ointment at the side of the mattress. Scooping out the final smears, he reaches for my hand.

When I hesitate to give him access to my wrist, he tips his head with a slow smile. "It's the least I can do to apologize."

I extend my hand and he takes it carefully, allowing my wrist to rest across his other palm while he sweeps the ointment across the emerging bruises. His touch is light, a sharp contrast to the strength he used before.

"I didn't expect to make it to the dryads alive," he says, continuing to brush the medicine across my wrist. The ointment cools the burning sensation and calms the redness right away. The dryads definitely don't muck around with their remedies.

"What happened to you?" I ask, gesturing at the wound across his forehead and the defensive wounds on his arms.

His lips press into a harsh line. "Fucking Banta and his new lieutenants."

Lucas's focus shifts to the room again, another quick scan before he returns his attention to me, a crease forming in his forehead when I continue to stare at him.

"Aiden didn't tell you about the wraith?" he asks.

My forehead creases. "What wraith? What new lieutenants?" I know about the Metalworker, but I assumed the other lieutenants were the same ones who nearly killed me.

Lucas's eyebrows lift, a momentary surprise, but his lips resume their hard line. "After you supposedly died, Banta gave Aiden the order to kill three of his lieutenants—"

My response is sharp, cutting him off. "Wait… what? Aiden killed them?"

Lucas stares at me, his expression like stone. "Aiden didn't exactly have a problem with it."

I shake my head, rapid, short shakes, as a thousand questions crowd my mind—not least of which is why Aiden didn't tell me. "They protected Banta from me. Why would Banta be angry about that?"

A fierce smile fills Lucas's face. "The official reason? They were supposed to rough you up and bring you back alive, not kill you. Banta claimed he didn't want you dead."

I squeeze my eyes closed. "And the unofficial reason?" I ask, already knowing the answer in my heart.

"Aiden needed someone to kill. Banta was worried about losing control of him."

I recognize Banta's strategy right away. He told Aiden that he didn't order his men to kill me. And then, he allowed Aiden to take revenge on them. If Aiden saw through Banta's ploy, he must have looked past it. After all, Banta gave his blessing for Aiden to kill the men responsible for my death.

I try to focus on the facts. "You said that three of them died. There were four. Which one did Banta keep alive?"

"Toad," Lucas says. "His skills are too important to Banta to lose."

Of course. Aiden mentioned Toad when we were at the warehouse. He is the snake shifter with the tracking abilities. Snake shifters are rarer than other shifter species, and solitary types—perfect for Banta's purposes. It would have been difficult for Banta to replace him.

Lucas's gaze rakes over me. "I was there when Aiden saw you through the flames. He fucking lost it when he saw that you were alive."

I draw a sharp breath. Aiden told me that he nearly lost control of his power when he saw me—that he could have burned the room. He got out of there before he did anything to draw attention to himself.

I pin Lucas with my glare. "You told Banta what Aiden saw."

Aiden didn't blame his brother for telling Banta that I was alive, which makes me feel like I shouldn't, either, but it was the turning point when Aiden went from being Banta's first lieutenant to becoming a target.

Lucas's hand closes around my wrist again, but it's a light hold, almost conciliatory, and his shoulders slump at the same time. "I didn't have a choice. Like I said, you don't know about the fucking wraith. She's as vicious as the Metalworker."

I grit my teeth. "Tell me."

"Her touch burns, but not like fire. Like acid." His thumb strokes across my wrist. "What was I supposed to do, Iyana? Use my non-existent power to fight back? I've worked hard to make myself stronger, but at the end of the day, I may as well be human, not supernatural." The snarl returns to his voice. "I didn't stand a fucking chance against any of them."

Frustration and anger give his speech an edge that resonates within me. Aiden chose to join Banta to protect his brother, but he regretted it, because in the end, he placed Lucas at Banta's mercy. Now his choice is coming full circle.

"How did you escape?" I ask.

"Banta's compound was attacked," he replies, startling me with this news.

"When? How?" I'm suddenly so agitated that I nearly jump off the mattress. All I can imagine is that Tessa came looking for me; that she attacked the compound trying to find me.

"I couldn't see much," he says. "Banta had me blindfolded and tied up in the wet room. Part of the wall exploded open, hell broke loose, and then I was free."

"Can you tell me anything about the explosion?" I ask urgently. "Anything about the magic? Even the color of it?"

His eyes narrow as he appears to think carefully. "Purple," he says. "But I can't be sure. I didn't take my freedom for granted. I fucking ran for it."

I lean back on my heels. Violet is the color of Maeve's magic. But it could equally have been someone else.

I try to calm my heart, uncertain whether I'm elated or concerned about the possibility that my pack might have attacked Banta's compound.

Tessa talked about going after him after we found her in the forest, but at the time, he was peripheral to Ford Vanguard's operations. Now that I'm missing, she has even more reason to take him down.

Even so, she's looking for me in the wrong place, and it's a little confusing to me that she hasn't located me here yet.

With that thought, I consider Lucas carefully. It took Aiden and me nearly two days to find the dryads. I'm not sure how he did it by himself.

"How did you find me?" I ask him.

"Aiden told me about the dryads months ago," he says. "He told me to follow the creek, so that's what I did. I damn near wandered for three days trying to find this place."

My brow furrows in thought because we only came to the dryads to avoid the Metalworker, who hadn't joined Banta's ranks months ago, so I'm not sure why Aiden would have told his brother about the dryads. Then I realize...

"He told you about the weapon the dryads are guarding," I say, taking a guess. "He told you to come find it if anything happened to him."

"Aiden was gone," Lucas says. "For the last two weeks, I didn't know if he was dead or alive. Coming here for the weapon was my only choice."

His grip on my hand tightens. He lowers his voice. "Have you found it? Is it here?"

I pause because it feels dangerous to share my knowledge of the weapon. But if Aiden already told his brother about the weapon's existence, then I can't lie about it. Especially because I vowed that there wouldn't be any more lies in my future. "It's here."

Lucas stares at me. "Then why haven't you taken it? Why are you still here?" He scans the room again, peering beyond the door, and I finally realize what he's looking for when he asks, "For fuck's sake, Iyana. Where is Aiden?"

Damn. How do I explain this to him?

I swallow. "It's more complicated than you can imagine."

His expression hardens. "Tell me."

"I can't tell you. I have to show you," I say. "But right now, you need to rest, hydrate, and get your bearings—"

"Like fuck I do." In one determined move, he rises to his feet, pulling me with him.

Now that we're standing, the full extent of Lucas's physical changes since I last saw him become even more obvious.

He's as tall as Aiden, but somehow, he never seemed as towering as he does now, looming over me, his chest, shoulders, and biceps thick with muscles.

Despite the tension I sense thrumming through him, his pale green eyes never waver from me—a kind of steely focus that he didn't have when I knew him before.

"Show me where my brother is," he says.

I consider the determination in his expression and his unrelenting grip on my hand.

"Okay, then," I say. "Come with me."

CHAPTER THIRTY-FOUR

I stride toward the door of my cabin, my eyes rapidly adjusting to the afternoon sunlight pouring across the porch.

Lucas overtakes me and prowls ahead, scanning our surroundings before he pauses in the doorway, blocking the way.

The brightness of the sunlight to the right of the door indicates that Clara is probably waiting for us on the porch, since the sunlight is never brighter than when she's nearby.

When I first arrived here, I had trouble seeing beyond my cabin's door, but my eyesight has adjusted over the last two weeks, and now I can make out the children playing in the gardens beyond my home.

I'm about to step around Lucas when his arm circles my waist, wrenching me back into the room. I gasp as my back presses against his chest, the hard planes of his torso and thighs like a wall behind me.

"Are you fucking crazy?" he snarls into my ear as he drops his cheek to mine. "You were about to step into the sunlight."

I guess it's strange that I don't even think about it anymore. Sunlight isn't as frightening to me as it once was. I trust the dryads and their control over the overhead canopy to keep me safe.

"It's okay," I manage to say as his arms continue to squeeze so tightly around my waist and ribs that I'm in danger of discovering once more how unrelenting his strength is. "The dryads' magic protects me. You'll see if you let me go."

He doesn't release me. His fingers splay across my waist as he lifts his cheek from mine, his eyes narrowed at the brightness of the porch and beyond it.

I'm suddenly aware of the stillness of the dryad children.

They've stopped playing and have turned toward us, each of them seeming paused in the middle of what they were doing—some hovering over new, simplistic plants they must have been creating, others stopping mid-step where they chased each other around the gardens.

They're suddenly all staring at us where Lucas grips me in the doorway.

"Do you trust them?" Lucas asks, his voice lowered.

"I do."

He makes a low hum in the back of his throat, as if he's unhappy with my answer. "Don't expect me to trust them so easily."

I spin in his arms, grateful when he eases up enough to let me face him.

"Then trust me," I say, taking a step back toward the porch, tugging him with me.

His eyes are still narrowed at me, his gaze flicking between me and the veranda, his shoulders and biceps tensing when I take another step. One more will see me move into the sunlight.

He braces but doesn't try to stop me when I step outside.

The canopy immediately casts me into shadow, and he lets out an audible breath when I remain there, unharmed.

Just as I anticipated, Clara is waiting for me in the bright rays of sunlight a few paces away.

"Lucas has a lot to learn," she says, her tone more judgmental than I was expecting.

He follows me onto the porch, his gaze raking over her. "You must be the wisp."

I'm surprised he recognized her power so quickly, since it took me a while to work out what she is.

She inclines her head. "And you're the brother."

The brother? It's a strange way to greet him.

The tension in the air between them is palpable, and I narrow my eyes at both of them, finding their exchange unexpectedly hostile.

Weirdly so, given that Lucas is a big guy and Clara is so little, and yet, it feels like she wants nothing more than to pick a fight with him.

"Lucas, this is Clara," I say carefully, wrapping my hand around his bicep, gauging the tension in his muscles.

"Right." He continues to glare at her. "You can't trust a wisp."

I thought the same thing when Aiden first told me we should follow the light along the creek. I didn't know much about will-o'-the-wisps then—only that their intentions were either genuinely kind or positively evil. They are never in between.

Clara arches an eyebrow at Lucas. "Just as you can't trust an Unknown."

Oh-kay. The instant hatred between them was unanticipated, but I've allowed this conversation to go on for long enough. Not to mention I'm beginning to bristle myself—since Aiden is also Unknown and he proved himself to be completely trustworthy. At least, to me.

Attempting to cut through the friction, I say to Clara, "I'm taking Lucas to see Aiden."

"Then I should come with you," she says, but I stop her.

"This is something we should do alone," I say, firmly.

Clara holds her head high, her skin glowing in the afternoon light. "If you wish. But I'm here if you need me."

When we leave her behind and make our way through the garden toward the north, I draw Lucas closer. "What the hell was that about?"

The scowl hasn't left his face. "Wisps always have another agenda," he says. "You need to be careful."

"How do you know that?" I ask, as we pass the group of children, who have resumed playing in the garden. "Have you met one before?"

He shrugs. "No, but—" He pulls up short, wincing, his hand flying to the wound at the side of his head. "Fuck, that hurts."

My grip on his arm tightens as I rise up onto my tiptoes to examine his head again. "You should be resting. Maybe we should go back. We can do this tomorrow."

His forehead is creased, a pained glint in his eyes, but he pins me with his glare all the same. "I need to see my brother."

"I understand," I murmur, acquiescing, since I was just as determined to see Aiden when I first woke up here, too. "This way."

I lead Lucas along the path until the canopy above us is knitted together so completely that the shadows are thick and dark. My feet move quietly across the moss-covered ground as I navigate around the white toadstools.

Finally, we reach the wash of vines decorated with little flowers that obscure the entrance to the life waters. The beautiful cascade of colors takes my breath away as surely as it does each day. I never get tired of seeing it.

"Aiden is in here," I say, pausing at the entrance. "But I want you to be prepared."

Lucas levels his gaze with mine. "I lived with a fucking demon for the last ten years. I can handle whatever's going on with my brother."

"Okay, then." I pull aside the vines and step into the circular clearing.

The enormous tree resting on the far side seems larger than ever, its branches thick and strong, and its leaves glistening in the light of the toadstools reflecting off the silver water.

Lucas freezes beside me, his focus immediately on his brother's still form, floating in the middle of the pond. The darkness gathered around Aiden's body obscures his features, but his silhouette is distinctly his.

My heart squeezes like it always does to see him lying there.

Other than last night, I've been able to keep my emotions under control for the last two weeks—tried to distance myself from the pain —but standing here with Aiden's brother brings home to me the fact that I have no guarantees that Aiden will wake up anytime soon.

Lucas lurches forward. "How the fuck did this happen?"

He doesn't wait for my answer, striding toward the water. I race after him, grabbing his arm. "Stop. Don't go near him."

Lucas ignores me, plowing onward, nearly lifting me off my feet. "That's my brother, Iyana. I'm getting him out of there."

"Lucas! You can't go in!" I shout, attempting to dig in my heels.

He turns on me, gripping my waist so that, suddenly, he's the one restraining me. "Why the fuck not?"

I'm about to tell him that the water will kill him, but then I realize it won't. He's Unknown. Magically repressed like Aiden. I actually have no idea what the water will do to him.

Aiden was unconscious when he was placed in this water—at least I assume he was, since I didn't actually see it happen. But I know his heart stopped before then. Clara said only one person can lie in the life waters at any given time, but I don't know what will happen if Lucas goes in there, too.

"All I know is that *that* water kills ordinary living things," I say, planting my hands on Lucas's bare chest, trying to avoid his wounds and failing.

He barely seems to notice that I'm pressing on the cuts. In fact, since he woke up, he hasn't once checked his own wounds. Other than talking about his head wound, he hasn't complained about the pain much, either.

He grits his teeth and his muscles tense, his hold on my waist relentless. "I don't fucking care. That's my brother."

A shiver runs down my spine as I remember what Clara told me about supernaturals who are magically repressed—they're more dangerous once they control their powers; then they should be feared.

I never really turned my mind to Lucas's power before, but whatever he's destined to become, it's bound to be something scary as fuck.

"I understand how you feel," I start to say, trying to figure out how to describe the danger to him.

At that moment, a leaf falls from the canopy above the pond, its small, green form twisting in the darkness as it floats downward.

"Look," I say. "Watch what happens."

The leaf drops to the surface of the pond near the water's edge, more easily visible because of the nearby toadstools. The contact is quiet, calm, but then the water bubbles, the leaf curls, and it begins to disintegrate before it disappears completely.

"Do you see? You can't go in," I say, glaring up at Lucas.

He remains tense, but he doesn't try to fight me again, shifting his balance and planting his feet.

"What happened to him?" he asks, his focus remaining on Aiden while he continues to hold me tightly, the hard lines of his chest and thighs pressed up against me. "How did Aiden get here?"

I start with our journey through the forest, the way we followed the creek, but I leave out the part where Clara's light guided us, since Lucas distrusts her. "When we finally found the dryads' home, they protected themselves. They knocked both Aiden and me out. I woke up in my cabin and Clara brought me here to show me that Aiden is okay. He's... sleeping for now."

"Why?" Lucas asks. "What's wrong with him?"

"Nothing's wrong. He's fine... but he's more like you than you thought."

Lucas's forehead creases. "Aiden and I are not alike. We never have been."

"I know it's a surprise," I say. "It was to me, too, but Clara said his power hasn't fully manifested. Once these waters draw out Aiden's power, he'll finally wake up in the form he's meant to take."

It sounds simplistic. Fantastical and unreal, almost. Waiting for Aiden to wake up is the reason I'm still here with the dryads.

Lucas's expression is unreadable. Distant somehow. He's impossibly quiet for a very long moment. Then he releases me—directing me slowly to the side—to begin a prowl around the pool and back.

He stops a few paces away, dangerously close to the edge. His hands are relaxed at his sides, but his fingers twitch, a muscle in his jaw clenches, and he fixes me with his now-shadowed gaze. "This water could draw out my power?"

I follow the tense lines of his bare chest, the quick rise and fall, and the way his gaze flickers across the pond.

"Don't do it, Lucas," I say. "Aiden's heart was stopped before he could be put in there. It could kill you."

"But it's worth the chance," he says, his jaw clenching again. "All my life, I've wondered what power I'm meant to have. Banta kept promising that it would be revealed after I turned twenty, but it hasn't." He shakes his head, a harsh movement. "I'm a nobody. Worse, an outcast."

He breaks my gaze, his muscles visibly tense again.

Stepping toward the water, he says, "I have to try."

CHAPTER THIRTY-FIVE

"*N*o!" I launch myself forward, tackling Lucas, my arms closing around his waist as I attempt to propel him back from the water's edge at an angle.

He loses his balance, his foot catches on something—a toadstool, most likely—and we go down together.

His arms fly around me as he hits the mossy ground heavily on his side. One of my legs is squished between his, but his shoulder is angled beneath mine so that I drive the air out of his chest when I land on him.

Damn! The impact jars through me, but I'm more worried about whether or not I've broken any of his ribs.

"Lucas?" I scramble to lift myself high enough to see his face and check him over, relieved to discover that he doesn't seem to have any new injuries.

He flops back onto the ground as I stare down at him.

"I am so fucked-up," he whispers, staring at the canopy overhead.

My hair falls past my face and onto his chest, where my hands are planted. "Yep," I say. "You really are."

He closes his eyes, but when I make a move to push myself up into a sitting position, his arms tighten around me.

"I think you were right," he says. "I should have stayed in your cabin. My head feels like it's about to fucking explode."

"Let's get you back there, then."

Still, he doesn't let me get up.

"Lucas?"

His eyes crack open just the barest. "You can put this down to my headache, since my judgement is currently impaired, but I'm never going to say this if I don't get it out now."

He pauses and I wait for him to go on.

"Aiden is fucking lucky," he finally says.

I understand Lucas's frustration. Not only does he not know what his power is, he has no way to make it manifest.

Right now, Aiden seems to have all the luck. Not that lying asleep in a pool of sparkling liquid is really that lucky.

I fight the need to look in Aiden's direction, fight the way my heart squeezes again.

"You'll discover your power when the time is right," I say to Lucas.

His eyes open fully and his hands stroke down my back. "Fuck, Iyana. I'm not talking about my power. I'm talking about *you*. He's lucky to have you."

I draw back a little, suddenly aware of how I'm lying on top of Lucas—in a way that could be misinterpreted.

Lucas is Aiden's younger brother, and I never really got to know him, but I considered him to be something like family, for the simple reason that he's *Aiden's* family.

Every time Lucas has touched me since he woke up, I've assigned platonic explanations to his actions—surprise when he grabbed my wrist, regret when he applied the ointment on it, worry when he stopped me from stepping into the sun, and falling just before was an accident, but now...

His fingers stroke through my hair, pushing the long strands back from my face, while his focus shifts to my lips, and the growing heat in his eyes is undeniable.

It's not that he isn't attractive.

Hell, the changes to his physique—the sculpted muscles and visible physical strength are sexy as fuck—but my heart isn't racing, and my body doesn't feel warm like it does when Aiden touches me.

If anything, I feel colder.

"You're right," I whisper. "It must be your headache talking."

I test his hold by gently pushing backward, needing to put distance between us.

He lets me go and I slip to the side, kneeling beside him and trying to remain matter-of-fact. "Let me help you up. You can lean on me."

He doesn't reject my offer. After accepting the arm I slip around him, his focus rises to the top of the cavern. "That's the weapon, isn't it?" he asks.

I don't need to turn around to know he's talking about the dagger entwined in vines above us.

"It is," I say.

He stiffens in my arms. "Why haven't you taken it? Why not come after Banta before now?"

I hear the accusation in his voice. With that dagger, I could have cut Banta down. I could have invaded his compound and freed Lucas weeks ago.

My response sounds empty to my own ears. "I can't get to it—"

"That's fucking bullshit." His arm encloses me again and he pulls me so close that I have to tip my head back to see his face.

His pale green eyes appear silvery in the light from the pond. Whatever pain he was feeling moments ago, it seems to have disappeared.

"The weapon is right there for the taking," he says.

My jaw clenches. "The dryads have guarded that dagger for hundreds, if not thousands, of years. It isn't a simple dagger, and taking it won't involve merely plucking it from the vines."

"How do you know that?" he challenges me.

"Clara said—"

"Fucking Clara." He releases me to pace around the water's edge again, his footsteps hard, his voice betraying frustration. "You should have taken that dagger weeks ago."

I grind my teeth, needing to defend my choices. "Not until Aiden wakes up."

Lucas's shoulders are tense, and his fingers tap his thigh as he draws to a stop a few paces away from me. In the silvery light, his chest somehow appears even larger than before, his muscles more sculpted.

He narrows his glittering eyes at me. "Aiden always comes first, doesn't he?"

I'm struggling to keep my own anger at bay now, fueled by his insinuation that I don't care about anyone else. "I won't apologize for loving your brother."

"*Love?*" Lucas asks. "If you loved him, you wouldn't have let him believe you were dead all those months."

"I couldn't..."

I couldn't leave Hidden House.

I was in pieces when Tristan took me to Helen. My body was wrecked. My mind was shattered.

I didn't exaggerate when I told Tessa that it took Helen six months to reconstruct my face and my body.

I had just reached a place where I was ready to step back out into the world when Tessa came into my life and then... she needed me.

She gave me purpose and a new place in life.

She welcomed me into her pack. A pack made up of women who care about each other and don't judge each other—and Cody, who lost his wolf and knows what it means to rise from the ashes.

Lucas advances on me. "Couldn't what, Iyana?"

I stand my ground. "We should head back to my cabin. You need to rest."

He catches my arm before I can turn, gripping my upper forearm. "Where were you all that time?"

I attempt to harness my patience. I've forgiven him for his blunt questions up until now because he's hurt and clearly having trouble controlling his emotions. Which isn't surprising if Banta has been messing with his head for weeks.

But I draw the line at revealing anything about Hidden House. "I can't tell you that."

"Can't," he murmurs, dropping my arm and taking a step back. "Or won't."

He presses his lips together before he turns back to the weapon with a harsh declaration. "Don't expect me to wait as long as you have. Banta's hurting people every day because of you. He's hurting others while hunting for you."

My heart sinks. I assume Lucas is talking about himself being hurt, but then he says, "Banta won't give up. He may have kept me alive for future leverage over Aiden, but he isn't so generous with his other captives. The day before I escaped, he brought in a woman and shot her—killed her—right before my eyes to prove how far he'll go to find you. He has a plan for you. He wants you for something—"

He shot a woman.

I don't hear anything else Lucas says. A shudder racks my body and a feeling of dread settles in my stomach. "Who was she?"

Lucas takes another look at me, a quick assessment. "I don't know," he says. "I'd never seen her before. But she was carrying this."

He reaches into his back jeans pocket.

As the small square card comes into view, the cavern tilts and my stomach heaves.

No... That can't be...

The card depicts a heart stabbed through with a dagger. It's the twin of the card I keep in my own back pocket—the heart torn apart.

Luna and Lydia have matching decks of cards.

Luna gave me her heart card, but Lydia...

Darling, strong Lydia, who is Luna's voice... She still had her heart card when I left.

Not anymore.

CHAPTER THIRTY-SIX

I can't stop the cry rising into my throat.

Shot and killed. Shot and killed...

I stumble backward, clutching my stomach, unable to remain standing.

Lucas reaches for me. "Iyana?"

Tessa and the others must have been looking for me. Luna and Lydia would have been trying to use their magic to find me.

Banta must have taken control of Lydia somehow and then he...

A wail tears from my chest. I slap my hand over my mouth, but it's too late to stop my cry.

Too late to stop Banta from killing Lydia.

Lucas's silhouette is a blur through my tears—freezing-cold tears, as cold as the nosebleed I had last night. He approaches me at a steady pace, looming over me where I crouch.

"Iyana?" He's still holding the card and it's all I see when he reaches for my shoulder, the thick, bloodied paper pressing against my upper arm as he wraps his fingers around my skin. "Did you know her?"

I curl downward, coiling into a ball, but he extends his arms around me and for a second, I forget that he isn't Aiden.

For a blessed moment, I feel warm, until the expanse of his chest presses to mine when he pulls me back to my feet.

And then I feel cold again. Too cold.

He grips my chin in one hand, my arm in the other, forcing me to look up at him. "The only way to stop Banta is to take that dagger. Until you have it, he will keep on killing."

I try to breathe, try to think. Try to remember why I haven't taken the dagger before now.

Fuck knows, I've plotted a path to it so many times over the past two weeks. I could have taken it if I really wanted to.

Yet... My instincts told me not to.

How can I justify my fucking useless instincts now?

Lucas's grip tightens. "You care about Aiden. You're worried that the dagger is surrounded with spells that could hurt him—or you. But there are other people out there getting hurt, Iyana. Your friends, whoever they are—they're in danger. Banta has more captives. He boasted to me about it."

Even Tessa and Tristan weren't sure that they would be immune to Banta's power. If he has control of them... Or control of Helen... Even control of Ella Griffin... Or Maeve with her magic... All of the women whose power I've been seeing in the flowers Drina has created. With them under his control, nobody would be able to stand against Banta Sol.

"You have to take the dagger," Lucas says, compelling me to believe him. "If I could take it, then I would, but there's no way I'd make it up to that branch without any power to my name. Do it *now*, Iyana. Take it and we'll go. We'll fight Banta Sol. Side by side."

He releases my chin so that he can point at the weapon, his voice vehement and thick with determination. "That dagger is the only weapon that can kill Banta Sol. We'll take revenge for Lydia's death and take back your freedom."

I tip my head back, my dark hair swaying. The dagger hangs so high above us—and yet, it's right there. The power to defeat the demon is so close. Such a simple weapon. But Clara's warning rings in my ears. *Water isn't water. A dagger isn't a dagger.*

I listened to her willingly, believed her warning, and took it to heart. But... to what extent was I willing to use her warnings as an excuse? To what extent have I been allowing my real fear to rule my decisions? A fear that is so much deeper than any concern about Aiden's safety.

Banta Sol beat me once. Very badly.

I'm afraid of *him*.

It doesn't matter how strong I've made myself. How strong I was, or how strong I could be.

He has the power of fear over me. More than my body or my mind, he controls my fear—and it's paralyzing.

By taking the dagger, I would be taking my first step toward him and into danger, not away from it.

My breathing is shallow and sharp, my ears are buzzing, and my arms and legs are barely under my command as I take a step toward the water.

"You can do this," Lucas says, and I'm aware of him watching me closely as I take another step. "Take hold of your future."

My steps are wooden at first, but then more fluid, as I focus on my goal and clear my mind of everything else.

Get the dagger.

Only hours ago, I mentally planned the way up to it. I've run through it in my mind so many times that I don't even need to think about it now.

Bursting into a sprint, I run around the edge of the water toward the tree, my footsteps quiet and sure as I build up momentum.

As I hit the closest safe point to the tree, I leap with all of my strength, the life waters glittering below me.

My arms stretch upward, reaching for the lowest branch, ignoring the water I'm jumping across and the danger of not making it.

I can make it.

My hands close around the branch and I swing myself up onto it, sensing the air whoosh around me as I land and straddle the thick bough.

Catching my breath, I focus on the next branch and the distance up to it. I don't have the benefit of a starting sprint this time, but I tell myself that I'm as light as air. That I can make this jump, too.

Balancing carefully, I bend my knees and push off, my hands reaching and closing around the branch I'm aiming for.

This time, I use my momentum to swing off that branch onto the next highest one.

Just when I think I'm going to make it, my palm slips against the rough bark, and I grapple to find a hold, desperately swinging my leg up toward it.

I grunt with effort and, somehow, I manage to gain enough lift to make it up and over the branch.

Stopping there, I take deep breaths and try to shake off the near miss. My hands are trembling and I fight the breeze around me—the empty space that beckons me down into the water—but I remind myself that I'm safe.

I close my eyes and focus on my next move.

I only need to make one more jump to a branch that sits a little higher up and to the right of my current position. It hangs at a level below the bough from which the dagger is suspended. That bough is too high and too much a part of the protective canopy for me to risk ascending onto it in case I'm exposed to the sunlight above its leaves.

My plan is to make a leap for the dagger from the lower branch, then land on one of the surrounding branches on my way down—assuming I can jump far enough.

The life waters glitter below me—a shiny mass—and they may as well be death waiting for me to fall into them.

Even from this angle, I can't make out Aiden's features. I tell myself that the time of waiting for him to wake up has passed. Lucas is right. I can't let Banta hurt another person I care about.

Gritting my teeth and focusing, I rise to my feet, get my balance, and picture myself making the jump to the next branch.

The air leaves my lungs as I launch myself up and to the right. My hands close around the bough and I swing myself up and over it, my chest now heaving with effort—but my focus is only on the dagger.

From here, I need to shimmy along this branch to get as close as I can so I can make the jump to the dagger.

My palms itch with the need to wrap my fingers around it, and I find myself crouching, balancing, and carefully making my way along the thick bough, hoping it doesn't break beneath me.

As I approach the dagger, it seems to gleam brighter, the light from the pond reflecting up across it.

The weapon is as simple as it seemed from the ground.

It has what appears to be a steel blade, although I'm surprised to see that the handle also looks to be made from metal, not wood.

The handle is possibly gold, although it seems odd that it would be fashioned from two different metals, but the gilded appearance is unmistakable between the vines that hold it in place.

Despite how sharp the blade appears, it doesn't seem to cut through the vines that twist so tightly around it.

I study the foliage as carefully as I can, although I'm too far away to make out the fine detail. These vines appear smooth, without any fiery fronds on their surface, but they shimmer, as if a child threw glitter on them in random colors.

Peering at them across the distance, it occurs to me that maybe these vines have a metallic substance in them, which allows them to hold on to the sharp blade without breaking.

The jump is farther than it looked from the ground. Even if I make it, the chances of me *not* plummeting into the life waters are slim. And now that I've seen how tightly the vines hold the dagger, I'm not convinced I'll be able to rip the dagger from them, either.

It's only when I glance all of the way down to the water's edge that I realize how far up I've come.

Lucas stands waiting, both arms slightly raised as if he instinctively reached out to catch me when I nearly fell before. The tension in his chest and shoulders is visible, even from here.

I slip my hand into my back pocket to brush the card resting inside it.

I'm convinced that Luna saw this dagger, that she caught a glimpse of my future. If only she had also seen the danger to her sister.

I have to do this for Lydia. No matter what it takes.

Just as I'm about to rise up on the branch—the soles of my feet tingling against the rough bark—my instincts prickle.

Wait... Lydia. Before I started ascending the tree, I'm sure that Lucas called her by name.

But I didn't tell him her name.

So... how does he know it?

Pausing, I peer down at him, suddenly asking myself again—could he be under Banta's control? But if he is, why would he urge me to take possession of the weapon that I could use to kill Banta?

I must have cried Lydia's name when Lucas first told me she was killed.

Shaking off my misgivings, I tell myself to focus. Calming my breathing, I make myself aware of each strong muscle in my body and tell myself I can make this jump.

Bracing, I bend my knees, harness my strength, and—

"Stop!" A girl's voice cracks through the cavern like a whip. "Iyana! Don't do this!"

I wobble on the branch, nearly lose my balance, and crouch to its surface again, whirling to face the cavern's entrance below.

What the hell?

Drina races through the curtain of vines, her small legs pumping and her dark hair gleaming red, as if it's streaming with rubies in the silver light.

Despite her cry to me, her focus is on Lucas.

His back is to me now and I can't see his face, but the muscles in his torso are coiled. His shoulders are hunched slightly, his feet planted as he braces as if to tackle her.

As Drina runs, a ball of light forms in her palm, its edges uneven, a concentration of crimson flames that seem to be crammed into the small sphere she raises above her head.

It's just like the will-o'-the-wisp light that Clara creates.

I jolt because that shouldn't be possible. Drina is a dryad—Clara said she was. A dryad doesn't have the power of a wisp.

It looks like she's running at Lucas, about to hurl the ball of light at him, but at the last moment, she veers to the right and flings the light across the pond instead.

"Wake up!" she screams, her voice piercingly shrill.

The ball of light bounces like a skipping stone across the pond's surface—a blaze of fire that hits Aiden's chest and explodes along his torso, lighting up every inch of his body.

Suddenly, I can see all of him, every part of his body surrounded by the crimson flames that continue to burn around him like fire on the surface of an oily lake.

His dark hair is longer than it was before, swirling in the water around his head. His expression is perfectly composed; his eyes are closed, his lips relaxed, but the angles of his face and body are sharper.

His arm muscles are more pronounced, his chest broader, his thighs bigger—as if that were even possible—so much bigger that the material of his pants has split in places, and his shirt has busted at the seams and barely clings to his shoulders.

Dear fuck. What's happening to him?

Without realizing it, I drop to the branch and reach for him, as if I can touch him from here, my arm extending down through the air, my fingers grasping nothing more than emptiness.

Despite Drina's scream—despite the fire raging around him—Aiden doesn't stir, and suddenly, my heart is pounding.

All I want is to leap down to him, scream at him until he wakes up, but I swallow the cries rising to my throat and wrench my attention back to the water's edge.

Drina is only a few paces from Lucas's position now. She raises her little hand above her head again, and another ball of light grows in her palm, but Lucas doesn't wait for her to throw it.

Lurching forward with an angry roar, he tackles her, swinging her off her feet.

Shock spears through me when he lifts her above his head, only to throw her onto the mossy ground so savagely that her body bounces, skipping across the ground like her firelight did.

"Lucas!" I scream. "What the hell?"

He spins, his jaw clenched. "She's with Banta! He must have corrupted her. She's trying to stop you."

My head spins, trying to make sense of it. "No... That's... Not possible."

Is it?

The memory of every meeting I've had with Drina flashes back to me.

Nearly every day, I saw her kneeling beside a new flower—purple roses, white sunflowers, flowers she said she couldn't control because their hearts were in cages.

And each time, they reminded me of people I love, tugging at my heart in different ways.

I told her to set herself free. To be wild. Now here she is, running at a man who may have the strength of a human but is twice her size.

Behind Lucas, Drina rises to her feet, uncurling slowly, and it's like she herself is a flower opening up to the sun.

I gasp when she grows taller with every inch she rises.

Her curves fill out, her arms and legs grow, and it's like watching a child become an adult within the space of seconds. It's so fast that her clothing tears and pulls across her chest and hips, her long pants splitting up the sides and her shirt tearing across her ribcage.

She raises her head and throws back her shoulders, her crimson-streaked hair falling down her back.

Her eyes are the same deep gray as before, her lips the rose-bud shape of the other dryads, but she glows around her edges.

She is as ethereal and as beautifully proud as Tessa.

Blood drips from a cut across her forehead and a graze extends down her right arm where she hit the ground, but her chest rises with a deeply indrawn breath as if she's breathing freely for the first time in a long time.

As she exhales, her whisper carries all the way through the air, across the water and up through the branches below me, to my position.

"You were right, Iyana, and I want to thank you," she says with a faint smile on her lips. "To set myself free, I just needed to be a little wild. Well, this is as wild as a wisp can be."

CHAPTER THIRTY-SEVEN

*W*ho *is* she?

She calls herself a wisp, but I'm struggling to believe that this woman, whom I thought was a dryad, is really a will-o'-the-wisp and has now transformed herself from the shape of a child into an adult.

I shake my head in disbelief.

Without waiting for a response from me, she turns on Lucas, her height now nearly equal to his, while light grows around both of her palms—burning crimson flames packed into spheres.

She takes up an attack pose, her back foot planted securely on the mossy ground.

The corners of her mouth turn down, her voice carrying clearly to where I continue to balance on the branch. "Iyana and Aiden are under my protection. You will not use them for your purposes any longer."

My forehead creases, my hands are shaking, and my head is buzzing. Confusion is not my friend and right now, I have so much of it that I nearly rock on the spot.

What the fuck is going on?

Lucas takes a step back from the woman who now stands in front of him.

He holds his hand toward me, beseeching me to hear him. "Don't listen to her, Iyana. She isn't here to protect you. She's here to make sure you stay weak. She wants Banta to control you."

My chest heaves as I focus from one of them to the other and then, as I try to make sense of everything, my gaze lands on Aiden lying within the water.

Aiden is the reason we came to the dryads' home. He told me the tree folk had a weapon that could kill any supernatural.

I trust Aiden. I do.

But...

Banta was the one who told Aiden that the weapon exists. Banta was the one who sent Aiden to find it seven months ago. Then Clara was the one who led us here, where the dryads stopped Aiden's heart and put him in the life waters. Clara was the one who told me that the dagger hanging from this cavern was the weapon we were seeking. She told me the story about it being the heart of Vulcan's son— revenge for the death of his secret love, Theia.

And now, Lucas is trying to make me take the dagger, and Drina is telling me not to.

But how do I know if *anything* I've been told is true?

I clench my fists so hard that my fingernails bite my palms. For the first time in weeks, my fangs descend in anger.

With sudden, heartbreaking clarity, I realize that I can't trust anyone right now. Not Lucas. Not Drina. Not the dryads. Not Clara. Not even... Aiden, because he acted on information that Banta gave him.

I only have myself and my own choices. For right or wrong. Better or worse.

I take a step along the branch. Away from the weapon. Needing to trust my instincts.

"Iyana!" Lucas roars at me. "Take the fucking dagger. *Now!*"

I draw a deep breath. "Or what?" I ask, my voice strong and clear, carrying in the sudden silence. "What will happen if I don't?"

Even from this height, I don't miss the slight narrowing of Lucas's eyes, the clench of his fists.

He stares up at me for a very long moment.

The longer he takes to respond, the more tense Drina seems to become, two perfect spheres of light growing in each of her palms so that she now holds four of them.

Mere paces away from her, Lucas purses his lips, and clicks his tongue at me, his expression cold and hard.

His demeanor changes so fast that it takes my breath away.

"Fuck," he says, his lips twisting with contempt. "I tried everything. Guilt. Remorse. Loyalty. I even flirted with you. But you're too fucking stubborn. You just don't know what's good for you, do you?"

He raises his hand toward me, and I sense a strange tug on my torso, the slightest jolt, as if an invisible hand plucked at me, forcing me onto my front foot, a step closer to the dagger again.

"You will either take it, or I'll *make* you take it," Lucas calls. "It's your choice."

Drina immediately draws back her hand, preparing to let her magic loose. "I won't let you hurt her!" she cries.

Lucas turns to her, nonchalant in the face of the power she controls. "How do you plan to stop me?"

With a scream, she releases the two spheres she's holding in her right hand. The crimson fire blazes across the space between them, but, to my surprise, Lucas doesn't try to get out of the way.

The spheres hit his chest and a cry rises to my throat as I expect them to explode against him, but there's a flash and, somehow, each sphere glances off him.

My eyes widen when he grins back at Drina. "Was that your worst?"

She backs off a little, her face pale, the remaining two spheres circling around her left hand. "What are you?" she asks.

I'm asking the same damn question.

Lucas doesn't reply. He takes a step toward her while a fine object rises from his back pocket all on its own. It's so small that I wouldn't have noticed it except that it catches the light. At first, I can't make out what it is, and then it untwines. A coil of... rope, maybe?

It lifts higher and snakes slowly across the air as Lucas advances on Drina. She spins and throws the two remaining orbs across the pond, adding them to the fire already burning.

"Wake up!" she screams at Aiden.

Her voice chokes as the rope twines around her neck and her hands fly to it, trying to stop it from breaking her skin.

I nearly leap off the branch I'm crouching on. "Lucas! Stop!"

He doesn't seem to hear me, focused on Drina instead. "Kneel, wisp. Before I take off your head."

A line of blood appears around Drina's neck as she drops to her knees, gasping for breath.

"Stay there and you'll live," he commands her. She struggles against the rope but remains on her knees, tears streaming down her cheeks.

"Why are you doing this?" I scream at Lucas.

Finally, he looks up at me. "Because we need to be who we're destined to be."

He walks to the water's edge and stands close enough that the liquid laps dangerously close to his toes.

"There's no escaping it. No escaping our purpose." He tips his head to stare at me while the rope pulls tighter around Drina's neck. "Now, I'm going to tell you one last time," he says to me. "Take. The. fucking. Dagger."

He's desperate for me to retrieve this weapon and I don't know why. Can't even guess. Aside from concluding that he's fucking lost it.

I don't know who Drina really is—or whether or not she's my ally —but I won't stand by and watch her die. If Lucas wants me to take the weapon, then I will.

And then I'll use it to find out what the fuck is really going on.

Switching my focus to the dagger, I plot my path as I rise back to my feet, ready to take a running jump.

My heart pounds as I calculate the odds of succeeding. Not good. Best case, I reach the dagger and manage to land on the next tree branch. Worst case, I fall into the water without even touching the weapon.

My feet fly as I run.

My muscles stretch as I jump as high as I can, straining as I power through the air.

The tips of my fingers close around the dagger's handle and a jolt of electricity passes through me. I expected there to be resistance, but the vines immediately retract, their glittering lengths whipping outward.

The dagger is free.

Clutched in my fist.

And then I'm falling, but I'm nowhere near close enough to the next lowest branch. My back arches as I draw the dagger back, attempting to plunge it into the side of the nearest branch to stop my descent.

Instead, a force takes hold of me, tearing at my insides, ripping through me, twisting me to the side against gravity. At the same time, my hand burns where I grip the dagger, and a scream of agony passes my lips, torn from me.

My cry echoes around the cavern as I plummet toward the water's surface, falling directly toward Aiden. His fiery body rears up beneath me, parallel to mine so that I'm about to land face to face with him. I prepare myself for the impact. For landing in the fiery water with him.

With a wrench that nearly tears my limbs from their sockets, I halt midair, floating on the spot only inches away from him. Drina's light flickers around us both, the fire leaping upward and scorching the air I'm breathing. Through the haze, Aiden looks completely at peace.

I don't know why I stopped falling or what power is holding me up, but I don't have time to think about it because my hand is burning and it's beyond any pain I've ever felt—a searing sensation rocketing through my palm and up my arm.

My focus flashes to the dagger, afraid it's somehow caught fire.

The golden handle rests within my fingers, the silver blade pointing down at Aiden's shoulder. Through the fiery haze, the metal glints, feeling molten, as if the longer I hold on to it, the softer it gets and, suddenly, my fingers sink into it.

Fear strikes through me. I can't believe anything Clara told me now, but she might have uttered one truth: This dagger might not *be* a dagger.

I scream as the golden metal seeps through the gaps between my fingers, spreading like thick blood across my thumb.

Rapidly, the metal rushes across the back of my hand and my fingers. The blade begins to drip—but upward—the silvery substance streaming toward my hand.

I try to let go, try to shake it off, but it keeps coming, a liquefied mass engulfing my hand and slipping along my forearm until it stops halfway toward my elbow.

Within seconds, the dagger melts into my skin and I'm left holding... nothing.

No more dagger.

Somehow, I've absorbed the blade and handle into myself. My skin looks the same, unblemished, but I'm screaming with pain as the weapon's fiery metal fills my veins, shooting through my arm and across my chest, where I'm sure my heart will stop.

That's when I float upward within the same force that stopped my fall, my body becoming vertical once again and rising high enough that my feet rest above Aiden's chest, and then, I'm being turned so that I'm facing away from him.

I take another breath, trembling, sweat dripping from my forehead as my screams stop and silence falls around me.

Lucas crouches at the water's edge directly in front of me, his arm outstretched, deep concentration on his face. When he moves his hand in a pulling motion, I move with him, like a puppet on metal strings that he controls.

His arm looks as if it's made from bronze, the gleaming metal covering his skin from his fingertips to his elbow.

"Don't worry, Iyana," he says, with a smile of satisfaction. "I won't let you fall."

Lucas pulls me across the water's surface, and I float gently to the ground, where he allows me to drop to my hands and knees.

I stare up at his bronze arm, which he doesn't try to hide, following the muscles of his biceps, shoulders, and chest.

Oh. Fuck.

No wonder his grip was so firm every time he grabbed me.

"You're the Metalworker," I say, my heart in my throat.

He squares his shoulders and inclines his head in the affirmative. "I am."

CHAPTER THIRTY-EIGHT

*a*nger boils within me and my fangs descend as I glare up at Lucas. "You fucking traitor!" I snarl. "You betrayed Aiden. Your own brother. Hurt him. Tried to trap him."

Lucas takes a sharp step forward, drops to his knees, and grabs my chin in his bronze hand. His skin is cold—far colder than mine.

"I control *you* now, Iyana. Completely. Vulcan's dagger has assimilated into your body—your blood has become metallic once and for all—and the final step in your transformation is complete."

"*Transformation?*" I search his face for answers. "What fucking transformation?"

His lips rise into a smile that chills me. "I take it you haven't seen your own face for a while. I nearly didn't recognize you when I first got here."

My brow furrows. I remember the way he spoke my name when he knelt within the circle of vines—it sounded like a question, as if he were asking whether or not it was me.

He holds up his palm in front of me. His skin is perfectly clear and smooth, a shiny metallic surface. My reflection gleams back at me.

I don't know who I'm looking at.

My eyes glint like a cat's eyes in the night, all silvery and glassy, and the new growth of hair closest to my scalp is a pale color, as if I have naturally silver hair and I haven't kept up with dying the roots.

It's too close to my head to see without a mirror, even when I pull the strands to the front.

My eyelashes are pale and so is my skin—although my skin color is not entirely new. The only part of my face I really recognize is my lips—and my fangs as they peek from my mouth.

Lucas runs his thumb along my hairline. "Clara did her job well," he says. "I may fucking hate that wisp, but she sure did a number on you."

"Clara's working with you?" My fangs descend so suddenly that they cut my lip and blood drips to my chin.

"She works for Banta," Lucas says. "But unlike me, her mind is not completely her own."

I jolt, try to struggle, scream with frustration when I can't punch his fucking face. "What have you done to me?"

"Me?" His focus follows the drip of blood down my chin, but since he has control of my hands, I can't wipe it away myself. "I did nothing. You did it to yourself. Drinking from the life waters every day."

I jolt. "Those vines weren't…"

He arches an eyebrow at me. "Come on, Iyana. You ingested the very water that is transforming Aiden as we speak. The power of the life waters is not a lie. It worked on you to draw out your inner nature, just as it's working on Aiden."

He cups my cheek, a gentle contact as he leans in and licks the blood off my chin, his mouth cold as he works his way up to the curve of my lower lip. "Now, you're like putty within my power. I can make you do whatever I want."

To demonstrate his point, he pulls my arms around his chest, and I can't do a damn thing to stop myself before I'm plastered against him, my head tipped back.

He strokes my hair. Light strokes that make me shudder. "I did try to do this the nice way." He lowers his lips to mine, hovering close. "Maybe you'll decide it's a good idea to be nice to me, too."

His lips are cold when he drops them to mine, and I jolt backward, but his power grabs me and forces me to stay right where I am.

The longer he holds me, the more his skin is morphing, slowly turning into bronze, so that now I'm pressing against his chest, which is half-metal from his hip to the opposite shoulder, the other half flesh and blood.

"What do you want from me?" I ask.

"I want what I was destined to have," he says, dragging his metallic hand through my hair. "I want everything. Power. Control. *You*."

I glare into his eyes. "You'll never have control over your life as long as you follow Banta."

Lucas shakes his head, tut-tutting at me. "Don't try to turn me against Banta. He's the reason I got control of my power. Without him, I'd still be nobody."

I can't move my arms or legs. It's like I'm in a vise, but I narrow my eyes at his head wound—the one he used as an excuse multiple times to evade my questions earlier.

"You really fooled me," I say. "Making me believe that you cared about my safety when you thought I was stepping into sunlight. Making me believe you were upset about Aiden being here—that you'd walk into the life waters to get him out."

Lucas strokes my face, following the curve of my forehead, cheek-bones, and jaw, his touch making me shiver. "Your flaw is that you're too fucking kind, Iyana. You tried to protect me when I got here. You worried that I was hurt. You believed me when I told you I needed to see Aiden. You brought me right here to the dagger. You wanted to see the *good* in me." He draws back a little, his lips pressed into a contemptuous line. "But you should have learned by now. Kindness is weakness."

"I don't believe that."

No. Tessa, Helen, Ella, even Tristan, in his own gruff way, they all taught me that kindness is more powerful than anger.

"Then you'll never win," he says. "Whether it's your freedom or your power, or even your life." He snatches hold of my shoulders, his grip biting. "You'll always lose."

I test his hold on me, lifting my hand to his face, my movement jolting as he gradually permits me to move. My fingertips brush the burn mark at the side of his face. "If Banta's wraith didn't attack you, then who did?"

His self-satisfied smile fades. "Your friends came looking for you. They didn't take kindly to the idea that I might have killed you." He presses a finger to his forehead. "Your little witch friend packs quite a punch."

Maeve. Of course. It was her, not the wraith, who struck Lucas.

"And these?" I ask, running my fingertips across the defensive wounds on his arms, testing the extent to which he'll permit me to move freely—apparently, as much as I want, as long as I'm touching him.

"She called herself your alpha. Her wolf was like nothing I've seen before. But, of course, she and the others didn't realize they shouldn't have been wearing metal buttons or zippers." He grins. "Or underwire in their bras. It was easy enough to make her and her mate back off once I drew blood."

I shudder at the damage he would have caused. "What about Lydia?" I need to know if he was lying about the card mage's death, but I find it difficult to ask. "Is she really... dead?"

He smirks as he lowers his face to mine and whispers, "You'll never know."

"Fuck you, Lucas," I say, jolting back from him before his power tugs and stops me.

"Ana," he whispers, using Aiden's old name for me, apparently unperturbed by my cursing. "Stop fighting your obsessions. You need to be with me. You'll understand soon enough that you should embrace your purpose. You'll know your place as soon as Banta explains it to you."

"You're taking me to Banta, then?" I ask.

Lucas pulls me upward, his hands rough. "Banta's already here," he says, making my heart sink. "He's waiting for us. Come with me." He angles his head at Drina with a snarl. "You, too, wisp."

She has remained behind me, just out of view, while Lucas was holding me, but her ragged breathing told me she was alive. The loose ends of the wire around her neck tug up and toward the cavern's entrance and Drina hurries to comply, remaining a few steps behind us.

I'm slower to obey Lucas, testing his control over me now that he's standing a pace away. He simply crooks his forefinger and my body jolts toward him, my feet dragging through the moss before he lifts me off the ground.

"I can walk," I snap at him.

He leans in toward me, wrapping his hand around the side of my neck. "But I like carrying you."

Turning his back on me, he pulls me along after him.

I attempt to dig my heels in—without success. The fire on the surface of the pond is dying down; the light inside the cavern swiftly fading. "What about Aiden?"

Lucas stops so suddenly that I bump into him—which he doesn't seem to mind, his gaze raking down to my toes as he half-turns back to me and wraps his arm around my waist, grabbing me once again.

"Aiden is staying right where he is," Lucas says, hoisting me off my feet and pulling me along. "He's the reason your friends haven't been able to find you. As long as he lies in the life waters, his power spreads through every tree, even the damn earth, concealing your location."

Damn. I thought it was because the dryads' home was so well hidden. Anxiety rages through me. My situation is like Tessa's when she was held captive at the Spire. We couldn't find her until she emerged from behind its protected walls.

Lucas continues. "We won't allow you to wake Aiden up until we say so."

They won't allow *me* to wake him up?

Lucas's choice of words doesn't seem lost on Drina, either. She tried multiple times to rouse Aiden with no success. She takes a quick glance at me, but I can't imagine what she's thinking. Or what Lucas actually means.

My head hurts as if I've been thumped. I need answers. Real answers. Not bullshit innuendo and half-truths.

Only with answers can I figure out whom I can trust and how to escape.

CHAPTER THIRTY-NINE

*L*ucas carries me along the path away from the cavern and toward the central territory, while Drina stumbles behind us. I can't help but notice that when Lucas's back is turned, Drina's expression changes.

She watches him. Carefully. And the glow around her fingertips is unmistakable. She's gathering her power, although I'm not sure what she intends to do with it.

Overhead, the sunlight is fading. Sunset might only be an hour away now and the dryads will be slowing down.

I catch glimpses of them through the trees up ahead, and at first, everything appears normal, but then I notice how the children are gathered around one spot and the warriors stand in an arc to one side.

Clara waits next to the group of children, just slightly apart from them, her childlike body bathed in pale afternoon sunlight. Behind her are two new figures.

One of them is Toad, the snake shifter. He's an indistinct man of average height with light brown hair shaved on one side, brown eyes, and features that allow him to blend in with his surroundings. He's wearing forest-green pants and a khaki T-shirt and, even with the bright foliage around him, he seems to disappear into the background. Especially because he stands so still. The only part of him that moves is his tongue.

While his pupils vertically constrict, indicating that his snake is rising, his tongue darts out, tasting the air.

He gives me a wide grin and licks his lips, apparently appreciating my scent.

Standing beside him is a woman I've never seen before. She's tall and thin, but that's pretty much all I can tell since she's wearing a long cloak with a hood, along with boots. Her hands are the most visible part of her body, her fingers longer than usual, her fingernails pointed.

When we draw closer, I can finally make out the outline of her features—sharp cheekbones and dark eyes, along with strands of blonde hair beneath her hood.

She reaches beneath her cloak and procures a long, metal whip, handing it to Lucas as he veers toward her. "You asked for this, Lucas," she says, drawing out her 's' sounds in a soft hiss.

The whip is long, judging by how many times it's coiled around, and it appears supple. Its handle is bronze while the surface is silver, and a small blade sits at its end. I shudder to imagine the damage Lucas could do with it.

He takes the weapon and clips it onto his belt, before he turns me toward the children.

Banta Sol sits in front of them. He's also wearing dark green pants and a khaki T-shirt. Even dressed in camouflage clothing, his presentation is impeccable, his demeanor unsettlingly calm.

His silver-gray hair is swept back as majestically as always, although, when I look a little closer, I notice that his beard is a little less neatly cut than the last time I saw him.

His pale brown eyes are filled with a gentle glow as he speaks quietly to the children.

"So you see," he says to them, as they sit wide-eyed facing him, "you must do as I say or your forest will burn to ash. Do you understand me?"

They nod their heads while their parents stand stiffly beside the group of warriors. I note Sunflower standing behind Mahogany, who is in turn located beside Rye. Their expressions are drawn, their shoulders tense, and their lips pressed into hard lines, but they remain completely silent and still as Lucas approaches with Drina and me.

Banta turns to me without rising from his seat—a seat I quickly recognize as a freshly cut tree stump. It's one of the trees that stands between the Sunlight Stones and provides protection to the playing children.

Lucas's hold on me is loose enough right now for me to tip my head back and assess the damage to the overhead coverage.

It's definitely brighter without the tree—despite the sinking sun. I can't imagine what could have happened to the rest of the tree's trunk since it's nowhere to be seen. But I consider the ground very carefully, and the new patches of sunlight streaming through, now that the canopy is thinner.

"Iyana," Banta Sol says, greeting me like a gracious host. "I've been looking forward to seeing you again."

He considers me from my hair to my toes, a smile slowly growing on his face. "You look perfect. Clara did her work well. As soon as she sent word that you were experiencing nosebleeds, we knew that your blood had transformed, and it was time to act."

He waves us forward. "Lucas, bring Iyana closer."

I sense the force clamped around me tighten before Lucas propels me forward. My steps are awkward, stilted—like a robot that can't move properly—and Banta's brows furrow with displeasure.

"Perhaps she can move on her own," he says to Lucas. "Since I'm sure she can see what's at stake if she disobeys me." He gestures at the children. "I would hate to hurt them."

I grit my teeth, but my knees buckle when the force of Lucas's power eases and my body is my own again. I remain crouched, the fingertips of one hand on the ground, my other hand on my knee.

I don't expect Banta to tell me the truth, but I ask anyway. "Do the dryads follow you?"

His eyebrows rise. "Not by choice, Iyana. In fact, until this afternoon, none of them remember laying eyes on me." His smile remains gentle and unchanging. "But I can see that you're confused. Perhaps Clara can explain."

He eases back into his seat while Clara sweeps forward, circling me, her power glowing in her palms.

"I think you know already that there are two types of will-o'-the-wisps," she says. "The inherently good and the mercilessly evil." She points to Drina, who clutches at the rope around her neck, her fingers bleeding now.

"Drina is good," Clara says. "I am not."

She continues to circle me. "I replaced her seven months ago—right after you 'died.' But it wasn't an easy task. I wasn't lying when I told you that the dryads' hive mind is difficult to control on an ongoing basis. It *is* possible to remove a memory and replace it with a new one, since the memory of one is the memory of all."

She smiles at Banta and I spin to him, putting some of the pieces together. "You took away the dryads' memory of Drina and replaced it with Clara."

The demon looks pleased with himself. "I told them to forget Drina, and that if they ever saw her, to immediately forget her again. Then I told *Drina* to cage her power and forget who she was." He waves his hand dismissively. "And of course, they all forgot I was ever here."

I shudder. "You can take memories like that? By telling someone to forget a thing?"

His expression remains benevolent as he leans forward in his seat. "You don't remember everything about the night you attacked me, do you, Iyana?"

Fear ravages my mind. What memories did he take away? And what false memories could he have left in their place?

He finally rises from his seat and picks his way between the children, who remain right where they are.

"Oh, don't worry," he says, bending to me and patting my knee. "I only had time to take away one of your memories of that night before you ran for your life."

Crouching beside me, he pulls aside the neckline of his T-shirt.

Two puncture wounds scar the base of his neck.

"It was the moment that you bit me," he says, his fingernails digging into my knee, suddenly painful.

I need to punch him—or at least to try to see how strong Lucas's control of me really is.

"You nearly killed me," Banta rumbles. "But you did me a favor, because that was the moment I realized how valuable you are. The opportunity of a lifetime was right in front of me. Unfortunately, your venom slowed my heart so much that my lieutenants thought I was dead. If I had been awake, I would have ordered them to capture you at all costs. Not kill you. It wasn't until they returned—bloodied and injured, barely alive after their encounter with Tristan Masters—

that I regained consciousness. By then, you were long gone. There wasn't even a sign of your body."

"What do you want with me?"

He answers me with a question. "Do you ever think about who you were before a vampire changed you?"

I'm surprised by his question. The honest answer I could give him is... *Sometimes. Most often when the darkness presses in.* That's when I wonder what kind of life I had before a vampire stole it from me.

I harden my heart and shrug, as if it means nothing. "I was human. Mortal. I'm stronger as a vampire."

Banta leans in, his voice a whisper. "What if you weren't human?"

I recoil. "Of course, I was human! Vampires can only turn humans."

He tips his head, an acknowledgement of sorts. "Granted, but what if you were only... *mostly* human?"

I shake my head vehemently. "That's crazy."

"Is it? Have you ever looked into your past? Sought answers about your thirst for mercury?" he persists. "Ever looked for your family?"

I wanted to. I may have left behind a loving family—a spouse, a home. Parents. Siblings. Possibly even a child, since I was old enough to have children when I was turned—the age I'll remain for the rest of my life.

"No," I snap. "There was no point. Whoever I was—she was gone when I was turned. There's only pain in asking those questions."

Banta sits back on his heels. "That's a pity. I guess we'll never know why you are the way you are." He dismisses our conversation with a nonchalant shrug. "Never mind. You're here now. All is as it should be."

Standing and spinning to Lucas, he says, "Put her on the Sunlight Stone."

I jolt. "What?"

Above me, the angle of the light has changed, but it's still shining strong and the nearest Sunlight Stone is a bright, burning patch where the canopy won't shade me. The light will turn my body into ash.

I'm lifted off the ground as Lucas raises his hands, crossing the distance to me while I try to fight back.

"No! Lucas!" I cry as I thrash midair. "You were worried about me stepping into sunlight before—I can't believe that caring about me was all a lie. You can't do this!"

"Don't worry," he says, wrapping his arm around my waist and pulling me against his cold, metallic chest. "If we're right about your transformation, then you won't burn."

"*If* you're right?" I attempt to thump his shoulder, but he stops my arm mid-swing. "What if you're not?"

He makes a rumbling sound in his throat that vibrates against my cheek as he holds me closer. "Then you'll die in my arms."

"And you're okay with that?" I ask, feeling colder by the second now that I'm in direct contact with his metallic skin again.

Lucas doesn't answer me. Pauses. But he resumes his path toward the Sunlight Stone.

I'm facing the dryads now and Rye has taken a step toward me, his brows drawn down, his shoulders hunched. His fists unfurl and his fingers extend. The grassy surface beneath me suddenly shifts, new fern-green tufts spring upward, and I picture the vines he might be about to create.

Across the way, Banta casually takes the hand of one of the children—a little boy—and turns to stare at Rye, who freezes. At the same time, Toad and the wraith crowd inward. Toad's tongue flicks in the direction of the young ones. Rye's shoulders slump and the vines he was creating slip back into the earth.

I wish I could tell Rye that I understand.

I'm probably about to die a horrible death, but at least I finally know that I can trust the dryads and Drina—at least, to the extent that Banta doesn't control their minds.

It suddenly occurs to me that Banta hasn't tried to control *my* mind yet. He has left the control of me entirely up to Lucas. It could be because he wants Lucas to feel like he has power in this situation.

Or it could have something to do with the changes to my body.

It doesn't matter anymore. None of it does. Because no matter how hard I try to struggle, no matter the force with which I attempt to hit and kick Lucas, I can't free myself.

The Sunlight Stone is only two steps away.

I close my eyes. Breathe in the clean air. And I make a decision.

If I'm about to die, then I'll do it facing the sun. Hell, I'll soak up those rays. The first and last time in my remembered life when I'll have the chance to know what daylight feels like. Even if it rips the skin and flesh off my bones.

I relax in Lucas's arms, testing his willingness to allow me to tip my head back, sensing his power ease enough for me to arch back over his arm.

He takes the final step.

Burning sunlight pours down over me, and I embrace it.

CHAPTER FORTY

*T*he sun is warm. Gentle. A little too bright.

I blink rapidly as I peer directly upward, the dazzling circle in the sky nearly blinding me until I'm forced to look away. My bare shoulders and arms are bathed in golden light and it's... nice.

So this is what sunlight feels like.

It's impossible for me to process what's happening to my body— or rather, what has *happened* to my body—so that I can now stand in sunlight without burning.

I'm suddenly aware of Lucas's arms squeezing more tightly around me. He's shaking.

"Fuck." That's all he says before he lowers me to my feet on the Sunlight Stone and slides to the ground to take a knee, but his hands grip both of my hips in a possessive move. "You're the one."

I take a chance to place my hands over his, a gentle move that he won't suspect is really a test of his continuing hold over me. I complete the move freely, but I can't assume that my freedom will last long.

Across the way, the wraith has drawn nearer to Drina, who crouches low to the ground. The rope has fallen from Drina's neck, another indicator of how shaken Lucas currently appears.

"Thank fuck," he whispers, turning his piercing gaze up to me.

The intensity with which he's looking at me now unsettles me more than the fact that I'm standing in direct sunlight.

I could hope that his concern means he actually would have cared if I'd died, but judging by the twist of his lips and the force of his gaze...

He's looking at me now, not like I'm a person, but as if I'm a prized possession. Some kind of fucking obsession.

"Let me go, Lucas," I say. "I can't be part of whatever fucked-up plan Banta has for me."

"No." His hands slide up over my hips and under the base of my shirt as he returns to his feet. His grip tightens and I sense his power take hold of me again.

"Do you believe in destiny, Iyana?" he asks.

I shake my head, giving him an honest answer. "I really fucking don't."

"You should." He cups my cheek with his hand. He lets out a quiet, bitter laugh. "If only you'd met me before Aiden. You might have been drawn to me and not him." He shrugs. "Then this would have been a whole lot easier."

He takes hold of my wrist. "You're too important to ever be free, Iyana."

Bronze metal ripples across his hand and fingers before he draws his metallic fingernail along the vein on the inside of my wrist and then presses it deeply enough to cut me.

"No!" I struggle again, but it's impossible to stop him.

I watch in horror as my silver blood pulses from my arm.

Lucas pulls back his hand and every droplet rises with his movement—against gravity—floating in perfect harmony to the tune of his fingers. He spins my blood slowly in the air until the droplets start coming together in a small whirlwind.

Gripping my shoulder with his free hand, he pushes me to my knees—where his power keeps me—before he transfers his hand to my wrist, holding it high while he covers my wound. Apparently to stop the blood from continuing to flow.

The silver droplets that he already captured begin to form a shape as he concentrates on them.

I gasp when he slowly molds my blood into the profile of a blade.

"This is your purpose," he says.

Behind him, Banta creeps forward, watching us carefully, anticipation appearing to make him tense. "Your blood is the key to making the ultimate weapons, Iyana," he says. "Weapons we haven't seen in millennia. Shaped by the hands of Vulcan's descendant. But they can only be created from the most special blood."

I squeeze my eyes shut. Like a dagger made out of a living heart. "Clara told me the story—"

At the side of the clearing, Drina suddenly cries out. "It's a lie!" Her voice is husky from her throat injury and audibly strained as she tries to speak up. "Nobody knows the real story. Least of all that vile wisp."

Clara hisses at her, but Drina focuses back on me. "It's forbidden knowledge," she says, punctuating her speech. "The story was hidden to protect the world."

I return her stare without giving away the turmoil inside me. She may be a wisp—not a dryad, after all—but I'm certain she somehow created the book she gave me; the one with the images she said revealed forbidden knowledge.

She claims that nobody knows the real story, but I'm betting *she* does.

"Until you know what really happened to Vulcan, you have no idea of the power you're playing with," Drina says to Banta. "It's why the dryads have guarded the dagger for all existence."

The dagger that molded itself to my hand and sank beneath the surface of my skin.

Banta scoffs. "Be quiet, wisp. I know everything I need to know."

At Banta's command to stop talking, Drina's mouth immediately closes and she sinks to the ground, subdued again.

Banta strokes his beard. "I've been searching for the perfect weapon all my life. Hundreds of years. Seeking the descendants of Vulcan. I finally found Aiden and Lucas. One born with the power to create the Forge Fire, the other born with the power to mold metal into any shape. Together, they have the power of Vulcan to create the ultimate weapons."

He leans toward me. "But first, they need the perfect metal."

"Me," I say. "My blood."

My cruel blood.

"The rarest of vampires, who consumes heavy metal and metabolizes it. If Vulcan could make a dagger from the heart of his eldest son, then the power of Vulcan can create countless weapons from your blood. You were brought together by destiny, Iyana," Banta says, a fanatical light in his eyes. "You, Aiden, Lucas. All three of you... The perfect pieces at the right time."

I stare back at him, at the pure, zealous belief in his expression—and at the way Lucas seems to hang on his every word.

I can't deny that, for someone who believes the mythology of Vulcan, the fact that two brothers have these powers could be convincing.

Add in the fact that my blood was never 'normal' for a vampire and it gives Banta all the hope he needs. Taking the dagger and assimilating it into my body must have sealed the deal as far as Banta is concerned.

Banta lowers his voice. "With weapons made from your blood, I will slaughter any supernatural who stands in my way. Including your alpha, Tessa Dean, and her mate, Tristan Masters."

A retort rests on my tongue when Banta leans back, his focus shifting to Lucas again, and an edge of tension enters his voice—especially when it's apparent that, despite Lucas's extreme concentration, the edges of the blade he's making aren't quite coming together.

"Can you do it?" Banta asks, a sharp note entering his voice.

A muscle in Lucas's jaw tenses. His hold on my wrist tightens so much that I think he's going to break my bones before he shoves my arm away, hovering both of his hands around the weapon he's attempting to create.

The blade he's forming seems to be fighting him—my blood dripping away from it in places. Each time he gathers my blood back, droplets float away from another point on the blade.

"Fuck," Lucas snarls.

They're both so engrossed that I suddenly realize neither of them is watching me as closely as before, and the more Lucas struggles with his task, the more the force around me eases.

A soft object tickles my fingertips where my hand rests on the edge of the Sunlight Stone.

I keep my movements small, swiveling my gaze to see the tufts of greenery growing around the stone. From the corner of my eye, Rye and Mahogany are suddenly swaying a little and, at first, I have no idea what message they're trying to send me and then...

It hits me.

Their quiet, synced heartbeats.

The sound to which I've trained for the last two weeks.

Drina seems to hear it, too. Her eyes close across the clearing and her posture relaxes as she sways a little.

Behind Banta, the children have quietly gathered into a smaller group. They aren't swaying, but their little faces are very calm.

Clara is watching Drina with increasing intensity while Toad and the wraith are watching the children. Clara knows how efficient the dryads' vines are, but the other two might not have any idea.

I concentrate on breathing and listening.

Hearing the unhurried beat like a drum.

I don't know what the dryads are planning, but I'm sure as hell going to be ready to go with it.

CHAPTER FORTY-ONE

*B*anta lets out a rumble of discontent as he remains focused on Lucas. "We need Aiden."

"I can do this without him!" Lucas snaps. "I don't need my fucking brother."

Banta shakes his head, his tone remaining calm. "Listen to me, Lucas. Your power is only one half of the equation. We always knew Aiden's power might be required, too. After all, Vulcan used fire to begin forging his weapons. Iyana's blood is too cold to sculpt."

Lucas's angry eyes flash at me, as if it's my fault he has failed.

"Fuck it," he snarls.

He flicks his hand, and my silver blood splashes across the Sunlight Stone in front of my bent knees, covering the new tufts of grass, which immediately stop moving.

Lucas yanks me upright. "You will wake Aiden up, and you and he will both do what you're told."

Thud-thud. Thud-thud. The dryads' heartbeats are so steady in my hearing now that I nearly sway into Lucas; my body responding to the beat, the need to close my eyes and allow myself to move with the warriors.

"No," I say, calmer than before. "I won't help you."

Lucas pulls me toward him, forcing my arms around his chest. "I can make your life very unpleasant, Iyana."

"You're going to hurt me either way," I say.

When he—the Metalworker—captured me back at the warehouse, he told me that Banta was going to bleed me dry. I thought it was a random threat, not a literal one.

"You won't stop," I say. "You'll take all of me—every drop of my blood—and never give me my freedom."

If I could fight him like I would fight any other opponent, I wouldn't even bother with this conversation, but he has complete control of my limbs.

I meet his eyes, my own gaze defiant, as I allow my body to go limp, forcing him to hold me—use his power on me—if he wants me to stay upright. "You'll have to hurt me if you want me to do what you want."

He wraps his arms tightly around my back, one hand gripping the back of my neck. "What are you playing at, Iyana?" he asks, his face close to mine.

For perhaps the first time, I realize that he has no scent. Unlike the earthy wolf shifters, and the fiery fragrance Aiden carries with him, Lucas's skin is cold. Lifeless.

I focus on the pulse at his neck. Then I lick my lips, drawing his attention to my mouth as I allow my fangs to descend.

"Maybe I'm thirsty," I whisper. "You tasted good the last time I bit you."

My bite had caused his power to recede. It was during our escape from the warehouse.

"The fucking bite marks took two weeks to fade," Lucas grumbles, but I'm not listening.

I jolt toward him, the sudden change in my posture having the desired effect on him. He doesn't resume control of me in time and my fangs graze his neck. My purpose is to alarm him, not to bite him, but he doesn't know that.

With a roar, he shoves me away from himself. His strength is so great that he flings me beyond the Sunlight Stone. I tuck my chin and roll, my training kicking in to diminish the impact of the fall.

I slide to a stop at Rye's feet. The dryads' heartbeats thud through me and every part of my body feels alive.

Lucas glares at me, but his expression falls as the dryad warriors shout in unison—a booming war cry that echoes around us.

At their call, a wall of vines shoots up in front of me, each blade with a fine, razor-sharp edge and amber fronds down the center. At the same moment, a circular wall of strong, thick vines rises around the children, while a second storm of barbed vines whip across Toad, Clara, and the wraith, driving them back from Drina and the children.

The wraith extends her palm, a poisonous mist gathering around her body that shrivels the vines before they can touch her and deliver their venom, but she isn't quick enough to stop the burst of greenery behind her that quickly twines around her throat.

Toad, too, rapidly disappears under a mountain of vines.

Clara fights back longer than the others before light bursts from her palms. Instead of aiming her magic at the vines, she drops to the ground, curled up over her knees, her magic bursting around her in a small protective shield.

The vines strike but can't get through, instead piling around her to form a cage. No doubt, the moment she lets down her magic, the vines will strike.

The last I see of the children, they drop and huddle before the protective wall closes over the top of them, forming a dome; layer upon layer of protective vines continuing to grow up around them.

Lucas roars with rage. Banta shouts a command, but the warriors' heartbeats drown out his voice.

Thud-thud. Thud-thud.

Just as I sense the tug of Lucas's power and my heart falls at the thought that my freedom was so short, sharp vines whip up around his and Banta's feet, slashing across their thighs, stomachs, and necks.

Lucas's power immediately bursts across his body, turning his exposed skin to bronze, and my stomach sinks at the realization that the venom in the vines won't be able to pierce his metal skin to knock him out.

He reaches for his whip, not even needing to touch it to control its sharp tip, which slashes across the air. The vines quickly adjust, twining around his wrists and ankles and toppling him to the ground.

He falls heavily, shouting and struggling to free himself while the vines continue to twist as fast as the deadly whip cuts them down.

Banta, on the other hand, remains standing, despite the pinpricks of blood around his neck where the vines bit him. "Did you think I'd walk in here and not already be immune to this poison?" he shouts.

Again, the dryads switch tactics, a barrage of woody stems

shooting up from the ground and forming a rapid prison around Banta before he can dart through the only remaining opening.

All of it happens within seconds and then the wall of vines in front of me rises too high for me to see beyond it.

Another wall forms behind me, and I find myself standing with the warriors and the other adult dryads in a corridor that extends to the right before it takes a turn to the left.

The forest shakes around us, the earth trembling and the branches above us shivering as the dryads work together to subdue their attackers.

Rye's big hand lands on my shoulder. "Go, Iyana," he and Mahogany say. "Drina needs to speak with you. We will keep the metal man and his master distracted for as long as we can."

Just like the first time I came to the dryads' home, the fiery fronds on the vines flatten in a ripple to the right, indicating they want me to go that way.

I only stop long enough to thank Rye. "Stay safe."

Then I'm running.

Running in fear that Lucas will take control of me again at any moment.

Before I turn the corner, I glance back at the warriors and the other adults to see them standing in two rows—their eyes closed, their heads bowed—and I can only imagine what's happening beyond the walls I can't see past.

No matter what happens next, I'm relieved to know I can trust them.

I've only taken two steps around the corner when I run straight into Drina. Her crimson-streaked hair swishes around her head, her hands still bloodied as she grabs my shoulders to steady us both.

She doesn't mince words. "You must go to Aiden and wake him up."

I recoil. "No! That's what the demon wants."

She grips me tightly, but unlike Lucas's hands, hers are warm.

"Please," she says, her voice lacerated from her ordeal. "I know you must feel like you can't trust me, but I need you to listen to me."

I force myself not to struggle within her arms, so triggered by Lucas's constant grabbing, that even the warmth of Drina's hands can't soothe my agitation.

She seems to realize it. Carefully, she lets me go and raises her palms.

"Please," she says. "I couldn't tell you Vulcan's story because I simply couldn't remember it. It was his brother who betrayed him, not his son. His brother stole all of Vulcan's weapons and created chaos among the old gods and the titans, but he kept one weapon for himself.

"He intended to kill Vulcan with it. But Theia... She was Vulcan's friend. Not his lover—although they cared deeply about each other. She stepped between Vulcan and his brother, and as she lay dying, she offered Vulcan her heart to make his final weapon. A weapon that would protect him because it would kill anyone else who tried to use it."

She peers into my eyes. "Do you hear me, Iyana?"

"I don't... understand..."

Her grip softens. "Banta Sol believes that absorbing the dagger has made your blood perfect. But you wouldn't have been able to touch that dagger if you weren't already... *you.*"

She reaches out for me again. "Theia was the Titaness of Gold and Silver. The dagger was equal parts of her, and now her heart is part of you. The only way you'll beat the metal man and the demon is if you wake Aiden and forge a new weapon. Together. A weapon strong enough to kill a demon. Strong enough to kill the descendant of a god."

I shiver. "You mean Lucas."

She nods.

I shiver, remembering all the way back to the Spire when Tessa used her power to see Aiden's instincts and she had suddenly seemed extremely wary, even troubled. Then, Aiden had taken hold of the old magic flames in the Spire's lamps and used them when he shouldn't have been able to...

"Then Banta is right?" I ask. "Aiden and Lucas are descended from Vulcan, the God of the Forge?"

"It's true."

I close my eyes. *Fuck.* It means that Aiden is old magic. Like Tessa and Tristan.

And Lucas, too.

Old magic creatures are immune to all other magic—except old magic. They are unkillable. Except by other old magic creatures.

"I bit Lucas and his magic failed," I say, feeling numb about the implications of my actions—the implications for me.

Tessa never used her power to see into my heart, but there was a moment when she looked from Aiden to me that... maybe... she sensed... I wasn't what she thought I was.

Drina's expression softens. "I overheard Clara tell you that a wisp can shine a light into the darkest places. But Clara can't see what lies behind the darkness."

Drina pauses. "I couldn't remember who I was, so I sought meaning in the life around me. I sensed the love you have for your family, Iyana. Every day, I found myself crafting blossoms that I believe meant something to you."

I exhale quietly. That must be why, each time I saw Drina, she was creating a new flower or object that triggered memories of Tessa and her pack. "They did."

"Your mind is dark, but light shines within you," she says. "You helped me escape from the cage I was in. You may never know if you are a descendant of Theia. But your power is strong. Stronger than you know."

Even though we don't have time, she waits for me to process what she said—precious heartbeats while the ground continues to tremble, the branches shake, and I feel as though my whole world just changed.

"Aiden and Lucas share the power of their ancestor," Drina says. "A power that could wreak chaos on the world again if it isn't stopped."

"I won't let that happen," I say. But deep in my heart, I'm forced to acknowledge the contradiction.

To stop Lucas, I need to create a weapon that can kill him—but I would be bringing into existence the very weapon that could be used to end the people I love.

The kind of weapon that could destroy the world.

CHAPTER FORTY-TWO

"*R*un, Iyana," Drina says. "Go as fast as you can."

I don't hesitate another moment, racing along the corridor that the vines created for me, my arms and legs pumping, my muscles straining.

The dappled sunlight is even softer now, and for once, night is not my ally. The dryads are the strongest during the day and their strength will wane with the rising of the moon.

I don't have long.

The path snakes toward the north, the foliage overhead becoming darker the farther I run, until I'm racing across the path lit by toadstools and hurtling toward the cavern.

It's deathly quiet inside and the silvery water glistens, but I don't stop. If it's true that Clara had me drinking this water for the last two weeks in some deranged effort to transform me into the perfect source of metal, then I'm sure as fuck going to wade right into it.

I plunge into the pond without slowing down.

I brace for pain, agony, or to experience some sort of tearing sensation, but it's simply freezing cold.

The water clings to my calves as I push deeper and, although the pond appears completely calm on the surface, I find myself fighting what feels like crashing waves around my legs.

I gasp as the pond deepens on my next step and I drop to my armpits in water that drags at my hips and chest—the push and pull of stormy water tearing at me and *now* I feel pain, the liquid like sandpaper against my skin.

Gritting my teeth and pushing onward, I finally reach Aiden where he lies at my chest height in the water.

Despite the fight to stay on my feet within the tumultuous water, I pause before I reach through the darkness that surrounds him.

"Aiden?" My fingertips brush his cheek, finding his skin colder than it ever was.

Despite my touch... nothing happens. He doesn't stir or react, and the shadows remain around his face and torso.

I have to face the reality that I have no idea how to wake him up.

I press my palm to his forehead and speak more loudly. "Aiden?"

Still, there's no response, and a deep despair grows within me. Everything that has happened today has been like this pond. It looks one way on the surface, but it's raging beneath and threatening to drag me under.

"Aiden!" I snap, loudly enough for my voice to echo.

I should know already that yelling at him won't work because Drina already tried that. In fact, she filled this pond with fire and still didn't get a response from him.

My hand closes over his shoulder and I shake him, another stupid move, considering I could push him under.

To my surprise, he barely rocks in the water, remaining so solidly still that I'm able to launch myself upward, climbing onto his chest and straddling his waist.

Water sloughs off me, but it's like oil clinging to my skin, making my top and long pants cling to my chest and thighs.

I lean down to him, descending through the dark haze around him, taking in his impossibly broad shoulders, the muscles across his chest, the way my arms have no hope of wrapping all of the way around him.

His hair swirls in the water, the dark brown strands the only part of him that's moving.

"Please wake up," I whisper, lowering my head to his shoulder and pressing my hand to his heart.

The silence seems endless, and with every passing second, the sun will be sinking lower and the dryads will lose their energy...

High above me, the vines that held the dagger curl across the branches, seeming aimless now that the dagger is gone. Like I took away their purpose.

My own purpose is in tatters.

Two weeks ago, I knew where I stood in the world. I was Tessa's supporter—a member of her pack. Someone who told Tristan to fuck off when he was being an asshole, and faced up to Tessa herself when she needed a whopping dose of truth and kindness in her life.

I felt like I knew who I was.

Now I don't.

I began my remembered life as an outcast vampire with a heart-stopping bite, and then—

I bolt upright.

When I bit Lucas, his magic began to fail. But Aiden was the opposite.

When I sank my fangs into Aiden's arm back at the Spire, the flames around his body had flared even brighter. I only managed to knock him out once I'd injected him with enough venom to kill ten men.

He told me once that *I* was his fire but I didn't believe him. I certainly didn't take his statement literally. The dryads said the same thing when Aiden and I first arrived here. I tried to convince them that he had no access to his power, but...

You are his fire, they said.

I lean over him, brushing his neck with my lips, tasting nothing of the flame that should be raging within him.

Resting my palm lightly across his cheek, my forefinger at the corner of his eye, I sense his eyelashes lying still.

My fangs descend.

I pierce his neck, deeply.

This time, I don't fight the rush of venom, allowing it to flow, embracing the awful euphoria that comes with it.

My heart leaps when his eyelashes flutter against my hand, but I keep going, pouring everything I've got into him.

His chest rises, a breath whooshing into him, and I pull back.

My silver venom leaks from the puncture points as I hold my breath and hope—counting heartbeats as I wait for him to wake up.

I wait impossible seconds, fear growing that I imagined his indrawn breath, that I didn't bite him for long enough. Or I bit him for too long.

"Wake up, Aiden," I say, knowing I don't have the heart to ask again.

And then...

My jaw clenches because I realize I've been calling him by the wrong name.

Lowering my lips to his ear, I whisper, "Wake up... *Vulcan.*"

His eyes flash open and he wakes with a roar.

CHAPTER FORTY-THREE

$\mathscr{T}$he water churns as Aiden surges upward.

Flames burst from his body and explode across the pond's surface—a wildfire burning in every direction—stopping at the water's edge but leaping dangerously close to the branches above us.

His arms clamp around me, drawing me close, pulling my legs around his waist and holding me above the water, the quiet cocoon around us making me feel truly safe. He left his torn shirt behind in the water and his bare chest presses to mine.

I groan with relief—and warmth. The first real warmth I've felt in weeks.

"Ana." His voice is rough as he strokes my back, my hair, presses his cheek to mine. Kisses the corner of my mouth. But his forehead suddenly creases. "Iyana?"

When I don't answer—can't answer yet because my throat is too choked up—the furrow in his brow deepens and his next murmur is a deep rumble. "Theia?"

I exhale, feeling like I'm dispelling years of stress. I have no idea who I am. Perhaps I'm all of them—Ana, Iyana, *and* Theia.

"Ana," I say, finally able to respond, choosing the name that fits me best—the woman who fell in love with him.

"You're Vulcan," I say, hesitantly. "Or... Aiden?"

His eyes glitter as he breaks into a slow smile and presses his forehead to mine. "Aiden." His gaze becomes introspective. "My power feels stronger. *I* feel stronger."

He draws back a little to see my face and his smile slowly fades. His gaze lands on my chin, then my bare shoulders, then his dark blue eyes flash down my arm to my wrist.

His voice is low and dangerous. "You have bruises."

Every damn place that Lucas grabbed me. In the firelight, the red marks are a nasty shade of brown.

Aiden demands answers. "Who hurt you?"

Telling him that his brother betrayed him is harder than I ever imagined. Especially because every second is precious now, and the conversation that I need to have with him isn't the kind that should be rushed.

"I... It's... This is..." I exhale slowly, as I try to figure out where to start. Shying away from discussing his brother yet, I start simpler. "Do you know where you are?"

"The dryads' home," he says, without hesitation.

"This water is a sacred place for them," I say. "You've been lying here for two weeks, and it's been drawing out your power. But your brother—"

He stiffens, suddenly alert. "Is Lucas okay?"

I close my eyes. *Damn.*

The tension leaves Aiden's shoulders and torso, but I sense that he's forcing himself to calm down, his own breaths suddenly deep. "You can talk to me," he says.

I meet his eyes, speaking carefully. "Banta Sol is here. So is your brother. But Lucas isn't the same person anymore."

Aiden takes a moment. A long, quiet one. He's very still as he processes what I said. "Lucas hurt you."

Again, speech sticks in my throat. *Why is it so hard to talk about being hurt? So hard to ask for help?*

In this case, it's more than that. I'm asking Aiden to believe that his brother—the brother that he spent his life protecting—is now his enemy.

I finally manage to say, "Yes."

Aiden's response is quieter than I expected. "Is Banta controlling him?"

I shake my head. "No."

Aiden is impossibly quiet. So still. Until he breaks eye contact with me, and somehow it scares me when he stares at the flames raging around us—the crackling fire—especially when the blaze leaps and dances closer to us at his mere glance. Then he studies the shape of my face, my eyes, my lips, up to my hair; a careful scrutiny.

"My brother is the Metalworker, isn't he?" Aiden asks.

I nod.

"And Banta wants the ultimate weapon."

Again, I nod.

"Did my brother try to make a weapon from your blood?"

I stare at Aiden. I'm surprised enough that he figured out on his own that the Metalworker is his brother, but now it's as if he's piecing together what happened today. "How did you guess that?"

Aiden's jaw tightens, his brows draw down, and the dangerous press of his lips is suddenly as scary as fuck. "Because I see you, Ana. I'm holding your body in my arms and you feel the way clay must feel in a potter's hands." His fingertips glide through my hair—his hold is gentle, and it sends tantalizing shivers all through my body to my core.

"Fuck," he whispers. "All I want to do is hold you. If this is the way I feel, then my brother wouldn't have been able to keep his hands off you." He squeezes his eyes shut before he snarls, "Fuck this power."

I gasp when Aiden draws me closer, his gaze tearing down all of my walls. "Do you trust me?" he asks.

"I do, but—"

"Do you trust that I will never hurt you? That I will protect you even if it gets me killed? Do you believe me, Ana?"

My lips part. My eyes widen. "I do."

He exhales and presses his forehead to mine again. "Then tell me what you need. Tell me, and I'll be there with you. All the way."

I take a deep breath and it all rushes out of me. "Banta trapped the dryads. They're trying to hold him off, but the sun is setting and they'll soon be exposed and vulnerable. I have to stop Banta and Lucas before that happens." I gasp in air. "I need you to make the weapon your brother failed to make."

Aiden stiffens as my final statement falls around us.

"From your blood?" he asks.

"Yes." I hurry on. "I know what I'm asking. I know the cost. Creating this weapon is a dangerous choice. If there were another way, I wouldn't ask."

Without hesitation, Aiden strides out of the fiery water, carrying me with him to the mossy expanse beyond it, where he places me back on the ground.

Water sloughs off us both, but the oily substance from its surface remains, plastering our clothing to our skin.

Now that I'm standing beside him, I can see the full effect of the life waters—the increased breadth of his shoulders and span of his thigh muscles and biceps. His damn pants are splitting in all sorts of places, *and* he towers over me.

He runs his hand down my arm, turning my wrist outward. "You'll have to help with this part," he says.

Unlike Lucas, Aiden's power can't draw my blood out or control its path.

I allow my fangs to descend, lift my wrist to my mouth, and pierce my vein with the tip of my fang, quickly withdrawing so I don't drink my own blood.

The pinprick is only deep enough to allow my blood to drip slowly, not the reckless cut that Lucas made in my left wrist earlier.

Aiden takes a knee in front of me, holding out his hands with his palms opposite each other, while a flame grows in the space between them. It lights up his chest and casts shadows across his face.

The heat from the flame grows until the temperature is like a volcano buffeting us, making the air shimmer and scorching my skin.

Sweat drips down my forehead and chest, but I force myself to concentrate, holding my wrist out so that the first slow drop of my blood falls into the flame Aiden is cultivating.

My blood sinks like mercury through water—a swirling silver droplet—but it slows and stops at the center of the flame. The next three droplets join it, gravitating toward each other into a perfect sphere that remains cohesive within the flames—there are no departing droplets this time.

Beads of sweat slip down Aiden's forehead. "Ana, I don't know how to shape it—"

Lucas's snarl sounds from the cavern's entrance. "Of course, you fucking don't. Making the weapon takes both of us."

I jolt and wrench my wrist away from the flame, which holds its shape and rises to my chest height while Aiden launches to his feet.

He spins to face his brother.

Lucas steps into the enclosure, still bare-chested—the long, metallic whip floating along beside him.

Fear strikes through me to see that the end of the weapon is bloodied. Lucas's skin ripples through alternating tones of flesh and bronze, neither of which hides the blood splatter across his stomach and shoulders.

"Don't worry, Iyana," he says, at my horrified look. "The children are fine. Clara's looking after them. It's a shame about their parents."

I swallow a cry of despair.

Rye. The warriors. Drina...

I leap forward, striding toward him. "You fucking monster!"

Lucas lifts his hands, and I'm jolted into the air. The freshly healed wounds in each of my wrists open and my blood spills freely. The droplets float across the space in front of me, drifting toward Lucas as he controls them.

Flames leap around Aiden's torso as he storms forward. The last time he fought his brother, Lucas didn't hesitate to use me as a shield against Aiden's fire, and I sense how hard Aiden's fighting not to release the flames at his brother now.

Aiden roars. "Let her go, Lucas!"

In response, Lucas squeezes his fist.

To my shock, my arms and legs splay, and my back arches, my limbs stretching painfully... feeling as if they're going to tear out of their sockets.

I try to swallow my scream as the pain reaches a new level.

Damn my body. Damn my blood.

Lucas snarls at Aiden. "You're going to do what we want now, Aiden. Or I will rip Iyana apart."

"*We?*" Aiden asks.

Banta sidles through the opening behind Lucas. His clothing is torn, his arms and legs cut where the material has been sliced open— by the sharp vines probably.

Deep red pinpricks dot his neck where he was struck, and a gash across his cheekbone and jaw cuts all the way down across his beard.

Toad and the wraith appear after him, taking up position in front of the exit. Toad is partially shifted, raised up on his snake body while his torso, arms, and head remain human-shaped.

The wraith pushes back her hood, revealing skin that is nearly transparent, so paper-thin that her veins and bones are visible underneath. She doesn't speak, but mist grows around her hands and Toad quickly slides a few paces away from her.

In response to their presence, fire bursts around Aiden's fists. "I won't do a fucking thing you want, Banta. Not anymore."

The demon doesn't hesitate, striding forward despite the fierce flames. "I don't have time for this. Put away your fire."

Two weeks ago, Banta's power would have forced Aiden to obey, but now the blaze continues to burn around Aiden's hand, growing brighter with every second.

Aiden's glare is even hotter.

Banta pulls up short. "I said—"

"It looks like your power doesn't work on me anymore," Aiden says.

Banta's glare is full of contempt. "You may be immune to my power now, Aiden, but you, your brother, and Iyana aren't immune to each other. You *will* do everything I say or Lucas will destroy Iyana." Banta lowers his voice, a soft threat. "I don't need her alive, Aiden. I'm sure Lucas can spill enough of her blood for my purposes before killing her."

Aiden is more tense than I've ever seen him. The sphere of flames in which my blood already gathered spins slowly beside him at shoulder-height.

He looks to me, his expression drawn, his jaw clenching.

I remain in the air, my arms and legs pulled taut, tears leaking down my cheeks against my will.

I told him I wanted to create the weapon. We can't do it without Lucas. If Aiden cooperates, we'll have the weapon we need, but the danger will be... who controls the weapon once it's made.

Aiden gives Lucas a terse nod before he pulls the sphere of flames forward, where it floats between his hands once more. "Get the fuck on with it."

Lucas steps up opposite Aiden so that they're facing each other. The brothers are similarly muscular, although Aiden is taller. Aiden's torso is covered in flames, while Lucas's visible skin quickly morphs into bronze—all the way up to his hair.

A look of concentration settles onto Lucas's face as he pulls the pool of my blood into the flames.

The droplets gravitate toward each other, forming a perfect orb within the fire. Still, Lucas pulls more of my blood toward it, drawing from the cut in my left wrist, until he makes a satisfied sound that is nearly drowned by the crackling of the flames. "That should do it."

As soon as he releases me, I drop to the ground, where I crouch and attempt to put pressure on my wound. I test his continuing hold on me in case I can move farther, but the weight of his power bears down on me so that I can't step beyond that spot.

Aiden is quiet, the firelight flickering across his features as he focuses on his brother. "How did I fail you?" he asks, his voice low. "When did I let you down?"

Lucas's response is cold. "Don't beat yourself up, Aiden."

Aiden shakes his head slowly. "I must have done something wrong. Or you wouldn't hurt the woman I love."

Lucas's lips twist. "Iyana is a means to an end. Ultimate power, Aiden. We can have it together. You just need to be willing to make sacrifices."

Aiden exhales heavily and the heat he's creating increases.

It's so hot now that the air shimmers all around him. New beads of sweat trickle down my face and I struggle to breathe.

On the other side of the brothers, facing me across the flames, Banta runs the back of his hand across his forehead, his face flushed.

Farther behind him, Toad and the wraith seem relatively unaffected—although Toad's tongue flicks out more regularly.

"I've already made sacrifices for you, Lucas." A muscle in Aiden's jaw clenches. "You have no fucking idea how many."

Lucas shrugs. "Then you'll have to make more."

He zeroes in on my silver blood within the flames, his hands hovering over the hellish sphere. Within the fire, my blood begins to form the shape of a new blade, and a triumphant smile grows on Lucas's face.

Across the top of the flames, Banta leans in with even greater anticipation.

Lucas works quickly, his fingers deftly shifting, pushing, and pulling as my blood forms the perfect dagger—the blade gleaming sharp, the handle ridged to facilitate a better grip.

It's larger than the blade made from Theia's heart. In fact, it looks big enough to cleave a supernatural's head from their shoulders.

My heart is beating faster now, every muscle in my body tensing as Lucas nears completion of the dagger. He must be only seconds away from drawing the blade from the fire now—and he has complete control of the weapon.

The only chance Aiden will have of taking the dagger first is if Lucas is distracted.

I push against Lucas's power over me—heaving with effort, trying to find leverage in the mossy ground—forcing him to glance my way, but his distraction is short-lived before his power clamps down on me again, forcing me back to the ground.

Lucas grins at the blade. "It's done. It's time to see if it works."

The air crackles as Aiden's biceps tense.

He moves fast.

His hands shoot through the fire, closing around the weapon while it still burns.

At the same time, Lucas's hand pushes forward, a savage shove.

I scream as the blade flies through the flames, slips through Aiden's grasp, and shoots directly at Aiden's heart.

CHAPTER FORTY-FOUR

The blade shatters against Aiden's chest.

Shards of metal fly wide, hitting the ground in all directions, one sharp piece impaling the ground beside me.

Aiden leaps back with a shout, every line of his body tense.

Lucas roars with rage as he tries to follow the broken pieces shooting like bullets around the clearing, his hand outstretched as if he's trying—but failing—to seize control of them.

Behind him, Banta appears frozen.

I stare in shock at the jagged piece of metal stuck in the moss at my side as I struggle to process what happened.

It didn't work.

The blade looked perfect, sharp—a beautiful, deadly weapon. Aiden's fire was supposed to heat the metal. Lucas was supposed to shape it.

The dagger should have killed Aiden, but instead, it broke. It may as well have been made of brittle ceramic the way it shattered against him.

"You!" Lucas screams at me where I huddle against the moss, my wrists still bleeding. "You did this! It's your fucking fault."

My head shoots up and my eyes widen. *How am I supposed to have done anything?*

He storms toward me, using his power to wrench me into the air again, pulling so savagely on my arms and legs that I scream with pain.

"I will fuck with you so badly, you'll wish you were never born," he shouts, raging toward me.

He doesn't make it two steps before Aiden tackles him with a fierce roar, flames pouring across his chest.

Fire engulfs them both.

Aiden's fist lands on Lucas's bronze jaw, splashing fire across his brother's face. It's so hot that droplets of bronze metal bleed from Lucas's cheek, splattering the ground around them and burning the moss to ash.

Aiden's fists fly, crushing blows that crash into his brother's face, chest, and ribs, driving him toward the ground.

Lucas lands heavily, his metal body creating a dint in the earth and, for a blessed moment, his power around me falters.

The terrifying pull on my arms and legs eases so that I can sag in the air, my shoulders hunched, my body aching.

A second later, Lucas fights back, his abandoned whip wrapping around Aiden's neck and dragging him backward, but not before Aiden follows up with a crushing kick to Lucas's chest that knocks him into the ground again.

Lucas leaps to his feet and rams into his brother, every punch between them making me wince.

Behind them, Banta paces from side to side, steering clear of the fight while his pale brown eyes zero in on me. Everything he planned for—his elaborate scheme—just went up in smoke.

Judging by the reddening of his cheeks and the way he drags his hand through his suddenly messy hair, he's angry. Fucking angry. And maybe a little confused.

The first dagger Lucas tried to create wouldn't hold together. This one held its shape, but it crumbled like a cookie on impact. It should have worked when both brothers operated together.

Why didn't it? Is it something to do with my blood?

As I continue to hover in the air within Lucas's power, I wonder: How could Vulcan make a dagger out of Theia's heart—a dagger that assimilated into my body as soon as I touched it—but his descendants can't make a dagger out of my blood?

I know nothing about forging a blade.

All I know is what I've seen in movies or in illustrations: the image of a medieval blacksmith working over a blazing forge, heating the metal and hammering it into shape, working to a beat known only to them.

A heartbeat all their own.

I gasp, trying to catch my breath as a cruel possibility hits me.

Drina said I couldn't have held Vulcan's dagger if I wasn't... *me.*

It's possible that the weapon can't be made from my blood but requires... all of me.

I raise my hands, considering the changes I've experienced over the last two weeks—my skin, my hair, even my mind—as I assimilated with the dryads' peaceful way of life and learned to listen to my surroundings.

I listen to my heartbeat now, as carefully as I listen to the dryad's hearts during training, even though I'm afraid of what I'll hear.

It's a solid beat. A little rapid.

As I listen more closely, a violent shiver rocks me, because the faint clang of a hammer rings above the deep thud of every heartbeat within my chest.

It's the sound of the forge that tells me what I have to do—even if it scares the fuck out of me.

As Aiden and Lucas continue to fight, I tip my head back, seeking the vines that curl along the cavern ceiling.

I picture the dagger hanging from the ceiling, but this time, I imagine Theia's beautiful heart in its place. I remember the way it melted into my skin and flowed through my chest.

It was her heart and now it's mine.

I close my eyes, breathe out, and face the truth: My blood isn't the metal from which the weapon can be made. My body is.

But to become the weapon, I have to subject myself to the forge: Aiden's fire and the hammer of Lucas's fists. Both of which could just as easily kill me if I'm wrong.

Only a few paces away, fire pours from Aiden's free hand while he attempts to stop his brother's whip from strangling him. The flames he aims at Lucas, who has half-risen, scorch the earth around them, and I fear for the trees, trusting that Aiden can rein in the blaze if it gets out of hand.

A fresh burst of fire explodes around Aiden's neck, turning the whip into putty that stretches and melts. He rips the dripping pieces away from his body and defends against Lucas's next punch, the two men colliding so fiercely that the ground trembles and the canopy above me shakes.

Lucas's control over me finally slips completely, and I drop to the ground again, dragging air into my chest. I'm free, but I don't know for how long.

To my right, only a few paces away, the sphere of flames that Aiden created—the one he used to heat the blade that shattered—continues to spin slowly in the air, abandoned.

I've already made my decision and I don't think twice.

I dart toward the burning sphere.

Its heat hits me—the hottest flame I've ever felt—taking my breath away when I collide with it.

I've never touched Aiden's fire before. He always kept me safe within a cocoon. Even when I bit him at the Spire, he withdrew his power before the fire could hurt me.

That flame was nothing like this one.

The sphere bursts across my chest, spreading across every inch of my skin like a hungry beast, destroying my shirt, pants, and under-wear in an instant, and adhering to every surface of my body—down my legs, my arms, up my neck, and into my hair. It's like plunging into a pool of molten amber liquid, beyond any heat I've ever experienced, and I fight the roar growing in my throat. Not a scream of pain, but a burst of energy that wants to tear out of me.

I suppress it. I can't make a sound. Can't draw attention to myself. Especially not now that Banta has retreated to the exit, hunched there beside his lieutenants, and Lucas is fighting desperately now that more of his bronze blood spills, and Aiden's face tells me... He won't stop until his brother is dead.

But I need Lucas alive.

Still, I'm forced to wait as my body processes the flame, as every inch of me heats until the fire is completely absorbed and my skin glows like embers.

I am metal waiting to solidify.

I acknowledge my fear of Lucas's fists. Somehow, stepping into Aiden's flame was easier than what I face next.

But my advice to Drina echoes back at me.

It's time to be *wild*.

I run butt-naked toward the fight between Aiden and Lucas, judging my timing, praying that I get it right.

I'll only have one chance at this. I need Lucas's fists—how many hits, I can't be sure, but enough to trigger the power I sense growing within me, waiting to be unleashed.

Ahead of me, Aiden lands another punch against Lucas's chest, driving him back, but the metal man digs in his heels. Parts of his chest are flesh and blood again, but his fist is still completely metal.

It's all I need.

He rages toward his brother, his bronze teeth bared, his hand drawn back for another attack.

I throw myself between them.

Lucas's bronze fist collides with my heart like a perfect metal hammer.

Pain explodes across my chest as the impact throws me back into Aiden, whose arms close around me a split second before the flames vanish from around his body.

"Iyana! No!" Aiden's fear-filled shout sounds in my ear as he wrenches me backward.

For a few moments, I'm facing Lucas and I'm a perfect target—a body shield in front of Aiden. The pure rage on Lucas's face tells me he's going to make the most of it.

Bring it on, you fucking monster.

He bursts forward, his fists ramming into me even as Aiden attempts to pull me away.

Lucas's metal fist crashes against my jaw, my chest, my ribs, my shoulder—every collision shuddering through me before Aiden succeeds in swinging me around so that Lucas's final hit lands on Aiden's back.

Crack!

The sound of Aiden's back breaking makes me freeze.

My eyes fly wide, a scream wrenching out of me as Aiden drops to the ground, collapsing so suddenly that his weight bears down on me.

He had subdued his power, doused his flames so he wouldn't hurt me, and that left him vulnerable to Lucas's powerful fist, and now…

Aiden's chin rests on my shoulder from behind. His voice is a low murmur. "Even if it gets me killed."

It was his promise to protect me.

This wasn't supposed to happen. Aiden wasn't supposed to get hurt.

His fall is so sudden that Lucas halts, pausing for the seconds it takes me to turn, still crouched, supporting Aiden with all of my strength when he slips to the side. His shoulder lands on my thigh, his head in my lap. He's facing me, but his arms and legs are motionless.

His navy-blue eyes blaze for a second, flashing from my face all the way to my waist.

I follow his gaze, taking in the silver of my skin, the way my body gleams like it never did before.

The strength I sense building within my muscles is far more than what it was when I was a vampire.

When I close my eyes and listen for the briefest second to my heartbeat, it hammers in my hearing, the sound of metal fully forged.

It worked. Aiden's fire and the hammer of Lucas's fists have made me into the weapon I need to be.

"Fucking beautiful," Aiden murmurs. "Before. Now. Forever."

Tears burn behind my eyes. My transformation might be complete, but it came with a cost that I'm not prepared to accept.

I bend to Aiden and press my lips to his. "You can heal yourself. Right now."

"Not without burning you—"

"You won't," I say as I press my cheek to his. "Nothing can hurt me now. Burn like you've never burned before, Aiden, and I promise you, I'll walk away from your flames." I press my hand to his heart. "But I will never again choose to walk away from *you*."

Aiden searches my eyes, about to speak, when Lucas cuts him off with a snarl. "You're both pathetic!"

The metal man's cheekbone is split, his skin showing through where his power has been diminished during the fight with Aiden. He grabs me—with his hands, not his power—pulling me so savagely away from Aiden that Aiden drops fully to the ground, and I scream with rage.

The way Lucas grips me tells me everything. I sense his power wash across me, sliding off me like silk, sense the growing tension in his arms, hear the sudden breath of surprise that he takes.

He can't control me anymore. I might not have been immune to his power before, but I am now.

I am... fucking forged.

Throwing me down onto the ground, he aims a kick at my head.

I roll toward the hit, my hands snap out, and I grab his foot midair.

His eyes widen in surprise a second before I use my upward momentum to flip him off his feet.

He lands heavily—all that metal making him less agile—and I wait for him to rise up, his chest heaving, his eyes full of murder.

"What sacrifices would you make, Lucas?" I ask, an impossible calm filling me. "For the ultimate weapon?"

His only response is a sneer, his gaze raking down my naked body as if he would like to tear me to shreds.

"Would you kill me?" I ask. "Kill your brother? Is there anything you wouldn't do?"

"To never be powerless again," he says, which makes me pause because I know only too well what it feels like to be defenseless, and how far I'd go to never feel like that again. Throwing myself into Aiden's fire and the path of Lucas's fists, to be exact.

But then Lucas goes on. "I would take you apart, pretty Ana, piece by fucking piece, and I'd enjoy your screams."

I exhale quietly, any sudden reservations I had about killing him disappearing at his declaration.

Behind me, there's an explosion of fire, the heat against my back scorching, so hot that the air dances with heat waves and buffets me.

I stand tall, unaffected now that my skin is impervious to all magic.

Aiden rises from the ground, stretching out his neck and shoulders, his skin glowing as hot as a burning coal.

I wait for him to focus on me because I won't end his brother if Aiden has doubts.

The pain in Aiden's eyes tears my heart out. He spent his life protecting his brother, only to lose him now.

But he gives me a nod.

I turn back to Lucas, my voice quiet. "If you want to take me apart, then this is your chance. But know this: If you decide that this fight isn't worth it, if you walk away right now, despite everything you've done… I'll let you leave."

I square my shoulders and wait for Lucas to make his choice. I need Aiden to know that I gave his brother the option to live, and what happens next is up to Lucas.

"Fuck that." Lucas spits. He plants his back foot before he launches himself at me. His metal fist flies toward my face, fast and hard enough to break my neck if I were human.

My hand shoots up. His fist stops in my open palm, my fingers close around it, and I stop him in his tracks.

At the same moment, my other hand whips out, my palm flat, cutting across his cheek, slicing through metal and bone like a knife.

He rocks on the spot as his bronze blood spills onto the ground at my feet.

"You're okay with sacrifices," I say, my heart cold. "As long as they aren't your own."

I ram my hand across his neck, my palm like a forged blade, severing his head from his body with a single cut.

CHAPTER FORTY-FIVE

I drop to the ground and close my eyes, trying to breathe. The fight isn't over—Banta and his lieutenants can't be allowed to get away—but the death on my hands is overpowering.

I try to harden my heart, to feel nothing, but it's impossible. There was a time—a long time—when I was a bounty hunter where I took lives without thought. Murderers, all of them—but what did that make me?

I know what it's like to have family now, to have more to lose—integrity, honor, love.

I tell myself to get up, but it isn't until Aiden's warm hand brushes my shoulder that I can rise.

He doesn't say anything, doesn't look in the direction of his brother's body—instead, he inclines his head toward the exit, where Banta and the other lieutenants are poised to escape.

"Get me out of here!" Banta snaps at the wraith, darting behind her as if he intends to use her as a shield.

She jolts into action, the mist thickening around her hands as she draws a large circle in the air that rapidly fills with a fog-like substance.

Damn. She must control some sort of translocation power.

I break into a run, my hesitation gone in a flash. If Banta gets away, he'll go underground. It will take years to find him again—even with Tessa's and Helen's help.

As I approach at a sprint, Banta yells at the wraith to hurry up, but her hands are shaking.

Her focus shifts wildly between me and the portal she can't seem to create fast enough.

I leap upward, my legs stronger than they ever were before, and crash down onto the portal, my arm cutting clean through it.

The mist disperses and the wraith's power vanishes.

Instead of attacking, she backs away from me—a defensive move that surprises me enough that I don't immediately go in for the kill.

I spin to the snake shifter, instead. He has shifted completely into his snake form, his serpentine body deadly and quick. Already sliding toward me, he leaps upward, his mouth wide open, his fangs sharp, aiming for my neck.

Before he reaches me, Aiden's fiery fist collides with the snake's head, punching him off course. As the serpent attempts to turn, Aiden grabs his tail, wrenches him backward, and shoots fire into his torso, then his head.

The snake's burning body drops to the ground.

Spinning back to the wraith, who has started drawing another portal in the air, I reach right through the acidic mist covering her body to grab her arm and stop her.

It feels like my fingers wrap around paper, as if she's barely made of anything at all.

She doesn't fight back, her pale eyes wide as she stares at me, seeming frozen—as though she's waiting for me to kill her—but then Banta screams from behind her where he cowers. "Kill the vampire!"

The wraith jolts as if she's been shot through with electricity, her pupils dilate, and *now* she fights back.

Poisonous fumes grow around her hands, but I breathe them in without any detrimental effect.

Reaching through the mist again, I grab both of her hands, clasping them tightly.

She takes a sharp breath, struggling against me. "Please," she hisses. "My family."

I freeze. My breathing is erratic as I try to control my anger. "Banta has your family?"

"My sister," she hisses, still struggling to obey his order to kill me, the poison filling the air around me.

Behind her, Banta screams at her again. "I said, kill her!"

The wraith jolts again, the mist thickens so much that it's like a deep fog around me, but this time, I understand that her actions are involuntary.

I let out a sigh. "I'm sorry," I say before I break one of her fingers.

She screams with pain, stumbling away from me when I let her go, nearly stepping into Banta, who continues to shout at her, his face red.

She stops and stares from him to me, her jaw dropping, and I sense the moment that she realizes she's free of his control. "How did you—?"

"Pain," I say. "Now get out of here. Don't let me see you again."

She nods and her cloak morphs and swirls within the fog, billowing around her paper-thin form. "Thank you for my freedom."

A fine black mist envelops her, obscuring her silhouette.

When it clears, she's gone.

Nearby, Aiden stands in front of the exit, blocking it. He could have killed Banta already, but I'm grateful he hasn't.

I need to do this.

Banta raises both of his hands, his usual calm demeanor slipping as he backs away from me toward the life waters. The light catches the paleness of his hair and beard, accentuating the lines on his face. "You don't have to kill me, Iyana. I can be a powerful ally."

I continue toward him, my footsteps careful and quiet on the moss. More than anything, I'm trying to control the killing rage that rises again inside me—a desire to make his end painful and not quick.

"You played with our lives," I say. "You controlled Aiden against his will. Turned his brother into a monster. Nearly killed me. Hurt *hundreds* of supernaturals."

"I can open doors for you, Iyana," he continues, trying to bargain with me as the light darkens around us now that every spark of Aiden's flames has dimmed. "I can get you anything you need. All the weapons you could possibly want—"

I dart forward and grip his shoulder.

"All the weapons?" I ask, rage building inside me as I stare him down, thinking of all the death he's caused. All of the pain and suffering he's inflicted during his lifetime. "I *am* the weapon, you fucking asshole."

My hand rips through his chest, closes around his heart, and crushes it.

CHAPTER FORTY-SIX

$\mathcal{T}$he silence around me is only broken by Aiden's steady heartbeat. A constant thud that pulls me back from the edge of rage.

I make myself stop before I run to him.

My right hand is bloodied, dripping with gore, and I keep it at my side.

I'm trembling, and it could be remnant rage, or it might simply be adrenaline—if a creature like me even produces adrenaline.

Not that I really know what I am anymore. A mercury-drinking vampire turned Titaness of Gold and Silver, forged into a weapon that can kill... anything. Anyone.

I'm afraid of the power I now control—of hurting Aiden without meaning to.

He crosses the distance between us without hesitation and pulls me into his arms, his breathing ragged. Resting my head against his chest, I take deep breaths, but I can't return his embrace, not when his brother's blood is all over me.

"I'm so sorry, Aiden," I say. "I'm sorry about your brother."

I ended it. Killed Banta and stopped Lucas, but it feels empty when the fallout has a cost.

Aiden drops his forehead gently to mine, his fingers splayed against my naked back. "I fucking hate him for betraying me. Fucking hate him for hurting you. But... I'm going to miss him." His voice falters. "He was my brother."

Tears burn behind my eyes, regret that I was the one who ended Lucas—even if I was the only one who could.

Being a weapon means nothing if I bring pain—if I'm a threat—to the people I care about.

The man I love.

My alpha.

My pack.

I'm a danger to all of them.

But if Tessa's experience taught me anything—if I learned anything on this road I've traveled—it's that even the deadliest creature can't walk through life alone.

When Aiden presses his cheek to mine, his arms enclosing me more tightly, I finally hug him back, bury my face in the crook of his neck, and accept that processing what happened in this cavern will take time. Weeks. Months. As long as it takes.

"Aiden," I murmur. "I need you to know that I never stopped loving you. Even when I was pretending to be someone else. Even when I couldn't let you know that I was alive."

He's quiet for a moment. "I love you, too," he murmurs.

A small weight lifts.

I bite my lip, begin to speak, but I'm startled when I realize that the shape of my teeth has changed. Running my tongue over them, I seek the sensation of my fangs, calling on them. I'm alarmed when I sense that they're bigger. I stop before I accidentally cut something—my own lips, for starters.

"I'm not sure if I should be around people anymore," I say.

He brushes the hair from my face, and I'm even more startled when I focus on the strands of my hair for the first time since I fully transformed, finding my locks streaked with silver.

"We'll get through this," he says. "No matter how rough it gets."

He leans in to kiss me and I return it carefully, the gentlest brush—the only contact I'm prepared to make before I know what's happened to my fangs.

"This isn't over yet," I whisper.

"The dryads," he murmurs.

I grit my teeth. "I won't let Clara raise their children."

His jaw clenches. "Then let's go."

We stride to the exit, but before I leave, I force myself to look back. Up above, a few of the leaves are singed, but that's the only damage to the canopy.

On the ground—the hardest to face—I'm startled to see vines forming across the bodies, thin ropes that quickly thicken and wrap around Lucas, Banta, and the snake shifter before they retract, pulling the bodies toward the life waters. It's quick and silent, and within seconds, they disappear under the surface, which becomes completely still again.

Dear fuck. I'm never drinking from those vines or stepping into that pond again.

Joining Aiden outside the cavern, I surge ahead of him, sprinting lightly as I lead him toward the center of the territory. He doesn't know the way like I do—or what to expect. The branches creak above us as the canopy shifts to conceal us from the moonlight—a familiar sound to me in the quiet—but Aiden throws sharp glances at the overhead branches.

"It's okay," I tell him. "I'll explain later."

Running along the pathway south, my feet are as light as air, my speed increasing so much that I need to make myself slow down around the corners before I skid into the vines that rise up along the way. They're burned in places as if they've been touched with acid and I can only assume that was the wraith's doing.

I round the corner at the end of the corridor, coming upon the battlefield at the center of the dryads' home. The cabins are in ruins. Branches and vines litter the ground. There are holes burned in the trees.

I pull to an abrupt stop, and Aiden halts a step behind me.

At the back of the clearing, the dome in which the dryad children hid appears to have remained intact. But it makes it very difficult to visually ascertain that they're okay.

Clara stands in front of the mound, doused in full moonlight, her small hands folded in front of her.

On the ground, laid out in neat rows, are the dryad adults and the warriors.

They look as if they're sleeping, glossy vines covering their bodies from their feet to their shoulders. I hold my breath and listen for their heartbeats, my hope dashed when I hear only silence.

Clara appears unconcerned when she sees me. "Don't worry,

Iyana," she says, as if we're in the middle of a conversation. "We're not complete monsters." She gestures to the protective mound behind herself and then up to the moonlight. "The children are fast asleep. They didn't see a thing."

She tips her head, craning her neck as she looks past us expectantly. It dawns on me that she must think Banta and Lucas are about to appear behind us at any moment.

The fact that I'm naked and gleaming like steel doesn't seem to have worried her. Nor the fact that Aiden stands at my side.

She must be *that* confident that Banta and Lucas are still in control.

"You must be Clara," Aiden says, relaxed beside me. "We followed your light along the creek."

"Ye-es," she says, faltering for the first time, still craning her neck.

"They aren't coming," Aiden says quietly, his hand brushing my arm as he steps toward her, picking a careful path through the fallen dryads.

Following him, I pull to a stop beside Rye, whose light brown hair forms a carpet around his head. Mahogany lies beside him, and I don't miss the way her fingertips extend through the vines, touching the tips of his.

Drina lies on the other side of them, and for a second, I think her skin glints a little. But it must be a trick of the light because when I listen, hoping to hear her heartbeat, I still hear only silence.

My anger grows again. Their lives were worth more than this.

Up ahead, Clara shifts a little, her voice sounding younger than it ever has. "What do you mean?"

"Banta and Lucas are dead," Aiden replies, stepping quietly toward her. The way he speaks, I could believe that his brother's death suddenly means nothing to him, but I know it's a façade.

I take a sharp breath, recognizing the face he's wearing. It's the mask he wore when Banta sent him out to kill someone. His target now is a predator masquerading as a girl. The wisp who leads people to their deaths.

Clara tips her chin up, glaring at Aiden like some sort of malicious doll. "That's not possible. Banta is invincible."

"Is he?" Aiden asks.

Clara takes a step back when Aiden keeps on, but then she stops.

"You can't kill me," she says with a snide smile, her power glowing around her fingertips. "You don't know how."

He narrows his eyes at her. "Then we'll have to figure it out."

Before we can reach her, a cry sounds behind us, a light grows, and I flinch as chaos erupts around me.

It's a sudden and beautiful chaos of vines and flowers, and a single ball of light that flies right through the narrow gap between Aiden and me to hit Clara in the chest, knocking her down.

My lips part in surprise when Drina rises up, surrounded by a sea of vines and flowers that move and grow with her as she races toward us, her crimson-streaked hair flying and her emerald-green clothing torn.

With a sharp glance at Aiden, we part, quickly stepping out of the way.

Drina glides across the ground as Clara struggles back to her feet. The branches above us—stripped back and blackened like the vines— shiver and tremble as a wind picks up, carrying Drina's quiet whispers as she practically flies at Clara. At the same time, her hands fill with flowers—so many of them springing to life that a cascade of petals and buds of all colors spills down her arms and onto the ground she hurries along.

With a snarl, Clara raises her hand to release her magic, but the earth around her suddenly erupts—also with gorgeous flowers— spilling up like a volcano and reflecting the moonlight pouring down on her in a glittering rainbow of light.

Clara gasps when the orb of power she was creating leaps toward the flowers, darting right out of her hand. She tries again, and the same thing happens.

"No!" she screams.

When Drina is only a step away, Clara roars with anger, both of her hands conjuring a light so brightly sapphire that I have to look away.

Drina's silhouette burns as she stands in front of Clara and all I can make out is a wash of flowers floating through the air and swirling around them both, absorbing every ray of light Clara creates until she slumps to the ground, her knees buckling and her shoulders hunching.

The sapphire light fades, the wash of flowers stops, and Clara doesn't get up. She's so still and her shape so rounded that she resembles a stone.

The flowers stop pouring from Drina's hands and she exhales an exhausted breath, crouching to run her hand over Clara's unmoving back.

Aiden and I approach, quietly.

"Drina?" I ask. "Are you okay?"

The wisp folds her legs under herself with a tired nod. "You can't kill a wisp by destroying their body," she says. "You must take all of their light and put it somewhere where it can't flourish." She looks up at me with a gentle smile. "Darkness can't flourish within true beauty."

Damn, she sounds so much like Helen right now.

I drop to my knees beside her, not quite believing that she isn't someone I dreamed up; her entire being giving me glimpses of the women I trust with my whole heart. "Who *are* you?"

"You know who I am. I'm Drina," she says, her smile becoming bemused. "A light in the dark."

My eyes are wide as she reaches out to me, a gentle brush of my shoulder, but she stops and gives me a knowing look. "My dear Iyana, you need some clothes."

I can't help the laugh that escapes me. Clothes are the least of my needs right now, but she isn't wrong. I'm pretty damn naked.

Aiden grins down at me when I glance up at him.

"I don't agree," he says, giving me an appreciative onceover. "You're wearing the perfect amount of clothing."

I press my lips together, blushing a little. It's weird how I don't feel naked now that my skin—my whole body—feels different, as if I'm wearing a kind of armor. But I have to acknowledge some basic bodily needs right now. I'm getting colder, I'm thirsty as anything, and I need to wash myself.

"What about the children?" I ask.

"They're fast asleep," Drina replies. "I won't disturb them until the morning. I want to clean everything up first."

"Aiden and I can help you," I say.

She gives me a nod. "I'd appreciate that. But first, you must care for yourselves."

I pick myself up, determined to put one foot in front of the other. "Do you have any clothing that might fit Aiden?"

"Well, actually," Drina says, looking him up and down, "I may be able to find something. I'll bring fresh clothing to your cabin, Iyana."

It's such a normal conversation. About clothes. Not death. Not survival. *Clothes.*

I miss a step as I pass between the dryads.

How can I think about clothing when they lie dead at my feet?

My knees buckle and I drop to the ground.

"Ana!" Aiden reaches my side in an instant, deftly avoiding stepping on anyone, while Drina appears on my other side.

I try to speak. "The dryads... I'm sorry..."

"They were badly injured," Drina says, rubbing my back. "But their bodies are like trees with deep roots. They will sleep until they're healed."

"They're not... dead?" I ask.

She exhales quietly. "Not in the way you think of death. They are like..." Her forehead creases. "Like seeds inside their shells. The outer shell may be burned, cracked, even beaten out of shape—but the seed inside still lives."

I slump with relief. Another weight lifts off my shoulders.

This time, when I pick my way past my friends, I pause beside Rye, kiss my fingertips, and press them to his forehead. "Heal well, friend."

CHAPTER FORTY-SEVEN

*R*eturning to my cabin, I pull the blanket from the bed and wrap it around my shoulders before I enter the little bathroom.

It takes a long time to wash the blood off my hands.

Aiden gives me space at first, taking his time looking around the simple hut, but I soon sense his presence in the open doorway behind me.

He gives a resigned sigh as he eyes the water pouring from the wooden faucet. "Another sink," he says, and I guess he's remembering trying to wash up in the bathroom at Mother Lavinia's place.

"Do you still hate water?" I ask, a little surprised, given that he spent so much time lying in the life waters.

He makes a disgruntled rumbling sound.

I spin so suddenly that I flick water around me—not deliberately, but at least it's clean after all of my scrubbing.

He dodges the droplets so fast, I'd think they were bullets.

I pull the blanket closer around myself. "I need a proper shower," I say, now that my hands are clean enough to handle my clothing. "I'm going to the real showers, and I'd like it if you come with me."

A quizzical crease forms in his forehead. "The *real* showers?"

I allow myself a small smile. "I'll show you."

I retrieve a pile of towels, some fresh clothing, and a few bars of sweet-smelling soap before I head across the room and stop on the porch to wait for him.

He follows me—but slowly.

Drina meets us at the bottom of the steps and places a set of clothing for Aiden on the top of the pile I'm carrying. "These should fit you," she says to Aiden, before she glides away again.

The clothing she brought him appears to be the same style as mine —emerald-green long pants and a V-neck top made out of the silky material that feels as light as air against my skin.

I lead Aiden toward the west, where the light overhead fades again and the canopy thickens.

Entering one of the shower cubicles, I draw him with me, giving him time to take in the glowing toadstools and the way the walls made of vines light up as soon as we step inside.

I'm desperate to bathe. Dropping my fresh clothing and the towels onto one of the larger mushrooms while keeping hold of a bar of soap, I shuck off my blanket and step beyond the row of fungi at the edge of the wet area.

I welcome the firm spray, the descent of the water down my hair, back, chest, arms, and legs, as I lather my body, scrubbing every inch of myself until I'm finally clean.

Then I tip my head back and taste the water on my lips. It's warm and clean. I drank water before, and I thought it was an aberration, but now I wonder... if I can walk in sunlight, then water may be my new source of hydration.

Opening my mouth, I allow the water to pass between my lips, swallowing a little before I gulp more. I'm so used to only needing a small glass of mercury that the amount of liquid I need now surprises me.

Swallowing as much as I can, I end up struggling to breathe, my chest heaving by the time I'm done.

As much as taking my fill of water satisfies my thirst, it also fills me with a deep fear.

I spin back to Aiden with a gasp. "What am I now?"

I find him sitting on one of the toadstools—a small miracle that it can hold his weight—where he's staying well away from the water's reach.

He rises slowly, every muscle gleaming in the luminescent light.

I remain under the spray, the water flowing down my shoulders, surprised when he steps into the shower with me, still wearing his pants.

A flame grows in his eyes, despite the water now pouring down on him. His hair falls across his face, damp strands against his cheeks as his palm curls around the back of my head, the weight of my wet hair falling across his hand.

Carefully, he brushes his thumb down the side of my neck, along the ridge of my shoulder. It's a slow movement, unhurried, and I close my eyes and welcome its calming effect on me.

"Do you need a label?" he asks.

I consider this for a moment. A name tells me what I am, but it doesn't determine *who* I am.

I shake my head.

"Then you're you," he murmurs, before he brushes the length of my arm and retrieves the cake of soap from my slackening fist.

Careful not to bump me, he lathers his chest and arms, then removes his pants to wash his legs. Finally clean, he lobs the soap to the side of the cubicle, tips his head back, and stands under the spray while the suds rinse off.

His body isn't quite as changed as mine is. His hair is still the same dark brown and his eyes are a shadowed, navy blue, but his muscles are even more sculpted—larger. Everywhere.

When I step forward and slip my arms around his chest, the water pouring around us, he gives a groan, pulling me higher and dropping his head to mine. His lips are heated, his tongue demanding access to my mouth.

I take a breath, give in to the need in my core, but I press my hands against his chest before we can go further.

"I'm scared of hurting you," I say, speaking my fears aloud.

When used as a weapon, my body could kill him without any effort at all.

"Hmm." It's a soft rumble in his throat as he draws my hand to his mouth, kissing the ends of my fingertips, nudging the side of my thumb, carefully tasting the soft, sensitive curves of my palm.

He draws back. "See? Not hurt."

I draw my bottom lip between my teeth, tasting the heady mix of earthy water and Aiden's fire.

Aiden focuses on my lips. "That's enough water," he rumbles, gathering me up against him and drawing me out of the spray.

He shivers, and heat blossoms around his chest. Within seconds, steam rises from his shoulders—and mine.

He gives me a lazy smile when the water droplets evaporate from our skin, but his smile vanishes as his mouth claims mine, his hands find my waist, and the evaporating droplets tingle against every inch of my skin as if he's touching me everywhere all at once.

Heat and need send my body into overdrive, and I moan as he hoists me upward, wraps my legs around his hips, and fits our bodies together.

He takes it slow, drawing out the moment, supporting and holding me up without anything behind my back, pulling me forward onto him.

Pleasure strikes through me, and my body responds with a fury of its own. Gripping his shoulders, I meet his thrust, my breathing erratic, my lips finding his and taking every sensation from the play of his tongue within my mouth.

He waits a beat—his eyes filling with flames, amber light playing beneath the surface of his skin—before he pulls me hard against him again. I gasp. Moan. Any concern I have about hurting him vanishes as he takes control, his movements as furious as mine.

We bump against the vines, veer into the wet area, get doused in water, veer out of it again and back into the vines.

Every thrust takes me higher, my body sensing each ripple of fire through his chest and hips, taking the heat he's giving me and returning it until the crash shakes my foundations.

We collide with the ground and I'm not even sure how we got there. I tip my head back, positioned on top of him, shivering with pleasure as he strokes my stomach, follows the curve of my waist, my breasts, my neck, before he trails his fingers down my chest again, each touch striking pleasure within me as if he's lighting a match.

The heat in his eyes is intense. "I want you in my life, Ana. Whatever it takes."

I bite my lip, my fangs descending as my heart warms. I rest down on him, listening to his steady heartbeat, and we lie like that for a long time.

Finally, he sits up so that I'm straddling him. He strokes my hair and back, his fingertips playing across my skin.

"I have my freedom because of you," he says, a deep rumble. "Now I need to decide what I do with it."

He brushes his thumb across my lower lip, skimming past the tips of my fangs. "There are other demons like Banta. Other supernaturals operating in the shadows. You once targeted them as a bounty hunter. You have the power—" He pauses. "*We* have the power to stop them. Together."

My lips part with a deep breath as the decisions ahead weigh down on me.

I have more power than I've ever had—literally, at my fingertips. I could choose to live out my life with Tessa's pack, protecting them. Not that they really need the extra protection. Now that the lowland packs are united, they're stronger than ever.

Or I could go with Aiden and walk the darker path, seeking out the demons and the criminals, the ones who prey on others.

When I hesitate, he murmurs my name. "Ana?"

"I have a family," I say. "I'm part of a pack. People who love me. It's not easy to walk away from them."

His breath suddenly catches. "Fuck. Ana. I'm sorry." His arms tighten around me, he presses his forehead to mine, and I sense the regret thrumming through him. "I had no right to suggest that you should give up your family."

Releasing me, he lifts me back to my feet, and a shot of worry races through me. "Aiden?"

He speaks carefully, his voice hoarse. "I've never had a home. Not a real one. I don't know what it's like. I once vowed I'd make a home for me and my brother, but the years kept passing and the dream started slipping away. When I thought you died, I let the dream go altogether."

He meets my eyes. "I took you away from your family. I separated you from the people you love, and I should have realized how much that would hurt you."

I stare at him, wide-eyed at the raw honesty in his speech.

"What if I want *you* to come with *me*?" I ask, softly. "To join my family."

He appears surprised. "A fire god in a wolf pack?"

I brush off his skepticism. "That's no stranger than a—whatever I am—in a wolf pack."

With a groan, he pulls me close again. "You know the things I've done. You know the crimes I've committed. I have too much to atone for. I can't let the dark places stay dark. Not now that I can do something about them."

He exhales heavily. "I want you in my life. I want a home with you. But I can't live out my days in peace knowing that I had the power to stop demons like Banta and I didn't."

My heart is in turmoil. If the power that I now control was meant for anything, it's to take down monsters like Banta.

And yet... I need my family, too. Aiden told me he shouldn't have asked me to give up my family, but it's still my choice to make.

Speech sticks in my throat and I'm quiet after that, and so is he.

We help each other dress and by the time we exit the showers, the light outside has changed. It allows me to see that the sheen on my skin has slowly faded, but I suspect that it will return if I draw on my strength.

I shouldn't be able to tell what time it is since the canopy overhead here is so dark, but I sense that daybreak is only minutes away.

"Dawn is approaching," I say.

Aiden is suddenly tense. "You need to stay under shelter."

"Not anymore," I reply with a smile.

As we walk back to the central territory, I tell him everything that happened while he was asleep and, for a while, I'm able to set aside the heartache of my future choices.

He has a lot of questions, but he's quiet again when I tell him what happened between me and Lucas before he woke up.

When we reach the cabins, I'm surprised to find the clearing free of broken branches and debris. Drina stands with her eyes closed, her palm pressed to the trunk of the nearest tree, while far above us, new leaves are growing to replace the ones that were destroyed.

"You're a wisp," I say to her, when she steps away from the tree. "I don't understand how you create plants like the dryads do."

"I, too, have rested in the life waters and come out stronger," she says, but her smile quickly fades. "It should have made me strong enough to protect the dryads from the demon, but he prevailed."

"Not anymore," I say, softly.

She gives me a quick nod. "Never again."

The quiet moment is broken when my stomach growls. Very loudly. I gasp when it feels like a yawning pit opened in my stomach. "What the hell?"

"You're hungry," Drina says, while Aiden remains a step behind me with a glint in his eyes. "What's the first food that comes into your mind?"

"Steak," I say, and then I blink with surprise.

Drina grins. "Then steak you shall have. Well, the closest I can get to it, anyway. How about you, Aiden?"

"The same," he says.

Drina tucks her long pants beneath her as she kneels on the ground and two pure white toadstools grow beneath her hovering palms. As she works over them, the toadstools elongate and change color until they resemble the juiciest pieces of steak.

"Aiden, if you wouldn't mind searing them for me?" Drina asks.

"With pleasure." Aiden kneels beside her. A flame flares beneath his palm as he runs his hand through the space above the steaks, cooking each side of them while Drina keeps them elevated.

It isn't until now that I truly appreciate the change in Aiden's power. Before now, he needed an external flame to access his fire. Now he's calling the flames from within himself.

"These are full of plant protein," Drina says. "I believe protein is what your body is craving right now, Iyana."

Dropping to my knees, I take the food from the leafy plate that Drina serves it up on.

I'm so hungry, I nearly inhale it. Chewy, juicy goodness. I groan as I swallow the last bite and lick my fingers. "Delicious."

I'm about to ask for another when the branches above us tremble. It's not the same shrieking warning that the trees made when Lucas arrived, but it alarms me enough that I jump to my feet alongside Aiden, whose palms flare.

The breeze picks up before the air pops.

Bright magic swirls in the air along the pathway toward my cabin, but I know this magic. I traveled within it once when Helen transported an army of fae to the Spire.

With a cry, I run toward the shimmering haze just as my friends appear within it. "Tessa!"

Her ruby-red hair swirls around her shoulders, the pull of Helen's magic plastering her flannel shirt around her chest, while her bright blue eyes are fiercely focused. "Iyana!"

Helen stands beside her, her dark hair pulled up into a loose topknot, her soft sweater also billowing. Her arms are outstretched, curved so that her magic envelops the people she brought with her.

Danika is crouched at the front, her light brown hair tousled, her hazel eyes darkly rimmed, and her hawk's wings spread as she poises, partly-shifted, as if she's prepared to fly if she needs to.

Behind Danika, Tristan is an image of pure ferocity—his wild, raven black hair falling across his eyes, his claws extended, and his chest bare, the tattoo of a snarling wolf's head seeming to leap off his skin.

Beside him, Luna is a petite figure, her loose skirt a flowing contrast to the other women's jeans, her sage-green eyes bright and her cheeks blushing pink as her cards swirl in a circle in front of her chest.

And then... Lydia steps out from behind Tristan, her appearance nearly identical to Luna's, her own set of cards intertwining with her twin sister's.

A cry of relief leaves my lips and I press my hand to my chest, but I force myself to pull up sharply before I collide with them, anxious again about my newfound strength.

Tessa's reflexes are second to none and she steps in front of me faster than my heart can beat, while the others fan out around us—a protective semi-circle. I sense Helen's magic building around all of us, as if she's about to create a protective shield.

"Are you hurt?" Tessa asks me, an urgent question, while her perceptive gaze flashes around the clearing.

I rush to speak. "I'm safe. I'm fine. I'm with friends now."

Tessa's intense gaze passes across the scene behind me. Crimson light floods her eyes as she assesses Drina and Aiden, before her focus drops to the sleeping dryads lying in the clearing and her face falls.

Helen appears to see the dryads at the same time and a cry leaves her lips. A deep sadness suddenly seems to weigh her down. "What happened here?"

My voice catches. "Banta Sol attacked them, but I killed him." It becomes a little harder to speak when I add, "Aiden's brother is also dead."

At this news, both Tristan and Tessa give Aiden a solemn nod. I haven't told them that I was the one who killed Lucas, but they know how painful it is to fight family.

Drina steps forward and introduces herself, saying, "Iyana must have a lot to tell you. You're welcome to stay as long as you need."

"Thank you. I'm grateful." The power fades from Tessa's eyes, which suddenly sparkle with tears as she darts forward and hugs me. "Fuck, Iyana. I was scared when you disappeared."

I return her hug, soaking up the warmth I find there.

Within moments, Danika folds her wings, Luna and Lydia put away their cards, Helen subdues her magic, and they're all hugging me. Even Tristan.

I exhale the last of my worries and hug them back, accepting the love they bring into my life.

CHAPTER FORTY-EIGHT

*T*he forest is peaceful, the light breeze brushing my skin as we sit talking for a long time on the soft, mossy ground beneath the shaded canopy.

Tristan takes up position at the side of our group, a few paces away, prowling around us, while Aiden retreats to the shadows on my right—a place he can't hide, given that his power makes his silhouette glow.

Danika keeps her wings folded but seems comfortable leaving them on display and I notice she has a new top that accommodates her wings now.

Luna and Lydia sit close to me, getting in my space, but I love their nearness. I always have.

Tessa rests opposite me, her discerning gaze relentless, and, while I tell my story without going into detail about the most painful events, I sense that she feels my deeper emotions—sadness, fear, turmoil.

Tristan prowls furiously when I describe my interactions with Lucas and Banta, his claws appearing again.

When the dryad children wake up, it's a reprieve from the retelling of my story, but it's heartbreaking to see them quietly run to their parents and kneel beside them, their eyes downcast and their little shoulders slumped.

It's at that point that Helen quietly approaches Drina and asks if she may assist the dryads' healing. "I can't heal them completely, but I can speed up the process so they will wake up much sooner."

At first, Drina is cautious. "I don't mean to question your healing skills, but a dryad's body is not like any other."

"I understand," Helen replies. "I've healed dryads before."

Drina blinks at her. Then peers at Helen more closely. "Mother Kadris?" she whispers, her jaw dropping a little. "Is that you?"

Helen gives her a small smile. "I must look older than the last time you saw me, Drina."

"And I must look younger!" Drina jumps to her feet and embraces Helen.

"As young as a wisp with your power should," Helen replies.

The two women are a similar height and build, and the wisdom and power between them feels like a tangible force.

I pipe up. "Drina looked younger yesterday."

Helen gasps as she spins back to Drina. "You aged yourself?"

The wisp gives a pleased smile. "I took some wise advice and broke the rules." She smiles at me before she gestures to the sleeping dryads. "I'm willing to break more rules if you're willing to help the dryads."

"Gladly." While Helen works over the fallen tree folk, the children gather around her, creating swaths of beautiful flowers to rest across the sleeping dryads' chests.

When Drina resumes her seat, she leans across to Tessa. "How far along are you, Tessa?"

Tessa doesn't seem surprised that Drina knows she's pregnant. "Only a couple of weeks, but it feels like more."

"Your son will be strong," Drina says, a gleam of certainty in her eyes. "A child of the gods. He will have immense power. As will Aiden and Iyana's children."

I'm startled. "I can't have children."

My declaration drops into a sudden silence.

Drina looks right at me, but it's Helen who lifts her voice from across the clearing to challenge my assertion. "Can't you?"

Within the shadows on my right, Aiden stands taller—the first move he's made since we sat down. His eyes gleam with firelight. And suddenly… there are so many possibilities ahead of me.

Children. A new family. As well as the family I already have.

But none of that will happen if Aiden and I don't walk the same path.

Turning back to my pack, I find myself, once again, the focus of Tessa's scrutiny, but she doesn't say anything about Aiden and me. Instead, she tells me about their search for me, the way they launched an attack on Banta Sol's compound trying to find me—only to be met with Lucas's power.

Danika's lips press into a determined line when she says, "We came here prepared." She gestures at their clothing. Not a metal buckle or zipper in sight.

I reach for Lydia, drawing her closer. "He told me he killed you."

She leans into my space, her tawny brown hair soft as it falls across my arm. "He nearly did."

Luna crowds in closer on my other side and I remember the card she gave me, anticipating what she wants to know as her big, sage-green eyes bore into mine.

"I found the dagger that was made from Theia's heart," I say.

Luna's cheeks blush more darkly peach and she glances at Lydia, who speaks for her. "Then you're the weapon now."

"I am," I say.

The clearing falls silent again, and even Tristan ceases his prowling.

Tessa is the first to move, smoothing down her flannel shirt and jeans as she stretches. "Iyana, will you walk with me? Maybe you can show me around?"

I give a quick nod, momentarily undecided about where to take her, and then I decide we should go south. "Along this way is where I trained each day," I say, when she joins me.

She tips her head as the canopy shifts over her. "Why do the branches move?"

"It's a protective mechanism," I explain. "The branches shelter the dryads so they aren't visible from the air. I imagine, from above, it must look like the boughs are shifting in the breeze."

As we walk, I point out the cabin where I've been staying, and describe the way the vines work to protect the territory.

When we reach the training area, Tessa circles the space at a slow prowl before she releases her wolf, its fur a deep green that blends with our surroundings. It sniffs at the ground, taking in the scent of the new environment, before it pads around the clearing.

"This is where I trained each day," I say. "It's designed acoustically to amplify the dryads' heartbeats so that they can move in sync."

I close my eyes and sway a little at the memory of training with them and experiencing the graceful dance.

"A little like Tristan and me," Tessa says.

I open my eyes to find her standing in front of me, her ruby hair falling across her shoulders, her lips pursed.

"You're in pain, Iyana," she says, quietly.

I can't lie to her. She's my alpha, but she's also my friend. A true friend.

I rest my hands at my sides. "I used to be so certain about who I am and what my purpose is. Especially when you came to Hidden House. Training you gave me a new path. Protecting you gave me a new purpose."

"And now?"

"I don't know where I belong," I say. "With you. Or with Aiden. I have a power I never dreamed I'd have. But it means nothing if I don't choose the right path."

"Where does your heart want to be?" she asks.

I'm quiet. I breathe out a controlled exhale. "My heart is pulling me in two different directions. You're my family, and I love you. But I also love Aiden, and he needs to right the wrongs of his past before he can find peace."

"Then don't choose between us," she says, surprising me. She takes my hands, squeezing them gently, her eyes glistening. "You can have both. You will always have a home with me. *Always*. No matter how long you're gone, or how far away you travel. You're part of my pack, Iyana. Time and distance won't change that. You can always return to us."

I try to swallow past the lump in my throat, try to stop the sob rising to my lips, but I can't. "Dammit, you're going to make me cry."

"I'm not sorry," she says, sob-laughing as she hugs me tightly. "I want you to be happy."

I hug her back and it's a long time before I pull away, wiping my eyes, and feeling grateful that she is... who she is.

"Thank you," I say. "For your friendship, and your love."

She gives me a smile, which quickly turns into a wicked grin when she rolls up her sleeves and asks me to show her how the acoustics work—to train her one last time.

At first, I'm worried about hurting her, and I take it slow, running through some of our old drills before I encourage her to close her eyes and listen as she fights. I don't have the heartbeat of a dryad that meshes with the environment, but I'm startled when she instantly moves in time with me.

"Your heart is a beautiful hammer, Iyana," she says.

I laugh. "I'll have to work on quieting it if I want to sneak up on someone, then."

An hour later, we return to the others, having worked up a sweat. I lead Tessa toward my cabin, intending for us to get water and wash up, but I slow down when I see Tristan and Aiden sitting beside each other on the steps of my cabin, deep in conversation.

Aiden is leaning forward, his elbows on his knees. Tristan's body language is more relaxed, but his brows are deeply furrowed. He gives Aiden a final nod before he clamps his hand on Aiden's shoulder and rises to his full height, taking the steps swiftly to reach Tessa's side.

"Iyana," Tristan says, gruffly pulling me into a hug that startles me. "I'm going to miss you."

I'm not sure how he knows I'm leaving. I can only put it down to his bond with Tessa.

Letting me go, he prowls toward Helen and Drina, who have continued working over the dryads while Danika, Luna, and Lydia are playing with the children.

Tessa squeezes my hand. "I'll ask Drina where I can wash up," she says, also giving me space.

I take a deep breath before I make my way to Aiden, where he sits on the top step. I slip in beside him, loving the way the fire leaps within his eyes when I draw near.

"Are you okay?" I ask.

"Yeah," he says, and I accept his silence when he doesn't elaborate on his conversation with Tristan.

I angle under his arm, pulling him around me and nestling my head in the crook of his shoulder. "Aiden?"

He presses a quiet kiss to my forehead. "Yeah?"

"I'm coming with you."

His heart skips a beat.

I look up at him before I go on. "When we're ready, there's a home waiting for us to come back to."

"A family," he says.

He tugs me closer, and I rest in his arms without regrets, accepting that the past is over, and the future is ours to create.

For the rest of the morning, I spend time with my pack: eating with them, laughing, sharing quiet moments.

Then I pack up the few belongings I have—the jacket, leggings, and boots I haven't worn in two weeks, but which, thankfully, the dryads cleaned for me. I even pack the bodice since it brings back a heated memory I won't soon forget.

Retrieving the book that Drina created from its hiding place beneath my bed, I flip it open to find that the pages have dried without any damage, although a silver sheen glistens across the pages where my nosebleed happened.

It has a lot of blank pages onto which I'm determined to write my own future.

When it's time to say goodbye to my family, I nearly can't do it.

Danika pulls me into a hug that brings fresh tears to my eyes.

"You were my first real friend," she says. "Look after yourself, Iyana."

While Tristan remains at the side this time, Tessa joins Danika in the hug. "Come back to us when you're ready."

As Luna and Lydia pile in around me, and Helen joins in, Helen's comforting scent overtakes my senses. It can't be anything but magical the way Helen makes us all feel loved.

These are the women who changed my life.

It takes a long moment for us to pull apart—a moment of knowing, in my heart, that it will be a while before I get to hug them all again.

Before I can change my mind, I spin to Aiden, who waits at the front of my cabin, holding our single pack of supplies. We'll go back to the warehouse first, see if anything is left of my belongings, and then we'll hit Banta's compound and make sure nobody claims his territory now that he's gone.

After that, well...

Slipping into Aiden's arms, I make him a promise. "We will go into the dark places. We'll bring fire and steel to the monsters who prey on others."

The light grows in his eyes as he also makes a promise. "And then, one day, we'll stop. We'll come home."

His heartbeat is steady in my ears, his power strong in my senses, making me even more aware of my own strength; the power that will give me courage in the days ahead.

Aiden's focus becomes distant. A slow smile grows on his face. "I have the perfect flame to jump into."

He curves his big hand around my head and his other arm around my shoulders and holds me close.

"Are you ready?" he asks.

"Always."

Flames burst to life around us, an amber firestorm spins from my head to my toes, and we jump.

EPILOGUE – TESSA DEAN

FOUR YEARS LATER

The night is still and calm.

Tristan's deep breathing would normally lull me to sleep, but tonight, I'm restless. Possibly something to do with the joyful drumbeat of little feet inside my four-months-pregnant tummy. Our daughter's legs are strong already, and I can't wait to meet her.

I snuggle back into Tristan, who lies behind me, one arm curled around me. My tummy is too big for me to lie comfortably on my back now—or on Tristan's chest.

I inhale his scent and it feels like the first time; notes of bitter orange, nutmeg, and cedar reminding me of running through the forest.

Our three-year-old son, Theo, nestles in front of me, his shoulder and side pressed against my tummy and chest while his other arm and leg are sprawled outward, taking up much of that side of the bed. He stirs, his dark eyelashes fluttering, and I stroke his arm to settle him.

His hair is as black as a raven's feathers, spread out around his head—the strands perpetually wild since he doesn't like having it cut. He inherited Tristan's features—crisp, green eyes and a strong physique—and he's already taller than the other three-year-old children in Tristan's pack.

But sometimes, when Theo looks at me, his eyes become a startling sapphire blue, a less-than-subtle change that tells me he has inherited so much of my power.

We've yet to discover if his wolf can separate from his body like mine can, but I don't imagine we'll find out until he's in his teens.

Like his father used to be, Theo is a restless sleeper. And like me, he's even more restless when we stay in the city. He seems to prefer the forest or the Spire where he can roam. The first time he disappeared into the trees, it scared the life out of me. When we discovered that Luna and Lydia's magic couldn't locate him, my fear only intensified. My entire pack—and much of Tristan's—set out in a panic, combing the forest, trying to find him.

I finally came upon Theo perched at the edge of the fae's ravine, seemingly unworried about sitting hundreds of feet above the river.

His little legs dangled over the edge as three rare Bright Ones floated around him. The little orbs of light seemed as unworried as he was, dancing around his head and shoulders, bouncing on his outstretched hand.

My son is fearless. Sometimes, he seems far older than his years. And yet... he is not immune to nightmares.

He settles now, his breathing deepening—but for myself, I have to admit defeat.

Sleep is not mine tonight.

Carefully extricating myself from Tristan's arms, I slip down the bed, trying not to disturb him or Theo.

When I finally make it to the bottom of the bed, my heart warms to see Theo and Tristan gravitate toward each other across the empty space between them.

Tristan draws Theo against his broad chest, while Theo nestles into his father's big arms.

Before Theo was born, Tristan went through a hard patch of self-doubt—dealing with a deep fear of walking in his father's footsteps; of failing to give Theo the love his son would need. It was heart-wrenching to see Tristan struggle with his fears when I never had a doubt that he would be an amazing father.

I made a pact with Tristan: We would help each other.

We've both had our moments—of being tired and challenged by all the responsibility resting on our shoulders—but we've never wavered from our promise to be there for each other.

We divide our weeks between the Spire, the forest, and the city in the western lowland—but in the last month, we've spent more time in the city.

The alliance with Ella's pack is stronger than ever and lately, there's been more movement between packs—members seeking mates across pack borders.

In the past month alone, Tristan welcomed ten new pack members, both male and female, some of whom already have cubs on the way.

Both packs are growing, and it fills me with hope for the future.

My own pack has grown, too. Along with my alliance with the fae, the dryads offered their help with repairing the damage that the witches did to the forest. Their skills have been invaluable in revegetating parts of the woodland—and they built me a new home that is invisible from the sky. A home I'm missing more each day.

Smoothing down my oversized shirt, I prowl into the kitchen, my bare feet slapping the tiles as I note the height of the full moon. The cityscape sparkles through the floor-to-ceiling windows along the left wall, a glittering sight that hides the town's darker spaces.

We brought peace to the lowlands, but there are always those who seek to cause harm.

I haven't heard from Iyana for months, and a small seed of worry has grown within my mind. At her last communication, she and Aiden were heading to Philadelphia, where they sensed that a conflict between powerful supernaturals was emerging. I haven't heard from her since.

Reaching for a glass of water at the sink, I'm distracted by a glow at the edge of my vision—a rapidly approaching light. It shoots through the far window, making me jolt. I nearly drop the glass before I recognize what the oncoming light is.

It's a Bright One. A glowing orb no bigger than my hand. The fae call them celestial stars. They're old magic. I've only seen them in three places: at the fae's ravine, at Hidden House, and when I fought the angels.

This Bright One zooms to a halt, stopping right in front of my nose—its light blinding me before it draws back, dancing around me and leaving streaks in my vision.

It's different to a will-o'-the-wisp's light, which burns like fire in a sphere. The Bright Ones are pure starlight, and this one is perhaps the most luminescent I've ever seen.

"Why are you here?" I ask, reaching out, immediately thinking the worst—that the fae are in trouble or that something's wrong at Hidden House—but then I study the Bright One more carefully.

Within its glowing center, I make out the silhouette of silver flowers.

The breath catches in my throat.

The last time I saw a Bright One as luminescent as this, it led me up the staircase at Hidden House and took me to the woman in the dark.

Her identity is a mystery to me. I don't know her name or her story. All I know is that her power has sustained the house for years. She healed members of my pack whose bodies were drained by dark magic.

It was her pure magic that hid me from my father when I was a child.

Years ago, Tristan promised Helen that he would be at Hidden House when the woman woke up.

I whisper to the orb, "Did the woman in the dark send you?"

The orb dances around me, gracefully gliding back and forth, bobbing up and down, as if to respond in the affirmative.

I'm suddenly frozen. I knew this day would come, eventually, but meeting this incredibly powerful woman whose actions influenced the course of my life, having her wake up is...

Frightening. Exciting. Painful, even, because, as Iyana once said to me, this woman sought shelter at Hidden House long before anyone else. She willingly offered up her power in exchange for a safe place to retreat from the world.

I still can't imagine what sort of pain would cause someone to seek the darkness of sleep.

Or what it means now that she's waking up.

My heart is suddenly thumping. We need to get to Hidden House as soon as possible, but I suddenly can't move.

My daughter chooses that very moment to kick me, and I wince, but I needed the boost to get myself moving. I whisper a 'thank you' to her as I rub my stomach.

Quickly gulping the glass of water, I return to my bedroom while the orb dances in the air behind me.

I slip quietly onto the bed, scooting in behind Tristan, and bend to nudge his cheek.

"Tristan," I whisper, brushing my lips against his stubbly jaw. "Wake up. We need to go."

His breathing changes, a deep inhalation. He will sense immediately the urgency in my voice, but he makes no sudden moves. He won't want to wake Theo or frighten him.

Tristan's question is a throaty growl. "What's wrong?"

"The woman in the dark is waking up."

Tristan's fierce eyes are suddenly wide open. His focus shifts to the orb floating in the air behind me, and his lips part, before his gaze blazes across me. "We need to hurry. I made a promise I'd be there."

I back away as, with great care, Tristan extricates himself from around Theo, pulls the blanket up, and tucks it around our son.

"Once we're dressed, we can take Theo to Danika," I say.

Tristan growls his agreement as he reaches for a pair of jeans off the floor to pull over his shorts. I quickly follow him to the bathroom while the orb waits patiently outside for us to emerge in record time.

Carefully drawing the blanket back, Tristan pulls Theo into his arms. Our son stiffens a little, his green eyes shooting wide—as immediately awake as Tristan was. "Daddy?"

"It's okay, buddy." Tristan shushes him, rubbing his back. "We're taking you to Aunty Dani. Go back to sleep."

I catch Theo's soft, trusting 'okay' before he settles against Tristan's chest and shoulder, his head buried in Tristan's neck.

Within moments, we've entered the elevator and are stepping out onto the tenth floor, heading to the first apartment on the right. The orb remains behind us as I knock, softly.

Cody opens the door. Now that he has to rely on his physical strength, rather than his wolf's power, his chest is broader, and his biceps are even bigger than they were before. He's a powerful figure and nobody messes with him.

Except perhaps… his beautiful little boy, who isn't sleeping well.

Cody's hickory-brown hair is disheveled, his sleep-deprived eyes shadowed. I suddenly feel immensely guilty relying on him and Danika when they aren't getting much sleep, but Theo is completely comfortable with them. Not that my son isn't comfortable with the other members of my pack, but they don't understand wolfish behavior as well as Cody does.

Cody is immediately on alert when he sees me. "Tessa. Is everything okay?"

"Can you watch Theo for a few hours?"

"Of course." He reaches for my son. "What's wrong?"

"We need to go to Hidden House," Tristan replies, carefully transferring Theo, who curls up in Cody's big arms. "The woman in the dark is waking up."

"Fuck," Cody murmurs. At that moment, Danika appears behind him, as bleary-eyed as Cody, her hair equally messy.

Their two-year-old son peeks around her legs, looking far more awake than he should at this time of night. He has his father's hickory-brown eyes, but his light brown hair is streaked with golden highlights, like his mom's.

"Oh, no," I say. "Not sleeping tonight?"

Danika rubs her eyes. "I swear James is really a vampire and not a hawk shifter." She tousles his hair gently, her gaze softening when he gives her a heart-meltingly adorable smile as he continues to cling to her leg.

"Go," she says softly to us. "We'll make sure Theo is okay."

"Thank you," I say. "Tomorrow night, let me know if I can watch James so you can get some sleep."

Danika lets out a laugh. "Be careful what you offer."

Minutes later, we've made it to the parking garage and are on our way. The orb stays with us in the SUV for a few seconds before it shoots ahead, traveling so fast that I can hardly follow it, before it disappears into the night.

When we pull into a parking space beneath Hidden House, we find Helen waiting in front of the elevator, her dark hair pulled up loosely, wearing a soft-looking sweater and jeans. Her posture and position remind me so much of the first time I saw her when Tristan first brought me here. The stark difference is the orb floating beside her.

I'm also a little surprised and curious about the chest-height stone fountain positioned at the side of the garage that is filled with softly burning flames.

Helen embraces me when we hurry up to her, angling to the side to avoid my already-big belly. "Tessa. Tristan. Thank you for coming."

"We came as quickly as we could," I say, while Tristan towers behind me.

"The fire?" he asks.

Helen gives me a small smile, but there are unusual shadows in her eyes when she says, "It's to help guide our family home."

A moment later, the fire bursts upward, exploding into a whirl-wind of flames that spiral and grow, the heat from the firestorm buffeting me.

I release my wolf so I can see with her eyes and, a second later, Tristan steps in front of me, shucking off his jeans and shifting, his enormous wolf snarling as he makes a shield of himself in front of me.

It's a protective move we perfected while I was pregnant with Theo. It's not that we're worried for my safety; we don't know what powers our unborn daughter will have, and we aren't taking any chances protecting her.

Ahead of us, my wolf walks right into the firestorm, unharmed by the heat or the hungry flames. She pulls up short when two figures appear within it, a brilliant cocoon around them.

Iyana's hair is even more silver-streaked than the last time I saw her, her eyes glinting with a sheen, like metal. She's wearing a body-hugging long-sleeved black suit that covers her from her neck to the tops of her knee-high boots.

Beside her, Aiden's body is like an ember, streaks of fire glinting across his bare chest and glowing through his black jeans. He's as big as Tristan, his biceps gleaming with sweat, his eyes ablaze.

My wolf howls and Iyana strides toward it, straight through the flames, seeming unconcerned by the heat. She crouches and reaches out her hand to my wolf. "Hello, Tessa."

At the same time as she speaks, Aiden rolls his shoulders, closes his fists, and the firestorm sucks inward, the flames disappearing into his body. His skin glows briefly before the fire fades completely.

Iyana rises up with a small smile. "Sorry about the dramatic entrance."

In front of me, Tristan shifts back into his human form, rapidly pulling on his jeans.

"Iyana." I hurry toward her and so does Helen, each of us hugging her in turns. It feels like forever since I last saw her. Far too long. "It's so good to see you."

While we hug Iyana for a long moment, Aiden and Tristan greet each other with respectful nods. They don't know each other well enough to be comfortable with each other—like Tristan and Cody are now—but I hope that will change in time.

"You made it," Helen says, releasing Iyana.

Iyana heaves out an exhale. "We reached the outskirts of Philadelphia, but the conflict between the angels and the dragon shifters kept us at bay. There are powerful forces of light magic at war in that city. We'll need to keep an eye on them."

"Well, I'm glad you're safe," Helen says.

At that moment, the Bright One dances between us. Iyana holds out her hand and it flits around her like a butterfly. Iyana's voice becomes hushed. "She's waking up, isn't she?"

Helen gives a quiet nod. "We should go quickly. She won't stay awake for long before she has to sleep again." Helen gestures to the elevator. "This way please."

I pull my wolf back to me and we all cram into the small space, the two men taking up a lot of it. My pregnant tummy takes up what feels like even more.

When the elevator doors open, we face a set of stairs leading upward. Three orbs hover in front of us and quickly dance up the stairs ahead of us. I take the steps far more slowly than the first time I raced up this staircase, picking my way through the silver vines that cover it.

Beside me, Iyana runs her fingertips across the plants cascading across the railing. "It's so good to be back," she says, looking around. "Damn, I miss this place. All of the memories…"

I reach across the space between us, a question in my eyes that I won't utter, because I need to give her the space to decide when she and Aiden will come home for good.

She's quiet, but when we reach the top step, she hugs me tightly. I sense that she's completely comfortable in her power now.

When she first transformed, she was full of turmoil, faced with making choices she didn't want to make. Now, she seems at ease with her decisions. It's not difficult to see why when she glances back at Aiden, whose entire demeanor shifts when she smiles. The sparks between them are palpable.

The silver glow filling the air grows brighter as we enter the large room where the ceiling gives way to a star-filled sky.

The pure light takes my breath away, even though I knew what to expect this time. Thick vines cover the floor, but they slip to the sides, creating a clear path to the pallet on which the woman rests.

Behind me, Tristan brushes his fingertips across my back, and I reach for his hand, entwining my fingers with his as we approach the center of the room together; taking up position at her head, while Iyana and Aiden stand beside us, and Helen stands at the woman's feet.

The sleeping lady is just like I remember her. Her hair is the purest white, flowing down the side of the pallet, and her skin glows as if starlight lives inside her. Her silver gown reaches her ankles and shimmers in the light of the orbs that sway above her sleeping figure.

A weapon rests beside her on the pallet. After not knowing what it was the first time I saw it, I did my research. It's a medieval weapon called a halberd, with two blades set on either side of a sturdy wooden pole. One of the blades is a deadly spike, the kind that could be driven into an opponent's heart from a safe distance, while the other blade is large, curved, and, in this case, bears an emblem that consists of a crescent and outward lines.

The weapon's age doesn't surprise me anymore. I guessed a while ago that this woman is older than Helen.

Yet, she doesn't appear older than forty years.

Practically ageless.

Her chest rises and falls to a deep rhythm and for a moment, I'm worried that Helen is mistaken about her waking up.

Then...

The woman's breathing hitches, her next exhale sighs from her lips, and her eyelids flutter open.

She blinks as she gazes upward, and I see the color of her eyes for the first time—the brightest green.

I don't dare to breathe as she lifts her hand a little.

Starlight wafts from her fingertips, pure and glittering. Then her focus shifts. Her gaze passes swiftly across me, Tristan, Iyana, Aiden, and finally, Helen.

"You found each other," she says, with a soft smile. "I hoped you would all stand together in this room one day."

She glides upward, slipping her legs to the side of the pallet, but her hand falls on the halberd's hilt and her focus snaps to it.

She pauses for a moment, her face downcast, her shoulders tensing.

"But this is the reason why I needed you here." She taps the weapon's curved blade. "This weapon belonged to my husband." She presses her other hand to her heart. "He was human. The best person I ever knew."

I'm startled that someone as powerful as this woman fell in love with a human, although her use of the past tense when she speaks about him would explain the deep grief in her voice.

"Where are you?" she whispers, as if to herself.

I gasp. Her speech resonates through me like an echo I've heard before, and I startle to realize... I *have* heard her voice before.

When I stepped into the Near-Apart Room at the Spire, the questions carved into the wall reverberated around me like the cries of people calling to their lost loved ones.

"You lost him," I whisper. "Your love."

"I did," she says. "And for a long time, I also lost my purpose. Then, you were born, Tessa. Not the first, but the one who made me realize I had a part to play."

My brow furrows. "What do you mean... not the first?"

"There are more like you," she says. "A new generation of gods arising. Some have been aware of their power for years, while others are only now discovering it."

She casts her gaze around at us. She's only been awake for seconds, but she hasn't wasted any time assessing us. "Tessa, daughter of the white wolf, bringer of war," she says, addressing me in her soft, but firm voice—the kind of voice that I could imagine once commanded an army.

"Tristan, son of Cerberus, indestructible," she says, her piercing gaze zeroing in on my mate before she moves on. "Iyana, weapon of Theia, the ultimate blade. And Aiden, son of Vulcan, master of flame. Each of you has the power to bring about the destruction of life as we know it."

Her expression softens a little. "Yet, here you are, joined in an alliance that has stopped war in its tracks."

Her voice hardens again as she taps the halberd, spilling starlight from her fingertips. "This halberd was blessed by dragon's fire and forged into a weapon of light magic. Its magic is purer than that of the angels. It has the power to open the earth, topple skyscrapers, and wipe hundreds of humans and supernaturals out of existence with a single swipe."

She looks directly at each of us in turn. "This weapon must be protected at all costs. Unlike each of you, it has no conscience. It doesn't choose where it strikes. My husband once carried this weapon and he understood its power, but others…" Her jaw tightens. "Others will try to misuse it."

Her eyes blaze, and I catch a glimpse of the tip of the power she controls; a power that keeps this house hidden from the world, that creates rooms within rooms, and that understands what I need and helps me find it.

"Nobody must wield this weapon," she says. "Ever."

"Why are you telling us this?" I ask, my voice a hushed whisper.

"Because I won't live forever. When I die, someone must take responsibility for protecting this weapon. Will you do it?" she asks. "Or if not you, then your children or your grandchildren?"

I consider the halberd, carefully. My melding bond with Tristan tells me that his thoughts are the same as mine: Only those who seek power would want this weapon. Between us we have too much fucking power to ever want more.

"We will protect it," I say. "As will our children and our grand-children."

Beside me, Iyana has taken Aiden's hand, an unspoken communication passing between them.

"With respect," Aiden says, speaking carefully. "Should you ask, I believe I could destroy this weapon in the Forge Fire."

The woman's gaze falls. She's quiet for a long moment. Her hand trembles where she rests it on the halberd's handle.

When she doesn't answer, I descend to my knees—not a graceful action in my pregnant state. "It's all you have left of him," I say, reading her impulses without needing to use my power. "You don't want it destroyed."

"Not while I'm alive." A tear trickles down her cheek, but she quickly swipes it away. "When I'm gone, if it isn't possible to keep it safe, then you must destroy it."

Aiden nods. "It will be done."

The woman lets out a soft exhale, her shoulders slumping a little. "I need to sleep again soon so that my energy can keep this house alive, but I have one more question for you."

She reaches for me, and I place my hand in hers. A jolt of power rushes through me at the contact.

"You must decide what legacy you will leave," she says, softly. "Will it be peace? Or war?"

"Peace," I promise, without hesitation.

"That is my wish for you, Tessa Dean," she says. "It always has been. I hope the other new gods feel the same."

I shiver, but I remind myself: The only actions I can control are my own. I can't predict what these other new gods might do.

If war comes looking for me...

I turn to Tristan, my fierce mate, whose growls are already sounding around me.

If war comes looking for us or our children, we'll be the ones who will end it.

~

If you loved this series and want to know about the war between the angels and dragon shifters, don't miss:
Hunt the Night (Supernatural Legacy 1)

An enemies to lovers romance with forced proximity and found family!

HUNT THE NIGHT: SUPERNATURAL LEGACY #1

The angels only let me out to hunt.

But it's not demons I'm sent to destroy—it's dragons.

I'm corrupted. My soul was impure at birth. I'm an angel born with an insatiable need for vengeance so intense that they caged me, branded me, and kept me in the dark.

I've been promised purity and redemption, freedom from my cage. Failure is not an option. My soul depends on it.

I must hunt the Dread—a merciless clan of dragon shifters whose true nature reveals itself in the dead of night. For once my killer instincts might set me free.

But one mistake is all it takes.

One moment that costs me my freedom once more.

Now, my life rests in the hands of Callan Steele, a Dread dragon whose touch sears my corrupted soul.

He makes a claim on me that can't be true. He tells me that my wings are not my own. That my strength is stolen. And that the fire in my angelic heart— the flame I've feared my whole life—belongs to him.

That *I* belong to him.

Some angels fall, but I won't crash and burn.

Content information: Hunt the Night is dark urban fantasy romance, the first in the Supernatural Legacy series. Recommended reading age is 18+ for sex scenes, mature themes, violence, and language. May end on a cliffhanger.

ASSASSIN'S MAGIC

To catch up on other series in The Ever Realms world,
check out the complete dark fantasy:

Assassin's Magic.

I am a hunter. The last of my kind.

Love is a risk I cannot take.

I've stayed hidden in the shadows, never revealing my power, but I can't stay
hidden any longer.

To avenge my mother's death, I must infiltrate the Assassin's Legion.

Easier said than done. They're violent. Unforgiving. And they don't welcome
women.

Staying alive will take everything I've got. Distractions will get me killed.

Distractions like Slade Baines.

He is relentlessly fierce. Destructively handsome. Disarmingly loyal. He
offers me an alliance and I have no choice but to accept.

But he's hiding his true strength and I don't know why.

The answer could destroy my heart.

*Content information: Assassin's Magic is dark urban fantasy romance, the first in
the Assassin's Magic series. Recommended reading age is 17+ for sex scenes, mature
themes, and violence. Ends on a cliffhanger.*

Tropes for the series include rivals to lovers, found family, close proximity,
academy romance, rejected bonds, Norse and Greek mythology, enemies to
lovers, and supernatural mafia.

*This series is part of The Ever Realms. A seven-series world by Everly Frost.

A SKY LIKE BLOOD

(KINGDOM OF BETRAYAL #1)

For more wolves, check out:

A Sky Like Blood.

I belong to the Vandawolf.
My heart and my power are his to control.

I am a Blacksmith, a wielder of the arcane magic that once scorched our land and brought blood-storms to our skies. Now, I live at the mercy of the Vandawolf, the dark king whose power forced the Blacksmiths to their knees.

But the price for my life is high.

When his enemies scheme against him, I cut them down.

And when the storms rage, I'm sent to fight the monsters that rise from our damaged land.

To fail is to betray the Vandawolf, and my family will pay the price.

Then a breathtakingly beautiful man steps from the blood-rain, and I'm faced with a terrible choice.

Do I end him or save him?

Is he a man or a beast?

Betrayal is only a step away.

Content information: A Sky Like Blood is fantasy romance, the first in the Kingdom of Betrayal series.

Recommended reading age is 17+ for sex scenes, mature themes, violence, and language. Ends on a cliffhanger.

Get your copy of A Sky Like Blood.

ALSO BY EVERLY FROST

<u>Stand-alone fiction - dark romance</u>

Corrupt Me: Immortal Vices and Virtues

ABOUT THE AUTHOR

Everly Frost is the USA Today Bestselling author of fantasy romance, urban fantasy and paranormal romance novels. She spent her childhood dreaming of other worlds and scribbling stories on the leftover blank pages at the back of school notebooks. She lives in Brisbane, Australia with her husband and two children.

a amazon.com/author/everlyfrost

f facebook.com/everlyfrost

o instagram.com/everlyfrost

BB bookbub.com/authors/everly-frost

g goodreads.com/everlyfrost

www.ingramcontent.com/pod-product-compliance
Lightning Source LLC
Chambersburg PA
CBHW050015120726
47903CB00006B/1778